HALF-LIFE
OF A
STOLEN
SISTER

ALSO BY THE AUTHOR

A Highly Unlikely Scenario
Good on Paper

HALF-LIFE

OF A

STOLEN

SISTER

Rachel Cantor

SOHO

Published by
Soho Press, Inc.
227 W 17th Street
New York, NY 10011

Library of Congress Cataloging-in-Publication Data

Cantor, Rachel, author.
Half-life of a stolen sister / Rachel Cantor.
New York, NY : Soho Press, [2023]
Identifiers: LCCN 2022058936 |
ISBN 978-1-64129-464-5
eISBN 978-1-64129-465-2
Subjects: LCGFT: Novels.
Classification: LCC PS3603.A5877 H35 2023 | DDC 813'.6—
dc23/eng/20221209
LC record available at https://lccn.loc.gov/2022058936

Printed in the United States of America

10 9 8 7 6 5 4 3 2 1

For my brothers and sisters, with love

This present moment had no pain, no blot, no want; full, pure, perfect, it deeply blessed me.   —Lucy Snowe, *Villette*

Writing, by contrast, is filled with the shame of visibility, of singularity, of the exposure of one's desire for recognition and love and existence. Writing, indeed, is the very sign of desire itself: it asks to be read. It is filled with the desire and the willingness to be known.
                    —from "The Uses of Doubt" by Stacey D'Erasmo

Part 1

YOUTH

LITTLE MOTHER—

in which a mother dies (as recounted by Maria)

Mama teaches the difference between us.

The pillows are all behind her. Around her, left to right: Branny, the closest because he's the Only Boy; Lotte, jostling with Bran, who's younger by a year but bigger; Em on the end, sucking her thumb; on the right, standing, Liza, holding a broom; and me, holding Annie, who sleeps with a sucker.

Annie, she says, you will always be the baby. No matter what you do, your family will love and underestimate you.

Annie opens her eyes, drops her sucker.

Emily, you will always care more for places than people. You will go away, but you will always come back.

Em puts a blanket over her head.

Branwell, you will try with your big heart to please, but until you learn self-control, you will only disappoint.

Branny whoops and throws a soldier to the air.

Charlotte, you care most for what you do not have; learn to care for what you have, and you will be happy.

But, Lotte says (she wants so much to understand!).

Elizabeth, your needs are simple; you will be forgotten, but you do not mind.

Liza holds her broom to her chest.

Maria. Are you there? Come closer, Maria.

I lay Annie onto the bed. She crawls to Em under the blanket.

I do not need to tell you who you are: you already know. You are the Little Mother, the one who fills the spaces.

I know this. I help Mama to lift a hand to my young face.

Because Mama is poorly she no longer: makes sockdolls, cooks cabbage, buttons dresses, shouts to Branny to stop pinching, counts the teeth Liza has lost, tugs at her pinafore, chews her nails, hums music by the dishes, explains puppets, says Scoot, makes faces at Annie, makes Lotte's little braids, makes anyone guess what's for dinner, says poems at the fire, calms Papa, a hand in his hair.

Lotte shakes the door and shouts. She draws pictures of happy Mama, happy Lotte, in crayoned blue and red. She slides them under the door; she tries to slide a cookie, a sockdoll.

I am eight so I'm the oldest: I yank Lotte away. But Lotte is strong. Strong with fear.

She shouts: Mama needs a doll from me!

She shouts: No, Maria. No!

Children, please!

Lotte wails by the water pot, placed there, before Mama's room, for the event of fire. Branny throws soldiers, Emmy won't nap, Annie crawls too near the stove, Liza scorches the sheets. Papa looks horrified—at all of it. He cannot read the paper for all the noise. I read to him. He shuts his eyes, his hands covering his face.

Auntie keeps saying, This isn't how we do things.

Mama teaches us what brings us together. You are one person, she says: you have one heart, one mind, one body. If one of you fails, all of you fail; if one exults, everyone exults; if one dies, you all die. It cannot be otherwise. You can live without me, you can live without Papa, but you cannot live without each other. Remember this. Emily, do you remember? Bran? Lotte?

Mama, let me get you ice chips.

No, Maria, she says. This is important. Lotte, do you remember? Liza?

Before she got sick, Mama braided my hair; she called me Beauty and sang me songs. We are both Maria: Mama Maria, and me. But now she's lost all reason, Papa says. Her eyeballs roll in her head and she sweats. Paddy, she says, the world is leaving me! Paddy, I am too young to die! Paddy, I fear there will be nothing after this, how can there be, if this is everything? Paddy, why won't you hold me? Make love to me, Paddy, I am still here, I am still here!

A Little Mother does everything the mother does, but less. She does what she can. Lotte is only five. She has feelings, so I hold her.

I take Bran to the park so he can run. I tell him to throw a hundred stones into the lake. He throws as hard as he can, he makes a lot of noise, sometimes he says a bad word. He can't count as high as one hundred, but when he gets tired I say, That's a hundred, and he's glad.

I take Em to the pound. She gives the dogs names and brings them treats. They climb on her face, which makes her laugh. If she laughs, she doesn't have nightmares. If she has nightmares more than twice, I take her to see the dogs.

Liza's nearly seven. She needs to talk. I ask her questions, about anything—the weather, what do we do to make Papa happy, is it time for washing. It doesn't matter. When Mama got sick, Liza didn't talk for a month; no one noticed but me.

The baby doesn't know anything. She needs to play. I tell the others that Annie must never be sad, we must never let Annie be sad. Everyone has to make faces at baby, everyone must play games. Ring Around the Rosie, clapping games. Annie laughs. Babies need to laugh.

Mama has stopped saying she's too young to die. She's stopped pinching her cheeks for Papa and telling us about ourselves. I thought I understood time, she murmurs as I sop her face, but I was wrong. Pain makes each moment huge, as does relief, yet a moment is still the smallest thing we have. I want more moments, she says. I want life, I want moments, I want time! But the vastness calls me, Maria. Forgive me! You must forgive me! I am so tired.

I am tired, too.

Liza and Lotte hide in the closet, wearing Mama's dresses and passing tea. The dresses have names we have mostly forgotten. Muslin, velvet, cocktail, other things. Auntie lets down the hems and gives them to the poor. Auntie arrived when Mama got sick. She's here now till school starts, then she's away. Who shall take care of them when I have gone? she asks. Paddy? Paddy? Aunt doesn't wear dresses with names, just good dresses, serviceable dresses.

Inside the shoes you see where Mama's toes stood. Now poor people wear Mama's pumps, her flats and mules.

The big bed where Mama died is gone, there's just a desk now so Papa can work, finally. Her body is with science but the important part of her's in heaven. Papa says it's time to forget. Aunt says, There's baloney sandwiches. Em says, I don't like baloney, Aunt says, Be grateful for protein.

Aunt makes sure we go to sleep and get up at the same time so we can have order. She makes meals and sews, but Aunt isn't a

Little Mother. She knows what children should become, which is little ladies and gentlemen; I know what we need now. We need to be together. I keep us together. I tell stories. About how Bran will buy us a Haworthy House worthy of the name. With six wings, servants, and pheasant for tea. Where we will have beautiful weddings with handsome swains and dresses with trains, and gossamer veils and tulips to throw.

The stories are how we know who we are, with no one left to tell us.

I will care for *all* the children, I say, in our Haworthy House. Everyone's children!

I'd like a garden, whispers Liza.

Ye shall have a garden.

I want a zoo! declares Em.

Ye shall have a zoo.

It's bags of gold for me! says Bran.

Bags ye shall have, say I.

Annie wants lovely toys, don't ye, Annie?

. . .

What do you want, little Lotte?

Lotte bursts into tears. I want all of it to be true, she sobs. I want all of it to be true!

We are all around her, left to right: Bran, Em, Liza, Lotte, Annabelle, and me. I hold Mama's hand but she doesn't squeeze. Branwell does a dance, Em gives her a flower, but she doesn't see. She looks at the ceiling. Her lips move, but she has no words.

She is a gorgon now, spitting and choking. No one has washed her hair. She would have turned the others to stone, so I sit with her, in her room, kept dark for sleeping, for not arousing love for the world. I say, It's okay, Mama, it's okay. She grabs my arm but I cannot hear what she says. She chokes again, and gasps and shakes her head and dies.

Her face is white, her mouth twists, her eyes are open. She is not at peace!

Papa said there would be peace! I try smoothing her hair. I try patting her cheek as she might pat mine. I say, There, there, and think, Maybe she *is* there, holding on! Maybe she doesn't want to go! I don't want her to go!

I look for stories to tell her about this world, to help her stay:

Liza is in the kitchen peeling potatoes, I say. She is wearing a shortish frock. Aunt says it's too short, she'll let down the hem soonest.

I say: Annie's with Liza, maybe in her chair Papa found on the street. Can you hear?

Her face doesn't move, it's in agony!

If she goes, I want to be with her! There can be no Little Mother without Mother: we are one thing: if one of us dies, we both must die. I tie my wrist to hers. I use the elastic from my hair, I use two of them. To get close so our wrists can be tied, I go under the covers. Mama's hip bone is sharp, her ribs are only a rack of bone, there is no softness where I can rest.

If I tell her about us, maybe she can hold on, she can hold on to me and not let go.

I whisper so only she can hear.

I say: Lotte and Bran are talking in their bunks, can you hear? Bran is dropping bombs; Lotte is getting cross.

Lunch, Auntie cries and the furniture shakes.

Kerblew, kerblew, Branny cries, the world is ending, the world is over.

Lotte says, Don't be stupid, penguin, it's all just as it ever was.

HUNT FOR MYSTERIOUS CARP—
in which children play

Okay, this is the thicket of wild woods that encircles the glass castle of the evil Lord

Right, and there are lots of poisonous berries

And wild boar

The three loyalist spies will have to be careful

I don't remember the spies

The spies sabotage the designs of the evil Lord and divert his attention from the rebels

Who are trying to reestablish the just and splendid reign of the Freiburg-Bonaparte dynasty

The spies are brave knights sons of the noblest in the land now imprisoned masquerading as mere laborers wearing rough-hewn clothes of flax

We need names

I'm Boron the Bold

Boron sounds like Moron moron

I am Bogomil the Bold

I am Elfron the Enigmatic

Rider is Rider

Rider can't play no dogs in Glass Town

He'll be quiet

He's never quiet

If he barks Aunt will make us stop

He won't bark

You always say that

GLASS TOWN: DRAMATIS PERSONAE

ROYAL MENAGERIE: Porky Porcupine, four flying horses, one Black Stallion named Buster, enough monkeys to fill one large tree, six talking squirrels: Frosty, Peculiar Eddy, Bambam, Tail of Woe, Mrs. Tail of Woe, Cheesecake

MENAGERIE ATTENDANTS: Quillmasters, Horse Traders, Monkey Shiners, Squirrel Grooms

COURT ENTERTAINERS: jongleurs, jugglers, jokers, jesters, jumblers, four genuine Genii

BEAUTIFUL LADIES: Lady Letitia Lambikin, Lady Renata Ramekin, Loretta the Galley Slave

---

What are you children doing?

Just playing a game Aunt

It's a very loud and disorganized game.

We're hunting mysterious carp

They sing riddles

Are you being fresh with me?

There are carp in the enchanted lake we need them to feed Prince Hal of Holbrooke

After we save the menagerie from Branny's bombs

There shall be no bombs in this household!

It's just a play Aunt

Don't talk back to me, young lady!

Sorry Aunt

Why are you wearing a tea towel on your head?

It's a disguise so the spies don't see us

No we are the spies

So the others don't see us I don't remember who

May I have my tea towel, please.

Sorry Aunt

When you start doing the washing, then you may wear tea towels on your head.

Sorry Aunt

Till then, no tea towels.

Sorry Aunt we won't wear any more tea towels

Do you have any carp we could use for our play

Preferably alive carp

I've had quite enough of your game. Where is Charlotte? Why isn't she watching you?

She is watching us she's Queen Sophia settling a disquieting mist on the guards

I'll settle on her a disquieting mist! She was meant to be mending. Does it look like she's mending?

Sorry Aunt can we go now the horses' wings are on fire

You children are all mad!

Sorry Aunt can we go now

I shall have to talk with your father.

Sorry Aunt can we go now

THINGS A KING CAN'T DO IN GLASS TOWN

1. Nap under the neem tree whilst his councilors meet
2. Bomb his councilors
3. Say shut up to his councilors
4. Call his councilors old women or warty old women
5. Go off to war when his councilors are meeting
6. Declare war on his councilors
7. Kill the councilors' horses or magic steeds

DEAR LADY—
in which Father seeks another mother

WIDOWER GENTLEMAN SEEKS LOVELY LADY

Dear Lady, How I long to meet you, and care for you as my own! You are all I think about during my leisure moments, which are few as I am an active man. I am recently widowed, and bereft, as any would be, having lost the singular-most jewel in his crown. Though I am slowed by grief, please know, I am not melancholy by nature: it is chiefly for my cubs I fret! Who shall be their mistress and tend to their hurts with a mother's loving care? Who shall teach my daughters the graces and obligations of womanhood?

More about me: I am a serious man of early middle age (forty-four and one half); I incline to hard work, and shall continue so till I am incapacitated by blindness or death. My origins are humble but honest, and I was educated to be a gentleman. I can be a lively storyteller, for I have inherited some of my Father's blarney (they call me Paddy: I am Irish by birth!).

My household is well regulated, even after the loss of my Wife. My children know to contain their boisterousness when dining or entertaining guests. The eldest four read, and this occupies much of their day. We enjoy dinners together, and

Sunday afternoons at the Park, where the children like to run and "be children." We also enjoy the "menagerie": our puppy Alabaster, Basket the hound, and assorted fish, birds, and guinea pigs. Our lives are simple; we know no luxury except that of being together. We consider ourselves abundantly blessed.

My work: I minister to the poor. I seek justice. I right wrongs.

Most humbling moment: Watching my Wife expire, not longer than a month ago. She retained her dignity almost to the last.

Why you should get to know me: I am an upright man with a rent-controlled apartment. I am called brusque but am a gentleman, and strive always to do Good. You shall never lack affection or good counsel. I can teach you Latin and give you a family with six precious children to make your life complete. Maria, my eldest, is a shining light. Eight already, she is as wise and virtuous as any Poet or Judge. Eliza (nearly 7) has an eye for beauty, and does well in needlework. She could assist you with the linens—both ironing and mending. Lotte (5), also known as Charlotte, or Charley-Barley, or Charlemagne, depending on her mood, is impetuous, but learning to be moderate. She would have you know anything which is on her mind, even if you would not listen, though if you did, you would be surprised by what you hear. Branwell ("Bran") is my Only Son (4). He is a brave soldier with an outgoing temperament (were I to allow it, he might make a life for himself on the stage—but I shall steer him otherwise). Emily (3) is old enough to talk but prefers her own counsel, and the company of dogs, or any squirrel on the street! Baby Anne is too unformed to manifest character, but she is petted by her sisters, and shall grow into a fine girl.

I know you shall love—and tolerate!—my wastrels as I do. If this profile satisfies, please contact me, so we might learn more about each other, with a view toward marriage by early spring.

Income: My funds are barely sufficient to support my Family, so you must be willing to bring your own. Also, my son's education shall be in want of subsidy. Your funds should be inherited or already accumulated, as your labor will be needed in the household.

What I'm looking for: A robust woman, unafraid of hard work. Ladylike manners. A modest woman of refinement. Cheerful, perhaps not desirous of additional children. Healthy. Love of teaching, reading, cleaning a plus. Because my Family requires much energy, it is best that you be under the age of 30 and unmaimed.

SWEETNESS AND OUR HEARTS' DESIRE—
in which Maria remembers Mother

Papa shall be home any minute! The children are ready, all six of them!

He probably doesn't realize it's New Year's Eve.

Only Maria remembers New Year's Eve. Mama made everyone's favorite, before she died: meat and veg for Papa; applesauce for Bran; bread, melon balls, egg rolls for Lotte, Liza, Maria. Em's favorite was everything because she didn't know, and Annie was barely born.

Mama would decorate the apartment with streamers and light, six colors for six children.

We are festooned! she would say. We are bedecked!

Mama liked to use two words when one would do.

Look, she'd say, hugging Maria, haven't we the most festive, most delightful Haworthy House ever? (Haworth was the name of their building. The children do not live in a house!)

When everyone was seated, Em on Papa's lap, Annie on Maria's, Mama would point at the meat and veg and say, Look, here are All Good Things, and here, she'd say, pointing to the applesauce, is Hope! Spinach, her favorite, was Prosperity, melon balls were All Things in Good Time, the egg rolls Happy Days, and the bread A Mighty Good Laugh. So we might enjoy Prosperity, and Hope, and All Good Things with our new year, she liked to say.

For that one night, everything was perfect.

Maria reminded the little ones of this earlier that week. She assembled them, which means they sat in a circle on the floor of the lounge.

But bread isn't my favorite, Lotte said. My favorite is always cereal.

It was bread at that time, said Maria.

I don't think so, said Lotte. It's always cereal, as long as I can remember.

My memory is better than yours, Maria said, because I am old and you are not.

Maria is nearly nine. Since their mother died a year ago, Maria has been their Little Mother. Papa thought he might find another, but none will have us, said he.

It was me, Lotte said, so I remember.

Lotte is six and three-quarters, which is almost seven, old enough to know for herself, she would have thought.

Maria knows better than to argue with children, who are unable to reason, according to Papa, but this was important. Do it right this year, and they might do it right next year, and the year after that. Do it wrong now, and that part of their life was gone forever.

Would you really want *cereal* for New Year's Eve dinner? Maria asked. What would you do then for New Year's Eve breakfast?

Lotte could see the sense of that. So the children conspired throughout the week, considering what details they could. Maria has a food allowance—for peanut butter and jelly, jelly alone, soup in a can, toast and sardines. To make things easy, Monday is soup-in-a-can day, etc. The allowance isn't enough for streamers, six colors for six children, it isn't enough to festoon or bedeck, but Liza has supervised drawings, each of a family scene, and on New Year's Eve taped them to the wall, though Annie's was more of a multicolored scrawl. Maria has collected what coins she could find. These are coins Papa is more or less giving away, as he leaves them in his pants. Still, she didn't have enough.

I will do without egg rolls, she said. The applesauce and melon balls would double as desserts—what their mother called Sweetness and Our Hearts' Desire.

So now it's New Year's Eve, and everything is perfect! Papa takes his dinners out, to have peace and consider his work, so probably he's eaten, but that can't be helped.

It's Monday so maybe he thinks it's soup in a can, but no! Maria has made something special, and here's Papa, turning the key in the lock!

Six children await him, more or less in a row. They have been waiting some time, so there has been giggling and some departure from the row. But now they stand, eagerly, each holding a hand, all holding their breath, girls wearing white dresses and pinafores on which Liza, inspired by their father's botany book, has embroidered *something*—poppy for Maria, violet for Lotte, pansy for Em, a modest daisy for herself. Annie wears a pale pink romper, gift of a mother upstairs, while Bran wears the whitest shirt he has, which is yellow, with shorts—at least they're not red or blue. Maria has found a comb and pulled the girls' hair, wet, into braids: maybe they will stay that way! Annie's whisper-thin hair, blond and baby fine, has received a red bow from a wrapping paper tie. All faces are scrubbed. Branwell later obtained jam on the chin (he cannot explain), which Maria wiped and pinched, though gently.

What have we here? Papa asks as he enters the foyer which serves as their dining room. Six children, so neatly dressed! Maria, you have done this, I suppose?

Happy New Year! Emily, barely four, says, though she has been instructed to wait. Already, she's fussing with her braids, already she's pulling an elastic from her hair.

There's turkey for everyone! Charlotte yells, for she knows this is what will make Papa glad, and in fact, turkey boils at this very moment.

The children are ruining everything: Papa was supposed to sit at the table lovingly set by Liza. He would affix his napkin to his collar and Maria would bring out the surprise! Turkey, boiled in six sealed bags (Em would share with Anne), complete with gravy, rich and brown. Papa would clap with delight and safely snip the bag tops and squeeze gravy and turkey onto their plates so no one would be burned, or soiled. Then Maria would bring out the frozen peas which she had boiled. A two-course meal, meat and veg!

Good work, Maria, Papa says, for no matter how the children ruin everything, he always knows. You have made dinner?

Maria nods, unable to speak.

We shall sit in ascending order, youngest first, Papa says, and Maria is relieved that the evening is Papa's now. She is tired. Organizing children is difficult! But Annie doesn't have her own seat, which Papa doesn't remember. Maria grabs Annie and sits, Annie on her lap.

Excellent, Papa says. Now Em, now Lotte . . .

Branwell comes before Lotte, Lotte says, which is true.

Just making sure you're paying attention, Papa says, but Lotte suspects that isn't true.

No, Branwell, that's my chair. Please sit in a child-sized chair. There you go. Lotte. Liza. Excellent. Ah, but now Maria, you must get the food, I imagine.

He hasn't done things right at all. Maria passes Annie to Liza. It's okay, she thinks, it's going to be okay.

Maria has a platter for the turkey boiled with gravy in individual plastic bags, she has a pair of scissors with which to snip the top, she has peas in a bowl. She has to explain the scissors and the bags to Papa, who at first looks dismayed rather than pleased.

Ingenious! he cries. What a clever girl (as if Maria had put the turkey in the bags)!

Papa does the honors, gently dropping turkey slices from plastic bags onto every plate, then squeezing gravy, which all agree is the best part. Maria distributes the peas.

There's a quiet moment when it's unclear if Papa will remember.

The turkey is All Good Things, Maria prompts.

It certainly looks delicious, Papa says. Good job, Maria!

And these, she whispers in Papa's direction, pointing at the peas, are Prosperity.

There is silence.

You're not doing it right, Lotte says to Papa, her chin cradled in her clasped hands.

Elbows, Maria says, and Lotte removes them from the table.

Because it is only right we enjoy Prosperity and All Good Things on this most joyous day! Papa says.

The children smile, though it seems Papa's face trembles.

Shall we toast? Papa says. But we haven't any glasses, he says, piqued.

Liza, who is seven and a half, is embarrassed. She moves Annie back onto Maria's lap and brings out water glasses, filled, one at a time so she doesn't drop, one, two, three, four, five, plus Papa.

Papa once looks at his watch and once down the hall as he waits.

To the New Year! he exclaims, raising his glass. We have much to be grateful for. Now you raise your glasses, he says.

This is how we toast the New Year. We raise our glasses, acknowledge our gratitude, and drink some of this splendid water.

I'm not thirsty, Branwell grumbles. Can I have new toys?

We have Sweetness and Our Hearts' Desire for dessert, Lotte shouts.

You are all my Sweetness and my Heart's Desire! Papa says.

Maria smiles. Everything is going to be okay.

BRAVE SOLDIERS—
in which Maria and Eliza, maltreated, die

The social worker comes and the girls are gone. Four girls, all gone.

Bran is with Baby in the park, so he and Baby get to stay.

Bran gets soldiers. Twelve of them. He gives them names, then comes up with new names. The names don't seem right, without the girls.

Hey, ho! Bran says to the soldiers, who greet him each morning with a smart salute. There is Aeschylus, and Tacitus, and Marcus Aurelius, and others, whose names don't always come to mind. Mornings, Papa teaches Bran Latin and History—which is necessary as Bran is nearly six—but sometimes Papa doesn't open the door.

Bran shows the soldiers to Baby, but Baby just dribbles, which is disgusting. Her diaper is also disgusting, so Bran drops it in the toilet and goblins come up from the basement with guns and hammers. They clang and make sounds that make Papa moan. Bran puts Baby in front of Papa's door, so he can remember where she is, but Baby is crawling now, so she isn't always where she's supposed to be.

There used to be a bed in Papa's room but Papa set it on fire, Branny's not sure how. That's when the social worker came. Now there's a bucket in front of every room, with water, and Papa's desk, tall and big, is where the bed once was. This is better, because it doesn't remind Bran of their mother, also gone.

The soldiers are very brave. There is George I, Henry II, Charles III, and so on. He pretends to share them with the girls: there's Maria Theresa, Elizabeth Regent, Queen Lotte, Empress Em, and when Baby gets a soldier, it's Princess Anne. More often, Bran is mad at Baby, because she won't stop pooping. As long as he feeds her, all she does is pee and poop.

Bran makes dinner from cans he finds at the dollar store, using coins he takes from Papa's pants. Baby likes soup, but when he's angry he makes her spaghettios, which she spits to the floor. Branny makes the soldiers clean it up. They are so brave.

The soldiers lost their sisters, four of them, stolen just like that, when the soldiers were in the park with Baby defending a town. Otherwise, the soldiers, being brave, would have fought them, they would have killed the enemy severely and taken away their limbs. Maria in particular was good at taking care of Baby, but she is ten. She bought diapers, she put diapers on, she fed Baby out of jars with other babies on them, but those are expensive.

When Papa opens his door, he teaches Bran about the wars, so many wars! Each with its own weapons: flails, and halberds, and trebuchets. His soldiers now have something to play with! A world war, a civil war, a revolutionary war, a thirty-years' war. He should go to the library more, if he's to write his reports, but he gets tired carrying Baby like a log. So he makes things up in his reports, which his soldiers get to play out beforehand; Papa doesn't seem to mind, which shows Branny something about history, how flexible it is.

In Branny's civil war, with its Minié balls and smooth-bore muskets, Lotte is master general, organizing battles and regiments. Soldier Em is their tactician, wily and ruthless. Maria is Nurse Nightingale: she holds the soldiers when they fall, until they live again. Eliza sees to the mess hall; she's very good at keeping things clean, not a mess at all. And Branny is Chief Bombardier, braver than anyone! It is he who single-handedly and against all odds continually rescues the stolen nurse, and housekeeper, and general, et cetera! *Kaboom!* He bombs the enemy and down they fall: one, two, three, all his soldiers, down from the ledge, where they were about to attack. *Kaboom!* One falls out the window. Oops! Branny picks up Baby like a log and goes to find the soldier. Baby cries, Papa moans.

Branny piles Papa's newspapers outside Papa's door, three or four a day. The piles are mountains on which his soldiers plot revenge.

The sisters are utterly gone. Rarely, a letter comes. We do not like this place, they say. It is nothing like our place. The food is not good, the people are not kind. Please bring us home. Branny would walk to the address on the envelope and free them if he could, but he can't, not carrying Baby like a log, which is another reason he doesn't like her. He asks Papa why the sisters are gone, and Papa says, They're better off, they're cared for. We can take care of ourselves, you and I, but girls are different. Bran almost says, What about Annie, but she's a baby, not a girl, so Papa's right about that.

Some days Papa puts on a waistcoat. His eyes are brighter then. He straightens the drawing room and goes out. This is when he returns with money and Chinese food. Branny doesn't like Chinese food and Baby can't eat it, so Branny pretends he's eaten. I didn't know you were getting Chinese food, he says. Can I have money for diapers? Sometimes he'll ask about the sisters. They're not happy, he'll say, can we go get them? They don't need to be happy, Papa replies. I'm not happy, are you happy? It's enough that they're cared for: there can be no happiness in this world.

It's usually when Papa sleeps that Branny enters his room to take money from his pants, he and at least six of his soldiers. He squeezes past the enormous desk to the cot, where Papa lies with his waistcoat over his face. Once or twice Bran has used the money to buy comics, but then he was hungry so he stopped.

Soon Baby is standing and no one has taught her! If she can learn things, she can be his pupil. He can teach her Latin and she can play games! Blabablabablaba, she says, laughing. That's another thing no one taught her: to laugh!

Another letter comes, this time from Charlotte. Please take us away. I think our oldest sister is sick, certainly she is ill used. I fear for her safety, and the well-being of all of us girls.

But Bran doesn't like how Papa looks when he talks of them, so he hides the letter. He puts a soldier in an envelope to send, or he tries to, but it doesn't fit, so he takes it out again.

Maria is the first to come home. She's eleven now, but there's no flesh on her, she's lost much of her hair, she covers scars with long sleeves. Bran tries to interest her in his soldiers, but she says she needs rest. Sometimes she reads to Papa. You were always my favorite, Papa says, which Branwell knows can't be true, since he's the Only Boy.

It's becoming difficult to carry Baby like a log—she squirms and once she fell, plop onto her diaper! So he puts her in a cloth bag and takes her out that way to get soup. You must hold her this way, says Maria from her bed and Baby climbs onto her and laughs. Sometimes Maria sleeps with Baby. When she does, it's easy to get diapers. Bran's arms feel empty then and light.

He tries again to explain about the soldiers: this one is Vespasian, this one Caesar, this one Caligula, but Maria asks for quiet, a little quiet. Now Baby is walking, she's running! You must clean this place, Maria says, but Branwell knows that cleaning's not his job.

Maria doesn't eat the soup that Branny buys. You must bring the others home, she whispers, but Branny knows this isn't what Papa wants, Papa was happy with just the two of them, and Baby. This one is Robin Hood, this one Friar Tuck, this one King Arthur, this one Guinevere. Please, Branny, I love you, but I need quiet.

Maria teaches Baby some words: Banny, Banny! the little one cries. Is that me? Bran asks. She's not saying it right. Branny throws out the newspapers so Maria can't read to Papa, but she's done reading. She doesn't leave her bed now except to crawl to the bathroom, which is dirty—it's no longer just Baby who can't keep her poop to herself.

You must *do* something, Maria says. Our sisters need you! Dear Bran, you must be brave!

I am brave, he says. I'm the bravest of them all! Look—this is the general, and this the lieutenant, this is the commander, and this the admiral.

Maria dies, so they bring home Eliza, whose bones are bigger than she, whose eyes jump out of her head, who sleeps in Maria's bed because she can't climb to her bunk. Baby pounds the bed, wanting to play. Baby won't leave and Eliza won't play, so Branny has to drag Baby away by the arms, and she screams and kicks, so he hits her and covers her mouth.

Lotte and Em come home to see Eliza die. Lotte slaps Bran's face: she is thin, all angles and bones, she has lost much of her hair, but she is not exhausted like Eliza, she has not lost her fire. Bran tries to give her one of his soldiers, one of the best, she can have any she likes. You should have saved us, she says. Em is silent, Aunt arrives to create order, Papa emerges from his room wearing his waistcoat. They never talk of this again.

SMALL LIFE—
in which Aunt Branwell restores order

I am returned to this accursed house. Paddy has only this to say: *I did my best, who could know, no fault of mine.* Also, *much missed, what shall we do without.*

The eldest two are dead, the younger four but skin and bones.

Words he does not use: *bereft, so young, maybe I should have, won't you help us please.*

What did she see in him, my sister? This preposterous man, with his muttonchops and stained waistcoat, around whom there is only death?

He did not help me with my trunk—in his world, heavy boxes lift themselves. For this I was required to tip a loathsome man in a blue jumpsuit. The man's distaste for this home was plain: he would not cross its threshold, and no wonder: it smells of sour milk. The boy—there is only one—showed his muscle—both arms!—then tried to *push* the trunk toward my room. He was ready to assume the mantle of *man* but his effort scraped the floor. Paddy watched, explaining our weather, warm for June—he has meteorological opinions to go with opinions on every other thing! Except the matter of children, the eldest two gone through no fault of his.

I had thought, being a gentleman, he would allow me his room but, no, I must sleep in the lounge. On a *couch*. There being only a kitchen and the children's room besides, where four must sleep on conjoined beds, two atop two. And a WC smaller than my pantry at home.

The boy Branwell makes comic faces hoping for reaction; his hair is red and flyabout. The girls are watchful, curious. Charlotte, nine, is eldest now; she's small, with sharp features on a square, unpleasing face; Emily is angular and undisturbed; Anne, the youngest, is light-haired and fretful. They remember nothing of my help when their mother died; they remember nothing of that year or me. I am a stranger, one they cannot bring themselves to embrace except as instructed: Kiss yer aunt, said Papa, when I arrived, and youngest to oldest pecked my cheek. I am not so deprived of human contact that I enjoyed their forced affection.

This visit shall be short. When my sister died, a week of succor became months became nearly a year. I returned home to learn my cat had died: the neighbor said kidney failure; more likely, he was careless with her life. My book group was taken over by a woman who favors *mystery*. Life—my life—continued without me. It wasn't a big life, but it was *my* life; I'll not risk losing it again.

Charlotte summons her council of faeries. I am but three days among them and already she has decided: I am a witch! Sit, she commands the younger and, knees touching, they sit. Assume thy invisibility caps! says she, and all put potholders atop their heads, square and soiled.

A: I can still see you.

C: That's because you're wearing the hat.

A: Can Rider see us?

E: All animals can see us. There is no question of that.

A: Even if they don't wear a hat?

E: Especially if they don't wear a hat.

C: I call this meeting to order. We shall commence to engage telepathically!

B: That never works.

C: Only because you don't try.

B: I try, I try very, very hard! Harder than anyone!

C: Try again. Close your eyes. The question is—concentrate, everybody!—what do we do about our predicament!

She presents the evidence (non-telepathically): Aunt is old, and ugly, which is true of all witches. I appeared "out of nowhere," which is what witches do. Also, I am nothing like their mother and therefore no true relation. Also, I want to take the place of their mother. Further, I don't love them: this is obvious as I give them bologna for lunch when cereal will do. Moreover, she has witnessed ceremonies, *evil* ceremonies, the particulars of which she shall not mention, lest the younger ones scream at night and damage her sleep.

C: You may now communicate with me telepathically. Bran, being second oldest, is first.

. . .

C: Try harder, Poopface.

B, *whispering*: *She's not so bad. I don't mind her so much though I don't like bologna.*

C: Adjust your cap! You're speaking out loud.

B, *shouting*: Invisibility has nothing to do with telepathic communication. I don't believe you've ever communicated telepathically with *anyone*!

C: I do! Every day! I do! I do! With *them*! Every day!

E: You've made Annie cry! We're going to the living room.

C: There is no living room, remember? *She's* taken it. Who likes porridge? Porridge is awful but she makes us eat it every day!

The boy proposes an all-out battle, with trebuchets.

B, *shouting*: We shall strike at dawn!

C: Don't be ridiculous. This wants a subtler approach.

A: We could tell Papa.

C: He is bewitched, chicken, weren't you listening? Em, what do you think? She has said your dogs are filth and want putting down.

(I thought but did not say it: Charlotte is a greater witch than I.)

E: We shall shun her. Aunt is a small-minded woman who likes small talk with small-minded people; we shall give her none, and she shall long for her little home and soon return.

C: This is a route more civilized than poison or magic spells, and more likely to succeed.

The children lay forth a plan for shunning: they shall pretend not to hear me when I call. Confronted, they shall not answer, but instead look over a shoulder or at their feet. Asked a question in their Papa's presence, they shall manage with shakes and shamefaced nods.

C: I adjourn this meeting of the faerie contingent!

To which all shout, Hooray!

I did not stand before the door as Charlotte rallied her minions; I do not lurk or spy. I was merely refilling the water pot before their door: Paddy's protection against fire.

This house is small, besides, and their voices loud.

I have only to put this house in order, then I am away, and gladly, shunned or no.

My sin, aside from being a witch who is not their mother? I insist on bedtime. I require protein and roughage. I critique their hygiene. When Charlotte was insolent, I removed her to the WC, taking the bulb with me. You shall stay here till the bells doth toll, said I, referring to the church carillon. She lost her characteristic bravery and screamed and begged for egress. Ghosts patrol the room, said she; the walls are red with clotted blood! Later I saw the door unlocked. I had to wee, Em said, the innocent.

Your action was extreme, Paddy said. Charlotte is but nine, and tender.

Nonsense, said I. I experienced the same at seven; it did me no harm.

I did not say that his wife, as child, escaped all punishment no matter the crime, dissolving always in preemptive tears. Charlotte, like me, is made of sterner stuff: she is not so easily broken. Like me, she shall have to learn self-control. Like me, she shall have to be strong.

Children require discipline, said I, even as they mourn. And care! I added, when he did not reply. None shall blame you for the elder two, but the remaining four are sticks! You do not feed them, nor are they dressed as girls and boys should dress. Do they have a change of underthings? I have yet to find them. There is a chill straight through your house, the hall is thick with dust, the shower without soap. Are your children clean, sir? Do you care? Have you given thought to their future? Soon they will be grown, young ladies and one young man—you must see to their manners and their schooling! They run like beasts, with no pattern except to sleep at night and dine with you, and no learning except what they might glean from whatever book they may find. You do not choose their books, Paddy! How can their morals be sound?

You shall not regulate their reading, was all the man could say.

They do not see you! 'Tis not right you should mourn if it takes you from the living!

You shall not regulate their reading, said he again.

Yer as mad as they, said I, and retired to my room.

'Tis a mercy my stay be but two weeks, one of them gone, for the noise even as four brush their teeth—a new practice, judging by the results—deafens me. They play but soon find fault—and rage, and scream, and scratch. Is screeching what children do? My sister followed me like a baby goat, and then I was off, working in a tea shop so she might learn.

The children tell one hundred tales of the "departure" of Eliza and her sister. They have flown away, or were eaten by bears; they hide in the basement, have been murdered by thieves; they are off in a huff but soon will be back. Maria shall again be their Little Mother, Eliza shall resume care of the household, all will be well. It is possible they do not know the facts.

They do not mourn their sisters, except at night. I leave them to it, for it is not right they rely on me, who shall leave them soon. Paddy is not *here*, properly speaking, for always he has a Thing that wants doing. They comfort each other, then—the younger two, Em and Anne, holding each other on a bunk as the elder two conspire, forehead to forehead.

Today I found Charlotte crying in the kitchen, holding a butter knife. Instead of hiding her tears, she threw herself upon me, saying, Aunt, oh Aunt! I had to pry her hands from my waist.

Find a tissue, said I, then we shall see about combing your hair.

Before I arrived, they had but one comb among them, and used it but rarely.

We do not talk of such things, Paddy said, when I asked him again. You shall not either, if you know what's good for you.

They quiet only when reading. And when constructing stories, for which they create masterful drawings, drawings I see only in passing for they are not to be shared with the likes of me. The boy being closest in age to the eldest is her natural ally and they write together, on scraps rescued from their father's bin. Emily and Anne compose tales together, about a different set of characters, all lords and ladies and crystal towns. The result is books small as postage stamps, which they hide, inexpertly. Eventually harmony gives way and shouting resumes.

I cannot think where they came from, these heathen children who rampage and desire my death! They have my brother-in-law's vices, his head in the clouds, and none of *her* virtues! My sister was gentle and obliging; they are harsh and emphatic!

Not even forty when she died, bearing six children in six years like a broodmare.

He was supposed to send them to school. I do not know why he did not send them to school.

I act as barricade, standing before their papa's door. If he is allowed a measure of peace, might he agree to spend time at their home? Charlotte tries to push me aside: she has a flower she wishes him to see. It is nothing so special, just a dying thing she's pulled too early from the ground. It can be made into tea to heal her father's croup, says she. If not, 'tis pretty to look upon and may cheer him.

Quiet will cheer him, say I.

No! she shouts. My flower will cheer him! Smell it—it's like a rose!

If she cannot learn control, she will not assume the life her father has laid out for her—a small life with no prospects, no purpose. Perhaps when the time comes, she'll be put to work so a younger may learn, so a younger may live a larger life. If she is lucky, the younger will appreciate her sacrifice: she will not choose a baby every year, she will not choose to die.

At dinner, Charlotte shows the marks I have made upon her arm, dragging her from her Papa's door. 'Twas my intention, says she, to tear her arm from her dying corpse.

Not now, Lotte, Paddy says, hands at his temples. I have a fiercesome headache.

You must stop her! Charlotte shouts, standing. You must do something!

Enough! her father shouts. You will apologize and sequester yourself. None may bring you dinner, not even your aunt, who loves you with a mother's tender love!

Six days to go. I have made an ally of the boy, which was not hard. I merely said, You look dandy, after he'd washed his head. His smile was something to behold! Now I must engage the girls in useful pursuit. I start with the oldest, as the others may follow her lead.

Me: Charlotte, are you ready to learn to sew?

C:

Me: It is polite to answer when someone speaks to you, Charlotte!

C: It is polite to address someone by their proper name.

Me: And what is your name, if not Charlotte?

C: Charlemagne, I've told you. Today it is Charlemagne.

Me: You have but one name, the name your parents gave you.

C: I have many names, depending on the day and the game we play.

Me: You have but one name as you are but one person.

C: I am as many persons as I wish to be.

Me: A child your age has no wishes, she wants only what her parents wish for her. And you have but one name, until you take that of a man.

C: I shall never take a man, or his name.

Me: Nonsense! Of course you shall.

C: You didn't.

Me: That's different.

C: How is it different?

I do not say that my youth was required so my sister might have hers. Instead, I say: Sewing time, child. You *will* learn how to sew!

I teach her to hem. Your brother and sisters will not stop growing, say I, so you must do this when I am gone.

You shall not continue among us, then? asks she, carefully needling the edge of a skirt.

You know very well I shall not, say I.

I know nothing of the sort, says she, insulted. I remember, again, how things are not discussed in this household.

I return to my home on Monday, say I, and check her face for joy. But she is crafty: her face betrays nothing but absorption in her task.

What is your home like? asks she. Is it very much like this one?

Oh, no! say I, and stop her hand, so she will not miss a stitch. I have a little house on a mountaintop, where I have lived my entire life. I have friends there, and a cat named Plenty.

We don't go to school, says she, so we have no friends.

You have each other, say I, having no other retort.

Papa says schools are ensnaring and propagate delusion. The delusion being that life is not fleeting, and we shall not be held to account.

Straighten your stitch, say I, wishing to avoid the subject of delusion.

So we teach ourselves. In the library. And other places.

Fascinating, I say. I'm sure you benefit greatly.

She nods. What do you do for fun in your house on a mountaintop? she asks.

I sing in a choir, and chair refreshments at the fête. And I'm in a book group with other ladies. Sometimes I garden.

Is that it? she asks, impertinent thing.

I haven't need for more, if that's what you mean.

Don't you wish to travel, and learn things, and meet famous people, and become famous yourself? A life lived wholly in such a small place must be very small indeed!

What appears to be small can be large in your heart. If it is your lot to give yourself to duty, you can learn to love that life.

That life shall not be my life, says she. I shall never have that life.

Very well, I say, and now you must redo every stitch.

My suitcase is packed. My hair is up, I wear my hat and gloves. The children are out, to spare us parting.

I: I wish you well, Paddy.

P:

I: I do not see that you have made arrangements. I have warned you that I am leaving. Who is to watch the children when I am gone?

P:

I: Some might blame you, leaving Maria and her sister in charge of the young, but Maria was sensible. Charlotte is neither old enough nor sensible.

P:

I: Paddy, say something. My car awaits. My home awaits, my cat awaits.

P:

I: You have no one, have you?

P:

I: You haven't money to hire a person. You have tried marriage, and none will have you. And my sister's inheritance? It was a goodly sum. Is it gone?

Paddy looks around, helplessly. I am to understand that it is gone, he cannot find it.

And my small life, Paddy? I think but do not say. Am I not to have even that? Am I to be a visitor in your home forever, living in my sister's coffin? I gave up everything for her and now must give up more?

At that moment, the children arrive, panting and red faced, talking all at once about the journey they have made to the wilds, the monster they found there.

They stop short.

You are still here, says Em.

I shall be your mother now, say I. Come, embrace me: I shall be your mother now.

HALF-LIFE OF A STOLEN SISTER—
in which four children learn and play

Bran is doing a jig. Through the seeing-eye-glass, Lotte spots him on a hillock, his arms outspread, his hair tangled and flying over his head.

He shouts into his headset: Branwell Brontey is master of all he foresees!

There is something essential Bran does not understand about being a spy.

You're talking about yourself in the third person again, Lotte says.

Lotte's spy-place is a tangle of bushes near a cluster of picnics. There will be much intelligence there, and none on Bran's hilltop.

The mission to rescue the Stolen Sisters—girls of all virtue with hair of fine-spun gold—was advancing. The sisters—Maria and Elizabeth—leapt from the tower of their imprisonment at the beginning of time, their hands entwined, only to be captured by the lurking Giants of Evil, who held them for eventual marriage to the ugly, ancient sons of the Everlasting King of Darklingland. The spies are proud of their progress. The state of Branny's britches, grass stained and soiled, however, is much less satisfactory.

It is Bran who presents their work to Papa: he alone is allowed in Papa's bedroom-cum-office. To read their report on Benedict Arnold, Ethel Rosenberg, Aldrich Ames, and all the Cambridge spies (a spy for each of their names), Papa sits at his desk, which is tall and broad; Papa too is tall and broad, big compared with every other man and possessed of a large voice.

Lotte listens through the wall to what Bran says, and broils with rage: his discussion of their studies is incomplete! Papa has no choice but to correct him!

When she was younger, Papa found her overcome by tears and sobs.

It's not fair! she said. I am the oldest! I am the one who chooses our day's study—I should be the one to report! He gets it wrong all the time! Papa, he makes us look like fools!

Passionate Lotte, Papa said, and it's unclear if he approves. If it is true, as you say, that Branwell misreports, oughtn't we allow him practice, that he may improve?

But we learned so much more than he said! she cried, stomping a foot. There is the truth of the matter, and there is what he says.

The truth of the matter, Papa said. That may be something we hold safely in our hearts.

I would share it, Lotte complained.

This is not how I would have you known, Papa said.

Lotte was unimpressed. How then, she asked.

Goodness, he said. I would have you known for goodness.

But I'm *not* good! Lotte said.

Exactly, Papa said, and that is that.

Sketching is a good way to spy. You can look at anything, watch anyone with a pencil in your hand. So they are at the Museum, sketching dioramas. Em sketches the rainforest. Beyond the tips of the canopy emerge the tallest buildings in the world, part of Glass Town, home of the Angels of Light, who have four names, one for each direction, and they are called: Charlemagne, Brancaccio, Emmeline, and Antidote. They stand tall against the Evil Giants, the insinuating Lords of Darklingland. Em quite forgets the leafcutter ant and cassowary as she draws crystal paths and jeweled walkways, and soon the diorama is all Glass Town, all shining light. In the upper corner, too far to touch, Stolen Sisters fly in gossamer gowns.

It is only while sketching that Bran is still. Otherwise, he has a motor that forces his legs to twitch, or run. Just as he has an amplifier in his throat that makes him shout when whispers will do. They hear through their headsets as he blows up a Kodiak bear. *Ka-blam!* he says, his voice low. *Ka-blam!* he says, louder.

Lotte pinches him. She sketches the same diorama, because she knows she will do better. She peeks at Bran's drawing: emerging from the bear habitat in the Dark Northern Land, crazed soldiers clutch at bayonets, each pierced through the eye or heart by an outsized arrow, dripping blood. Green men perch in trees, holding daggers in their teeth. *Ka-blam!* Bran shouts. A bomb falls now on one and all—all of them doomed, soldiers and green men alike.

Shh!

Bran and Lotte look over their shoulders. As Bran offers his usual apology (*I'm sorry! It was immoderate of me*), Lotte whispers into her headset: Troll sighted. Request backup!

It is at night they make most progress locating the Stolen Sisters, for it is then they write about Glass Town. Lotte and Bran, being older, occupy the top bunks, while Em and Anne, eight and six, sleep closer to the ground. Each has an identical notebook: red, orange, yellow, and green, youngest to oldest. Together, they define the landscape: boroughs, enchanted and enslaved; island kingdoms, populated by serfs and tsarinas; bridges controlled by demons who traffic in information and magic charms. Always, new obstacles, more enemy agents, more criminals who must be caught, beasts who must be tamed through the judicious use of spells and potions if the sisters are to be saved, always more evil, and only the four of them—four Angels of Light, four Geniuses, four cardinal points—on the side of right. And tonight, a new troll, wearing gabardine and holding keys, a troll with impossibly long, multijointed fingers, for poking and prodding, sent by whom? The Giants of Evil! The Lords of Darklingland! The Everlasting King himself! The children write their stories separately, each in his own way, in print small enough to resemble typeface, though often, come morning, Annie is curled by Em, her sister's pencil in her hand.

The bells toll, and Lotte hears them, the Stolen Sisters. Save us, they whisper. Save us! We are so scared!

We're coming, Lotte whispers back. Wait for us! We're on our way!

They breakfast in Auntie Brontey's room, which used to be the living room, before Mama died. Auntie's not a Brontey, not really—she's a Branwell, but Ant-y Branty, no matter how you pronounce it, doesn't sound quite so *well*, and what's more, Branny won't have it. Everything about the Only Son deserves respect, says he, especially his name, which will carry forward through the generations. Who else will take care of you, when the time comes? he asks.

It had better be Bran, because the sisters will not marry. They swore an oath to this effect and solemnized it at the Great Fountain. They promised to die together, so none would ever have to be alone. Then they licked a poisonous leaf in turn, and survived the ordeal.

Auntie makes oatmeal on her hot plate: the whole apartment smells of oatmeal. In Auntie's room, two space heaters, two layers of rug—who'll take care of the young'uns, she says, if Auntie takes a chill? The children share folding tables in pairs, not speaking till spoken to; when Auntie judges they're done, she brings out her sewing, a wicker basket with tapestry top and pink satin interior—Lotte wishes it for picnics, but Auntie says No!

If Aunt has her way they'll soon be at school, but for now they teach themselves.

Shoo, she says, handing out bologna sandwiches. Back before dark.

The children file out of the building, one after the other, eyes on the ground so they don't have to see the doorman, whom they know to be savage. He smells of smoke and his cuffs are soiled. Rent control, they've heard him say. Six of 'em in three rooms. Oughta be a law.

He thinks them deaf, in addition to cretinous, for the children have heard other things:

Run wild in the building till I put a stop to that.

Mother lovely lady, poor soul. They put her in the grave.

His lackey, one of three goblins who inhabit the building's nether regions, an assortment of weapons attached to his belt, says, The tall one'll be a looker someday.

At this, Em's head doesn't snap up, for she is the tall one. Bran considers whether he must fight the goblin, but decides the time isn't right.

The four are out the door—free!

There are things they no longer do, not since the sisters were lost. They do not split up; they do not travel the city alone or in pairs. They do not seek a talking eagle in his aerie, nor look to survey Glass Town from above. Their search has a different logic: stay close together and close to the ground.

They ask a librarian, the nice one with the burnt mouth, for an important Maria, a brave Elizabeth, for each of the stolen ones. So Lotte and Bran have Betsy Ross; Em and Anne have Marie Antoinette. Tonight, Betsy Ross will sew a flag for Glass Town: a colored stripe for each cardinal point—red, orange, yellow, green, youngest to oldest—a star for each Stolen Sister. Then Marie Antoinette, vile encroacher, will battle Elizabeth Regent, Virgin Queen of Glass Town. Bran will see to it that all the soldiers die, then Lotte the Geniius will raise them up.

Last week, Lizzie Borden set fire to the Enchanted Forest, while Mary Queen of Scots was exiled to the Land of Frozen Ladies for her betrayal of the sisters. Through it all, Marie Curie seeks a cure in her Glass Town laboratory, asking: what is the half-life of a Stolen Sister?

Lotte doesn't like library days; it's on those days they speak most strongly.

Save us! they say. Help us. *Lotte! Please!*

Outside each room is a bucket of water. Inside each room, a fire extinguisher. Papa takes no chances with his darlings. Sometimes when they must enact a battle scene, they wear their gas masks to the basement, their hair flying behind them, the girls distinguished now only by their height and the quality of their screams.

Annie was feeling sad; she had a nightmare. I saw them, she whispered from her lower bunk. They looked just like us. Did they? Did they look just like us?

They were crying, Annie said. They wanted to be saved.

Lotte has also been dreaming. When she dreams, the sisters aren't sad, they're angry. It was you! they say. *You* were supposed to save us! Why didn't you save us?

At dinner, they submit to their father's questioning.

What is virtue? he asks the youngest.

Obedience and self-reliance in equal parts, answers Anne.

What does the future hold? he asks the Only Boy.

Brilliance, Bran answers, and sorrow, in equal parts.

What is the good life? he asks the tall one.

It is here, she answers. It is what we have.

What do we seek? he asks the one who chews her nails.

We seek what's stolen, Lotte would like to say. *We seek what we have lost.*

Forgiveness, she replies. We seek forgiveness.

The next morning Lotte describes a vision she's had. It is almost true, what she says, depending on what you think of visions. In this case, it's something she has imagined and almost saw, or would have seen, had she opened her eyes. A vision of kindly Maria Theresa, speaking from her cloud throne. Go to a small garden, she bade us, and in that small garden, find the smallest tree, and on that small tree, find a golden pear. When we eat that pear, taking equal bites each of us—she looks at Bran—we will learn a vital clue. Everything will be different.

Where is it, asks Em, who already knows.

You will be blind children today, Lotte says. I will lead and you will follow.

Annie is happy, she likes wearing blind-girl glasses.

Bran is happy: when they eat the magic pear, everything will be different, which means he can be Brancaccio, the Italianate Prince and his sisters will be Italianate Under Princesses!

Only Em is not happy. And Lotte. But Lotte is never happy.

The children put on their dark glasses and take their sticks from under Annie's bed. It pleases their father to think they will hike today, in the all-healing sun.

Lotte takes them to the subway, three blind children with sticks. She makes sure they get seats. They softly sing a blind-children's song. Three blind mice, three blind mice. Lotte closes her eyes: she sees two girls, waving, two girls dressed in white.

Out in the air, Emmy pales. Though she cannot see, she knows where she is.

It's wrong! she says. Charlotte! You know it's wrong! and she opens her eyes. And coughs, and chokes, as if swallowing smoke.

She does not say it: Lotte has taken them to the Land of Unwholesome Fire. Where the Stolen Ones were lost.

Annie does not understand, Bran understands only that action is required.

Tag! he shouts, punching Anne. You're it! and off he runs, back down to the subway.

Reluctantly, Lotte follows. If you breathe very hard, Lotte thinks, some part of them comes back to you, part of them on the wind.

Em is silent that night as Bran and Lotte map the Land of Unwholesome Fire. There is the valley of boiled bones, the plain of ash, the scorched forest where nothing can grow. Bordering this Land, a line of golden pear trees.

Anita, the Italianate Under Princess, falls asleep in Emme-lina's shaking arms.

———

Lotte takes them to the art museum, but first they dance in the rain. Water drips down their faces as they smile to the sky, white dresses flying. Bran runs down the hill shrieking: I am Master of the universe! Lord of the upper and lower realms!

Payment being voluntary, they walk through the queue, faces down, hair dripping. They will sketch still lives from Distinct Artistic Periods. Em and Annie sit before Dutch tulips. Bran has found a bloody hare. Lotte, on a different floor, sits before a guitar, a newspaper in pieces, they remind her of the world shattering. But then she sees, from the corner of her eye—a white dress fluttering!

Lotte can't believe it! She drops her sketch pad, her pencil, and runs, and shouts into her headset: I've seen them, one of them, they're here!

A gabardined troll grabs her; the dress turns another corner and it's gone.

I saw her! Lotte screams. She's there! You have to let me go!

The trolls do not believe Lotte is home-schooled. They do not believe she's in the Museum alone. They do not believe her name is Lotte Brontey or that her father does not own a telephone. She has no nails left to chew. She tastes blood. Two of her fingers bleed.

They examine her talkie-walkie. Hello? they say. Hello? They will not let her go, she will not say where she lives, there is no Reverend Pastor Brontey, Esq., in the directory, there is no Auntie Brontey. They sit her atop the Information Desk, so she might be claimed. As the Museum closes, she sees Bran, Em, and Anne linger by the door. She gestures with her chin that they must go. This is something they swore they would never do, but they cannot all be captured.

The troll examines Lotte's sketch pad, the dioramas, the drawings of Maria Theresa on her cloud throne. Marie Antoinette stabbed by the Virgin Queen. Marie Curie laboring for her cure. We will call the police now, the troll says. It will be unpleasant for your parents.

My mother is dead, Lotte says. We killed her with our stuff and nonsense.

The troll visits the coat check, to see if a coat is there, or maybe a bag. Lotte runs. Out the door and down. Down, down, down! No one chases her, but still she runs. Into the park, and up a hillock, up up! She runs as if lifted by wings, and she is, lifted—by girls in white dresses, two of them.

The world is silent now, except for the wind. Below, she can see the park, she can see Branny's hillock, the bushes where she listened, looking for clues.

One of the sisters says, not unkindly, You were supposed to look out for us.

I was looking out, she whispers. Truly I was. You went to get clouds for Maria Theresa's throne.

You looked away. You were supposed to guard the door and count.

I counted, she whispers. I did!

They fly through clouds now, clouds thick and dark. Lotte breathes them in, their dust fills her throat.

This was the condition by which you were allowed to play with us, Lotte.

I lost count, just for a moment, Lotte cried. It was the airplane, it made me look up, it made a crashing sound.

We called out to you, we called out to you in your ear.

You asked me to save you.

We did, but you didn't.

I couldn't get in the door! There was so much noise. They pushed me away. Oh, Eliza! Maria! I tried! It wasn't my fault.

The clouds through which they fly are ashes and bone, they are flame, the little girls fly.

TROLLEY—
in which Branwell attempts to do Good Work

We take a trolley. I ask for quarters and dimes so I might show how well I count and apportion them. I hold on to a pole and imagine the men I shall meet. They wear ragged black coats held high with rope belts, and shoes with holes at the heel or toe. They hold caps when Papa arrives; when he passes, they touch his jacket, murmuring thanks.

The trolley twists and turns with no care for the riders within. I nearly lose my footing and step on my pater's toe.

If there is a lesson I would have you learn today, my Papa says before we open the door, it is to be humble, for any may fall into life's morass and, once fallen, find it difficult to arise. We must extend a hand to those who fall; it is through such acts that we are known.

I can do that, I think. I can extend my hand to any who lie upon the ground, though I am small for my age, somewhat, and may have a hard time bringing him up.

'Tis well to see one's pater stand tall amongst lesser men. Several persons rush to greet him. Papa praises their efforts, for they do Good Work. I do not like the way they greet me—very much as one would a small child. I am polite, however, and explain that no, I'm not in a "grade," for I am home-schooled and therefore have no favorite subject, though I do enjoy translating Latin, and also writing poems. Their eyes open wide with admiration! Papa is displeased. I begin to feel angry inside for it is my view that if a person troubles himself to accomplish something he should then have the right to share that thing with others.

They return to their work, which is nothing more than ladling stew. The men do not have rope belts, nor do they wear caps. I may have learned something about imagination, then recall that what I had imagined was in fact a color plate from Dickens, so it is not my imagination which is to blame but his.

I am struck by inspiration. Perhaps I can help, Papa?

He looks upon me, all pride. I was hoping you would offer.

He puts a plastic jug of water in my hand. And some plastic cups.

I would have you offer water. If it is your wish to stop a minute to converse, you may do so.

I must look stricken, or unsure.

You may talk freely upon many things, says he. The weather, or you may ask how they find the stew. I should not ask about Current Events, lest you reveal your new friends to be ignorant. Go, he says, and pushes me toward the first table.

I stand at its head a moment. I am unnoticed.

Water? I ask. One man, clean shaven with a scarred neck, waves me over. I am to pour water into his cup, though it is nearly full. I find my hand shaking and spill water upon his shorts. He jumps up and says something I may not repeat.

Do you not even apologize? the rough man asks. I nod and turn quickly to another table. There, I manage to pour without mishap, and then, because a man asks my name, I offer it.

A good name, says he.

Thank you, say I and ask, How do you find your stew, good man?

At which point every man at that table did laugh.

I turn, ears burning, and approach a new table, at which men sit who know each other.

Water, gentlemen? I mumble, with none of my former enthusiasm.

A swarthy man, heavier than one might think a hungry man to be, says, Well, here's a fine-looking red-headed chap, and gestures that I should sit.

I guess the stew be good, to see you so jolly, venture I.

You haven't tasted it, young gent? he says, smiling so I know he means me no harm.

I am to eat after you. Leftovers, say I.

This was not true, for I had eaten stuffed cabbage at home, but it would have been my father's answer, to demonstrate humility.

If ye've not et, ye must be hungry and weak, says a second, who is smaller, and not jolly.

I am not, say I, for I eat regularly and can withstand a late lunch. Also, I am of a strong constitution, though I am small.

Still, says the jolly one, who says his name is Terry. Still, you should sit, for ye've been serving a while now, and I would guess you're not accustomed.

No, sir, you are right. This is my first time at the soup kitchen dining room, at which they laugh, and again I burn. Soup-serving place, I say, whatever. Do you want water? I say. Also, I have cups.

I have something better, says Terry, still jolly. I have juice in this container here, and he shows me a flat metal bottle. We've been sharing. Let's call it apple juice. How old are you, son?

Nearly twelve, say I, for it was nearly true.

Plenty old to share juice with some well-meaning lads. You'd like?

I consider what my pater would prefer.

Yes, please, I say. I should like that very much.

Jolly Terry looks around. Here, he says, you sit here, between Jim and Pet.

The two make room.

Take a nice deep gulp, says he. It's good for ya!

One sip and I know it isn't juice. No fruit makes a burning sensation down one's throat, and travels so warmly, and settles so nicely in one's depths. I take a second sip, and pass the contrivance, which Terry calls a flask.

Ye like it, says unsmiling Jim.

I do, quite, I say.

Ye'd like some more, asks he.

With pleasure, say I. And so we continue, passing the flask, I asking questions about the stew and the weather, they replying with well-considered answers (the stew lacked seasoning, the weather is warmish but they fear rain), and soon we are the best of friends. I cannot understand why I had found these men forbidding or strange, when in fact they wish me only well! Emboldened, I tell them of my prowess with Latin and Greek, and ask if they know anything of Current Events, though it was perfectly alright if they did not, and Terry laughs, and Jim and Pet laugh, and I laugh most of all, until my pater arrives.

Up, says he.

I'm none too certain on my feet. He sniffs my face. What have you been doing? says he.

Enjoying conversation with these fine gentlemen, I say, and giggle. As you said I should.

He slaps my face.

I do not feel manly then—so shocked by his attack that I begin to cry.

You have been drinking alcohol, he says. I can smell it.

Never! say I, sobbing. I wouldn't! I would never drink alcohol.

Yer bonny boy wished it, says Terry. He took a shine to it, I think he has a future here.

You said it was apple juice! I protest. They said it was apple juice! explaining, though my words in my sobs were none too clear. I thought it was apple juice!

You believed it was apple juice? Papa says. If so, I shall apologize. If you did not know you drank alcohol, I shall expel these three men, and they shall never return.

I look at my friends. They had ought to lose, for they had no need of my father's good opinion whereas I would need it every day of my life!

I nod.

You understand what you say? If they are hungry, they may not return here. They shall deserve to be hungry if they have given you whiskey without your knowledge. But if you speak an untruth, they will go hungry and the sin shall be upon you. Is this what you mean to say?

I nod again.

The world turned unpleasantly, as if we were on a trolley and I might at any moment fall.

DEAD DRESSES—
in which Charlotte abandons everyone

It being an odd day, they meet on Emmi's bunk, Emmi being the odd one. Tomorrow, they will meet on Anni's bunk, Anni being the even one, even though Emmi is twelve and Anni eleven, almost. Branni, on a top bunk, is the leap year: look! he leaps from bunk to bunk, how odd! He leaps because they are three now, not four: Lotti, aka Naughti, is back at school, she's back at boring boarding school, abandoning them all to Papa's silences and Aunt's sewing hour. She writes excited letters: I'm learning Geography! I'm learning Arithmetic! As if hills and numbers were something to talk about.

In leaping, Branni slips and all but falls between the bunks. His leg dangles, already he's screaming, and not just because Emmi has taken a bite of his thigh.

When Papa sent Emmi to boarding school with Naughti, she famously stopped eating.

I was more dead than alive, she explained to Anni. They had to send me home.

What was it like, almost dying, Anni asks, not for the first time.

It was very, very quiet, Emmi says. Every anomalous day, it was quieter.

It sounds nice, Anni says. Everything quiet.

Emmi doesn't like it when Anni talks like that: You will never

die, Em says, because we will always be together. She squeezes
Anni under the covers.

But if we weren't, Anni says, reasonably.

Branni continues to scream.

The reasons Lotti is naughti are self-evident:

She abandoned them.

She likes it where she is.

Where she is is very stupid, but she likes it.

She tells everyone she likes it, she doesn't care who hears.

She says she misses them, but if she did, she wouldn't be
there, she'd be here.

She acts like they should want to go, too.

She writes letters, but not often enough, and when she does,
she writes about being *there*.

She thinks she's better than everyone, because she knows
about numbers and hills.

Before they talk of Glass Town, Emmi and Anni must:

Show each other their roosters. They must touch each other's
roosters, but only a tap. They must touch tongues (three times).
They must say magic words.

The rooster thing happens in the bathroom, where the
girls pee together, despite Auntie's admonishments. Touching
tongues happens under the covers.

Actually, they don't show their roosters anymore, not since
Emmi started sprouting, soon she will be an animal, not a rooster.

The magic words happen in each other's ears.

The princess is held captive in the evil Lord's dungeon, her hands
in irons over her head.

She groans wretchedly, says Emmi, under the covers.

Yes, says Anni.

But no one can hear.

Except the imprisoned old man, remember? The one who gave away the secret of the castle when he was a boy. He has a beard down to his knees which covers his . . .

His choo-choo, I remember, but he's dead.

Oh, Anni says.

The princess doesn't have to look at that.

I've got a secret, Branni says from his bunk, casually, as if to himself.

His voice cracks and creaks because of the apple in his throat: it's easy to ignore him.

The girls lie close together, Emmi's arm around Anni.

Evil Lord Castlering makes her take off her clothes, Emmi whispers. He lets the servants look at her. He makes her show them her rooster.

Maybe her hair is long enough to cover that, Anni says.

No, says Emmi. This is when she cries abundantly.

Can the fairy godmother arrive? asks Anni.

There is no fairy godmother, Emmi says.

It's a really good secret, Branni says. If my sisters are nice, I might tell them.

The girls ignore him. The princess does not fare well in the dungeon, Emmi says. Just when she thinks she's slipped free of her shackles, an ogre arrives with a maggoty meal. Just when she convinces the ogre to release her, evil Lord Castlering arrives to slice the ogre in two.

This shall be your roommate, he guffaws. *Nay, your double room-mate! Hahahahahaha!*

It is unclear what the princess has done to deserve this fate, except to be good and pure. The walls of the dungeon sweat drops of her tears.

If Branni were allowed to tell this story, he'd assemble great masses of soldiers to storm the dungeon; they would draw, quarter, tar, and disembowel the evil Lord, and release her to great fanfare. Lotti would help, because he and she tell their stories together—she would marry the princess to dashing Lieutenant Livermore. But Branni isn't allowed to tell the tale, and Lotti is away. Telling stories to her new friend *Nell*!

The secret has something to do with all of us, he says.

Go away, says Emmi.

Emmi teaches Anni what it's like to be dead.

First you lie perfectly still. No—arms by your side. Yes, like that, touching nothing. Now you think about absolutely nothing. Go ahead, try.

The two girls lie on Emmi's bunk perfectly still.

I keep thinking about thinking nothing, Anni says. Then I think about lunch.

Keep trying.

Anni keeps trying.

I don't think I can do it, she says.

It takes practice, Emmi says.

Can you do it? Anni asks.

Oh, yes, Emmi says.

Anni tries again, then scratches her nose, because she's thinking about lunch.

I think you'll find this is when a girl is most fine looking, Emmi explains.

Is this what *they* looked like? Anni whispers. She knows not to say their names.

Oh, yes, Emmi says.

I remember, Anni says, though she doesn't.

You're always going to be ugly, Branni says from above, especially when you're dead.

The girls ignore him, thinking about nothing.

Because that's when worms crawl in and out of your nose.

The princess has escaped! She rides the moors on a wild black stallion, who likes to rear on his hind legs and roar. They haven't decided yet if he can fly, because they're not sure where the princess must go. For the moment, it's enough that she gallop on the moors. Under the moonlight. In a white dress she found on a clothesline—otherwise she'd be nude.

Emmi and Anni take a break from their tale. They have two pillows behind them.

My hair is longer, Emmi says, but yours is wavier. That makes us even.

She fingers Anni's curls, and her own frizzy locks. Anni nods.

And I'm taller.

But you're older, Anni says.

I will always be older, Emmi says.

Anni nods.

So really, I'm ahead there, Emmi says. I'm even taller than Naughti, and she's older than everyone, so I think I win on tallness.

My eyes are violet, Anni says.

My eyes have no color, Emmi says.

They're gray.

That's no color. So we're even there.

Will I ever tell stories like you and Lotte?

Emmi considers. No, she says. You're very nice, but I don't think so.

You're both toadstools, Branni says from above, and he throws his pillow onto them.

Emmi puts the pillow behind their heads.

Hey, give me back my pillow! Branni yells. Give it back! Give it back!

You'll have to come get it, Emmi says, and you wouldn't dare.

Emmi's right: he wouldn't dare.

They plan what to do when Naughti comes back for the holidays.

Will we call her Naughti? Anni asks, still under the covers.

Always, Emmi says.

Even to her face?

To her face we'll call her Your Fourteen-Year-Old Royal Greatness, Your Most High and Mighty Aloofness, Your Royal Higher-than-High Who-Cares-About-Your-Snootiest Snootness. We shall say, Tell us about your hills and numbers, then we shall fall asleep.

Emmi laughs.

I miss Lotti, Anni says.

Naughti.

Naughti.

Well, she doesn't miss us. She's happy without us, remember? With her new friend *Nell*.

Will she die at school?

Naughti will never die. She'll outlive us all. She's not beautiful enough to die.

You guys are ugly artichokes, Branni says from above, and I'll never tell my secret.

Bran walks with Papa in the park, while the girls fall behind in their white dresses, arms entwined. In their mind, they carry parasols; servants tend to the pugs; swains wait at every turn, hoping to toss waistcoats onto puddles but none is rich or handsome enough for ladies such as they. Papa and Bran discuss Current Events, while Emmi and Anni note the arrival, over the horizon, of the demon Ahasuerus holding a scepter of fire and snakes, flanked by three dozen of his grisliest flesh-eating giants, their arms outstretched . . .

Anni screams!

When Naughti visits, she must win Emmi over. You're looking taller, she says, then catches a look in Emmi's eye, but not too tall, she says, just the right height, for right now. She asks to see Emmi's stories, which Emmi refuses, saying they belong to girls who stay at home. She offers to teach Emmi about hills and numbers, but Emmi laughs. Before long, Naughti heads back to school, looking over her shoulder to see if Emmi waves (she does not). Branni gives her a hug; they bump heads so their brains might mingle; Papa offers a hankie, Aunt gives practical advice. Anni cries all night. Emmi says maybe Anne should join Naughti at school, where surely she'd die.

Branni has a secret, and it's so big he doesn't know how to tell it.

Neither Emmi nor Anni has outgrown Auntie's sewing hour. After tea, Aunt retrieves her basket from the sideboard and they sew for the poor, often mending Anni's outgrown dresses, which have passed from sister to sister, and are barely white, despite assiduous application of bleach. Some are so old they're from the oldest sisters, whose names must never be mentioned, which causes Anni to consider them *dead dresses*. Since Emmi became bigger than Lotti, she has taken to labeling her dresses, so Lotti might remember whence they came once they come to her. Property of Queen Emmi, she writes in marker inside the collar, so darkly it can be read in red reverse around Lotti's neck, a palimpsest bled into muslin.

They sew rag dolls for the poor in Aunt's parlor, which is also her bedroom, out of linens that cannot be saved. Anni has become adept at sewing doll hems, for her eyes are fine.

I thought *we* were poor, Anni says.

Hush, Aunt says. You don't see anyone giving us rag dolls, do you?

Anni shakes her head.

You've always had a rag doll of your own, haven't you?

Anni nods.

Before they enter Aunt's doubly heated room (she maintains two heaters to keep off the chill), they submit to inspection. Dirt behind the ear, Aunt says, will dash many a match. As often as not, Em is sent to scrub her fingernails.

While they sew, Aunt talks about comportment and family history. Emmi nods as if listening, but in fact she imagines the princess sisters—there are two now, surrounded by evil-looking men in torn-up clothing, raggedy men with half-grown whiskers, and whiskey breath, who whistle and whisper things the girls do not understand. As the men sidle closer, stinking of tobacco and bad deeds, their necks sweating, their teeth broken, the girls clasp hands, murmuring each other's names. They would rather die than be taken! But taken where? Emmi doesn't know. It's not a dungeon where girls are taken, it's not a place, really—it's a state of being brought about by time in which girls *change*. Emmi has seen it—not in her own family, of course, but around them. She has seen girls change, ferocious girls who used to beat Emmi for standing on the wrong side of the sidewalk—now they simper, hobbling on stilted shoes.

Men's ruling desire is the ruination of women, Aunt has said (and Emmi has no reason to doubt her, for Papa ruined their mother, and he is the best man she knows), but what Em doesn't understand is why women consent—why they rush to ruination, simpering and hobbling!

Her own sisters, older than she, chose to die rather than face this ordeal! Emmi hopes to find an easier way.

I shall never marry, Emmi announces, interrupting Aunt, who is explaining the several ways in which ladies might prevent food from lingering betwixt their teeth. You'll change your mind, Aunt says, accustomed to Emmi's non sequiturs—truthfully, she has hope only for Anni.

I never change my mind, says Emmi.

Aunt nods, then reaches for Emmi's rag doll. Its facial expression is frightening: two lopsided eyes, and a crazy smile, sewn shut with cross-stitching.

You shall not make of yourself a seamstress, either, Aunt says, and commences to unravel the face.

The girls, seated on the floor beneath the grandfather clock, discuss the best words. Hair should be *tresses*, or *golden locks*. A forehead is always a *brow*; when possible, it should be *clear*. A dress is always a *gown*, never a *frock*. There are no good names for bosoms, or roosters, or belly-bottoms: these should never appear in stories, not anymore.

Branni has traveled seven hours to see Lotti.

I have met this Nell, he says from the bunk above. She is not much of anything.

The girls ignore him, whispering under the covers. The princess sisters have concocted a plot, and it is daring: they shall set fire to the place where the ragged men congregate, after ensuring that the men are closed within.

She still doesn't know as much as I, says Branni. For

example, about Latin or Greek. I have quizzed her on the Peloponnesian War.

The princess sisters are about to light the flame, but they are stopped by Lieutenant Livermore, who argues in favor of another punishment: the men shall be stripped of their land and holdings, for they are quite wealthy, being the forgotten sons of the world's richest man. These holdings shall go to the sisters, so they might build a fortress.

She was pleased with the Glass Town tales I showed her, Branni says. She says they are continuous with those she and I fashioned together. I could show them to you, if you want. One is illustrated quite nicely with dragon guards and artillery.

The sisters hold the lighted match and consider the pros and cons.

One of the sisters falls in love.

Emmi is white faced as she decides this.

Not with one of the scraggly men, no, not with Livermore— with a different one.

Oh, no, Anni says. What is she to do?

The man is the long-lost son of the Emperor of Light, the one who was kidnapped as a child by the Monster of the Everglades, remember?

I don't, Anni says.

The monster wanted all the world's light and twenty years later, the Emperor was still gathering it as ransom.

Anni looks blank.

It was a long time ago, Emmi says. He's spent all these twenty years finding his way to the moors, having escaped at the age of six. He has had multiple adversaries since then.

Like who?

It doesn't matter. What's important is that when he emerges, a ray of light catches his countenance and the sheen of sweat on his arms, alerting the girls to his ominous presence.

I think he's very handsome, Anni says.

Emmi is silent a moment, then nods.

In a flash of an instant, the man . . .

Whose name is Ashwell!

Whose name is . . . Philip the Strong. Philip the Strong falls in love with Eliza, the younger. But tragically at that very moment, the elder, Marie, falls in love with him, for he is dark with chestnut curls, and his expression is superior, and he can fight an entire army. She faints, of course, but Philip doesn't tend to her, he sees only Eliza, who kneels to her sister's aid.

Oh, says Anni. Does this mean they have to die?

This means they have to die, Emmi says.

Bran offers to share his newest toy—a machine gun that can wipe out an entire garrison, though it looks like a broom handle with glued-on buttons.

Come on! he says. It's better than your stupid dolls!

Emmi and Anni's rag dolls sit at the edge of Emmi's bunk, attending to the story. Each wears a placid expression. Neither is bothered when Branni murders them with his gun.

The girls prepare for the wedding of Philip the Strong and Eliza, only Marie, they decide, will betray her sister to the evil Lord Castlering, who has been hunting her with slavering dogs. Marie will then substitute herself for her sister. Philip the Strong will think she is Eliza, because she will be wearing her sister's dress.

Bran is dropping pages of his latest story onto their heads, complete with realistic illustrations of the latest Glass Town massacre, sixty rebels dead, their fingers severed and worn, sewn together, about the heads of the victors.

The rag dolls will be maids of honor. They are too stupid, Emmi says, to recognize the substitution.

Look! Branni shouts. I can write with both hands! and he drops more papers, which Emmi bats to the side.

Anni is not certain about this turn of events, as the sisters have always had each other and now what do they have, but she trusts Emmi.

Branni is roaring in his bunk.

Shut up, penguin! Emmi shouts.

I can't help it, he says. The lions have gotten loose! *ROARRR!*

You're like Eliza, Emmi says.

She has located a torch and they have made a tent with their knees.

Because I'm younger?

And prettier. Marie is tall, and her hair frizzes. She is not guaranteed to marry a prince.

Does that mean I have to die? Anni asks.

Emmi doesn't know: it remains to be seen.

I promise you, Branni whispers from his bunk, you wish you knew my secret.

I promise you, we don't.

It has to do with Lotti.

Naughti.

I shall never call her that: she's better than both of you combined.

She's better than you, that's for sure.

Say that louder one more time to my face!

I'll say whatever I want, and you can't hit me: I'm a girl!

I can't hit you but I can pinch you so hard you'll squeal!
You can't! I'll show the bruises to Papa and he'll strike you!
He won't! He never strikes me! I'm the Only Boy!
He would! He has! I've seen it!
You lie!
He struck you when you bombed Anni's face with soldiers.
Branni is silent. Emmi is right.
My secret is too good to tell.
Tell your soldiers, Emmi says. They want amusement.

Eliza learns of her sister's plan because of a loyal courtier named Chestnut. Weeping, she drugs her sister using a tincture of opium, masking the telltale odor with cinnamon and, still weeping, gives her to evil Lord Castlering, who mocks her tears. Rather than marry Philip, whom she despises for coming between her and her sister, Eliza drinks the same tincture and lies down by the edge of a cliff, so she might tumble into it whilst sleeping.

Why do sisters always have to die, asks Anni, because she's too young to remember.

The sisters lie in state, reunited in death, young and beautiful in their white dresses, mourned by all who knew them. The sisters always die in Emmi's stories, so new sisters must be born: Mariella, Marietta, Mariposa, Marina, and Mariquetta; Libby, Lizzy, Betty, Bess, and Elizabeth. Today, for the first time, they die for a man.

I liked it better with Lotti, Anni says. When Lotti's here the sisters don't have to die.

Emmi slaps her.

She's coming back, Branni shouts. That's the secret! She's coming back! She's staying here forever! We'll do stories our way and you can't join us! Ha ha, ho ho!

Anni holds her cheek and cries.

Part 2

DUTY

A FISHMONGER'S COMPLAINT—
in which duty is explained

After they have passed through their New Year's Eve rituals, admiring All Good Things, which is a stew Aunt has made, which is not very good, and Prosperity, which is not-so-prosperous-looking weeds, boiled to perfection, and toasted a small portion of port and exclaimed their gratitude for Papa's work, Auntie's good offices, Lotte's diligence, Branwell's brilliance, Emily's elegant *tallness* (this last offered by Lotte with a laugh), and Annie's estimable *Annieness*, and food has been served, and praised, and partially covered up by bread, Papa gets down to business: Emily, he says, is rude to the fishmonger.

I've naught to say to him, says she, and he so very much to me.

He merely passes the time, says Aunt, who has apparently received the complaint.

He *wastes* time—does he think I have an endless supply? I am there to purchase fish and be gone, so I may do my real work, which is to *think*.

Your real work is to be of service, says Aunt.

I serve my mind, says Em. It is a heavy taskmaster.

Paddy, say something, says Aunt, offering yet more Prosperity. He says he greets you, she continues, addressing Em, and you say, Six fish! He is not a mind reader, he does not know which fish you desire.

I desire fish! We shall be happy with any he provides, provided he be an honest man who provides honest fish. Whereas I shall not be happy discussing fish—with anyone! Really, Aunt, you shall not convince me that the world's happiness depends on my chitchat.

Paddy? Say something! The girl is sixteen. How shall she make friends or one day wed?

Emily laughs. Then Lotte and Annie laugh. Aunt scowls.

Emily, you would do well to make yourself agreeable is what your Aunt is trying to say.

But Aunt is not done:

They run without purpose throughout the town, their arms outstretched as if to fly!

But Papa believes in exercise, he believes in fresh air. He cannot find fault in this.

Annie finds a new subject: How she enjoys Lotte's lessons! They have been learning about Rome's eight hills—or is it seven?

Annie well knows the number of the hills, but wishes Lotte's involvement, for Lotte seems abstracted. For three years, she has been teaching Annie and Em. They have long moved beyond anything Lotte learned in school, so Lotte is both teacher and taught.

But Aunt is not finished: Really, what is the use of knowing Rome's hills? Can they prepare you for life *out there*? Certainly, they shall not help you find a job. Certainly, when you meet a young man, you shall not entice him with talk of hills.

We learn, Aunt, because learning makes us ladies, Lotte says, not caring that Aunt is unlearned: is she not a lady?

And you do an excellent job, Lotte! Papa says. I know your sisters appreciate it—and Lotte lightens, and smiles.

Thank you, Papa! Perhaps you can advise on next week's lessons, for we discuss *poetry*!

No need, Papa says, no need. You do a splendid job. How go your studies, Branwell? I believe you translate *Odes*?

Yes, they teach me much about *poetry*. Perhaps I could offer the girls a lecture?

Bran asks this of Lotte, who kicks him.

Splendid! Papa exclaims. So glad to hear it.

But is that what a university wants? Aunt asks, again proffering Prosperity. Poetry is fine for *girls who would be ladies*, but shouldn't Branwell learn something *profitable*? Poetry shall not support you, much less your sisters, should they decide marriage beneath them.

And here Branwell, all of seventeen, begins a disquisition on poetry, and the effect of Latin on the developing mind, and behind her napkin Emily giggles, and Lotte pinches her, and also giggles, and Branwell, who finds his manliness insulted, throws a bread roll.

Lotte is the first to recover.

How goes your work, Papa? she asks, though they are treated quite regularly to summaries of all Papa does for the poor.

Splendid! Papa cries, though our funds are short, and I would benefit from an assistant.

Oh, I could help you! Lotte says. She would abandon her sisters' education, and her own, to carry her father's briefcase and assist him with . . . with . . . well, she's not sure what, but she is confident in the power of her intellect and the soundness of her judgment.

Oh, no, my dear. Such is not suitable employment for a girl such as yourself—I see much that is ugly. I do think that next year you shall leave us for employment, however. Yes, I think that is certain. You are, what—eighteen? It is coming time now, don't you think?

Well, no one can reply to that.

DEAR SIRS—

in which Branwell and Charlotte seek encouragement

Dear Sirs,

I would like to recommend myself to your attention. I am a young man of eighteen, well-read in the Classics and Literature—to wit, the Greeks, Romans, and Romantics. I could produce pieces for you on a regular basis displaying my knowledge of said topics for the edification or even (sometimes!) the amusement of your readers, of whom I have been one for eight and one-half happy years. If these topics be not of urgent interest to your outstanding editorial staff—though they should be! they should be!—you have but to name a subject and chances are I have some knowledge of it and can produce pieces of illumination upon it. Truly, I have matched wits with the sharpest minds I know, which are many, and have reason to think mine the subtlest and most refined, which you shall see as soon as you request samples of my work, which I will send you promptly, together with some Poems. You have only to say the word.

I look forward to a long and mutually profitable relationship.

Your humblest servant,

Branny Brontey

Dear Mr. Poet Laureate,

Please forgive this trifling missive from a poor young person who would become a Writer. I have striven all my nineteen years to write poems and tell tales as might both entertain and instruct, and have created upwards of four hundred pages this year alone. I have the will, you see, to make of my life a Writer's Life—I need only assurance that I should. I pray that I can call upon your patient kindness to read but a few of the enclosed pages and make for me an assessment, for I know not one soul who could otherwise make it for me, and trust not my own judgment.

I await your reply with trembling hand.

Yours sincerely,
C. Brontey

Dear Sirs,

I have yet to hear in reply to my letter offering my services as Writer for your esteemed magazine. Perhaps my letter has not reached you, or maybe you are one of those arrogant sorts who believe the only minds of worth are those already encountered! That one cannot be found outside one's sphere of limited experience! This is not true, my friend! Out here in the "hinterlands" there are many a man of intellect willing and, in my case, able to share his thoughts in an electrifying manner, as befits your magazine. Perhaps you are now convinced and will request some of my "little pieces." Believe me, I have a number ready to go which will please your readers, just as they have pleased my numerous friends and widespread acquaintance.

I look forward to hearing from you, and entering into a lifelong "friendship of letters." I enclose one of my Poems, in case it argues in my favor.

Your humblest servant,
Branny Brontey

Dear Mr. Poet Laureate,

Thank you for your prompt reply to my letter: it was elegant in its brevity. I fear, however, that you have misunderstood my intent: I did not wish a *blurb* from your august hand—not knowing what a *blurb* might be—nor even a recommendation (and I am at a loss as to what you might *recommend*—a book, perhaps? But I have read nearly everything worth reading, though not, alas, *your* entire oeuvre, though I do rather enjoy perusing your latest volume on sticky nights when sleep is hard to come by. Be reassured: if it were *book* recommendations I wanted I would seek the aid of a *librarian* or *bookseller*—I would not trouble our Poet Laureate!). I fully appreciate that you have a *policy* which you would apply blindly against any who *would* ask for a *blurb* or a *recommendation* and I applaud you, for any policy should be applied blindly if it is to be applied at all. I did, however, appreciate the eight-by-ten glossy which you so graciously enclosed, and felt there was instruction to be had from *that,* for how stately and grave is your appearance, as you stare abstractly into a black-and-white distance, your pipe nearly forgotten in your hand! When I asked about the Writer's Life (and some small measure of encouragement), I imagine it was *this* I wanted to know: how I might affect such *gravity* and *stateliness,* and such a model you have given me to follow! I am distinctly grateful! Thank you also for the *discount coupon*! I might now save nearly a dollar when purchasing *your* latest book, which could make all the difference.

I regret that you found it *disconcerting* not knowing whether I was accomplished *gentleman* or dilettante *female*. I can appreciate that this knowledge may have influenced your reading of my poor work, and indeed been determinative, had you read it, but as you did not, by your own confession, I conclude no harm was done by the omission, and am very much relieved!

So thank you—or rather, thank your kindly assistant, Miss Frumm—for her little note, which I shall frame forthwith as a stellar example of efficiency, wit, and style.

Yours eternally,

C. Brontey

OBSERVED TODAY, PT. 1—
*in which Charlotte finds a job, and Bran does not
(as recounted by Anne)*

**Being a Notebook of Anne at Fifteen (and Sixteen)
Containing Occasional Character Sketches, Dialogue,
and Such Description as Might Aid a Future Writer**

Winter: sky milk-white, ground a blinding light

It is decided: Charlotte will into the world! She is nineteen,
her future will not wait. She is to . . . nanny! It is not clear why
she must <u>travel</u> to nanny: she dreads being away! She dreads it
so much she is unable to enjoy <u>today</u>. I think we should view
each moment as distinct from that before or any other, and so
understand it on its own terms and not <u>relationally</u>. Em is a
master of this, so much so that (unlike me) she does not need
to articulate the skill.

Lotte might <u>exert</u> herself to find work closer to home—but
how often we act for reasons that little contribute to our best
interests or even our dearest wish!

She leaves after guiding our studies for four years—a veri-
table headmistress! How we laughed with Don Quixote and
Apuleius's Ass, and puzzled over geometry, and gasped over
Dante's punishments! We allowed our hearts to swell with
Byron, Gibbon, and Shelley's *Frankenstein*. Lotte found a chalk-
board and waved an eraser, shouting *Capital! Capital!* when
one of us spoke wisdom. I accepted her pronouncements, at

first—she is vehement while I am unlearned. Of late, though, I have been fashioning my own thoughts, which differ sometimes from hers, or if my thoughts do not arrive, I examine hers carefully to at least confirm that I agree. It is in this spirit, the spirit of finding <u>my own voice</u> that I begin this notebook: what does <u>Annie</u> see, feel, experience, want, and think?

In Lotte's absence we shall have no instructor: Branwell is not amenable and Em insists that learning must be <u>intuited</u>: it soaks into her, says she, with no words rising to the top—she cannot, in other words, <u>teach</u>. Truthfully, I cannot follow that mechanism nor see its point.

Overheard: "Annie is on the verge of womanhood." Lotte speaking to Em, who unlike Lotte is all industry, <u>baking</u> something. "She sleeps with a doll but when she considers something seriously, she looks quite wise, as if holding within her a very old woman. I like this characteristic in her very much," Lotte says, though she sounds far from decided. "Perhaps as an old woman she will have the innocence of a young girl."

Lotte is ever one to "sum a person up"; methinks it be her favorite thing.

I do not sleep with a doll, of course, merely a pillow in the shape of an owl.

Winter: snow blackened, crystallized, seeping

Bran sits with Lotte as she prepares her trunk.

"I'm running away!" she says. "Don't tell!"

Bran mumbles something. He must be tired after last night.

"Have you no curiosity? Pass the books, please," by which she means the poetry books she has taken from our shelves, though they belong to all. "I decide between Tahiti and Antarctica.

Which is better for a person who burns in summer but is always cold?"

Bran:

"My heavens, how you mutter! Have you a headache? . . . Well, that's your problem, and best you learn it now: drink has consequences . . . No, I won't release you! You must stay as I pack, and advise me: beach or berg?"

Bran:

"Valhalla is out of the question: I haven't the stomach for spicy food . . ."

Bran:

"Did you just say it will not be as bad as I imagine? . . . No, I won't lower my voice! . . . What do you mean, <u>why</u>? Must I list my shortcomings to you who knows them well?"

Bran:

"I shall humiliate myself for your pleasure and to win the point. First, I have no talent for friend-making, yet I require company, else I crumple. What? You <u>know</u> I cannot find satisfaction in <u>small talk</u> and <u>shooting the breeze</u>. You have seen me attempt to 'chat with the grocer'—you know me incapable. Second—may I continue? Second, had I friend-making talent, I should find no one to friend as <u>nanny</u>, no one who invents worlds, and is motivated by art, no person of feeling and wit. Third, I can't say I'm fond of <u>children</u>, much less <u>boys</u>! Where are you going? No, really, you must stay! Pass the soldier . . . Yes, I am taking it with me . . . To remember you with, silly! . . . No, I shan't lose it. I have never lost a thing in my life."

Bran:

Lotte laughs. "Except my innocence! Yes, that's long gone!"

Bran:

"Yes, I have other tokens: a lock of Annie's hair, a locket from Em . . ."

Lotte laughs again at something Bran has said.

"You're trying to make me feel better, but the place sounds like death and I wish to live. But I shall manage death, temporarily, <u>for your sake</u>, if you promise to write and keep our stories alive! I must know what happens with Count Trimaldi's plot to conquer Lower Lands . . . No, you may not kill Mistress Teeter; there may be no Teeter slaughter! I depend on her to save the noble line of Tartarian . . . Yes, do away with the wise goatherder, if you must: he is tedious and a scold. But I am not done! You must let me finish my rant or I shall never make my point. I shall tolerate all that's un-tolerable if you use what I earn to establish our future! I shall work hard every day and every night so you may have what you need. This must ever be on your mind, how you shall help us by helping yourself. Promise! . . . Bran, I must hear it: knowing you shall apply yourself will buoy me! . . . Thank you . . . Yes, I believe you, why shouldn't I? Those little shoes there, please . . . yes, I know they are quite the littlest things you have ever seen . . . Oh, please, I have never applied them to your backside! And stop cradling your head in your hands—you look ridiculous. Okay, go, lie down. We'll talk again in six years' time, when I am back, an unrecognizable spinster with bunions and warts. I am trying not to be scared but, yes, go ahead, go! You're quite the worst brother I have ever had."

Winter: puddles of slush splashing in galoshes

At the door, Papa offers Lotte a well-made pen, so we may hear from her. She straightens his tie, which he does not appreciate, preferring not to be fussed over by <u>females</u>. Em and she touch foreheads; "I shall write ye," she whispers. "Not if you expect a reply," says Em. "You know I'm not one for <u>self-expression</u>." "You shall learn the trait, for my sake," says she. "Not likely," says Em. "Then think of me—tell me you will think of me!" "That's easy," says Em. "I shall think of you every time I pass your bunk!" At which Lotte bursts into tears. "You tease," says she. "You mustn't tease!" "Well," says Em, "you mustn't cry at the drop of every hat!" but squeezes Lotte liberally. "Be a good girl," she says to me, as if I were ever anything but.

Branwell she finds hardest to release, he being her other half, or so she says. "How shall I manage without you?" she says. Bran cannot say a word for the tumble of her words and flow of his tears. "I shall make ye proud!" he manages, as she wipes her cheeks and his with a sleeve.

Winter: new snow silences

The house does not shift easily to its new configuration. Silences are loud, gaps in footfall a confusion to our ear. The kitchen, the hallway, our bunks startle with their spaciousness. Conversation stutters because we expect someone to contribute who is not there: the joke is missing, the jovial reply, the witty retort. We expect our day to be upended by a mood, we watch our words, lest we injure. Then we settle, the vacuum is no more.

Aunt has discovered fur-lined boots—a gift from Bran for being a "right good old lady." She says they allow her feet "tolerable" warmth, and she doesn't at all mind their clomping sound, though all other sounds, which is to say our sounds, "pluck her very nerves."

Note: I would learn about myself, but write only of family: it is <u>they</u> who fascinate! Is this the lot of the youngest? I would <u>be</u> myself, but don't know what that is!

Also, I have set myself the task of describing in ever new ways the <u>weather</u>: if I must <u>set the scene</u>, I would do so <u>originally</u>. I shall persist in this discipline, but it does not sit well: I care as little about weather as I do <u>dress</u> or <u>furnishings</u>: *Emily sat on a crooked chair in a wrinkled frock, fretting about the <u>rain</u>, which fell as all rain falls—wetly!*

Spring: faint clouds, a rolling wind, Bran might exit in short pants, the rest would cover up

In her letters, Lotte mentions no friends, no books, no ideas. She writes about boredom, misery, and daily slights, all of which she is willing to bear, to help Branwell make his way. The fact that he has yet to identify, much less make, his way concerns her not. If I were away, I would keep my mind fresh, no matter the circumstances, and if I suffered, none would know it.

Summer: spring or summer, depending on whom you ask

Bran has purchased for himself a cravat; heaven knows whence he procured the cash. He stands in poses before the glass: "I beg your pardon?" he says, and (new pose), "Branwell Brontey, charmed!" When he sees that I observe (because I laugh) he chases; Aunt chastens.

Papa, unaware that Lotte has for ages <u>neatened</u> his desk, wonders at the mess; he knows not whom to blame. He has introduced Emily to a shooting range, explaining that she has <u>aptitude</u>. One may pursue a thing only if one knows one will be successful, is his circular logic, which is why I shall not be similarly introduced.

"I feel one with the pistol," is all my sister will say.

I have not <u>stamina</u>, like Charlotte, who could move a universe (though she chooseth instead to <u>nanny</u>), nor imagination, like Em, to define what has <u>not</u> occurred in worlds that cannot be. Asked where my aptitude lies, Papa says, "Somewhere, dear Anne, and we'll love ye still if ye don't locate it." He may not note it, but I <u>have</u> aptitude: for seeing what is there and giving it form. For observing what is real, and near. It is wholesome to recognize one's limitations; wholesomer still to make good one's strengths. I do not care that neither he nor any other knows it!

Autumn: rumblings of thunder, wet leaves dissolve on the ground
Lotte, visiting, makes up for lost time. Yesterday she and Bran continued a furious letter-writing campaign to interest eminences in their prose. This followed a furious story-telling campaign betwixt the two (involving twelve elves, some bridesmaids, a dozen macaroons).

Also, Bran made her sit for our "portrait," Bran having already dispatched Emily and me (I look like a mouse about to bolt!).

Today, Papa bids she visit <u>ladies</u>, to "enliven them" with her "youthful charm." Lotte's reply: "If I have charm it is only that associated with youth; if I have youth it is only in relation to those ladies, so I shall go, if only to feel charming and young, for I do not believe my presence will uplift anyone, unless the lady wishes sweets, in which case she should thank Em, for it shall be she who does the baking." She says this after Papa has left the room, then asks if I will join her so she may avoid "getting lost" in our building or "captured" or "kidnapped."

Each lady, we learn, has affection for at least one <u>thing</u>, and through such <u>things</u>, keeps her heart aflame. Miss Allen collects souvenir plates; Miss Fetch knits extra-long scarves. None feigns interest in the books we offer, referring to poor eyesight, arthritis, a preference for "real life." Their worlds are small, having shrunk at a greater rate than even the ladies themselves, yet they are brave: they tell of lost loves, lost dreams, lost sisters; fingers tremble as they point to photos of themselves as belles, as bridesmaids, always as bridesmaids.

After our visit, Lotte is white-faced. She believes she has found her fate, as a lady with commemorative plates. I believe we fashion our destiny, first by identifying a goal—one nobler, one hopes, than collecting crockery—then by mapping a path toward it. I, for one, have determined my purpose: I shall write! I have started <u>small</u>, as befits my inexperience, practicing observation and description, and shall continue till I have found my voice and a habit of apt expression—so I may end <u>big</u>, having written a book—I'll say it now!—by the time I am Lotte's age! That is four years from now: all manner of thing may be accomplished in so great a time!

Winter: wind slaps icy rain

There shall now be two away, as it is Bran's turn to fly. He is, finally, to seek his fortune, as they say (our fortune). He has taken all necessary steps, says he, and then some.

He spurns traditional suitcases, preferring a knapsack to fit over his shoulders.

"This way I shall have my hands free should I need them," said he.

"But your suit shall wrinkle," demurred Papa, who has strong feelings about suits.

"I shall not wear a suit," said Bran. "They shall see me as I am, in my natural glory!"

"I insist you wear a suit!" Papa said. "What well-bred boy does not wear a suit when petitioning for his future?"

"A modern, well-bred boy," said Bran. "These men shall appreciate my style!"

"I would have them appreciate your substance!"

"Substance in this case shall be reflected by my style."

"I am becoming cross with you, son. You know we depend on you."

"Then you shall trust in me," said he, "to know what is expected in this day and age—which is different from your day and age. Improved, if you don't mind my saying."

"Tell me at least that your dress shirt does not miss buttons."

"I shall wear a T-shirt," said Bran. "It contains a witty slogan that shall reflect my style."

"Tell me at least that it hath no stains!" said our father, despairing.

"I have not looked on it recently," said Bran, but by now I think he teased.

Our father has not much humor, however, so voices were raised.

Winter: some of this, some of that

Branwell is returned, though not wrapped in Glory. His knapsack is lost and anything in it. His eyes are streaked beneath with black, they hold a wildish look. There is a *substance* in his hair: Aunt says it looks like *glue*, how does a boy get *glue* in his hair?

"I have presents for ye," he mumbles, gesturing to his knapsack which is no more.

There is a smell to him which is not nice. I should be more specific: writing requires specificity, but I cannot name the odor, it being new to me and unfamiliar.

I would not like to be the one to tell Charlotte she labors for naught.

Figure of speech: It is as if rats died in his overcoat.

SEND. DELETE.—

in which Lotte longs for word from home

I'm arrived at my aerie, one mile from the ground. I am spared much dizziness, as my chamber is windowless, an alcove off the kitchen with beaded entryway.

The boy, I am told, prefers not to knock.

There is no bookcase in this room, Bran, nor any kind of shelf.

I don't know where we'd put it, said the Lady when I asked, and she is right.

SEND.

Tell me, Bran, does Auntie still make oatmeal on her hot plate? Does she still hand out bologna sandwiches and say, Back by dark! Does she speak of Lotte? Does anyone?

Two weeks and I do not hear from Em. Do she and Anne still fly through the town, daring the wind to lift them? Has Em befriended the fishmonger? Does she still shoot? She shall not *email*, I know, but she may yet form letters: I have seen her tiny scrawl. Pinch her arm, and if she looks at you with vicious intent, tell her it was I who did this thing and if she is angry she may write and tell me so.

I must go: the Little Prince wants a washcloth. The cat, he says, doth need a bath.

SEND.

How you berate me! When I asked if Aunt made oatmeal, I did not suppose she had changed course. Our Aunt does not change course. Your sister is sentimental: she wishes you to share this vice, if vice it be. Still, if Aunt should stop serving oatmeal, I should hope to hear of it.
SEND.

Dearest Bran, Have you taken your test? I know you shall do marvelously, and make your sisters proud. If you have yet to take your test, I beseech you: answer questions briefly, offer no unwanted analysis. Above all, answer no question in Latin! They could fail you out of spite, and shall if they feel your learning exceeds theirs, as surely it does. Then shall our efforts be insubstantial, like melting snow, like the smile on your dear Amelia's face. If only /
SEND.

I am sorry to be continually interrupted. I do not wish to be one of those ladies who sends unfinished sentences into the world. Little Prince Darkling has a computer, but he would not have me use it. I'll "ruin" it, he says. His mother agrees with this logic. She does not wish to replicate patriarchal structures in her home; therefore little Prince Darkling must be indulged in all ways and never treated harshly, no matter how thoughtless his actions.

I paraphrase.

So until they invent a computer that cannot be ruined by my poor typing, I shall have to steal time when the Prince is with his piano teacher or his boxing master, and the Lady absorbed in her magazines, ready always to abandon my missives—but you shall forgive me, for one of my fragments contains more affection for you than the uncounted tomes of anyone else.
SEND.

Again you berate me, but I jest: why should I not approve of your Amelia? She has ringlets of fire, which is no small thing. Also, her mouth purses prettily when she's "making her sums." I'm not sure she has the hips to make you fat, ugly babies, but given time to grow into her mother's girdle, she may.

You have not said when this test is to be! How can I hold my breath all day and send messages of luck and love on the wings of the fleas of the parrot of the Empress's fool, if I do not know when you are to be examined? I know you shall do us proud! And when you are a famous astronaut, or skydiver, or bombardier, flying wherever your soaring heart takes you, you shall rescue us, we sisters who toil for you, and we shall make a new Glass Town, where all of us may be Angels again. **SEND.**

Yes, Bran, I am aware that Em does not labor for you, *strictly speaking*, and do you hold that against her? You would not had you seen how she paled at school, how she paled and pined and fairly starved herself to death. Had you seen how I was required to stay with her every night, urging her to live, all day shouting at any who would hear: *My sister ails! She will not eat! She must return home!* She lives now because I pulled her back to life. If she helps Aunt keep house for you, it's toil enough, as you would know had you ever cleaned a toilet.

I, on the other hand, am strong and fit, and able to work double-time so I can pay you half my wealth, so you might prosper—do not disappoint us! I know you will not.

As for your Amelia, you shall have to judge for yourself whether I tease or disapprove, just as you must judge for yourself whether she and her mother's corset shall do you for a lifetime—this is a decision I would not wish to influence. **SEND.**

Do not talk to me of Amelia's precious feet! Am I one of your mates in the tavern, that I should marvel at her feet? Has she no inner virtue? No habits of mind, no imagination, no learning, no ideas? Do not talk to me of your mates at the tavern! Do you not know what each of your drinks costs me?

DELETE.

If you knew how bleak my life, you would not speak to me of shade trees and days made for sketching! First, I must tend to the Princeling and the squalling babe, preparing one for his Tutor, the other for a day staring at mobiles. (What? You did not know a babe was attached to this household? Nor I, till I arrived.) The child shouts commands, the infant screams, while the mother sees to her coiffure. She would not see me idle as the baby sleeps, so daily she discovers chores I might do, as a *special favor* to her ladyship, for she is mindful that I am not a *housekeeper.* (Pity me, for she hath discovered I can sew, which means new curtains for every room and closet in the house.) It is this mother's fantasy that babies require constant "stimulation," so that when the thing wakes, I must recite poetry to it, though it be no more than an open mouth, sucking milk and screaming. Thus, she believes, it shall become genius.

After the child returns from his tutor, I supervise homework, which oft he will not do, and the mother is in agreement with this as well, for it does not do to turn learning into a *chore.* In the evening I supervise *television* viewing, my hand ever on the remote, ready to switch selections should an offering become too violent for the boy's sensitive nature—only I have yet to switch selections for when my finger makes ready, his Sensitive Nature lets forth a growl so fierce I fear for my safety.

We would not impose *routine* on the Prince, so it may be ten, or later, before he nods; should I carry him to bed before he is fully asleep, he screams and wakes the babe, and day stretches further into night. It is rare he sleeps with clean face or clean teeth.

I am, in short, trapped in a Tower where daily my mind is beaten down and dulled, where if ever I have a pleasing thought, about Glass Town or my worthy home, if ever I hear the distant cry of myself as I once was or could be, a whole person, a real person, awake and divine, some gnome asks me for a *thing*, which I must provide with a smile. By the end of the day, my head droops. I cannot read, or write for the *Gazette*. I have not one sensible person with whom I may speak. I experience barely a glimmer of what life might be, lived as it ought. You, who always have people about you, who are satisfied with your Amelias and your mates, cannot imagine how alone I feel. So, pray, do not speak to me of shade trees and days made for sketching unless you are ready to free me from my tower, that I may enjoy them with you.

DELETE.

Tonight, Ms. Nosebleed introduced me to her book group as her favorite drudge (I paraphrase). She described my modesty (my silence as she complains of her lot), my ladylike behavior (my willingness to do extra work). I restrained myself, as I have learned to do: I *hold* everything—my breath, my arms against my chest, my tongue. I have a dragon within whose fire could set the whole world alight; I hold that, too!

The ladies chirp: how nice to have a drudge, and one so neat about her person!

The book they read is tripe: the cover makes this clear. A winsome girl gazes at a roiling sea, her clothing a diaphanous veil. They have the leisure to read tripe, while I, who once held *real* conversation about *real* books, am asked to "whip up" some of Annie's delicious scones.

I endeavor to *hold* but instead run off in tears.

If only, Ms. N. says later—and I mustn't take this *the wrong way*—if only I weren't so *sensitive*, if only I didn't take *offense* at every little thing, I might be happier, oh how she wishes I could be happier.

I, too, brother, I, too.

SEND.

I am guessing you did not pass your test, Branny dear, and this is why you do not write. What shall we do if this is so?

DELETE.

Dearest Bran, would you really forsake me, when I am friendless, when I labor only for you? You have passed your test, surely, and prepare for university in a few "short" weeks—short because you have every good thing about and before you. I can wrest no joy from my weeks: they are interminable. I pray you never know interminable time. But if you do, know that I would never leave you, but would stand ever closer. For me, those would be the shortest weeks of all.

SEND.

I look from our aerie into the depths and think, Shall this day be my last? A slant of light makes me think of Glass Town then, its diamond towers and shining steeples. I see all of you there, you, Zamorna, everyone, and Maria appears, our Little Mother, with regal gown and scepter. She smiles on me and I feel safe almost, as if my soul does not drain from me drop by drop. I *shall* be an Angel of Light again, I think, one of the four cardinal points. I shall, and stay in this place another day.

DELETE.

I am glad to hear from you, but you worry me! You quite forget your punctuation, and your sentences stray! Do you write from a tavern? Does someone write for you, someone without your learning and grasp of syntax? When you say you throw your life away and will I catch it, what, dear Bran, do you mean? I have such small hands and your life is so large /
SEND.

Annie says you did not sit for your exam, though she is quiet about the reasons. Papa, she says, would have you learn a trade. What is it to be, Bran? Are you to be a plumber, you who never had to clean a toilet? I am wretched for you, and for me. I had thought you would learn, and teach us, but I can manufacture no interest in wrenches and pipes.
DELETE.

My "performance," I am told, is wanting. I lack enthusiasm. I am too often "in another world," I am "testy," my Lady will not ask for things lest my expression darken. Could I not whistle while I work (I paraphrase)? I will do better, I say, I promise!

Instead, I sit in the Prince's court, watching an expanse of wall, white like a page. The characters of Glass Town appear there—Princess Mary-Anne, with her jeweled scepter and beaded gown; dashing Count Zamorna; demonic Alphonse with his band of sixty thieves; the golden triplets with their magic monkeys and dainty hats, good Miss Staple minding them all. In the distance, shimmering, Glass Town itself, and at the foot of our great Towers, your legions: the Elbow Regiment—your first creation, remember?—the Royal Archers, the Cavalry and Bombardiers, and at their head, Prince Brontey! You assemble our troops with a roar, your great stallion rearing, its forelegs lifting, your bugles sounding a rousing call!

But—what's this? You lead our forces away from me! I reach for you from my wooden chair, I reach! Who shall save me? The mother fairly shouts: Really, says she, I had to address you three times! The Little Lord wishes his tea!
SEND.

A neighbor writes to say you are seen entering a vacant residence where hallucinogens are found and that our Em, whom you malign, must retrieve you from this place, and also find money with which to pay your debts. Perhaps you are not resigned to your future life as plumber. Perhaps you find your Amelia wanting, perhaps you regret asking me to work fifteen hours a day to finance your vices. I do not know because you will not say.
DELETE

Today, while endeavoring to prepare *two* hyper (or is it hypo?) allergenic, macrobiotic meals tailored to the very specific nutritional needs of their most high highnesses, I found myself unable to breathe, as if some ill being gripped me about the neck. As I choked, my heart charged near fully out of my chest, so frantically did it beat, I experienced the chill of February, though the apartment was well warmed, and my limbs shook, though I could not move. You would not credit the terror I felt, the sense of black doom as dread closed upon me. I felt I might die on the spot, and all I could think was, *Is this it, is this all there is?* When in fact, the only real danger was scorched peas and a ruined pan.
SEND.

The Child has taken issue with my discipline, I have taken issue with his insolence. He advises that he has always known I have stolen from him, by which he means, I have used his computer without his consent. He has, moreover, because it is *his*, felt free to read my scribblings thereupon, which is to say, my messages to you; soon he shall share them with his mother. I told him by way of reply that he is a spoilt, useless thing, indulged beyond reckoning, and shall always be a leech upon society, contributing nothing that is original or good. I told him that he took every advantage, every gesture of caring, every moment of love, and wrung all goodness from it. He replied that at least he is not ugly and small, at least he will not be a spinster.

I hit him then.

He wants money, of course. I dared not say my brother drank it all.

I await now the return of Mistress Nosebleed, that I may pack my things—my three gray dresses, my toe-pinching shoes. Your *Gazette*. My intractable attitude, and too great sensitivity, my inability to adapt. It shall all fit within the smallest of bags.

Do you suppose if we had our mother, life would be different? Would she have taken our hand and prepared us to live in this world? I cannot imagine what is expected of me, I know only that whatever is wanted, I *want* it. I had hoped these last fifteen months to do well here, to make myself indispensable, perhaps even to effect improvement in this child, but some defect in me will always out! I had hoped through love and constancy to save you, but those are weak, small qualities in me, for I have failed.

You claim to remember our mother, though you were small. You say she had pretty teeth, and laughed easily, that I am nothing like her. I remember only that she was a place where I might cry, I remember that she would hold me up. Do you think she watches us, do you think she cares for us still from her porch in the sky?

I have stood all morning, my back to the Prince and the mite, staring at the sky—as if I might see something there, the Stolen Sisters flying, a sign, a crack of lightning, God's smile, anything that might say, there is a place for you in this world, and I will show it thee: follow, follow.

DELETE.

OBSERVED TODAY, PT. 2—

in which Anne fails out there (as recounted by Anne)

**Being a Notebook of Anne at Nearly Sixteen
(and Seventeen and Eighteen), Containing Character
Sketches, Dialogue, and Such Description as
Might Aid a Future Writer**

Summer: the air is hell's blanket

Lotte is home, her job as nanny having "run its course." Our papa has found new labor for her, this time as <u>receptionist</u> at the firm of Roe Head.

When she thinks of it, she can barely breathe and takes to her bed.

"When I was young," she whispers to Bran, who squats by her side, "I heard the bells with impatience. They marked the hours before our future, and our future was so bright! I wished they would move along! Now, I cannot help but fear: they presage nothing! Brother, you must save me! Save me! Amass your armies for I shall not survive it!"

Bran says a thing in her ear, to which Lotte's reply is a sob and an embrace.

What that boy can have said, who never spoke sense in his life, I cannot imagine.

"Where is our shining future?" she asks of us later, still abed. "We must find a purpose and attach ourselves to it, firmly! This cannot be our life, sisters!"

"My purpose," says Em, "is to remain without purpose as long as I can."

"That may suffice while you are here," Lotte replies, "but how long shall that be?"

You are eighteen now, is what Lotte means but does not say.

"We shall join the circus then," says Em. "I'll be an aerial artist and Bran a sad-faced clown. Annie shall shoot apples off my head—large apples—and you, Lotte, shall charm the wildebeest."

Lotte doesn't know whether to laugh or to cry.

"Laugh," says Em. "Ye might as well!"

I will not share *my* purpose as my sisters will laugh and possibly injure my resolve.

Later, Em, her hair wisping from humidity and toil, brings Lotte dinner.

"I am not worthy of your stew," says Lotte.

"Perhaps not," says Em, "but this is casserole," and leaves the plate by the door.

Winter: I should have allowed an extra half hour to navigate by bus, for we are slowed by ice

Lotte writes: "I have made enough of a name at Roe Head Roe Your Boat—through diligence if not aptitude—to bring a sister on as <u>Stenographer</u>. I think Annie would do best—she's seventeen, I believe? Her temperament is well suited to office life. Tell her not to worry: I shall teach her."

I am tired of being taught by Lotte, but if I am to be imprisoned it might as well be within her reach. Emily manages a *sorry* look, for as the elder between us, it should be she. Though we all carry in our hearts the memory of her, collapsed, at school.

I shall make no fuss with trunk or goodbyes. And none shall offer me a well-made pen.

Spring: buds awaken

It is four months and I write not of the office, nor of the city, nor even of my sister out of her habitat. I manage barely a postcard: weather lovely, wish you were here! I <u>do</u> wish they were here: Em, Bran, even Aunt! Lotte works two jobs, which is more than I am required to do, being "delicate" and barely of working age, so I see her but little. Even our "lunch hours" do not coincide. Still, I find cause to pass her desk—she is at the center of our maelstrom; always she has her head in the phone, two phones, three phones! Or she is buried in paper, or taking instruction from a troll. She wishes very much to please. I found her weeping once in the WC: someone had found fault with her typing. "I am not a typist," she cried. "I should not be judged for my typing!" She wishes to succeed. I wish only to survive.

I am practiced at slipping through and behind these walls, attracting no one. No one speaks to me, though they do speak *at* me, which is to say, through me, which is to say, via my stenographer's pad. Lotte was right: dictation is nothing so much to learn and I have learned it.

After work, I creep to my room, which I share with a certain <u>Elaine</u>, who spends what nights she can with her "boyfriend," a married man named Tom. There in our room, which is decorated in half—flounces on her side, books on my own—I read, allowing but four hours' sleep, maybe five. Poetry from the library, also the works of certain moral and aesthetic philosophers (I wish to know the <u>origin</u> of art! I wish to know its <u>purpose</u>! Also <u>our</u> purpose!). When I read, I am no one, seen by no one.

Which explains my reluctance to write: how can <u>no one</u> write of <u>anything</u>? I find that one requires little food if one is no one: I subsist on melba toast and, on Sundays, jam.

Autumn: I don't know

Charlotte is at my side, for I have fainted in some room. I call out for Prince Gallant, for Mother. Lotte sits on the floor and holds me. "Be still, my darling," says she, for I thrash. "I will care for you." She strokes my face. I clutch at her with my whole self and bury my face in her gray dress, which smells of flowers and soap. "Take me from here," I cry, "promise you will take me!" She helps me to stand.

"Out of my way!" she shouts, when a secretary, gawping, blocks the door. "Out of my way!" she shouts, when an Associate rushes forth. "Do not impede me!" she fairly roars as she helps me out of Roe Head, into the lift.

I shall never mock my sister again nor think of her as other than a fury on the side of right. She did not give one thought to her own future at that place. She was a lioness, a giant, an angel avenging! No force, no power could come between her and her task, which was to protect me and bring me forth, all the while speaking kindness: "You shall be well, dear Anne. I shall see you safe. Be brave, dear Anne, for soon we shall be home."

There can be no question of my going back. We do not retrieve my garments—let Elaine have them! Let the library wonder at my unreturned books! We go home!

Tale: A girl judges her sisters for their frailty, their unwillingness to go into the world. She gets her comeuppance, of course (is this not the purpose of literature, to teach each character their flaw?): she enters the fray and is smacked down and sickened—a jolly tale but who would read it?

Winter: the children outside are louder now, playing in the snow

B: So Tooley rests himself on the settee and I am off to bed, to encounter the ghost.

C, *on a lower bunk next to B, eating grapes*: Who doesn't trouble itself with sleepers on a settee.

B: A normal bed, it was, such as normal people rest on in normal houses . . .

C: Not a bunk, in other words, nor a converted couch.

B: Ye gather my point! So I rested myself on this normal bed, which was neither bunk nor converted couch, and no sooner did I fall asleep . . .

C: Unaided by alcohol . . .

B: I didna say that, wench!

C: Continue yer non-bunk story, though it be bunk! I am wan and in need of a good ghost story!

B: This is no *good* ghost, sister: have ye not been listening?

E, *from above*: Tell yer damned story!

B: This place be much more pleasant when Charlotte's off recepting, have ye noticed, Em? Though we did miss *you*, Annie-bee! Are ye comfortable? Do ye want anything? Another blanket? Carrots fer building up yer strength?

Me, *under cover in my lowly bunk, shakes head, weakly*:

B: No sooner did I fall asleep but a terrible, horrifying power I could neither see nor name lifted me up to the air and threwed me across the room!

C: A good thing ye weren't on yer bunk or ye'd have broken yer head!

B: I've always been a lucky boy!

C, *laughs*:

E, *from above*: Enough! 'Tis time for Anne to sleep.

B: Ye don't believe me! I have proof, sisters! On my backside! Move over, let me stand: I shall show ye . . .

C: Hie, brute!

B, *sitting again*: If yer not careful.

Spring: *I don't know I don't care*

I am moved to describe our Things, so happy am I to be home. I trawl with notebook, prepared to describe—but instead look, at Emily's apron, gift of Bran because of the blue bears, to touch, Auntie's sewing basket, our father's books! To smell: porridge! wet dog! I shout (for I am alone): Home! I am home! I am home! I sneak a scone, I look, I touch, I smell, then I am content to shut my eyes, to simply *be*.

I am no writer if I am content to look touch taste smell hear *be*!

Then Emily arrives, dogs barking and begging for bones, hair in a lopsided knot, face flush with heat and health.

"Who wants bagels?" she shouts, waving a white bag.

EVEN EXCHANGE—
in which Branwell sells three sisters (but not an aunt)

When I get home, I assure the girls they'll be well looked after:
Yer brother has taken care of ye!

Shh, says Em, arriving from the kitchen, you'll wake the regiment!

What, I cry! Do my sisters sleep? Is their labor so tiring they
must sleep *all* the time?

Did you not hear the bells? 'Tis four, says Em, and at least one
of yer sisters be off working.

I cannot make out which that might be. I am sure I saw both
yesterday!

Lotte is slave at Roe Head, and I am soon to join her.

If Lotte is away, then she'll not be disturbed by my rude action!
But do not worry: yer futures are secure! I've auctioned ye
off. Annie hath found her match in Bryan, for his business
selling fish. He needs someone to slice and scale, and Annie's
so obliging.

Ah, says Em, and what did you get for her?

A surfboard, say I. I've a mind to surf.

Will ye surf our river, or do you plan a trip to the sea? asks Em, taking over my jacket, which is momentarily caught at the elbow.

Working on the details, say I, and put an arm now free about her neck. Have you nothing to eat, Em, for it's been hours.

You don't spend yer money on ought but booze, so I'll wager twenty-four, since I fed you last.

Could be, say I, there's a lot sloshing there, and I point to my belly.

She laughs. You can always count on Em for a laugh.

What are Lotte and I worth to yer mates? She's looking now in the fridge for whatever Aunt has made. You got nothing much for us, or you'd admit it.

Nothing much for Lotte, I'll say it. What can she do? She's not obliging, she doesn't laugh like you, she doesn't even bake.

You'll not give her away, I hope, says she, putting toast in the oven.

Nah, say I. I've traded her for a bag of monkeys, when they become available. I'll turn 'em into a show, and profit off 'em. She's found a plate for me, and a knife, but I push the food away.

Now yer talking sense, my sister says, and for me? I hope you've got yerself at least a book worth reading.

I got a price above rubies. Yer to work the bar, where yer long arms and no nonsense will assist. For this I am to have free beer, and the occasional chaser.

Yer a businessman! says Em, pulling on me to stand. Have you not traded Aunt?

Nay, say I with a gesture. She likes me, you know, very much unlike the rest of you.

I don't like you but I do love you, says Em, balancing me with both arms.

D'ya think I'll amount to something? I ask from a place on the floor I find comfortable.

As an auctioneer? Decidedly not.

I made this picture of you, say I, and take a crumpled bit from my pocket.

That's me, is it? My expression is sour.

Yer disappointed in me is why.

How can I be disappointed if I had no expectation? She lifts me with my help.

Which is worse, say I. D'ya think I'll amount to nothing then?

Y'ask the wrong person, Muffin. We are only what we are and

what we decide we'll be. This is for you to say, not me. She's maneuvering me, but gently, down the hall.

I'll chew on that as I sleep, say I.

Help me in the removing of your sweater, says she.

Not sure I can, I say, after trying. I'll probably not, say I, and my shoulders heave.

You'll not what? I've done talking of sweaters.

Not amount, say I! I don't think I can be what you want.

So you said last night, though you were quieter about it and didn't cry!

What is it you want from me? say I. I'm just a boy!

Yer a man of twenty-two, in case ye hadn't noticed! Maybe you might help me with these shoes! By standing, not kicking.

'Tis too much for one man! I canna do it!

Might I convince you to lie before you spew?

I ponder this. My shoulders heave.

You didn't! Muffin, you didn't!

I'll clean it in the morning, I promise, just help me to my bed.

MINUTES—

in which Emily fails out there (as recounted by Em)

Attendees: Mr. Roe, Mr. Head, assorted associates. Also, Desiree, to rub the head of Mr. Roe. And one Emily Brontey, Junior-Secretary-in-Training.

Members not in attendance: Mr. Roe.

Welcome: The Roe Head Roe Your Boat Partners and Assorted Associates Meeting was called to order at 11:05 A.M., having been delayed five minutes by Mr. Head, who *trudged*, then by Desiree, who strove to keep the coffee orders straight. Then Mr. Roe looked upon Junior-Secretary-in-Training and said: Was this what Miss Brontey had always looked like: he recalled a *little* person, whereas this one was quite *tall*. Desiree explained in sentences that were sometimes hard to follow that *Junior-Secretary-in-Training* was younger sister to *Receptionist*, having been hired on a probationary basis because of the elder's exemplary performance—at which point Mr. Head interrupted: was not *Brontey* the less-than-hearty though otherwise satisfactory *Stenographer* who collapsed after a mere nine months' service, never to return? Different *Brontey*, explained Desiree, hoping to hide her exasperation. That was an even younger *Brontey*! The elder being little, persisted Mr. Roe. The elder being little, Desiree confirmed. By Jove, said Mr. Head, who still looked confused, perhaps because the youngest, though not the younger, Brontey *was also little*!! The coffees arrived, none looking particularly distinguished, which discomfited the partners, who depend on extra foam to set themselves apart; the meeting finally commenced at 11:21.

Approval of Minutes and Reports: The minutes were approved as presented. The partners tabled discussion of finances till such time as greedy associates were not present. Desiree commenced to do a little dance based largely on her understanding of ballet. The associates clapped but were embarrassed as the partners did not clap. Desiree then took her place on Mr. Roe's knee.

Old Business, New Business: Junior-Secretary-in-Training became distracted during this part of the meeting as old business did not differ from the new. At home, each day resembles the next, and from this sameness, from this "old business," something *new* may arise. In this creation of newness, every minute is an hour, hours pass in a minute, and life is timeless— which is not the same as endless. A person cannot spend her life endlessly, even if such is how she may earn a living, which is to say, she cannot remain in a place where the new stands *not* in relief to the old. Junior-Secretary-in-Training would prefer to live in the park. So she quit, effective five minutes ago.

Said termination should not reflect upon *Receptionist*, who implored *Junior-Secretary* to "stick it out," by which she meant murder her soul minute by minute. *Receptionist*, being better able than the younger (and youngest) to *accommodate*, shall kill her soul "sticking it out"; do her the kindness of dismissing her before the damage be too great.

Adjournment: The Partners and Assorted Associates Meeting was adjourned at 12:05 P.M. Minutes submitted by (ex) Junior-Secretary-in-Training, E. Brontey.

OBSERVED TODAY, PT. 3—
in which Charlotte fails out there (as recounted by Anne)

**Being a Notebook of Anne at Nineteen and a Half
(and Twenty), Containing Occasional Character
Sketches, Dialogue, and Such Description as
Might Aid a Future Writer**

***Spring: the children outside are louder now, looking forward to
the park***
Em: I say, Settler, you seem to have enjoyed your breakfast.

Dog: Bark!

Em: Yes, well, if Papa would not have my eggs and ham, you
should have them.

Dog: Bark, bark!

Em: He's wrong to say omelets are unhealthy. He has no basis
on which to make that proclamation!

Dog: Bark!

Em: Eggs are healthy whether or not they have things within or
aside them, before or after them. To say otherwise is just plain

silly. You must be glad I'm back. I expect you were fed only oatmeal by our aunt when I was gone.

Dog: Snuffle.

Em: It was a bad idea, a bad bad wholly bad idea, going away. But trust in Em, dear Dog: I shall never leave thee again. Even if we must take shelter in the Post Office, I shall never leave thee.

Dog: Bark, bark!

Em: What's that? More omelet? You are an immoderate thing: that is why I love thee. But you shall not get fat; I think instead we shall go to the park! Shall we? Cavort in the park? I shall bring your ball, the rubber chewed one which is your favorite. Shall we bring Rover II? Though she be a lazy thing? We shall: you shall teach her to cavort, for this is another area in which you excel! Rover! Rover II! Gather thy things for we be off!

Dogs: Bark, bark, bark, bark!

Em: We shall also invite Master Branwell, who is *very* good at playing. *BRANWELL MONKEY GET YER COAT! WE FROLIC NOW WE DO!*

Spring: light returns

Now that Emily is returned, we tell tales once more, in the park now, under a tree, garlands on our heads—starting with the privations of the royal clan of Boiseberry as they flee the banks of Mount Trefoil from Mad Prince Edgar, grateful for their seven magic envelopes and seven seeds of invisibility. Emily insists that the children be crippled by want; I agree, but only if they be lifted now and again by brightly shining birds.

Summer: steamy, brains boil up out of the head to coat and mat the hair

Lotte, visiting, tells us of her "love life," which is no life. We walk arm in arm around the table, wearing such hats as we have found—a hunting cap, a boater, something Lotte calls a cloche.

"A man at work," she explains, "wishes me to volunteer for his cause, educating unwed mothers about vitamins. 'Unwed mothers need self-control,' I said, 'and sense. They do not need me.' 'You are dutiful,' said he, 'and efficient. I would have you reconsider, over coffee.'"

Emily laughs. "He asked you for a date!" she says, which fact Lotte acknowledges, also with a laugh, then Em says, "Shh! We'll wake Aunt, and have to learn about early birds! Let me guess," she whispers, "he wore a dashing cravat?"

"He wears plain clothes; his hair is badly cut. His eyes gleam with the brightness of a fanatic."

"Heaven, hell, and the realms in between!" cries Em, throwing up her arms. "What are we to do? Become helpmates to boors? I would rather pick food from garbage cans."

"He finds me dutiful," Lotte says, addressing Em, her back to me. "What would he say if he looked into my mind and saw my brain's peculiarity, the millions that throng there, wanting expression? If he visited my heart, and saw how quickly it quickens?"

"Screw 'em," says Em, sitting down on a kitchen chair and taking off her little boots.

"That's fine for you to say," says Lotte, moving a chair next to Em. "You are content to be your singular self, single forever, I not so much. Should I have gone out with him? Should I?"

Emily shrugs. She has had her fill, already, of this talk.

"A receptionist at my night job," Lotte continues, "describes a worthy *brother* . . ."

"A worthy brother?" Emily drolls. "What is that?" but Lotte is not deterred. I pull up a chair to sit beside her, and I take her hand.

". . . his prospects, his talents, the difficulty he has <u>finding the right gal</u>. I smile and say, 'He sounds just grand!' It does not occur to her," Lotte says, her voice catching, "it <u>shall never</u> occur to her, to introduce me to this paragon. She is kind, but not blind: she has seen my face which does not please and my figure which is slight. She would not 'do that' to her brother, whom she loves."

We do not contradict her, for we know: we are women who do not attract.

Lotte is possibly unaware how tightly she grasps our hands as she endeavors not to cry.

"She has seen me shed tears by the shredder, for the tedium of my task; she knows me to be 'prickly' and 'sensitive,' and 'incapable of fun' (I do not *drink* with the gang or *carouse*). But I would like to meet him, for he is serious about his studies and wishes to see the world!"

Em puts her long arm over Lotte's shoulder, for Lotte is now near tears. It is ever Lotte's way to volley without notice from ecstasy to tragedy, from comedy to despair.

"What am I to do?" she asks, her voice wavering. "Men look through me on the street. Even the ancient do not see me! Time is slipping, sisters! I do not know what to do!"

Consider that your sisters might be in the same boat, is what I think, if not a smaller boat, a narrower boat, a boat that already sinks, but Emily is quick to embrace her.

"I would not be alone forever," Lotte manages, sobbing onto Em's shoulder, and her cloche falls.

"Ye shall not be," assures Em. "No reason why ye should be."
"You'll always have us," say I, which does not help.

Autumn: wet leaves stick to windows, galoshes

Crisis at Roe Head. Charlotte will say only that she has forfeited a fortnight's wages to "get the hell out of there." "Enough," she says. "Enough!" Asked what "enough" is, her eye twitches and her mouth sets. She is only twenty-four but the lines by her lips are hard. "One has a limit," is all that she will say, and puts her keepsakes on their little shelf: a tin soldier, a lock of someone's hair.

Winter: bells echo through naked trees

Another season. We may well ask: whose turn is it to venture out and fail? Em shall not leave us: this is plain, nor should we wish her to. I am considered our last resort, though it is two years since my collapse at Roe Head. Branwell it should be who leaves us, but he is disinclined.

Papa looks upon us with worried eye: what is to become of you, he thinks.

I feel a strange lassitude. I should write, but cannot manage it.

"'Tis time we took in boarders," Bran says, attempting humor.

Spring: a brazen few march without overcoats or gloves

Emily wishes to take up the matter of the Paisley Twins and the howling Wolf of Eidertown by the fountain at the park; I decline. She shrugs and writes poems, page after page of poems. Our troubles do not trouble her—she is inhuman that way.

Summer: they say it is summer; time will tell

We walk around the table, wearing hats. Lotte proclaims our Glass Town dead. "If we are to be drudges, let us not ponder what is shining and bright! We have no need for romance, for regal lords, the great gleaming sea. Let us tell *drudge* tales! The drudge is noble, in her way."

"Balderdash," says Em, who invites her to our tale-telling only to be kind.

Rover chewed my notebook; I do not feel the loss. I wish I had hope to share with Lotte but I have squandered mine, I know not where. What shall wake me?

Autumn: rain follows sun follows cold follows rain

Bran has determined that he shall sell comical drawings of tourists in the city. The outlay we give him for his room and board shall quickly be recouped, says he. The money shall pour in.

Father's reply: I am glad to see initiative. Of course we shall subsidize your latest harebrained scheme (I paraphrase). Lotte's reply, were she here and not walking angrily in the park: May we see a plan, to know how many drawings must be sold and at what price to recoup this outlay? Aunt's reaction, as she brushes away a tear: Must you go so far? Bran's reply: The people in this town are rubes, they know nothing of drawing (he points at his painting of we three, from which his face is effaced, he having been unable to settle on a nose). Em's observation: Bran is a showman, he shall attract attention and do a serviceable job—we have seen his work, we know this to be true—and besides, have we a better thought?

Little Anne's conclusion: it shall soon be necessary for me to pay Branwell's future debt.

I have not long in our little house.

Part
3

HOPE

PRESENT PERFECT—
in which Lotte & Em find a teacher abroad
(as recounted by Charlotte, mostly)

Dear Diary.

The world is new! Em and I run through the *piazza* as if it were our park, never minding strange Italian stares: we are free! We run across a bridge, an *isola*. We laugh as we run through a market, as if we were children still, and run—we run! We pause by the river again and see in the water's black reflection, *ourselves*: all stars and a bright, white moon. The world is a wonder, a never-before-seen wonder, marvelous in its newness: we are *free* and we run some more!

Dear Diary.

I can hardly believe we're here! The credit is all mine, *I* made this happen! Dutiful Charlotte, obedient Charlotte! *I* did this! The knowledge I shall gain here shall make of me a teacher, or so said I to Aunt. She would not have me travel alone, so I prevailed upon Em—our Embly-Wembly, our homemade homely Emily, who's only ever been six months at school, who nearly died of homesickness there, who could not manage an *internship*—to come here, too.

We chose Rome because we wish a city of *layers*, we wish all roads beneath our feet—a Renaissance road, where journeyed Michelangelo to bargain with the pope; a medieval road, where Italians and invaders did bloody battle; a Roman road, where once strode emperors, patricians, and slaves. We wish *everything* beneath our feet!

I have never wanted anything as I have wanted this! I shall sleep but three hours per night, so I might spend every minute looking, feeling, hearing, reflecting; every minute here shall be as one million minutes at home—thus I shall make of this an *eternal* journey, one that extends for the rest of our lives. I feel particularly that I have done well by Em: she was ready to grow old in our home and die. We shall both be changed—eternally!

Whether we shall pursue teaching is a question we need not address—not here, not now, not in our present perfect.

Dear Diary,

I think it right, when one begins a new life, to offer an accounting of oneself, that one may more easily shed what is outgrown, or dead on the vine, in favor of new growth. I am Lotte, aka Charlemagne, aka Charley-Barley Brontey, oldest of four, upper two-thirds of six, motherless but possessed of much father and possibly too much aunt, late of a high and worthy home, abandoned so I might explore new worlds, to wit, old worlds, to wit, an *eternal* world. I am small and insignificant, rarely noticed, even when I stand on my head, which is not often, as I am prone to headaches and other nervous ailments— the result, Papa says, of too much *thinking*; of not enough cod liver oil, says Aunt; of disagreeing with him, says Bran; of too-tight drawers, bawls Embly-Wembly; of insufficient exercise, suggests Anne, who immediately qualifies, then withdraws her suggestion, in an agony of regret.

My insignificance is reinforced by my plain wardrobe—if anything can be reinforced whilst attracting negative attention. I have three dresses which I alternate, depending on my mood: all are gray, all are gay, all, in fact, are identical, so I must be fastidious in examining my mood, to determine which best suits the day. I wear my hair pinned up so my ears may stick out: I do this because I have much to learn, or so I'm told: I allow nothing to hinder my hearing.

I am the veteran of many wars, all lost before I arrived in this *bella città*, to wit the nanny wars and the Roe Head Roe Your Boat temporary-receptionist wars, through which over four or more fulsome years I was miserably and utterly vanquished. Being a mere twenty-six years upon this earth, I trust my battle wounds shall heal and those who regard me shall notice neither a walking limp nor a habit of waking, screaming in the night.

In addition to being insignificant and quiet among strangers, I am of above-average intelligence and tolerably well-read. I am lazy, however, and this above all: I would study more and noodle less. This is my resolution now that I am here: to see and hear and feel things I have not seen and heard and felt before, and through these experiences change, for the better! To be open to all that befalls me, so Italy's refinement might refine me. I am a block of half-made marble, I am paint that wants mixing!

Emily wonders aloud from her hotel bed that my navel is so worth gazing at. She derides my journal-keeping, as well she might: being transparent to her own self and ever the same, she has never to ask, Who am I, what am I doing on this green earth.

It is time we made our way into town, she says, and she is right.

I shall add only that I shall write fully and completely here of our experiences—not slavishly reporting on every sight and sensation, like some *tourist*, but rather recording what is *significant*, so I might better understand it, or make use of it. I shall speak only the truth, even when it does me no credit, as shall often be the case, if my life's history is any guide.

June the 13th, Embly-Wembly Brontey. Aunt will be feeding Rider if she hasn't forgotten Papa will be righting all wrongs in the City, wearing his cape. Annie babysits the Robinsons Branny walks the aisle of his railroad car shouting Shhh! Shhh! so all can hear. The Antarctic wasteland readies for rebellion. Lotte scribbles and looks furtive. The dying Jesus upon the wall looks bored at this rate it will take a long long time for him to die. Here is a drawing of the Market when I find tape I'll transfer it here that moving motion is Lotte gone before I arrive.

Dear Diary.

We spent a pleasant hour by the Trevi eating bread and sardines, imagining what happened to the duplicitous courtier Saldino. I am not so familiar with Saldino, he being a creation of Em and Anne, but I am very familiar with duplicitous courtiers. Still we disagreed about whether he might subvert the planned marriage of Jennifer of Orange with addled Rex Stuart, King of the Lowlands—Em saying yes, because this is how the story may move forward; I saying no, because there can be no satisfaction in such a tale. It was a pleasant hour, as I have said, and for the length of it, I knew not that I was in Rome, by the *Fontana di Trevi*, eating bread and sardines, but rather imagined I was in a settled kingdom of Antarctica, made warm and habitable by the Geniis Emmi and Lotti—this troubled me, it troubles me still.

Dear Diary.

Our lodgings are of the least expensive sort. The room is simple, as befits our budget: a rickety four-poster, shared by Em and myself, a low bench for our packs, a sink that runs cold water (*non potabile!*). The towels are to be provided by ours truly, so for the moment, we dry our faces on our sleeves, which are as clean, or unclean, as the sink itself, for it is there we must wash them. The faucet plip-plops all night long, reminding us that the toilet is down the hall, which is the same as many blocks away. There is a cross above our beds, a dripping Christ affixed thereto, I suppose for our devotions, were we devoted. Our view is of a tufa wall.

But it is time to wander. A girl who shares our bath wishes to join us. I haven't the opportunity to oblige or offer a palatable excuse: Emily says, loudly, simply, No.

Dear Diary.

Em is curt. She does not understand that I do not wish Glass Town—or rather, she understands, but cannot see why. She has offered to create another land with me, only let us not abandon our tales! I tried to explain about the present perfect, but she shook her head angrily: 'tis possible to do both, said she. Look where we are! said I, though we were in a grotty hostel, nothing distinguishing it from a room in any other land. This is all I need, said I, and it is true.

I want so much from this voyage! I want to see everything, experience everything! Emily needn't fear: I shall not leave my imagination behind, but wish it *rooted* in what I see. This is the difference between us—or between I as I was and the me I wish to be. When I stand amidst the broken pillars of Rome, it is Rome I wish to see—ancient Rome, Rome of any time or day—not the settled lands of Antarctica. This is my resolution. Emily shall have to bear it with me.

Dear Diary.

Yesterday, we walked a broad street and found ourselves by a subterranean *ruin*, of the sort that fill and organize this city. To the rough eye, the ruin is but dust and stone, knocked from earlier heights, lying random and unintelligible about the ground, but the sensitive eye discerns pattern and purpose, and imagines the grandeur that once was. The ruin, I learned upon opening my guide, had in fact been four temples and a theater, where once proud Caesar stood—and was murdered! How deeply did I sigh to think of such a history—then Emily saw the cats, who twist themselves about each column—ugly, bony things, which Em insisted we must feed.

All eight thousand? I asked.

If need be, said she, and off she went with our lunch money. The cats dined on *fegatini*—little livers, said she—while we made do with bread.

We wrote reports of what we'd learned, together with a sketch of the ruin and an imagining of its past. In my imagining, Cicero exhorts his countrymen to display Roman virtues, chiefly discipline and self-sacrifice. In Emily's, war is declared, a virgin slaughtered.

Often we come across a thing we assume to be of late date, only to find it is of Roman construction, which has given us much to ponder—specifically concerning the deception of appearances, the nature of truth, and so on—which in turn has resulted in splendid reports, mostly by Em, who has the talent of seeing straight to the heart of things.

Alas, we have calculated and discovered that our funds dwindle at a rate more rapid than anticipated. We shall have to (a) cut short our stay, (b) eat fewer meals, or (c) stop feeding the cats (*Never!* says Em).

June the 20th Embly-Wembly Brontey. At home Papa is gathering Aunt and Branny for a Friday Dinner maybe a roast even in summer. He is able to tell of the good things he hath accomplished, putting things right in the City Aunt tells of the lovely things she has sewn for the Poor and Branny says nothing because nothing is excellent on the Railway. Lotte is happy here, her face wild sometimes. Here is a drawing still no tape of Annie surrounded by beastly Robinsons she is the one who looks shipwrecked. General Fortescu hears rumors of rebellion.

Dear Diary,

In the Borghese Gallery I take the unprecedented step of using my composition notebook as journal, so I might write *in situ*, for remarkable things have occurred, and I fear that by delaying, I shall lose some of the detail which is so critical to the telling of a tale.

First it must be said that I was piqued with Em. It short, she does not brush her hair.

I am as Baal made me! she cries, when I object, because she stands by an Egyptian statue. Look, she wishes me to understand: I can attract more attention through bad behavior than bad appearance. She need only raise her voice among strangers to win any argument from me.

It was then I saw him, a most peculiar man. He was observing us from behind black pince-nez. He seemed at first glance quite deformed, with his agitated hair and muscular shoulders all out of proportion with his slight frame, which would give him the aspect of an ape, were it not for the extraordinary intelligence of his eyes, which sparkled like rare black stone. His dress was, to say the least, flamboyant—loose trousers, pointy shoes, showy cravat, affected beret. Of course, I burned to note that he observed our bickering—Em, in her dishevelment, me in my scolding, as though observing us *in our essence*; I quickly left the Egyptian gallery to find another. Contrary sister be damned! Deformed man, double damned!

Dear diary, he followed me! When I understood this, I thought to lose him in a sketch. It was Bernini's *Daphne* I attempted to draw, though it is a masterpiece well beyond my ability to render, its metamorphosis being altogether too subtle for my rough pen, which meant that he did, impertinently, peer over my shoulder to catch a glimpse! I slammed shut my notebook and betook myself to the Ladies' Room, where I felt *reasonably* certain he would not follow, and there I trembled in my stall. I tremble there still, perhaps discomfiting travelers who wish to relieve themselves—but I too need relief, in my notebook! Who is this man!

Dear Diary.

Outside the Borghese it rains determinedly, and Emily is determined we should stay, though I have pressed her to leave, feigning illness. The man is of no consequence, she says. He is no danger, unless you were to love him, in which case he should be danger indeed.

Like all men, was her implication, for she can have noted no particular peril with this one, having hardly afforded him half a glance.

I blushed fiercely, both as a result of her words and the loudness with which they were voiced. Sometimes I think this is her purpose in life, to vex me: she can have no other, as she is without ambition and will speak to no one outside our family in anything other than a monosyllable. Yet vexing me is no worthy ambition, for it is so easily accomplished.

Here, since I have ruined this notebook entirely, is a sketch of Em communing with King Tutankhamun, as I imagine him. They recline, eating grapes, and talk of Baal, how he has made them contrary, and too tall, and frequently unwilling to untangle their hair.

Dear Diary.

I write this in the hall of our pension. The light is dim, and though it is late, I hear Italians at the *ristorante* across the street, dining *al fresco*. They are most loud and uninhibited, caring little for those who wish to sleep. One would think that dining at this hour would be disadvantageous to the digestion, but they sound happy, and hale.

The man—but now I can give his name, it is Signor H.— has given me his card. He did not leave the Gallery, he did not leave *us*; rather, he persisted in observing us, approaching me finally before a painting of *Saint Catherine*. I was so absorbed in the beauty of that work that I had nearly forgotten his lurking self. I probably stood before that painting longer than is usual for a *turista*, for I could not rid myself of the impression that Catherine wished to speak—not with me, of course, but with her creator. She sat before that superior being, exposed—oh, she was clothed, but *spiritually* she was naked, *intellectually* she was exposed. Exposed yet silent; the tension overwhelmed me. What did she wish to say? There was that quality in her eyes, which I recognized, which said, There is an infinity within, I would share it with you—and the knowledge that the being with whom she would share it knew already anything she might say.

I imagine I looked quite pitiful in my absorption: mouth agape, eyes softened and tear-filled, posture quite forgotten.

You feel he loves her very much, this painter, a voice said in English, buzzing close to my ear like a fly. I turned on my heels, I'm sorry to say, and stared at this man, who was not much taller than I, whose skin had a rough, open-pored quality that did not inspire confidence.

You feel he loves her very much, to have captured her vulnerability and sorrow.

I nodded, for he was right: I did.

This outline, for example—he pointed at her bare shoulder, and I could not help noting how beautiful his hands were, how well tended and nicely formed. It is tender, no? This can only be the work of a man in love, for this is how a man *looks* at a woman he loves, is it not?

I could say nothing, for I know nothing of men in love. He smiled—though whether at my speechlessness or what he was about to say, I cannot know—and his face transformed, as is often the case with ugly people (myself included, I rather hope): he was radiant like an angel.

This thinking is rubbish! This man did not love this woman, this man loved no woman—

I must have looked puzzled.

This man loved *boys*, he said, and again the words, and the volume with which he spoke them, caused me to blush. And this, he continued, referring to Catherine, was no boy!

He stopped speaking to regard, and appreciate, the frank *womanliness* of the lady.

But surely, I ventured to say in Dante's Italian, she doth love *him*.

He laughed. He laughed with a heartiness I'd rarely heard in anyone, at least not any adult, as Papa and Aunt are more likely to chuckle than *laugh*.

This, my precious foreign visitor, he replied, again in English, is the famous Adriana. A courtesan. She is practiced in this look of love, she offers it to any who would pay for it.

Which is when he gave me his card.

I am an experienced guide, he said. My charges are in the other room, with my wife, he added, learning about Etruscans. Where do you stay?

I shook my head, as if to say, I shall not say.

Of course, he said shaking his head, you misunderstand.

He took the card from my hand and turned it to its reverse, on which was engraved the words H— Boarding House, reasonable rates, in both English and Italian.

You shall meet my wife, then you shall transfer to my house, he said, where I shall right your mistaken ideas about art, and life, at less than the cost of your current accommodation. A pair of Danish girls has left today; the room can be available tomorrow.

I don't know, I said.

We have hot water, he replied.

I shall speak to my sister, said I.

My sister said no. She cannot trust a toff, and that, says she, is that.

Dear Diary.

I have effected a compromise, which shall please both Em and myself. We shall move to the establishment of Sr. H., assuming we approve his wife, and the setting, and the linens, and verify the hotness of the water, and Em shall continue having my lunch money for her cats.

Dear Diary.

Now that we are settled in the establishment of Sr. H., I must confess I did not repeat the whole truth here, though I swore earlier that I would. Return we must to the scene before the saint. We had just spoken of courtesans and . . . boys, but he had not yet handed me his card.

The gentleman said, What do you know of this lady, this *saint*?

I opened my Baedeker; he took it from me.

I see, he said, that your studies are somewhat desultory.

Not so, said I. Lacking in plan, yes, but not enthusiasm.

This saint is Caterina of Alexandria. This wheel here, do you suppose it to be decoration?

I suppose nothing, said I. I note only its felicitous line and coloring.

She refused to marry anyone not as intelligent as she.

He looked at me pointedly, as if awaiting a reaction; reaction I had, for I had from the age of three said as much to any who would listen, but I withheld my thoughts, concealing emotion, which bubbled and boiled, behind a face stony like that of Daphne.

She died a virgin, of course.

At this I could not help but blush, and again Sr. H. laughed.

You mock me, sir! I burst. I may be a plain thing, and insignificant, known to few and possessed by none, but this does not mean I am unworthy of love!

He smiled, as if expecting—nay, *desiring!*—this reaction.

My dear Signorina, he said, we speak of a painting and a saint—surely, you are neither! She was to die by that wheel there, he added, but one touch and the wheel broke in two. You did not know this, did you? The sword, alas, had no such scruples and another martyr was achieved.

It was then he gave me his card, and issued his invitation.

You wish to learn, said he. This is good. But you cannot be both pupil and instructor.

I took his card, then pressed my case with my sister—why, we might well wonder.

Because I *do* wish to learn, because everything I do not know burns me with shame.

Because he wishes to teach me.

Because before long I shall be back in the wars, fighting to save my soul, and learning is all that shall comfort me.

Because I have never imagined conversation such as this.

June the 23rd, Embly-Wembly Brontey. Our new accommodations are tolerable we no more have to eat sardines like starving whales. There is no dying man upon the wall but a large number of chattering females. Lotte's face is a coat of many colors red with indignation as one female uses her towel green with envy as she observes another's comb set white with horror as a third explains her system for capturing men the complete Italian flag. General Fortescu holds a summit for the head of Antarctica forces. Lotte is enthralled by Mr. H. because of his learning. I am disgusted by the brownness of his teeth.

Dear Diary.

I see that I have not yet described our new home, though we have been here nearly a day. Sr. H. runs a school of sorts for well-brought-up ladies who wish to learn something of art, thus his *pension* acts as both dormitory and place of instruction. It is less expensive than our former lodgings, though our fee includes board and lessons, because we share a room with six others. I suspect their costs are heavier than ours, and it is the departure of *Dutch* girls (not Danish!) that makes possible our stay, for their fees—this was stressed by Sra. H.—would *not* be refunded.

Sra. H. is a delightful creature, all smiles and welcomes, till one tracks mud into her *salone*, then she becomes all dragon and shrill retorts. I think she was not pleased with our addition, as truthfully, our fees can do little more than cover our meals. Also, Sr. H. introduced us as the *most intelligent* Miss Bronteys, which I think rankled.

This one, he said with a grin, has learned Italian from Dante!—an announcement neither she nor I found amusing.

I have described the misses crosswise, as both one thing and its opposite. I do not understand inconsistency—a person should be one thing or another. Perhaps I shall write a composition on this topic.

Lessons began three weeks ago with Egyptians; they have now passed Minoans, Archaic Greeks, and Etruscans, whoever they may be. Tomorrow we begin with Romans; the weekend next, Sr. H. shall catch us up, a gesture for which I am grateful (Emily less so: I care nothing for Etruscans, says she).

We are sixteen altogether, with Em and myself being the oldest. Most would seem about the age of eighteen or twenty, though their manners suggest children of six or seven—though not in the Brontey household, for Aunt would never have abided lip smacking and gum chewing and nail biting and hair twirling, not even in a *wee bairn*.

The *pension* consists of two apartments: on the lower level, our rooms: two dormitory rooms, a bathroom, and instruction room, filled with books about art; on the upper level, accessible to us only at certain hours, a sitting room, our refectory, and beyond that, the private apartment of the H.s. The rooms are furnished simply with bulky wooden commodes and fresh flowers. Many look out over a charming courtyard, in the middle of which stands, improbably, a palm tree. Others look out over the street, which is like any street in this quarter: noisy, cobbled, full of industry and boys playing soccer.

I think I shall be happy here.

Dear Diary.

We walk everywhere, which is fine for Em and myself, less so for the ladies, who lag, complaining that Sr. H. wishes to save on the cost of a coach. They wear frightening slippers that strap up their legs and increase their height by two or three inches, causing them to waddle like ducks. Which is unfortunate, because Sr. H. does not talk merely when we arrive, as if our way were without interest, but along the route, and the ladies, with their clucking and waddling, miss this. Not I, for I am right at his side (Em being a few steps ahead, which fact I attribute to the length of her legs and not to any rudeness on her part).

Our first stop was the Roman Forum! My heart filled when I saw that vast graveyard of Roman stone! Immediately, as Sr. H. described what we saw, I withdrew my sketch pad, as did Em, to begin drawing the site, to better fix our impressions. The ladies stared. I don't suppose they felt a need to fix their impressions, the entirety of their murmured conversations being about a young man who darkly ignored his parents by the Arch of Titus. Which is a shame, since Sr. H. marvelously distinguished ancient skeletons one from the next—*this* being a temple for Castor and Pollux, *that* being a Julian Basilica, the other being the *Senate* building—giving vivid life to a vanished world.

On our way back to the *pension*, I queried our teacher about one thousand things. I asked when he would receive our compositions, for I could see how I might profit from revising my piece about Cicero, now that my knowledge had grown—oh, how the man laughed! You wish to write a composition? His laughter drew the attention of the ladies, who tittered. Naturally, I said. There is no better way to fix information in the mind, to make it one's own—and I confirmed that yes these would be in English, not medieval Italian.

Very well, he said. I wish to see this composition over *colazione*. I shall read it when my wife takes you to the archeological museum. Shall I expect one from your sister as well? he asked. You best not ask, said I, for if you seem to expect one, she shall not do it; this is her nature, and no amount of chiding on my part has convinced her to change.

Again, how he laughed!

Dear Diary.

It is the practice of the young ladies to exit by evening and return before the doors lock at night, smelling of beer and tobacco, their lipstick smeared. I wonder that Sra. H. does nothing to stop them. I shall certainly say nothing, for their absence allows us to complete our work. One of them, a *perfumed* girl with pug nose and pointed chin, stooped to examine Em's sketch of the Forum. Pretty, she said, but why not get a card? Why not get a brain, Em said by way of reply.

Dear Diary.

I think that I shall never write again. Sr. H. has seen my composition of Cicero, and laughed! He writes, *Who is this Cicero? What do you know of him* really? Well, Sr. H., I know a great deal about Cicero, having read many of his works in the original, having translated several as well. Did I say this to my teacher's face? I did. Then, alas, before I could properly note the effect of my revelation, I broke into sobs and ran to this room. When the girls assembled for *cena*, I resolved it were better I starve than appear in public ever again.

Emily shakes her head. Her composition, which treats the march of History, earned her high praise—I could see the exclamation points from here: they cheer her on, though punctuation is ordinarily her declared enemy.

I was so happy this morning, and so desolate today—and tomorrow? I shall have no feelings left by then.

June the 25th, Embly-Wembly Brontey. Lieutenant Brandenburg has declared his intentions to General Fortescu's ward. If Annie were here we'd have a jolly old time instead I have Lotte who wraps herself in her blanket and feigns a cold. Decent old Mrs. H. offered tea I said leave her she'll get lonely soon enough.

Dear Diary.

Sr. H. has clarified his comments. He came to see me in my room this morning, where I still lay prostrate, devoid of spirit.

He did not mean, he said, to suggest I was ignorant of Cicero. No, he said, most seriously, I should never accuse you of that! I blame my English, said he, and I nodded, for while his English is serviceable it is in no way elegant and is likely to be misinterpreted. What I mean, dear Lotte, he said, taking my hands! I meant only this, and I would have you listen carefully so we may be clear: I know Cicero and I don't give a rat's ass about his exhortations!

My ears turned red; I endeavored to release my hands, but he held them firm.

What I mean, he said—and his face was transformed: his eyes sparked and flashed, and his expression, again!, was that of an angel—is what should we care for the scoldings of that old man? Have we not heard enough from him? When I said what do you *know*, I meant, what do you know in here? and his hand, so warm! covered my chest. *Here* beats a heart, yet we see nothing of it *here*, he said, raising my composition with his other hand. *This* is what interests me, what *Lotte* sees in the *Foro Romano*, what she feels, how she understands what is around her. Repeat after me, he said: Cicero is a silly, boring man.

I could not help but smile.

Repeat after me, or I shall not continue, he insisted.

Cicero is a silly, boring man . . .

And I am a brilliant young lady. Come on!

And I am a brilliant young lady??

So, I hereby swear,

So, I hereby swear,

Never to write on him

Never to write on him

When I might write upon myself.

At which point my dear teacher removed his hand from my chest. I didn't know whether to laugh or to cry—so I cried. And cry still.

Dear Diary,

I forgot to mention that all this occurred while the rest of the girls, Em included, were at the archeological museum with Sra. H. I continued to sit in my bed long after Sr. H. left me, stunned, still feeling the heat of his hands on my chest. What can he have meant by what he said? Write upon myself? Who could be interested in what happens to insignificant Lotte? Two hours have passed, and still I have no notion.

But, lo! He returns!

Dear Diary,

Our conversation continues!

He is come to tell me I may lunch with him, the progress of my composition permitting—but immediately he sees I have not moved, not to dress myself, nor to put pen to paper.

You have a look of puzzlement! he says, and again I fear he may laugh.

Indeed! I say. I am puzzled! Greatly puzzled!

Look! he cries. She gesticulates! You are perhaps at heart *un'italiana*!

I think not! say I, and I do not know what you mean when you say I must write what I see and think and feel on seeing the Roman Forum! What I see and think and feel is Cicero!

That is most perplexing, says he, and he sits by my side. And why would that be?

Because this is what I imagine, sir!

And what does Cicero mean to you?

I endeavor to explain: Roman virtue—duty, restraint, self-sacrifice! The very virtues that guide my life! I sacrificed for duty! I restrained every inclination, I held back every desire, every wish that was mine alone. To bring money to my family so my brother might make his way. And now he works for the railway!

You are right! cries he, handing me a monogrammed hand-kerchief. I do not know what this is like! You must tell me!

I'm sorry? say I.

This is what interests me! At last you understand! Passionate Lotte! Tell me what it was to restrain your inclinations, and he hands me my notebook. Lunch, he adds, I shall bring you.

June the 27th, Embly-Wembly Brontey. Lotte weeps. Mr. H. rejects her composition calls it stiff and prissy. Mrs. H. hovers with her damned tea the chattering hens gather on their roosts. Cecilia Watt-Curlicu is betrothed secretly to Commander Lettice. If only Alabaster were here I would have someone intelligent to talk to.

Dear Diary.

I have written a tale of Lotte restraining her inclinations by the Temple of Saturn: she wishes to run but instead stands properly, she wishes to shout at beauty but instead listens, and thus she learns, and by learning, prepares for the future. Signor has not liked this story, not one bit, he has writ upon it one large, ugly line. Emily, meanwhile, continues to deserve her exclamation marks. This one, she writes like a man! Sr. H. said proudly to his wife over *colazione*; Em just stared at her breakfast, neither acknowledging nor caring for the compliment. The wife narrowed her eyes, as she is wont to do whene'er he mentions a Brontey.

Were I to write like a man, Sr. H. would draw ugly stripes through my page—I wish I knew what he wanted!

June the 29th, Embly-Wembly Brontey. He is barbarous when he rages Lotte's hand shakes when she hands over her wretched papers neither has any more sense than my cat. We have seen all the marbles of Rome in just one week yet there are more. Fortescu suspects that Brandenburg doth spy. Annie writes amusing tales of beheaded Robinsons.

Dear Diary,

He has been kind to me this morning. Stay with me, Lotte, he said, and again took my hands. Let the others roam! and he laughed at his English joke, though it was not his first telling. I nodded my assent, my hands shaking in his, though it was clear he did not mean to reproach me. I have not been clear, said he. And I call myself teacher! Is it possible no instructor has asked you to speak of yourself? I have had no instructor, I said, unwilling to explain four semesters of *boarding school*. I was home-schooled, I added, because he looked stricken. Of course, he said, as if speaking to himself, that should have been clear. And your *mamma*? I have no mama, I said, and there my treacherous lip trembled, and tears began their now accustomed course over my cheeks. Your papa, then, surely. My papa, I said, is of a mind that girls should listen, not speak. Will you accompany me? he asked. I wish to walk. I shall, said I. Perhaps you should wipe your face, said he. He awaits me even now!

Dear Diary,

It is some days since I have written, though not for want of incident! There has been rather a surplus of incident, all for the good! The day I walked with Sr. H. has changed my life! The things he said, they resonate! The careful way he listened, the questions he asked. He has the natural gift of a teacher, to make *learning* natural, to disguise it as conversation. The day was mild and we walked through the streets of this quarter, ignoring urchins and dark boys on motorbikes. As we walked, seemingly at random, following no pattern, he asked questions—about Papa, for example, his pedagogical theories. I told him of the learning we undertook when we were young, the reports we wrote. Tell me more of your papa, he said, and I warmed and told him of Papa's good works, his liking for order. I told of his excellence in learning, his translations of History. He was your Latin teacher, then? Signor asked. Oh, no, said I, and explained how I learned such things from Bran, who learned from Papa, and from it extrapolated Dante. And your aunt? he asked, smiling, and I said more, about her doubly-heated room, her fear of drafts, the sewing she does for the poor. She doesn't particularly *like* children, said I, but she has managed to be mother to us all. You should hear Bran imitate her country music—and how she affects to be angry with him. I described Bran, his red hair, his theatrical nature, how he makes us laugh—and cry, and described our disappointments. I talked about the work I had undertaken, as nanny, then at Roe Head. My desk there, with its view of rich, fat Lords of Nothing bustling importantly to and from the WC. The partners, who did not see me, gliding through our halls like malevolent wraiths. I talked at length of those years, how time, once my friend, oppressed me, how weighted I was by the bitter thought that this was *everything* that would ever be, duty without joy, toil without ideas, crowds with nary a *companion* for the rest of my life. I took in breath at that point, for never had I shared such matters.

My teacher grabbed my arm, and I stopped short. Lotte, he cried, and how I wished he'd take my hands! *This* is your subject. I shall hear no more of noble Romans and their alleged virtue; *this* is what I would hear. You would hear about the Lords of Nothing and despair? I asked. I would hear *any* of it, he shouted, catching the attention of a *fornaio* who was shutting his shop for *siesta*. I would hear of sewing hour, and wraiths, and prodigal sons! Yes, I would hear of desperation! I would hear about life—*your life*, passionate Lotte! Duty is the enemy of inspiration! *Your life, that* must be your inspiration! Learn this, and my work is done. I looked up and we were in a most magnificent square. He turned me about and we were home.

July the 3rd, Embly-Wembly Brontey. Mr. H. says foolish things he compares Rome to Russia sneaking glances at me as he knows I will fight him on paper if not with my fists. My compositions improve for he has a strong eye at least for syntax and how it may be diverted and dammed to great effect. He strikes out all my similes asking what in fact is similar to any other thing this I don't care to argue so I retain the simile in my mind where "in fact" it is more comfortable (like a child resting after a day of play). Lotte wears a superior smile I think she is in love with Mr. H.'s beret I hope this is the worst of her secrets. She has become a person no one can talk to. I write no more of home because I miss it too much.

Dear Diary,

We are familiar now with what is Roman—Roman baths, Roman theaters, Roman arches, Roman frescoes . . . We have been to palaces, marketplaces, mausoleums, temples, even the entire ruined town of Pompeii. *He* emphasizes the architecture, *she* the ornament, though I have no doubt she dresses his ideas as her own. The young ladies moan now at anything *Roman*; the fact that we move on to the *Romanesque* assuages them not.

We are familiar, too, with the extent to which Romans stole ("borrowed") from the Greeks, the Etruscans, even the Egyptians! Everything is imitation! Rome has no deep originality: originality can stem only from experience; experience is the only thing authentically one's own! I wonder that Sr. H. does not teach this to Emily, for she continues to write of ideas, never of anything felt, seen, or otherwise experienced. Yes, I have snuck glances at her compositions, she leaves them about, as if to say, Delight in my exclamation points!

For my part, I write day and night, about what is my own— the Darkest Monsters of Darklingland, clomping down the hall, mud on their boots, hair sprouting from their ears. The Ladies

Caroline, Shaniqua, and Desdemona, with whom I shared quarters—Caroline, in particular, who affixed a man's tie to our door when she wished me to sleep on the couch, the crick in my neck I acquired therefrom. I write of our high and worthy home, our childhood. Branwell running down the hill, his red hair flying, master of all he foresees. I write ever deeper, ever sweeter, I feel my heart strongly as I write; I offer everything that once cushioned it to him!

It is better than Antarctica, better than Glass Town, better than edifying reports. I write about my Self! She is a small thing, and tender: I love her!

I have found for her a finer, simpler language—I begin to think I hide behind my sentences. They are straighter now, and plain, like arrows pointed at my heart. Look here, they seem to say, and find me, *know* me! I am profusion!

My teacher says nothing, I believe so I may be free to write. He is a generous man, effacing himself so I might learn.

Emily looks at me strangely, as if to say, The sister I know is leaving me, but why.

Dear Diary.

In my teacher's continuing silence I lose all calm. I wonder at this Self which I found so lovable—how can it be thus, if he love it not?

Dear Diary.

My teacher does not look upon me, as if I have done something disgraceful. I try to catch his eye, for I would share another walk—I tire of the constant company of *girls!*—but he does not see me. I allow my fingers to touch his when I hand over my reports, so he might take my hands as once he did (*little Lotte! passionate Lotte!*), but he will not. I wonder if it is Sra. H. who causes this change, for he would not withdraw for *no* reason. Her spoon clangs with *especial* loudness when she serves spaghetti onto my plate. Her meaning I am certain is this: I am none so intelligent as you, and while I must bore this man and can never be his equal, I yet carry his child, so he must be satisfied, and so must you, without him! Oh, yes, she is with child, and a right balloon: I have seen the *cornetti* she eats at breakfast, stacked high like armaments. I wonder that she can stand at all, much less stand the person she's become.

Undated. Embly-Wembly Brontey. The days are too much the same to attach a date they do not pass except one like the other. Lotte cries she no longer stands by her triumph whatever that was. Poor Lotte she was never so strong as her emotions and they change by the hour, leaving her battered and confused but ever proud she shall not discuss her landslides with such as I a tall ill dressed Brontey monster with a rock inside that cannot be moved. Mrs. H. looks askance the more he tends to us the less she tends her stove soon all our dinners shall be burnt. I have no heart for Lieutenant Brandenburg I do not know that syntax is worth it.

Undated. Embly-Wembly Brontey. She has written of our sisters. She has concocted a fable according to which their death is her fault. She is monstrous it is monstrous that she should behave so exposing her self our selves our lives and what does he care I have seen his eyes grow hard as she minces and sighs. I have destroyed it come what may our sisters are not hers. And now she is in a flying rage shouting at girls as if they had interest in her compositions accusing them one by one tearing at their pillowcases. I have known you hated me because of my special relationship with our Teacher she cries oh no, dear Sister, it was I it was I.

Dear Diary,

I have told our teacher about Emily's transgression. He should understand why I have no composition to give him, but he laughs. I have not sisters, said he, nor brothers. I envy you your spats, and with that he turned to his toast, which was burnt by his wife, the witchy portly one—yet he spread marmalade on it, as if it were nectar! Anything she does delights him, anything I do he treats with a yawn and a sigh. Look at me! I wish to say. I am more interesting to you than toast! It is I! Lotte! *Your* Lotte! I knew not that I was passionate till you made me so! I have shared with you my heart's desire, I'm sorry it does not stir you!

Surprise! he says today, and even the proper young ladies bestir themselves, but all he means is one church atop another atop a pagan temple. Tonight I have in mind a different *kind* of composition, containing all that I have learned about cosmatesque marble, see how he likes that.

Dear Diary,

Aunt has died. My first (ignoble) thought: has she left us something so we may stay? My second: let Emily go; I was Aunt's least favorite. My third: home I go; she was like a mother to me, or certainly she tried. My final thought : will my teacher see that I have gone?

Undated, Embly-Wembly Brontey. Aunt hath given away Alabaster also Rider, and the parakeet named Ferdinand she shall have their company in heaven. Lotte weeps over her correspondence with that man Annie and I go to the sea. Is it the lack of Robinsons makes you glad I ask. That and the boundless sea says she none are confined in the sea all may be free. On the train we are Lady Millicent Hallifax her paramours Mordor and Mulligan Sr the aging Countess de Rackenstein the swami the lion tamer the woman who dreams

AT HOME—
in which Branwell tends a dying Aunt
(as recounted by Aunt)

I brought you a present, Bran says! Look, Aunt, a clementine!

My voice doesn't work by way of reply, nor my hands, so the boy feeds it to me, bite by bite, then wipes the juice from my chin. I smile, despite myself. The boy rolls his eyes, as if praised. Be a good girl now and sleep, says he. You remind me of my Uncle Jim, I think: big talk, tall tales, dead at forty. I suppose it's out of the question that I might have a drink.

Where are they, the girls? I ask. The boy sits at my bed. You remember, says he, but I don't. Annie's with the Robinsons, he says, Robertsons, I forget which—awful people. McMansion, rude children, ring a cowbell? Really, Aunt, you must *try*. I say nothing, because it *doesn't* ring a bell. Em and Charlotte're studying, he says. A bit old for that, aren't they? say I. Overseas, says he, delivering the punchline. Who let them do a foolish thing like that? I ask. Why Papa, the boss around here last time I checked. He says this pleasantly, but wishes victory for his sex. Paddy's no boss, I think. He's weak; you all would have died were it not for me six weeks before your father noticed. Good thing I got sacked by the railway, the boy says. Else, who'd take care of you? The others, say I. Where are they? He sighs: Long gone, Aunt, long gone. D'you need a rolling-over? I am not a piecrust, say I.

At home, no one's nursed by a fella, but here I am, cared for by one, and likely to die for it.

Honestly, say I, is this the best you can do? It's takeout, Aunt, you know I don't cook. It's disgusting! I thought you liked Chinese. I never! A pouty look, never looked good on a boy. Give it here, then! I'll take it I'll take it: you want me to starve! The boy laughs. You watch I don't make you eat with chopsticks, says he. That'll be a hoot. I'll hoot you, I say, but again I smile. The boy always could make me smile.

Hand me my sewing, I say. There is no sewing says the boy. What no sewing? Don't be a fool! Annie took it with her to the Robinsons. Annie hates sewing. You lie because you don't think I can thread a needle or be steady. I lie, says he, because I want you to myself.

Rub my feet! He rubs my feet, but I can't feel them. My hands are dry. He pushes lotion onto them. My arms are stiff, he kneads them. No! he says: I'll not touch thy legs! He brings a pot and washes my head. What've you done, boy, did you wash my head with laundry detergent? He looks at me cockeyed. Yer correct that yer hair ain't right. Should I cut it with a knife? I think a moment: Go ahead, my days as glamour-puss are done. I don't think he's serious but he returns with scissors. It's wrong but I consent: easier than saying no. His eyes aren't right, he doesn't walk a straight line. Never mind, say I: 'tis easier now. Paddy looks at my head with horror, as if I'd done this thing myself. I allow him to think it: the boy does his best. There was a time when conscience said, Marry this man, for your sister's sake, but I could not do it and he didn't ask.

I cannot count the bells: is it morning or is it night? The meals the boy brings are indistinct: porridge, soup, at any time, all food I can eat without teeth; we've decided: teeth are more trouble than they're worth. Usually when he arrives I am asleep, so who can know if it's night or day. When he stinks, I think it's night.

Where are the girls, I ask pleasantly. Eaten by lions, says he. No way to talk to your aunt who's trying to be pleasant. Alright, eaten by porcupines. Better? He's reading a book and doesn't want to be disturbed. You remind me of my Uncle Jim, I say. I know, says he, dead at forty. Don't worry, I say: plenty of time. And the eldest, what's-her-name? Which one, he asks. There are so many eldest. What am I to do with you? ask I. Send my sister in, I say: I tire of you, I really do.

He investigates my face with a flashlight. His eyes are red: he fixates the light upon himself when I jump that I may see. Only me, he says, and what can that be? he adds. *Me*, he says, answering his own self, and sits on my bed. Where does my beginning end and my end begin? Can't say, say I: I expect where it always has. He nods, vehemently. You may be right! I may be old, say I, but I am often right. I have brought you a picture, he says, the one I painted of the girls. I have placed it at the foot of yer bed so you shan't be alone. Have you anything to drink? ask I. I burn. Grundy 'n' I have drunk it all, says he, though Brownie helped, then he sighs and crawls up onto the bed. I push at him, his arms surround me; he snores.

I cry because it hurts and I forget where I am: where I am is only pain sometimes, never a room, never a place, never my home. My home is a small place in the mountains. I have a cat. I have a window box, a Victrola, three rag rugs. A boy who cleans my gutters, not this boy. *This* boy arrives to hold my hand or brush my hair, telling tales to make me forget where I am, only this forgetting is better than mine. There is a lord and lady and a terrible prince, and they get up to things. I never know how these stories end, maybe they never do.

What happened when you went to the city? I ask, because I never knew. He only shakes his head. All sorts of things, said he, things that add up to no thing, none of them the right thing. Did you get lost, Bran, did you try your best, did you meet a bad one, a woman perhaps, did you change your mind, we'd have understood if you'd changed your mind. Old woman, says he, I love you, but I'll not say. I'll take the secret to my grave, say I. And that'll be soon enough. Nonsense, says he, you're fit as a fiddle and he fiddles, singing a song from my home and jiggling about the room. Always he could make me laugh.

Has my father been to see you? Never, say I, and it may be true, nor the girls. You're the only one who loves me. And love you I do, says he, and truly. He has taken to lying with me because it stops me crying. His hands are small like a girl's, though he smells of refuse. How old are you? I ask. A quarter century, or thereabouts, says he. Old enough to know better, say I. Alas, says he, 'tis true.

Stop your talking, say I, and tell him a tale of my home. He holds my hand, and wipes my face with a cloth, because it's hot, and he waits, because there are spaces between my words, long spaces: the words are hard to find, in fact, sentences are hard to find so I use just words: rocking chair, mountain, ivy, honey, a barn, a dance, a sunset on the green, young man, tea shop, red, blue lavender. I see, says he, I see it all. How lucky you are to have such a home! He kisses my hand, as if he'd been there, as if he'd seen the young man feeding me honey on the green while I wore lavender and held daisies in my hair, as if he'd seen him kiss my hand.

The truth is he's not here when I need him, not always. It's hard to be alone. I emptied myself out for them; there was nothing left for me. They needed me, little rabbits, what was I to do, so many of them, but now? No one waits for me, no one waits on me. The pill has expired, I'm thirsty, I hurt.

I have seen it! he exclaims and I see that it is bad. His face flushes red, his shirt is torn. I have seen it and it is everywhere, it is nowhere! he exclaims. I know what alcohol does; this is not that. But stop! he cries. 'Tis not fair! Not fair! He tears at his hair, really tears, and cries, pitiably. I cannot do it, he cries, you do not know me, this is not for me! You stop, I say, but he does not hear. If I could get up to hold him, I would. Where are his father, his sisters? Why is it always I who cares for all? I sing a song, a song from home. His eyes focus. Aunt, he exclaims! Do you need a thing? I am going to the store.

The spaces between my words continue to grow, filled with pain and more space. I've brought you a fan the boy says, but it's a breeze upon my porch. The clementine is honey on my chin. I don't know what to do with my life, but it's Uncle Jim, his arms about my waist, saying little girl, little girl, what to do with a little girl. The boy kisses my hand. Please don't leave me! says the grown man with the hat. I shall be alone if you leave! But they need me, say I. The little ones need me. And they do.

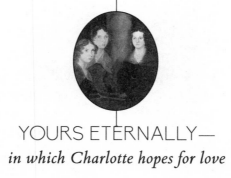

YOURS ETERNALLY—
in which Charlotte hopes for love

Dear Esteemed Teacher,

I am so grateful for the condolence letter you sent Papa! Aunt cared for us with selfless devotion—seventeen of my twenty-six years!—never liking our city, perhaps never liking *us*. You know her well for the portrait I have painted of her eccentric ways. Today, her overheated room has cooled, but our hearts have not.

You were kind also to praise the sisters Brontey, which words moved our papa much, as he likes to hear that we have done well in the world. I am sure that Em was brought to you fully formed—it often seems she was so formed at birth!—but I became praiseworthy only as a result of your intervention. For that I humbly thank you.

We are fortunate in this sad time to be all of us together, though briefly: Em, my sister Anne (granted leave from her position as *nanny*), my brother Bran (who, dismissed from the railway, nursed our aunt). We draw comfort from each other, as we always have—I suspected once that we should be our own closest friends forever, for all the sorrows we have known—but this was before I had such a friend as you. I do pine for your City, I think of her *eternally*. I had not known before how small my home, how small my *life*! It hath not one drop of *eternity* in't, though the days are long enough. If you took pity on lonely Lotte, she would reply and think you saved her Life.

With affection,
Little Lotte Brontey

My Dear Sr. H.

Our family thanks you again for your kind thoughts; we all enjoyed your letter addressed to each of us in turn (except Anne, who is returned to the Robinsons). How surprised we were to be understood so completely—Em especially, as she imagines herself invisible, despite being as plain to view as Gibraltar's rock! You would not know her, my teacher, so thoroughly is she absorbed in our household's maintenance—she has no fancy ideas now, except those pertaining to potatoes, and laundry powder.

We think to put ourselves out as instructors, Em and I, though our connections are few. I allow myself hope between the bells of one and two, when I await the post, though each day, the post doth disappoint! Meanwhile, I do not read or write, for fear I may go blind. I perhaps did not mention that weak eyes afflict our family—Papa is now quite unable to read his *Times*.

I should make an exception for a letter from you.

Your especial friend,
Lotte Brontey

Dear Professore H.

We have quite failed at *instructing* for none would have us! I cannot regret this, for I have not your passion for *teaching*. (It must have seemed an endless task, filling my empty vessel: I had *everything* to learn about *everything*. But pour you did, and generously—and my vessel proved strong, I think—strong enough to retain what you gave me for a lifetime, maybe longer—for *eternity*.) I find other occupation for my time—for example, organizing my writing. You do not know this, but I was writing long before I met you! I have over my twenty-seven years created volumes of stories, poems, and tales, on all manner of theme. There are perhaps one thousand pages here; I did write once, to a man of letters, enclosing samples of this writing. He praised my style—yes, the very style you found so *unacceptable*. I am given hope by his approbation, for he is a man so distinguished that surely you will have heard of him, even in your Town. Some stories are accompanied by my own illustrations, many quite fine. Truly, the perusal of them must offer hours of delight.

I would be willing to share any of these, should you but ask.

Your Lotte

Dear Sir,

I have received your letter and quite understand! Your lady doth restrict your letters to one per quarter, to be addressed to my entire household! Excellent woman! A man does well to be ruled by a woman of such good sense! I hope she also advises you when to walk talk and think, for one mustn't trust oneself to walk talk and think without a most excellent guide!

Still, you do not say *I* must not write, which I understand to be encouragement. Were you to write a letter for my eyes only, I should keep your secret, and fully admire your independence.

Little Lotte

My Dear Sr. H.

I apologize for my *snappish* tone: you dealt me a fearsome blow! Please know, I am grateful for any news I might hear, whether or not addressed to *Papa*. Days weeks months pass with nothing to distinguish them. Branwell, with whom I once shared tales, is gone. Emily is immersed in *poetry*. I can imagine no future for myself, except that of drear—returning to serve the Lords of Darklingland.

Many days, I do not stir from bed, preferring the darkness of my dreams to the darkness of my every day: in dreams at least I may return to you.

My family worries that I dwindle, though they cannot guess the cause.

Do not forget me! Spare me but one letter, one letter for me alone! I cannot describe how bleak it is here, or how a day—a month! a year!—might be brightened by just one line from you! There is a reason you lifted me above the others: we share an affinity—yes, I say it!—our souls do long to speak. So speak, dear teacher, *speak!*

Your Lotte

My Dear Teacher!

I understand—*only now!*—that Papa has asked you to suspend our correspondence, *such as it is*, more than two years since I was expelled from your shores! He thinks your letters make me ill—how little he understands! It is their *absence* that sees me so reduced—yes, I am smaller now: I have no interest in food—even the sight of Emily's stew arouses in me none of the hunger I felt at your table, in your sight. If you heed my papa, I shall vanish altogether!

You took my hand in yours, you looked deep into my eyes (and dare I say my soul) and offered a vision of who I might become. You opened in me the habit of *openness*, dear teacher, then you locked the door that wants opening! It was cruel, you are cruel, though with just one word I shall forgive.

Please, beloved man! One word so I may live!

Your Lotte

NO NONSENSE—
in which Branwell reveals Big Plans

It is possible to commemorate the dead without speaking of them; so it is in our household, where on New Year's Eve, we think of Maria's turkey-in-a-bag, Mama's streamers, six colors for six children, Aunt's indifferent stew. Charlotte cannot smile, but Emily can cook: we will enjoy her chops and think of All Good Things; her greens taste of Prosperity, for they are salted and well spiced.

Branwell alone wears black. It is not our habit to display mourning. We cannot know if he wears such to express grief, our aunt months gone, or to gather free drinks at the pub.

It is good we are together, Papa says, after serving All Good Things. He has forgotten that Annie toils at the Robinsons, though her income pays for our chops and Branwell's mourning gear, including his black hat.

Branwell has let us know that he's expected elsewhere: he shall not stay for Sweetness nor Our Hearts' Desire, which tonight is a double-layer cake. Emily experiments often now with layered things: poems with multiple meanings, bright sweaters over a dismal dress, thoughts of a bunk where above she exults as a sister weeps below.

Emily would listen were her sister to talk, but Charlotte wishes to be asked and Emily is not one for asking. Besides, she knows the source of Lotte's distress and likes it not.

Still, the Bronteys are grateful. Branwell (whom Lotte has taken to calling *Brindle* in her disgust) shall not say it, but he is grateful for Emily's food, and the work his sisters do to buoy their father, who too easily gives in to gloom. Emily is grateful to be home, alone with her imagination, which explodes! Papa is grateful to no longer be alone with Branwell, whose moods he cannot comprehend, whose life feels like a reproach, though he would rather not think why. He is grateful, too, for his daughters—home again!—for they pet and cajole and tend to him. Charlotte is grateful for . . . well, Charlotte is not grateful. She is subsumed. The world is a heavy and dark place, a terrifying place—because the heaviness, the darkness are without end. It is enough most days that she combs her hair.

We toast the New Year and Papa surprises us all:

Branwell shall be a civil servant! he says. I am so very proud!

Alas, no, Branwell says. Did I not say?

You must have forgotten to say, Papa says. What has changed?

They wish me to piss in a cup. I shall not piss in a cup!

I'm afraid I do not understand, says our good father.

T'would violate my liberties! Bran insists. I shall not piss in a cup!

Working would violate his liberty, Lotte mutters, *serving* and doing so *civilly* would violate his liberty.

One must have principles, Papa says. Precisely, Branwell says. Em contrives to drop a pork chop on his lap. Tell us a story of your travels, Papa continues. I never tire of thinking of you in that ancient place.

It is unclear to whom Papa speaks for he examines his greens.

Lotte wishes Emily to answer, but Emily does not oblige, she will never oblige. The question discomfits Branwell, too, for he remembers being excluded from everything.

If only you had gone to Paris, Bran says, you might now *teach*. All men of quality study French.

We are not all men, Emily rejoins.

Perhaps if you had improved your Latin, Branwell persists, you might now profit.

You are the only one who has ever profited from our labor, Lotte says.

Don't be crass, Little Lotte. I speak only the truth.

So what is your plan now, truth-teller? Shall you profit from your Latin? You are soothsayer now? Oracle? Shall we find you in a cave divining fortunes with a chicken bone?

Never you mind, Branwell says. I have plans, big plans. You shall see.

Branwell shall make us proud, Papa says.

No one knows if Papa believes such things, but he is quick to say them.

Name one, Lotte says. Name one of your big plans!

Well, I have published poems. You might not know that. In papers of note.

If they are published, then they are not plans. What are your plans, your very big plans? Do they involve spending money you have found on the *railway*?

Lotte, that is enough. Nothing was proven against our Bran, Papa says.

I am to teach with Anne, if you must know. She has arranged an offer from the Robinsons. I am of a mind to accept.

You are to be . . . a nanny? Papa asks.

Tutor, Papa! I shall train the next generation of Robinson men—a noble pursuit. For which I shall be remunerated far in excess of little Anne, who has only to supervise the wardrobe of two young *girls*.

There is silence about the New Year's Eve table.

We shall look forward to profiting from your labor, Lotte mumbles.

Don't count on it, Branwell replies.

MR. FIVEPENNY MEETS THE GIRLS—
in which Papa's assistant arrives at a bad time

The curtain rises. We are in the Brontey sitting room: tiny with heavy, dark drapes. On one wall, a painting of three girls who look like ghosts. To the left, a single bed with rosy, ruffley spread; a lady's desk on which lies discarded sewing, a fire extinguisher; a tiny embroidered footstool. In the center, a disused fireplace with mantel, on which rests an urn and old-fashioned photo of a young woman's face in a bronzey frame. To the right, a hallway is visible and, across the hall, a door on which is written in a childish hand "WC."

Papa, sixty-eight, sits in a chair by the fireplace. He wears a smoking jacket–cum–dressing gown, the buttons of which may not be aligned, or possibly a vest from which pocket hangs a gold watch chain. He wears thick glasses, yet still he peers, seeing with great difficulty. His white hair is overlong, his part not straight; his mutton chop sideburns, at least, are well shaped. At his feet sits Rider, an ancient dog, who does not move. Mr. Fivepenny, twenty-seven, clean shaven and alert, occupies a chair also by the fireplace. His suit is inexpensive and/or worn.

PAPA: And that is the story of how I raised myself up from the poverty of my ancestors.

MR. FIVEPENNY: Fascinating!

PAPA: Were your ancestors very poor?

MR. FIVEPENNY: Undoubtedly!

PAPA: If one goes back far enough.

Mr. Fivepenny nods vigorously.

PAPA: I expect you'll meet them soon enough.

MR. FIVEPENNY: My ancestors? I hope not!

PAPA: My daughters! They're around here someplace!

MR. FIVEPENNY: Excellent! I have heard tell also of a most worthy son?

PAPA: Eh?

MR. FIVEPENNY: A son? I've heard of a most worthy son?

PAPA: He's around here someplace. I expect you'll meet him soon enough.

A woman's wail is heard offstage. She would appear to be in agony. Mr. Fivepenny half stands, looking to Papa for elucidation.

PAPA, *sadly*: That would be our Lotte. She is of late returned from the Continent.

MR. FIVEPENNY: I would attend her!

PAPA: She'll be in with tea soon enough.

Mr. Fivepenny sits. The woman wails again.

PAPA: It is a happy time, for we are all together. Annie is returned from service, Branny, too. Em is back from the Continent. They are all orphans, you know.

He indicates the urn, the old-fashioned photo.

PAPA: My beloved Maria, dead these twenty-four years. Do you wish to see?

He stands on the dog's tail, who yelps piteously, and begins walking uncertainly toward the mantel, his hands waving. Before Papa can knock over the urn, the loutish voice of a man can be heard from the hallway. He appears angry and possibly intoxicated. Papa turns to face the door (more or less). His expression is angelic, one of doting love.

PAPA: That would be our Bran. I shall greet him. The urn is there, should you wish to view it.

A short man with crazed red hair enters the room. It is Bran, twenty-eight. Though he appears not to see the people in the room, he shouts—or rather, he raves. He wears semi-fashionable clothing, including an ascot. Though he is small, he seems to take up all available space.

BRAN, *shouting and gesticulating*: And I said to the Poet Laureate! . . . For once in your life, should I! . . . It's as if! . . . I can't understand it I *cannot*! It is not right! I love her, man, I do!

Bran begins to rend his garments and to weep. A small arm reaches into the room and pulls Bran out. A small plain head can barely be seen at the door's edge—it is Lotte, twenty-nine.

LOTTE: Don't mind him. Have you no tea? I'll get you tea.

Lotte leaves, pulling away the weeping Bran. A door slams and it is quiet again.

MR. FIVEPENNY: Perhaps I can help with the tea?

PAPA: My daughter is perfectly capable of making tea, Mr. Fivepenny. Do you think her incapable of making tea?

MR. FIVEPENNY: I think her distressed and occupied by her brother.

PAPA: That would be Bran, Our Only Boy. Takes after his mother. Did you see the ashes?

MR. FIVEPENNY: Perhaps I shall see them later.

PAPA: He has known disappointments, but he shall rally. The girls are penniless. When I die, they shall be out on the street, unless Bran can be convinced to make something of himself.

MR. FIVEPENNY: Surely not!

PAPA, *whispering*: Rent control! Their aunt, lately deceased . . .

Papa waves his arm to indicate the sitting room; Mr. Fivepenny is not sure what he's meant to see.

PAPA: . . . has left them something, but not enough to live on, poor chicks. Lotte thought she might make of herself a teacher, but that has not worked as planned . . .

MR. FIVEPENNY: You say she is of late returned from the Continent?

PAPA: Three years hence. A melancholic return, I know not why. But here she is with the tea.

Lotte arrives with a tea tray. She wears a trim gray dress and sensible shoes. Her mousy brown hair is pulled back in a tightish bun. Her face is puffy, her eyes red. She moves as one who is weary. She places the tea tray down on the small desk, pushing aside discarded sewing, and picks up the teapot. Her hand shakes. Mr. Fivepenny jumps up.

MR. FIVEPENNY: Allow me, Miss Brontey!

LOTTE: Do you think me incapable of pouring tea, Mr. Fivepenny? I assure you, Mr. Fivepenny, whatever else I may be, I am capable of pouring tea.

PAPA: Mr. Fivepenny, meet my eldest: Lotte. Lotte dear, this is Fivepenny, my new assistant.

LOTTE, *wryly*: Charmed.

Mr. Fivepenny, still standing, bows.

LOTTE: Sugar? Milk? Soy?

MR. FIVEPENNY: Yes. Please!

Lotte, smiling to herself, pours rather a lot of everything into Mr. Five-
penny's tea. He accepts the tea, though in the shaking of Lotte's hand,
much of it spills onto the saucer. Lotte pours tea for her father, who takes
the stuff black. The two men sip. Lotte heads for the door.

PAPA: Is Annie about? I would have her greet my guest.

LOTTE: She is indisposed, Papa.

PAPA: Not sick, I trust.

LOTTE: No, not sick. But she has taken to her bed.

PAPA: Retrieve her if she is not sick! It is her duty to attend to
my guests!

LOTTE: If you like, I can force a dress on her, and carry her out
here, though I'm not sure I can bear her weight . . . Perhaps if
I drag her . . .

PAPA, TO MR. FIVEPENNY: You shall meet my youngest on
another day.

MR. FIVEPENNY: I hope she shall be stronger then.

LOTTE: I, too, for she leaves me with the washing.

Lotte again turns to leave.

PAPA: Lotte, do not leave. Pull up a chair. Sit with us a while.

Lotte looks around, notices the tiny footstool, looks at Papa a moment, then drags the stool to a point between Papa and Mr. Fivepenny, taking care not to trod on the dog. She sits on the stool, endeavoring to find a modest position for her legs, so close to the ground.

PAPA: You would not think to look on her, but Lotte is quite the scholar!

LOTTE, *both pleased and displeased by the attention*: I am tolerably well learned.

PAPA: Tell him the languages you speak!

LOTTE, *rolling her eyes and looking away*: Italian, German, Latin, some Sanskrit.

PAPA, *proudly*: And Greek!

LOTTE: Papa, I do not speak Greek. You declined to teach me, remember?

PAPA, *scratching his chin*: I do not.

LOTTE: You taught Bran.

PAPA: I didn't teach you?

LOTTE: You didn't teach me anything, remember?

She rises and wipes Papa's chin, or makes some other infantalizing gesture.

PAPA: An oversight.

LOTTE, *bitterly*: What Latin I know, I learned from Bran. Only he is a poor teacher; he frequently got it wrong.

PAPA: How is your brother? I hardly see him these days.

LOTTE: You would hardly wish to see him. He is not worth seeing.

PAPA: Tsk, tsk. I would not have you say such things about your brother and the Only Boy.

Mr. Fivepenny nods with much gusto, then, unable to control himself, stands, facing Lotte.

MR. FIVEPENNY, *ardently*: Miss Brontey, I am a plain but honest man . . .

Bran comes in again. He is as before, his clothes disheveled and now torn, only now he has what appears to be red jam on his chin. As he raves he lurches about, bumping into furniture.

BRAN: I am dying! Oh, angels: weep! This illness shall be my last! Verily, I cannot withstand the pain! O, sorrow! O, grief! It is more than a mere man, more even than an exceptional Only Boy, can tolerate! It was only yesterday. And yet! And yet!

PAPA: Branny, we shall have to have a word about your Latin.

Lotte stands and points Bran toward the hallway, then gives him a little shove. He exits, still raving. Offstage, a door slams. Mr. Fivepenny cannot take his eyes off Lotte.

PAPA: I am something of a versifier! Shall I find you some of my poems?

MR. FIVEPENNY: By all means.

Papa stands, and steps again on the dog's tail, who yelps piteously and returns to sleep. Papa makes his way to the door, bumping into such furniture as comes his way.

LOTTE: His poems are quite edifying. You shall be well instructed by them.

MR. FIVEPENNY: You were in some distress earlier. I should like to be of service.

LOTTE: Distress?

MR. FIVEPENNY: I thought you did cry out.

LOTTE: I had only misplaced my pincushion, Mr. Penny.

MR. FIVEPENNY: Fivepenny.

LOTTE: Even were you five times more valuable than I thought, I should have no need of you. I misplaced my pincushion, then I found it.

Mr. Fivepenny stands again, and holds his hand over his heart.

MR. FIVEPENNY: Miss Brontey, I am a plain but honest man . . .

LOTTE: The one doth surely prove the other!

MR. FIVEPENNY, *confused*: I beg your pardon?

LOTTE: That you are willing to admit the first doth prove the second!

Mr. Fivepenny still looks confused.

LOTTE: Mr. Fivepenny, it is plain that you are both plain and plainspoken, but you are not to declare yourself to me! I shall not have you and that's that.

MR. FIVEPENNY: That's that?

LOTTE: My heart belongs to another. He will not have it, but still that's that.

MR. FIVEPENNY: That may be that, but it's not the *end* of that.

Now it is Lotte's turn to look confused. Luckily, Papa returns holding some papers.

PAPA: I have found them. A longish poem about manly virtues. Courage, all that.

LOTTE: Uh, no, Papa. Those be lawyer's papers you have found. From the Robinsons. A restraining order, for he who has never known restraint.

Papa: Are you quite sure?

Lotte: I worked in a lawyers' pit on your instruction, slaving to serve the future of that one there, the boy who raveth—so yes, I recognize the paper, the seal, the language.

Papa peers down at the pages.

Papa: You may be right, Lotte dear. I see many flourishes here, but no verse.

Lotte: And nothing very edifying, I'll warrant.

Papa: We may yet discourse on noble virtues. Sit down, Lotte. Sit, Mr. Fivepenny.

Mr. Fivepenny returns to sit in his chair; Lotte returns to squat on her footstool.

Papa: I believe man's noblest feature is his willingness to sacrifice for others. What say you, Lotte? What do you say is man's noblest feature?

Lotte, *without hesitating*: Brilliance of mind.

Papa: And you, Mr. Fivepenny, what say you?

Mr. Fivepenny: Kindness. Any man might aspire to be kind, regardless of his gifts . . .

Lotte: Or woman . . .

MR. FIVEPENNY: I find, Miss Brontey, that ladies do not, as a rule, lack kindness.

LOTTE: You have never been in service, Mr. Penny. Or a girls' dormitory!

MR. FIVEPENNY: I have but small experience of ladies. Which deficit I hope to correct very soon.

LOTTE, *ignoring Mr. Fivepenny's meaningful look*: Ye shall find no ladies in these parts, Mr. Penny. We are all beasts here, rude and savage spinsters, all of us ineligible.

MR. FIVEPENNY, *standing*: I fear I may have overstayed my welcome, Mr. Brontey. I shall look forward to hearing your poems . . .

LOTTE, *also standing*: And being edified by them.

MR. FIVEPENNY: Certainly, and being edified by them, on another occasion.

PAPA: Blasted poems.

MR. FIVEPENNY, *in a small voice, to Lotte*: Have you perhaps a *gabinetto*?

LOTTE: A what?

MR. FIVEPENNY, *in a smaller voice*: A *little room*?

LOTTE, *smiling*: You are standing in the smallest we have.

MR. FIVEPENNY, *in an even smaller voice*: I require a . . . young men's facility?

LOTTE: Speak up, Mr. Fishpenny! Is it the water closet you are wanting? If so, I shall have to disappoint. Emily is there. She has commandeered that room as the only place where she might have the quiet she requires. It is hers, she claims, until her bread has risen, which by my watch shall be another two hours.

Mr. Fivepenny looks crestfallen and rather uncomfortable.

PAPA: Lotte, do something to assist the man!

Lotte shrugs and exits the room. She pounds on the door marked "WC." From within issues a roar. Surely a lion rests therein! A lioness protecting her young!

LOTTE: Emily, dear, you must exit. We have a young man here with urgent need.

Again, that roar.

LOTTE: I assure you, Em. His need is pressing! You must exit!

The door of the WC opens and Emily Brontey, twenty-seven, bursts out. She too is disheveled; tall and ungainly, she wears a long, high-collared, unflattering dress. She is secreting pieces of paper in her pockets and inside her dress. Her hands are black with ink stains.

EM: If you had been but patient, I had nearly finished.

LOTTE: Mr. Firepenny, it has been a pleasure meeting you.

She ignores his extended hand.

LOTTE: Papa, shall we get you some dinner?

PAPA, *to Lotte, not seeing Mr. Fivepenny*: Good man, that Fivepenny. Has a passion for the *poor*. Em, be a dear and scratch my back.

THE END

IRON-POOR BLOOD—
*in which Charlotte makes plain her distaste for Mr. F.,
if only to herself*

Dear Diary,

Mr. Fivepenny tires me with his solicitations. Miss Brontey
I feel you are not well Miss Brontey I fear you have iron-poor
blood Miss Brontey you grow too thin Miss Brontey may I
prescribe walking twice around the park a brisk walk brings
roses to the cheeks! He speaks without subtlety, does Mr. Fivepenny, he speaks without *punctuation*, for his meaning is simple:
he would feed me chicken livers, *he* would walk me around
the park, conversing on *assistant* matters, he would bring roses
to my cheeks. Mr. Fivepenny, roses never occupied my cheeks,
my cheeks were ever wan, I am not brisk, I have never been
brisk, I am not brisk by nature, except in mind, and my mind
requires *punctuation*, it requires elegance and grace, it requires
subordinate clauses! I shall ne'er eat your *livers*, nor make 'em for
ye, nor watch ye eat 'em. I'll not be healed by *simplicity*, there
is no *recipe*, no *regimen*, that can bring *roses* to my cheeks. I am
moved by abstractions, not *recipes*, not *regimens*, and certainly
not *chicken livers*, and certainly not you.

BAD SAD DAYS—
in which Bronteys dwell in sadness

PAPA *talks to his dead wife*

You may as well know it, Maria: I cannot see, this is the truth of it. I must rely on Fivepenny to bring me here, and he has much to do, as I am little use to our business now. He has spent a moment pulling up weeds; I shall have to trust that your resting place is not overrun. You have bouquets, but these are chosen by Fivepenny, so we shall also have to trust in his taste.

I confess it: I do not trust in his taste, nor his fastidiousness in the matter of weeds. Fivepenny is a plodding man—capable and diligent, but unimaginative and, shall we say, unconcerned with beauty. Which makes us a useful pair: what I can with my genius for imagining *envision*, he can with his genius for plodding *execute*.

But he is a dull topic for our meeting: you would wish to know of the children, you would wish to know about me.

These are, in fact, troubling times. If I am to see, I must submit to the knife! I have spoken with a doctor: he insists! He assures me that the operation is no great thing, yet I must sign a declaration absolving him should I die! I might as well absolve him now, for how shall I manage it when I am dead? Our doctor is a practical man.

Dear Maria, for all my imagination, I cannot imagine *this*: how our children shall manage when I'm gone! They are strangely unformed, our little birds, all baby down and quickly beating hearts. All are returned from work; all have failed. None can enter the world without suffering collapse—one month of *work* requires six of convalescence. Annie is become quite small with sadness. Lotte weeps whenever she gets the chance. She claims it is for my good she remains at home—go! I wish to say. Go! All of you, go! But I cannot say it, not when they so clearly wish to stay.

They are like you in their delicacy. I wish *for their sakes* we could have bred this out of them, I wish they might have inherited my *sturdier* qualities (though not my eyes!); failing that, I wish I could have weaned it from them. I tried: sensing their fragility, I pressed them to be independent, I did not coddle.

They bicker, too! It is awful to behold: they snipe and pick at each other like children! Lotte has done harm to Emily, who will not suffer her presence. All reprimand our Boy, for the strain he puts on their nerves, and the washing. I treat our son with kindness, for what use is condescension when you wish to encourage good? Our daughters I treat with stolid courtesy, for what good is affection when you wish to encourage self-reliance?

None shall marry—this is plain, and not just because they are plain: the girls haven't the strength to bear young, or compromise, or please themselves with domesticity: their ideas are so childishly *grand*! Em cannot take the direction of a superior, nor recognize anyone as such, while Lotte feels too strongly her own cares, wants, and desires. Both are possessed of eccentric habit, which at their age may be forever set. Our Anne disappears in company—poof! she fades away! Who shall see her? Only a wizard, and there be none in our witches' den.

Our boy, meanwhile, receives notices forbidding contact with a *married lady*. He adheres neither to his sisters, nor to me, nor to anyone, but only to drink and childhood dreams of

greatness. I have asked why he does not attempt literary produc-
tion. The publishing world, being a closed and narrow place,
cannot accommodate genius, or so he says. He would rather
discard paper and pen than allow know-it-alls and do-nothings
to contemplate his words. Yet he scribbles; they all do.

What shall they do if I die? I would make provisions, but my
estate is slight—so sayeth our solicitor, whom I have also seen
this week—he is another practical man. I leave them nothing
but my example, and what I have taught them, which may be
small comfort when they collapse and starve.

And each other, of course: I leave them each other.

Maybe our son will see his duty, and find a way to care for
them. Maybe our girls shall venture boldly into the world.
Maybe they shall sprout wings and fly—this seems as likely!

Mr. Fivepenny fidgets: it must be time for us to go.

He is another practical man. I mourn the woman he marries,
for her spirit, delicate or lively, shall be crushed by *practicality*.

ANNE *observes without leaving her bed*

We are a strange family, comprised of sisters who do not
leave their bed. Across from me, Charlotte exclaims, blanket
covering her chin, though it be summer: "I am near three
decades on this earth, most spent in this worthy home. I look
at our vista, once universe, now lesser hamlet[1] and wonder: are
they gone, our best years?[2] When were they exactly? If they
have gone without making themselves known, what of the year
that is now, what of future years? Our town now feels ugly
and mean; I cannot enter it without thinking of another life

---

[1] Note, she does not look at a vista: she is firmly implanted in her bed

[2] Note, she asks questions but wishes no reply

elsewhere.[3] I failed at nannying, and office drudging. I thought to make myself teacher, only to learn that sans degree, I cannot! Still, I cannot believe I was made as I am, with these talents and this sensibility, to no end, with no end in sight.[4] This belief is a single thread which I must find and tug—gently, so it does not break! I would not be lost forever without hope!"

Emily replies: "If you wish to talk to yourself, do so in the street where none shall be disturbed by your gabbling." She wishes silence, she says, in escalating tones: she deserves silence, surely for once, we may offer her silence!

Emily has commandeered both upward bunks and is engaged in a project involving pen and paper, the nature of which she won't discuss.

Lotte, even when she does not talk, sighs too loudly, according to Em, and turns with too great emphasis.

"Ignore me," Lotte says. "I do not wish to disturb your important pursuits!" to which Emily replies, "It is all you wish! You *need* more than all of us combined. I am busy: stop your sighing and your rolling!"

Lotte holds her breath and lies still as a corpse.

"Is this better?" she asks.

Emily screams.

I look but can find no good in the world.

LOTTE *starts letters she does not finish*

Now that we are home again, we bump elbows constantly. Our little room with its four serviceable bunks has shrunk to half its erstwhile size—even as Bran takes over Aunt's room,

---

[3] Note, she wishes someone to ask about elsewhere; Emily does not listen and I haven't energy to oblige

[4] Note, she does not mention my talents, our talents

which we might have been glad to call *living* room had my brother been a *man* not a muffin. The kitchen is become our sanctum, which no man (save Rover) may enter—even Father's new assistant, a certain Mr. Fivepenny, whose *maleness* is not so certain.

I am too weak to rise—too weak in body, too weak in mind. If I am to love no one, be loved by no one, if this is my fate, what is my purpose? If there is to be nothing special in my life, no goal I might pursue, no pleasant surprise, no reward to buoy me, why is this a life at all?

Papa is testy and will not be read to; he shakes off any guiding hand, with the result that there are many broken things about the house. I purchased a shammy, so his spectacles would not smudge and he might see *something*. Thank you, Anne, he says, for in fact he sees *nothing*, and fancies he can tell us by our tread or the smell of our hair.

I am afflicted by an all-over *debolezza*. I exhaust my energies daily with small bits of ironing and mending, and give thanks that Em, not I, caters to us or we should starve. She alone carries live blood within her. The fire, which once leapt in all of us, will not catch flame.

Emily let slip an amazing thing to *Brindle*. She said Anne had "better things" to do than wash the spew from his britches. Like what, pray tell? was his response. Her life is a shell, no pearl lies within. Like write a novel, was Em's reply. I quizzed Anne. 'Tis nothing, is all she'll say, just a thing, a plain thing, a lowly thing. Yes, she's written pages—a number, in fact, of lowly pages, plain pages. Step by step, page by page, you watch, she will finish this thing, this lowly thing, and it shall be a good, if small, thing, a clear and steady thing. Our Anne is writing a novel, little Anne! I have celebrated by sharing with her my favorite pen, gift of Papa when I first went *out there*; heaven knows I have no use for it.

The Only Boy was moved then to claim a novel of his own, though his is no small thing: no, it is a Big Thing, an Enormous Thing, a Thing swollen with Importance, on the biggest most noblest most *manly* subject, about which he has done all possible *research*, for he has lived this Thing, and it has rent his soul and wasted his mind. His enormous, swollen subject: star-crossed love. *Consummated* love, says he, with a baleful look on his maiden sisters, love *consummated* yet frustrated by forces *external* and *malignant*. Love of a sort virgins cannot imagine!

Where is this Thing, we ask, because none believes in it.

In here, he says sagely, and taps his unwashed head.

We need an infusion—even Anne, steady Anne, is pale and not so bright. I fear a dangerous pain afflicts her, a *spiritual* pain. (Em sleeps through Annie's sobs, she and Rover snoring in their respective bunks.) I shall begin with the obvious, though Em does not like obvious things: I shall begin with her mattress.

EMILY *rages*

Lotte has been into my private things she has found my Poems. We Shall All Write Poems she declaims We Shall Send Them As A Book. She shall never be my friend again she is a monster who knows no feeling except for herself and her misshapen lover the flirt the hunchback the apelike Mr. H. I wonder does he encourage her still. Annie does not understand for her poems are simple things by reading mine Lotte has killed me.

Part
4

WORK

A COMEDY IN FIVE ACTS—
in which Charlotte finds poems!

1.

Emily (*red-faced, shouting over the stew, brandishing a wooden spoon, her hair, never tidy, flying from her pony tail*): In sum, you have killed me!

Charlotte (*sitting stiffly at the kitchen table: she does not move, she cannot move*):

Emily (*straightens her dress, as if her wits could be found there and collected by straightening*): My poems, how did you locate them?

Charlotte (*hoping to communicate honesty and simplicity*): I looked.

Emily: What made you think of the watercolor box? Was it the first place you looked?

Charlotte: No.

Emily (*pointing, repeatedly*): Then it was a serious pursuit, a diligent pursuit, a devious and relentless pursuit! Where else did you look?

Charlotte: Other places.

Emily (*arms akimbo*): Name them.

Charlotte: I searched under your mattress, inside the drawer that holds your underwear, behind the food you keep for Rover, before finding them in your watercolor box. (*quickly adding*) But the merit of your work excuses my actions!

Emily: Lotte their merit cannot excuse your actions! Lotte you are unforgivable, Lotte what you have done cannot be forgiven! Lotte you have taken a sister's gift which is *trust* and wrecked it!

Charlotte (*standing, to give herself extra footing, though Em is taller and much more in the right*): I am unforgivable. I cannot be forgiven, you shall never trust me again, but your poems are magnificent! They shine with the brilliance of originality, of truth, of rare mental force. Yours is a voice that has ne'er been heard!

Emily (*again waving a spoon*): Yours is a voice I would not hear! Go! Ye shall not eat my stew!

Papa (*entering the kitchen, looking for his midday meal*): What is this then? Lotte?

Emily (*sighing*): Papa, 'tis nothing. We've stew for lunch.

2.

Emily (*slicing onions with a louder-than-usual chop*): My poems are private. They are nothing more than more of the same.

Annie (*pretending to occupy herself with setting the table*): Glass Town?

Emily: They are Glass Town, though perhaps something more.

Annie (*as if distracted, attending to the serving bowl*): May I read them?

Emily (*chop!*): They are not meant for reading.

Annie (*adjusting the serving bowl*): Still, they are Glass Town, so maybe I shall?

Emily: You had a hand in Glass Town, I admit. But these are something more.

Annie (*mildly*): Then I should have more reason to read them.

Emily (*loudly, so Charlotte, listening in the hallway, might hear*): You must first pry them from the troll in the other room. I shall not ask her, for I'll not speak with her again!

Annie: I have poems, too. I should be glad for you to read 'em.

Emily (*with an extra loud chop-chop*): Everyone has poems. Even the Only Boy has poems!

3.
Papa (*surveying his children, seated 'round the table, his hands a steeple*): Children.

Bran (*rolling eyes*):

Papa: You are nearing an age when you shall not have me to organize you, to call you to account, to create peace among you, for I am old, as you can see, and infirm.

Lotte: Papa! That's not true!

Annie (*playing nervously with collar*):

Lotte (*bursting into tears*):

Papa: No, 'tis true, and as it should be. I've had a good innings, as they say, and if I have regrets they are not as regards my family, for you are all fine children, who have done me proud.

Bran (*looking pleased, not noticing sharp glances from at least one sister*):

Papa (*voice thundering*): But!

Annie (*starting*):

Lotte (*tears falling afresh*):

Papa: I shall not die in peace if you be not peaceful with each other. Anne!

Annie (*starting*): Yes, Papa?

Papa: What have I said of the four of you?

Annie: That we are the remnant. We must live the lives of six.

Papa: And? Em?

Em: We must make our mama proud.

Papa: And? Bran?

Bran: All should follow the Only Boy.

Papa: And? Lotte? You are the oldest, yes? I expect more of you.

Lotte: We are one blood, one heart.

Papa: Yes! You are good children. Now make your peace that I may die in peace.

Bran (*crying out*): It's their fault! I had nothing to do with it!

Papa (*waving his hand, leaving the room*):

4.

Lotte (*eyes wrecked by tears, face pinched and worn, extending her hand to a seated Em*):

Em (*ignoring Lotte's extended hand*): You do not sway me with weakness.

Lotte (*returning her hand to her side*): I leave my weakness behind.

Em (*looking at some far-off point*): You do not sway me with tears or emotion.

Lotte: There shall be no tears.

Em (*looking fiercely now at Lotte*): You shall not wear me down with flattery.

Lotte: I would not insult you.

Em: You shall not bore me.

Lotte: I offer you argument.

Em (*hands on lap now*): I'm listening.

Lotte: My argument concerns idleness.

Em: Continue.

Lotte: One aspect of idleness is a refusal to act beyond one's sphere; the narrower one's sphere, the greater one's idleness. Scribbling requires no great *commitment*. But bring these words before another, allow them to act upon that person, and this is another order of action!

Em: Are you saying that I am idle? I do not wish flattery, but I cannot see how *criticism* shall help you.

Lotte: Em, it is not you I speak of! It is Anne!

Em (*interested now*): Anne?

Lotte: Our Anne has poems! I know this from various channels.

Em: Because you listen to our chatter.

Lotte (*hands sweeping to encompass their cramped living quarters*): Would I had a choice! She has poems, she wishes to share them, yet she lacks confidence.

Em: It is not easy being the youngest.

Lotte: Sometimes she must feel quite outshone.

Em (*glaring*):

Lotte: If only because we have seen more of the world.

Em: Quite.

Lotte: I propose a volume of poems. We three shall write it and with it make a name. Those who look down upon Anne, who think her mere *nanny*, shall see her new. She shall see herself new!

Em: The same could be said of you: your pride is injured by the indifference of others.

Lotte: I wish our *family* name to grow, else I would go my own way, publish my own poems.

Em: When was the last time you wrote a poem?

Lotte (*stepping one step closer*): It has been a while. Okay, yes, it has been some years, but they stand. You shall scrutinize them and tell me if it is not so. I am sure Annie's shall stand as well, for she is a hard-working girl, of keen intellect and feeling.

Em: She is.

Lotte: Then we shall do this thing?

Em: This thing for Anne?

Lotte: This thing for Anne.

5.

Anne: This will see Em's poems into print?

Lotte (*whispering*): It is the only way. We must be with her or it shall not happen.

Anne: I am happy then to do this thing, if you are happy to include me.

Lotte: Em has specified: we are not to use our names.

Anne (*nodding*):

Lotte: Em wishes to be known as Rover.

Anne (*nodding*):

Lotte: Annie, I joke! Do you never smile?

THE BELLES—

in which three sisters create a book (as recounted by Lotte)!

Dear Diary.

I smile all day long. I have never smiled as I smile now, as we sit amidst our poems, picking, choosing, sorting, testing. We are unsentimental, we are harsh, we are fierce as we debate each line; we have Art to protect, and our good names (though we shall hide these under *assumed* names). We wear the armor of discrimination and taste; we seek power and depth and good rhyme and images clear and true. We are the Genii of Glass Town again, the Angels of Light, the four cardinal points, though we are but three—Emmy is bright enough to be two Geniis—three even! I am glad to be even a footnote, Annie too.

Children know such moments of happiness, when, the rest of the world forgotten, they become so lost in fellowship and play that the present is everything, and the past and future—wherein lie all sadness and care—are nothing. Their faculties train on that moment, which is therefore perfect. Some individuals of a strongly *spiritual* nature (I count my sisters among these) can approximate this feeling through encounter with *Nature* or *The Spirit*, but at its strongest and most powerful, we experience this state only through a union of minds, a union of intentions. I had quite given up my dream of achieving such a union—only to find it *at the age of twenty-nine* with my sisters! They see into my mind, they see into my spirit and heart, and esteem them; they see all of my faults, which are legion, and love me nonetheless for what I am!

The poems I contribute are old ones, though this makes them not the less beloved by me. Most transpose a theme from Glass Town, fixing one moment from that narrative and expanding it into the timeless realm of poetry; I feel they stand. Annie's poems are plain things but they too shall not detract or distract from our main enterprise, which is bringing Emily's poems into the world. I may achieve little in my lifetime, but if I succeed in this, it shall be achievement enough.

Dear Diary.

We laugh at the kitchen table, testing authorly names. We consider the obvious: Carlotta, Emmilicious, Annetchka, Emmelina, Annika, Embly, Lotte, Annabelle. Then Em suggests we take *un-female* names, and we agree. I am Carter. Em is Emerson, and Annie Artemis. For family name, we consider *Branwell*, for our aunt, but consider it too close to *Branwell*, the Only Boy, and shorten it to *Bell*, which we think has a bright and clear sound, a *resounding* sound! Also, it allows us to call ourselves belles, which makes even Annie laugh.

Dear Diary.

I am to be our businesswoman. Annie is no *negotiator*—she would give the poems away—and now that our poems are fixed, Em cares little for them, the enjoyable bit being already complete. So it is left to Carter Bell to find our publisher. I have learned already that no self-respecting *agent* will look at our efforts, much less represent them, there being no *money* in poems, or so I am told. How this can be if every child must memorize poems, if every university student must (I am told) write about poems, if every learned man must *cite* poems in his speeches, I wonder but do not ask. It does not do to try to create interest where, a priori, it does not exist. I have gone to our bookshelf and found the names of reputable *publishers* of poems, but when I have called these, they profess no interest. Publish some of these poems, they say, then return to us. I do not bother to confront them with the circularity of their logic.

But persist I do, and I have found the perfect match! An establishment called *Universal Publishing*. I would have thought *universal* suggested a want of discrimination but they assure me that, no, not everyone can be published by *Universal Publishing*, and what's more, they have published dozens of books of poetry (though none, I dare say, by a trio of *belles*!). What's more, in contrast to Big Publishing, as they call it, we Bells may have with *Universal Publishing* a strong hand in matters related to cover, design, font, and the like, which suits us, being all of us handy with a sketch pad and accustomed to making our own little books! So it is done, the one caveat being that for this level of control, we must contribute funds toward publication. We have gone too far to stop now, say I, and the papers are signed!

Dear Diary.

A most distressing development. I have signed our contracts C. Brontey, as representative of the three Bells, which *Universal Publishing* has understood to be *Mr.* Brontey, so Brindle has received our galleys and opened them! *Though they be addressed to C. Brontey and he cannot have mistaken that letter!* At least this is how I reconstruct events. All I know for certain is that the package is opened and the galleys strewn. We cannot go to Papa, of course, for Papa would not approve our book: he would not have us *upstage* the Only Boy, who with his scattered appearances in print is understood to be our *literary* member, though of course our sobriety and decency *daily* upstage the Only Boy.

Dear Diary,

I have requested a resending of the galleys, though this shall cost us extra. I have blamed Emily's dog, I have called that blameless beast a cur that knows no control. Rover is of course all control compared with our home-grown cur: Rover does not foul his nest, as Brindle does nightly, but who would credit the Only Boy with the destruction of Literature?

Dear Diary,

Brindle, home after a night of debauchery, sobs in the hallway—I can hear him from my bunk. Why would you not include me? A literary endeavor might have turned my life around, it might have been just what I needed, you know life has not gone easy with me, why degrade me like this before my fellows, they shall know you have rejected me, you three slight girls, though I am the poet of this family, our one true artist! Why, Emily, why?

His misery is so acute, I am tempted to feel for him! It's not his fault he was raised to think himself *king of the universe*: he was intended to be king of our family, which was his universe, yet never was he given tools of self-examination or restraint which might have made him worthy of veneration. But then I hear Emily cry, Let go of me, brute! You bruise my arm!

Dear Diary,

The thrill of publication was more in anticipation than in fact. The *fact* is, the font is not as we imagined, the pages are cramped, words are misspelled, which an editor might have noted had there been an editor, but we have achieved something that is nonetheless to our liking.

No one buys our little book, however, nor do they review

it, though our publisher *universally* assures us that it is available to *any* who wish it. We therefore have decisions we must make. Whilst Branwell carouses and Papa dreams, I shall call my sisters together, for we must have a plan!

A BOLD IDEA, CLEAR AS A BELL—
in which sisters decide to write novels (as recounted by Em)

Papa falls asleep, so I extract his plate that his beard might not dampen in sauce. Our papa, once asleep, is not easily awakened, so Lotte speaks.

Speak, Lotte, speak!

Sisters, she says, we must confab. And stands, to more fully gather our attention.

Aunt's bequest, she says, is much diminished, thanks to Branwell's profligacy and our failure at selling *Poems*. Papa, moreover, is quite unable to see.

Annie agrees: Fivepenny must accompany him everywhere, to ensure he arrives safely and can find the media, podia, et cetera, without injury or humiliation.

It was with great delicacy, I said, addressing Lotte, that you guided him to table tonight, so he might not bump and bruise his person.

But Lotte has not yet achieved her point:

Sisters, we must prepare for a time when Papa cannot work! We need a plan!

I do not speak because Lotte, however much she may search the ceiling for inspiration, has a plan and is ready to speak it.

Anne does not see it. Shall we return to work? she says. 'Tis months since I am returned from the Robinsons' . . .

I *spit* (metaphorically).

Annie continues: Perhaps I am refreshed?

Wait! Lotte says, as if an idea strikes her with great force. She may have to sit for the force of it! I have an idea! she says. It is bold, it is clear as a Bell! Shall you hear it?

We allow Lotte a *suspenseful pause.*

We must, says she . . . write novels!

I have been expecting this and do not welcome it. Ahh, I say. Oh, says Anne.

Lotte allows us a moment to absorb.

Think of it! she says. Our imagination is best suited to narrative, with the exception of Em's, whose genius runs to anything. Every day we hear of persons who haven't half our artistry gaining fame and income from their work, so why not we? Our books must sell, of course, which means they must have much in them that is desired by the public, such as love and adventure. Also, I insist: they must instruct!

I do not welcome the idea, but can offer no alternative to destitution.

An adventure in instruction, say I.

But Lotte is serious—so serious we may not say no: she would not survive it!

Annie, she says, I understand you have begun one?

I have, she whispers. It concerns a *nanny.*

I have ideas, I allow.

I am undecided, says Lotte. My imagination, fertile so long, is silent now, but I trust that with application, and your kind patience, it shall again grow large!

My sisters welcome this endeavor, Lotte with joy, Annie with quietly held ambition; I know it shall clamp me down and strip me bare. If I am to face destruction, however, it may as well be with them, in service to Art.

Annie looks for and finds the port.

Hooray! we cry. Hooray!

THE PROPER EXERCISE OF GRIEF: A WRITER'S OCCASIONAL NOTEBOOK—
in which Charlotte imagines a novel from real life

Notes from a sleepless night

I have achieved my end, though my sisters are not glad.

Emily walked from the room.

Annie, I said.

She retrieved Emily, saying I don't know what in the kitchen.

What, Emily said. I just went for peanuts. If I am to be a monkey doing tricks, I should at least be well-fed.

Are we agreed, then? I asked. If so, let's have a toast!

Annie ran to get the bottle, while Emily crunched peanut shells and spat them to the ground.

Commodious notes

I sit in our well-lit loo, wondering: what shall I write? I felt no such anxiety writing poetry. 'Tis no great thing to render *one* moment (in a poem), but a *lifetime* of moments (in fiction)? Moments that bear the weight of cause and effect? Moments peopled by . . . *people*? I am stymied! A bad poem wrecks but a day (and from it one may salvage a line to seed new work), but a novel? A novel can wreck a year or more! I have no year to spare for wreckage!

It was not so long ago Someone locked me here, thinking to teach me; restrained in this space, I imagined *everything*: evil, abandonment, blood seeping from the walls. Now, grown, I see only plain tile, overused towels frayed at the edge. I have no imagination at all!

I *should* follow the path given me by my teacher, which is to plumb my life and heart, but who would read about a lowly Receptionist beaten lower still? Or a nanny and nighttime filer? If an author be not happy with her life, how, I wonder, may she plumb? I have no romance to share, only hopeless dreams; no feats, just groveling and loss. To plumb Lotte, one must plumb grief.

Notes written on the back of a shopping list

I write on a park bench, groceries tumbled at my feet for I have imagined a tale! A brother and sister, each in love with persons unavailable. The brother's *amour* takes advantage of his inexperience, manipulates his self-regard, while the sister's beloved is noble, trapped with a woman whom honor does not allow him to reject. That woman is infirm, let's say, and ugly, and dependent, which adds to his bond, while the sister still bears the dew of youth, and youthful energy, and youthful love to share. Unlike the brother, she has principles and pride; when her position becomes clear, she leaves the man, while the brother degrades himself by sneaking. The health of both suffers, but the brother *externalizes* his anguish in selfish acts: he demands attention, chooses fiendish friends, harasses his lady, who in any case has little *true* interest; eventually, dissipated and brought low, he dies, perhaps in a gutter. The sister *internalizes* grief, engages in acts of selfless devotion. Perhaps she performs good works in Africa, where she meets a man who admires her character. They are content to live a life of service. Possibly they are separated by misunderstanding, brought together again by truth.

But no! I cannot see it! I cannot see the *missionary* who must be this girl's reward: who can tolerate someone always in the right? She may, if she's a dull sort of girl, but our reader certainly will not!

How can her love be other than her *teacher*?

Notes after a fine beef stew

We walk around the table, holding hands, each of us wearing something pink, for we are *in the pink* (we think): I a pink sock, Anne a pink napkin by way of a bib, Emily the *idea* of pink (which must suffice).

Anne relates more of her tale as we walk—or rather, she enlightens me, for I can see from Emily's complacency that she has heard it. It is Annie's tone, her observations, her descriptions that stand out; she catches wonderfully the *milieu* of a family as it tries to reconcile new wealth and leisure with liberal ideals. Her critique is sharp, but the tale lacks *incident*. Also, who can care for a *nanny*, especially one so plain, with so little fire? Her tale-teller is something of a tattle, relating the wrongs of others; *she* does not act, except in one calamitous way, and not to further her own fortunes but rather to aid her *brother*, which while praiseworthy in Real Life is less so in Literature. Her predominant emotion is *regret*, which is tiresome and never instructive.

I do not say so, we being still new at our rôles, but I shall share my thoughts, bit by bit, as if they arrive slowly, over a period of evenings, and kindly, so they may be well received. Though in fact her book is half done, so perhaps I am too late to influence her direction. I can yet applaud her efforts, and do, with an uproarious clapping of hands, for while her book may not be my cup of chowder, it could well be that of others, and besides, I admire her seriousness, and application, which to this point far exceed mine.

I am, in fact, disgusted by my girl! She does not deserve the teacher I would give her! Look how she whines! She sits by his door like a pup, wagging her tail, begging for *something, anything*. She crumples when questioned. Tears pool in the waiting-room of her eyes, ever ready to spill. Who can *care* for a protagonist such as this! Where is her dignity! Where her self-respect!

Notes while all else sleep

Again I write "commodiously" while others sleep. We took time from our day to sit (uncomfortably) on a hill in the park; there Emily's tale emerged. It is a strange and disturbing thing. There can be no offering *her* direction, for she will not have it, nor would I know where to begin. She read passages aloud, and when she was done, we could not speak. One must be very strong indeed to retain one's vision and voice proximate to hers! It is a good thing Anne, in particular, has initiated her tale, for while she could never emulate Emily's depth or ferocity, she could not in their presence maintain her own sharpness were her style not fully established.

I shouted *Hooray!* when she was done, startling the birds of our park. And yet, and yet, I do not doubt that this book is not what the Public wants.

Laundry notes

From the bowels of our worthy home, perched in a plastic chair as the laundry spins, I write—*as the teacher!* What a solution! He shall see my girl's *qualities* and I shall not have to rest inside her noisome head! He shall overcome trials, show his mettle, his independence, his *worthiness*, if not to her—for *she* shall see straight to his heart immediately—then to the reader. A brutish brother he shall have, and indifferent relations, but he shall out from under! Now that I see my project I am all into it, and resent any interference, namely, the need to wash, converse, and eat my soup. Spin washer spin! Dry dryer dry!

NINNY NANNY: NOTES FOR A NOVEL—
in which Annie imagines a novel out of life

Little Annie Nanny wishes to write a novel? Little Ninny Nanny? What does Ninny Nanny know of *novels*? She's never been one for *imagination*, never been one for *making things up*. She prefers "real life"! She's not a novelist at all!

She begins, then, with "real life." She begins where it all began! In a well-to-do suburb. An impatiens suburb. A patient, impatiens suburb. This is the **setting**: white clapboard houses, faux Tudor, slate roofs. Boys on tricycles followed by nannies. Girls with tennis bracelets and convertibles. **The house** is three storeys, old brick, white shutters, long lawn, blue pool, tennis court, balls clustered at the net. Nestled amongst old trees, a gazebo. A drained birdbath. **Inside:** antiques, purchased, not handed down. Eight bedrooms. What you'd expect.

What do I, Annie Nanny, know of settings? But I like the gazebo, I like the tennis court! The nanny's brother (we shall call him . . . Branford) can meet . . . Mrs. Richardson in the former, and they can court, so to speak, in the latter.

The *people*. **Mr. Richardson:** A prematurely aged man of sixty-three, cared for by a quiet nurse in a closed-off wing of the house. He dribbles, he can't make himself understood. At one time, he was a dynamic, though never a *kind*, man, never a *good* man.

Mrs. Richardson: An attractive, *aging* woman of forty-three, well-preserved as a woman may be who has never worked a day in her life, who maintains her figure through weekly *purges* and daily visits to a gym, and *Jason*, a very personal trainer. Her hair is *done*, her eyebrows and fingernails are *done*, occasionally she disappears so her neck and stomach may be *done*. She thinks fur barbaric and has opinions about the environment (chiefly, that it is *good* and should be *saved*), and has been known to raise money to "combat" diseases (which she knows to be *bad*).

But no, this will not do. The wife is not *simple*. She is *not simple*! What she did to *him*, to Branford, is simple, but she did not do it *simply*! First she gained the trust of the **nanny**! Not only the trust, the *love*! Without the love and trust of the *nanny*, nothing happens!

Stupid nanny. Stupid stupid nanny! She feels sick in her soul.

The daughters: Frieda, perhaps, and . . . and . . . Jane. Not Jane—Jane is too serious. Frieda and . . . shall both their names be Frieda? Frieda the Younger, Frieda the Elder! Fourteen and fifteen when the nanny arrived, now an enchanting sixteen, seventeen. Pleasant girls, but can one expect depth of feeling?—well, yes, about their *wardrobe*, the attention to which they're entitled. Can one expect *imagination*?—well, yes, about their prospects, their *rightness* about everything. So yes, let's say these are girls of feeling and imagination! It was not out of the question they might inherit the wealth of the father, then insist on an unsuitable match.

The son: Richie Richardson IV is not *entirely* spoilt: one feels there might be hope for him, but he lacks energy, fortitude, a sense of destiny. He crumples, usually onto a sofa; he can go nowhere without dragging his feet, his shoulders aslump, his posture the very picture of a draining sack of sand. For what does he save his energy? For tantrums, for kicking and screaming epithets and hitting out, chiefly at the nanny, for it is *she* who must turn off the TV, she who must brush his teeth and carry him to bed.

The nanny: The nanny does not command respect. She is small and quiet, she yearns to please. At home, she is the baby; at work, she is the poor little one, who knows nothing of fashion, of boys, of men. Because she is never seen, she sees everything.

For two years, this has been the nanny's lot: being kicked at by a boy, ignored or mocked by the girls, the mother being *unavailable*, the nanny unqualified, to exercise discipline or insist on corrective action. Any surprise she is lonely? Any surprise she is wretched?

The tutor: Any would want Branford as a brother! He is smarter, faster, stronger, funnier, more brilliant than any other boy! At twenty-five, he knows everything about everything! Ask a question and he replies in Latin, then tells a story from Tacitus, a *funny* story, a *naughty* story, then applies its lessons to current events, comparing our leaders to dissolute emperors in such a way that his sisters, or anyone, experiences hilarity and horror in equal measure! As a lad, it was *his* energy, *his* imagination that ignited that of his sisters, *his* soldiers, *his* drive, *his* readiness for battle, *his* insistence that the story not rest. Men crowd him now, to laugh and stand him a drink, that short man with the bristled hair, the *Irish-looking* chappie with big gestures, tall tales, ever ready with a joke and a laugh.

How his sisters pet him, how his father attends him, how they *sacrifice* for him, and he, so good natured he doesn't even *notice* their sacrifice, as long as through it he gains for himself, all the while *dreaming*—of wealth, independence, fame above all. It seems only a matter of time, a matter *decided in heaven*, so obvious it requires no focus or *effort*. So he doesn't sit his exams, or attend university, though all of us worked to make that possible. Instead, he gets a job at the *railroad*, just a stopgap, for he is *writing*—oh, he is writing! Poems and tales—essays and scholarly pieces and opinions, too, if only he could find someone to *help*, someone to recognize his *genius*, and lift him from us, like an angel. Oh, Branford, you were not lifted: you were *dismissed* from the railroad—your *accounts* did not gel. You sent letters to people who *might help you*, for you could see no way of helping yourself: you had never learned to help yourself. This time it is the nanny who shall save you! *Hah!*

We arrive, finally, at the *plot*!

The plot: Do I begin by describing the ruin of Branford? What use have we for suspense: as soon as the reader meets innocent *him*, pleasure-seeking *her*, the outcome shall be obvious, as shall be the outcome of the outcome, which is to say ruin.

No, the plot begins with the *plot*, it begins with the nanny.

The nanny is barely twenty-three but she has been with the Richardsons two years when our tale begins. She is retained because of what she is not: she is not a thief, she is not messy, dirty, late, uncomfortable, fat, a crier, obtuse, a chatterbox, a woman of noxious habits; she does not ask for things, she does not smell. If she has a fault, it is that she is too generous: she thinks the mother *unfortunate*, slave to her brute of a husband. Mrs. R. tells Nanny about her trials, how her husband, when he was well, *abused* her, mentally, physically, even between the sheets. She is lonely, and sad; she erred in marrying him, but what can she do? He's an invalid! How could she leave him, this house, her position!

Nanny is moved! Sometimes the lady asks about Nanny's family! What an honor! Nanny describes Papa, his good works; her sisters, their labors and talents; above all, her brother. Pink comes to her cheeks when she describes his exalted qualities. He sounds lovely! the mother says, dreamy-eyed, and Nanny, legs black-and-blue from the boy's kicking, conceives a plan. Ninny Nanny! Damn her plan!

She produces a photo—he is more handsome even than that! Really, she does not think of the mother—how could she? She knows his tastes, she knows he does not require *acuity*, just bouncy curls, a flouncy manner. She knows the Friedas, how silly they are, how unformed. With only a decade between he and they, surely one will want him! And through such a match, the nanny's fortunes would be made. Her sisters could give up hateful work, Papa might *retire*.

Nanny sighs: how she misses her brother, she says—his wit, his high spirits, his generous nature, which sees humor in everything. How he enlivens a house! What a marvel he is with *boys*: they look up to him, cast themselves after him, for Branford is an upright man, a manly man, a paragon of all the virtues she could name, and good at playing boyish games, at throwing balls, and catching them. Nanny delivers this balderdash over *weeks*. Oh, I have another letter from my brother! What a darling he is, yet he does not find a position suited to his talents! Oh, I have heard from my brother! He has published another poem! Oh, yes, he has published many poems! If only you could read them! If only Mrs. R could meet him!

If only Mrs. R had never met him.

It will take a year to write a novel such as this! Would I spend a year with a *ninny*?

Ninny Nanny makes headway. Now the mother *asks* about Branford. How is that paragon? Look, says Ninny Nanny. She produces another photo: his color is high, his smile large. Nanny has been saving this photo for the right time: they are in such a large and empty house, the mother and her family, so many rooms want filling.

I have an idea, says the mother. You will think me fanciful, for surely your esteemed brother could not want to be . . . my baby's tutor????????

Ninny Nanny affects shock. She puts hand to mouth, following a sharp intake of breath.

I do not know, Mrs. Richardson! It would not hurt to ask . . .

Is it true, Ninny Nanny? Is it true you did not imagine a liaison between *madame* and your brother? Did you really think he might find interest in those adolescent girls? Perhaps you imagined that an affair *with the mother* might raise you in that family's esteem? The boy might not kick, the girls might consider your feelings, you might enjoy dinner with the family, no more an exile to the kitchen for meals with a toothless gardener? Did you not imagine that such a liaison would bring your family *faster* to their wealth, the husband being always about to die? Will you say this possibility *did not cross your mind*? Pimp! Procurer!

I am sickened by *Ninny Nanny*—she is not a *likeable* character: she *has* no character.

Where was I? Outlining the Plot, or rather, the role of the plot in the Plot. Crafty Nanny!

And so it comes to pass that Branford, a strapping lad of twenty-five, is hired by the Richardsons . . . At a salary exceeding that of Ninny Nanny, I need not add.

What else is there? Only the unfolding of the affair: the intrigues, the tennis, the laughs. For two years, a scuffling behind closed doors, mussed hair, misplaced laughter; tawdriness, tardiness, looks held too long; the word *we*, and *us*—but Nanny is none the wiser! She has hope for the Friedas, she sees only the brother she has always known—spirited but honorable.

Incident shall be easy to identify, though painful to imagine.

Do they love each other, the mother and Branford, or do they merely lust, this antique matron and half-formed boy? Mrs. R wishes to think herself child; the boy wishes to think himself *grown*. Lust grows in a hothouse such as this; as for love, I should have difficulty rendering it, having never seen its image.

There is the matter, then, of discovery, and denouement. It shall be the gardener, for he is loathsome. He shall spy them. To make it more dramatic, I shall place them by the seaside. The family goes on holiday, leaving Branford behind! But he cannot be apart from his beloved—so he follows, on the sly! The lovers dally in the changing house; they are seen by the gardener! He is faithful to his employer or, more likely, senses opportunity for gain—he blackmails, but does so clumsily, or dobs them in out of spite. Whatever the case, the husband is roused.

Why is the gardener on holiday with the family? I know not but I shall work it out.

The mother insists the gardener is mistaken, for where is this tutor, this *boy* who could hardly interest a *woman*? Not here! Presented with proof (what? a photo? a letter? a dropped ribbon?), the wife *breaks down*! She insists he *forced* himself, or rather, he insisted but *she resisted*! She would never betray Mr. Richardson! Why did she not come forward, why did she not see the blackguard sacked? Oh, beloved Richard, I did not wish to trouble you, your health being delicate. But of course, dismiss the boy, you know what's best. And the sister, too: she'll look at me funny now.

Out goes a letter from the lawyer and, when Branford will not exit, when he continues appearing behind shrubs, whistling for his lady, leaving notes amongst the tennis balls, which she does not see, having no one now with whom to *play*, a restraining order.

But before all this, the nanny. What of the nanny? There shall be an earlier climax for her: she shall finally learn what is obvious to all. In shame, *before* her brother is found out, she shall leave the house, returning to her family home, a stranger there after four years. Her departure may in fact alert the gardener, who, suspicious now, follows the misses—but this is not Nanny's concern—it is their *coupling* for which she takes responsibility, not their *discovery*.

Yes, this is it, this is the story I wish to tell.

SEPARATION & SEPARATION—
in which Branwell longs for his Lady (as recounted by Em)

I: Here are All Good Things, which are ribs; here is Prosperity, which is cabbage. Do we appreciate Annie's napkin folding? What of her tulips?

Papa, Lotte, Annie, *nodding, assenting, passing food*:

Branwell, *face ravaged, napkin affixed to his collar*:

Papa, Lotte, Annie, I, *eagerly toasting, acknowledging gratitude, trying to smile*:

Branwell, *sighing, then sighing some more*:

Papa, Lotte, Annie, *eating the food, sharing anecdotes, praising the food*:

Branwell, *moaning*:

I: Branwell, you neither toast nor acknowledge the cabbage. What's up?

Bran: My Lady remembers me. But her agony be so acute, her doctor insists she suspend contact!

I, *enjoying ribs with my fingers*: Your separation brings Mrs. Robinson agony, therefore her *doctor* prescribes more of it!

Bran: Her love brings her to the edge of collapse! Though it break her heart, she sees the sense of his proscription, for she hath not a strong constitution.

I: Pray tell, what be the difference between separation and separation?

Bran: I am to stop sending poems.

I, *enjoying cabbage*: To the Robinson household.

Bran: Yes.

I: Where her husband might see them.

Bran: He is none too acute, but yes there is that.

I, *breaking a piece of crescent roll*: She does not wish a divorce.

Bran: T'would be impractical.

I: For then she should be left with nothing.

Bran, *standing*: Not nothing! She would have me!

I, *enjoying my crescent roll*: Which is as I have said: she would have nothing.

Bran, *sitting again*: Her husband is not a well man.

I: You wait till he dies when she should have something, in addition to your nothing.

Bran: T'would be convenient. She wishes to share everything with me.

I, *passing ribs*: Everything except poverty! But perhaps we have room for your Lady here, in our worthy home! Her children could live in our kitchen, or maybe with you in the lounge.

Bran: You understand nothing of Love!

I: I understand by your example, and hers, that Love requires money—I understand that much!

Lotte, *standing, words escaping—whoosh!—like air from a balloon*: The lady is cruel! She fans your love, which is unforgivable! Why else would she encourage you with false tales of agony and a weak constitution? Her constitution was strong enough when she wished to *consummate*! She requires love but will not love! The fact that you love her is more important to her than the love itself. She is cruel, your mistress, and no Lady!

Bran: She loves me enormously, so shut yer traps, both of ye! Annie knows the truth, don't ye, Annie? Tell them: the Lady is sincere!

Annie runs like a child from the room.

Papa: Pass the cabbage, please.

THE RED ROOM—
in which Charlotte, tending Papa, imagines Plain Jane

Day 1

I may not dwell on the failure which is *Teacher*, for Papa's surgery is complete!

Can he not recuperate at home? I asked.

If you can wheel him in his bed fifty miles or more, his surgeon replied.

Thirty days? I asked.

A small time, the man said, if at the end your father sees!

I booked a room for his recovery, in J—, by the surgery, where, tended by me, our father shall grow strong. With a bath, a *kitchenette*. All of it, mysteriously, *red*. Red upholstery, red carpet, red tea cosy! I would tell Pater this because he cannot see, but he also may not converse. He shall not know, then, about the *redness* of this room till his bandages be gone. I may let in no light, save what escapes this blind. Maybe, writing by this blind, I shall myself go blind, to be tended by Papa, who shall re-blind himself by the blind, and so on.

I had rather a different vision of *recuperation*. Papa and I in a room—perhaps not so *red* a room—he bandaged but ready for badinage. I would read the paper to him; we would discuss events of the day. He would teach me things—Greek, for example. Teaching would give him *strength*, for he would have purpose, and be proud of my progress. We would joke about my cooking, for he knows it is not my specialty (in fact, oatmeal is all he will have: when he is hungry, he weakly raises a hand; I pour hot water onto a packet and he is satisfied). I did not imagine we would talk *every moment*; I thought we might sit companionably, he contemplating what we had discussed or planning our next lesson, I writing, and he might ask what I was writing, and I might acquaint him finally with *Poems*, and read to him from that book, and if he were encouraging, I might, all atremble, read to him from *Teacher*, and he might say, *Publishers be damned!* You must continue, Lotte! You must write another!

It is good my writing be invisible to me in the dark, for my dreams are pathetic things, and I a pathetic girl.

Day 2

We are visited by an *aide*, whom I fairly attack: How is my papa, how is he *really*? He recuperates as he must, says she. Yes, but can anything be said of the operation's success? How can one speak of success while bandages still encircle his eyes, says she. Is it certain he shall be better? I ask. If you do as the doctor says, and are quiet and forbid the light, there's a good chance. But you need not stay every moment! adds she. I protest: Of course I shall stay! *Does she have no father?*

Papa does not move unless he is washed by this aide and set at a new angle. You must do this, says she, or he shall ache and develop sores. Sores from lying still? I ask; she assures me it is so. He hates it when I touch him, I say. Do not be a useless thing, says she. Okay, she does not say this, but she thinks it. All the same, says she. So I push our father to his side, he groans and flails his arm weakly. When he groans I say, More oatmeal? Have you need for a commode?

It seems he lies beneath a shroud, I his only mourner.

I have slept badly, on my chair and ottoman. We did not give proper thought to where I might sleep in this room, having thought only of Papa's bed, which goes up and down for his comfort (though thus far, he gives no indication that he wishes to be anything but prone). I might sleep on the *red* floor, for the carpeting is soft enough, but I would not have Papa wake and miss my shadow. I believe the aide must give him medicine to force his sleep for he is a vigorous man who would not otherwise consent to lie so still.

I have thought to add berries to his oatmeal, for added strength. Papa spits them out like a cat. I have determined from the absence of light by the blind that it is night.

Day 3

I must write a new book—what else may I do in this *relentless* room, this eventless room? I position my chair and pencil by the crack beneath the shade, but am besieged by thoughts—of the publisher who sent *mimeographed* judgment about our work. He misspelled *Emerson* and wished us good fortune *placing our work elsewhere*, as if it were only a *table* we wanted. Then, sneakily, he signed himself *Editors*, as if he were many, as if his opinions were so unanimous within himself that he might as well be both plural and anonymous. In my mind I stomp my feet and shout the brilliance of Emerson, the sharpness of Artemis, the small virtues of *Teacher*, the short-sightedness of *Editors*. I become agitated with words and retorts and snide asides, and before I know it, an hour has passed, and I have spent it putting specters in their place, and have even blackened my notebook with paragraphs of a letter I cannot read and shall not send, and when my rage is spent, I confront the hurt that lies beneath: when all we wanted was encouragement, in the form of bindings for our books, this Editor, whose power surpasseth his understanding, did dash us.

My book, I tell myself (for now I weep), is not so bad as he says, or since he did not *say*, as he *thinks*: or is it? Am I a silly *female* who cannot *write*—and if not, what may I do? On and on it goes, till I *sob* outright because of this multiform *Editor* who will not name his many selves, and call myself names, awful, vicious names: *Ugly! Dull! Useless!* I shall return soon enough to the *receptionist* wars, the nanny wars, the dogsbody-to-a-nobody wars, my life over at thirty before it has properly begun—and as I say all this to myself, I have written not one word of anything *new*, just given words to what is old, a story of defeat. And so my paper fills, and while I have much notion of myself as small and ugly, I have as yet no notion for a book.

Unless I write a woman unable to write in a red room, for all her tears and fears. Though she would have to be a child, for who would credit a *woman* with sentiments such as these?

Day 4

To not think of the girl in the red room, I pace this room, devising tasks:

Sketch the darkness. Be faithful to the lines in the dark, and their shapes.

Describe the redness of this room. Consider all synonyms for *red*. Recall which items in this room are crimson, which rose, which ruby, which scarlet. Imagine the room *green*. Imagine that grass grows from the bottle-green carpet, moss from the emerald-green walls.

Remember what you can, the more useless the better. What was the stuff of the dresses we wore at school? What foods did Mother make when we were ill? Did Papa smile when she was alive? Did he tell jokes? Was he always afraid of fire?

Try to touch the ceiling. Stand on your head and try to touch the ceiling.

Sit on a pile of Papa's books and command your subjects. Invent new laws to please them: Everyone eats pie! Pretty girls must shave their heads! Editors must learn to read!

Recall the face of Bran when he was five, when he was eight, when he was twelve, when he was twenty. Imagine for him a different life.

Remember a Glass Town tale, act out each part, improved upon. Die as Diana Diamond dies when she learns of the Duke's duplicity—dastardly Duke! Devise sentences that rely on the letter "D," the letter "I," the letter "E." Die, Diana, die! Imagine Diana's funeral: who attends, who attends in secret, who in disguise, who is too broken-hearted to attend but visits her grave by moonlight. Imagine her dress, her hair laid about her, her expression in death. Imagine what flower she holds as she is lowered to her grave.

Recite Milton. Recite Dante. Make your way along the ridge of Purgatory. Imagine who suffers here, who walks alongside. Do not settle for Virgil, that pompous know-it-all. Find someone gentle, composed, who does not doubt. Maria it shall have to be: she knows her way to heaven. Remember, says she, holding your hand as you walk the ridge, you must be brave! But what if I slip and fall? Over the edge, this ledge, to Hell, what if I fall into that red *eventless* place? You cannot slip and fall, says she, for you are inside your mind: where would you go? No place is more slippery, you say, no place so dangerous! I could fall without end, and who would know? Take my hand, says she. You can always take my hand.

It was once Maria's game to leave me in the dark. Guard the castle, said she. Let the castle guard itself! I replied. I am only a girl! but she said, You're a big strong guard who takes on all comers, and off she went to conquer ghosts. I tried to guard the castle, but was vanquished by the dark, the creaking, the lights that slid against the wall. I had to cry out, and she ran to me. Lotte! she said. There's nothing here, look, there's nothing anywhere for you to fear! This is just a closet, here are your clothes, you can smell them, they are known to you, come, little Lotte! How brave you are! How strong!

I'm not brave, said I. Look how I cry!

You are brave, she said. Did anyone attack the castle? A demon or an animal?

No one attacked the castle, said I. It was I alone in the dark.

This is what courage is, she said, completing a task, though you be afraid.

Really? said I.

Yes, she said.

I could try again, said I.

Tomorrow, she said, and laughed; I, too.

And now I wonder: *is* this all courage is, completing a task though you be afraid? If so, trembling Lotte, Lotte tormented by *thoughts* and *fears*, is the bravest of them all!

Day 5

I lie on the red, red floor and think of the girl who cannot write. She is not a writer, of course: she is only a girl, shut in a red room. Things happen to her, things that are not *nice*: no story may arise out of *niceness*. She is an orphan, loved by no one, this is plain, perhaps *because* she is plain. Locked in the red room, she sees this, that she is *seen* by no one. She fears, she is frenzied. Always she knows that even if she gains, the red room, where she is alone with her pain, the plain pained nature of her unloved self, will ever be with her.

There can be no comfort for such as she.

Day 6

I sit, grim, beneath the slit in the shade, and will myself a theme. By which I mean a man.

The world hath no interest in your *teacher*, say I.

So he is not a teacher, I reply. He is something else.

What do you know of something else? I ask. What do you know of *him*?

Nothing, say I. Therein lies my mastery! I can create anyone! Anything!

Mystery, not mastery! A spinster hath no right to write about *love*.

Nay, cry I, my inner voice rising: I have every right to write about love, to imagine it, to broadcast it and spin it out, to imagine a *happy ending*.

For whom? say I. That *girl*? That withering thing in the red room?

I do not know.

You do not know. This sounds a rip-roaring tale. Are there ghosts in't? Or demons? An I-don't-know girl shall not carry a story far.

She is a plain girl, an insignificant girl.

You'll need plenty of ghosts then, and a house fire, and a mystery. And beautiful ladies. What has happened to him, this man, that he loves an insignificant girl?

Certainly he is humbled, say I. Certainly he was once large and now he is, now he is . . .

He would have to be crippled to love an insignificant girl! And blind to love one so plain.

No! I say. He has always loved her! This is his greatest trait, his ability to see her, to see beneath her surface, to discern her *character*.

If you say so, say I. If you are content to write a *fairy tale*, about children, for children.

No! say I. I will write a woman! 'Tis as woman she enchants him . . .

Enchants him! You are a dreamer, a spinner of tales, a lol-lygagger, a . . .

I insist! She enchants him! She enchants him because of who she is. Because she is not like the others.

She sounds an unlikely sort to capture so great a man . . .

He *is* great! That is why he cannot be enchanted by others. They flash like glass diamonds, whilst she . . .

Flashes like real diamonds?

She does not flash, I say. She is made of burnished gold.

Burnished gold. And he is enchanted by gold.

He is enchanted by her, he is enchanted by what is real. It is her *character* he loves.

He would be the first man to do so. A rare find!

On it goes.

Would I could banish myself from this red room; I would do it.

Day 7

Sleep is made difficult by a pounding tooth. I thought nothing of it at first, but now, if I forget it, it announces itself anew, *sharply*. So I am awake, ice pack on my jaw.

It is cloudy and no light slips underneath the blind? When the aide is here, I ask the day, and she says, *Thursday*. And I say, yes, but which *Thursday*, so she must give the date, for how do I know if one day or eight have passed? You might consider going outside, says she. And leave Papa? Never! say I. She shrugs, and applies a wet cloth to my father's face.

Earlier, I tripped and cried out. Papa bestirred himself: Lotte, he murmured, and I did hearten: he heard me! he cares for my safety!

I would have porridge, said he.

Is it possible to disappear in the dark? The aide shall return to find only my boots and a blackened notebook. Were there a mirror, I should see only a semi-person: a shade, a shadow.

I am two days (at least) without sleep.

Day Other

Another bad night, my tooth aching now with sharpening pain. I grasp my chair with both hands so I do not cry out. Perhaps I do cry out. I seem to recall standing over my father's bed, holding my jaw and shouting about injustice, his injustice, that he should never teach me, as he did Bran, or discuss events with me, as he did Maria, or practice *shooting* with me, as he did Em, or devote any thing to me alone. That he should never have congratulated me on a drawing, an essay, a thought well expressed, that he should never have seen anything in his little Lotte.

I recall this shouting but I can't have done it, so it must have been a dream.

In this dream I slammed my hand against the wall. It is a testament to the strength of my imagination that I can still feel the blow.

Day Next

I have stopped trying to track our days.

There is no solace in this world, I say.

None? asks Maria.

When you are young, comfort may be had from a sister, or friend.

But?

It is not enough. A sister is not a mother, a friend is not a father.

We had a mother, she says, a father.

We have always been orphans.

Our parents loved us. All parents love their children.

So you say. I do not remember being loved. What is it, to be loved?

Lotte, you are loved! And when our parents are gone, we shall have husbands to love us.

We shall have no husbands, say I.

You don't know that.

I am past the age of freshness. I can find no way of making plain what's within, and were I able, it would not matter, for my outside is plain.

Who would you wish to love you?

I do not know him.

But you can imagine him.

I cannot imagine him.

Who is he, Lotte?

Do not make me imagine him.

Is he good, Lotte? Is he strong? Does he perceive what you hold within, does he behold character and beauty without?

I cannot play this game, sister: it is too cruel.

Say one thing that he is.

No.

One thing. I would hear one thing that he is.

He is good.

And another!

He is strong.

And another, please!

I can do no more! I say. It is too great a pain to imagine what I cannot have. You may not ask this of me!

One more thing!

I cannot!

I have twenty more days in the dark. I fear for myself, really I do.

Day After

A voice wakes me. I think it is the aide but it is Maria.

You must wash yourself, says she. You must wash your dress. You must make yourself a meal.

I blink.

You say that you know what you are. This is not what you are.

What am I? I ask, sitting up in my chair, because truly I do not know, but she is gone.

I know not what I am, but I do know what I am not: a layabout: I am not a layabout.

I am startled by the rankness of my hair; I had not realized it was so warm in that room; my dress sticks to my good self! I wring out my dress, but I am not sure that it can be cleaned. I convince myself that the window behind the blind may be opened, just a little.

I have seen to my fingernails, the dirt behind my ears. I sit in fresh undergarments waiting for my dress to dry. I have eaten four muffins, and all the aide's soup!

I think of the girl in the red room: that poor child! That poor dove, that lonely bird! Will no one care for her? (I slap the wall and stomp a foot.) Will no one hear? How she sobs in her red room! Who has locked her there? Do they hear her cries and turn away?

Day Again

You speak a great deal about character, Maria says.

I am making tea. I bring it back to my chair, my crack under the blind.

What else may we rely on? I ask. A hand, even a man's hand, can be withdrawn, a mother can die, a sister can die, a brother can be unreliable. Life creates all manner of burden;

character determines how we respond. It is the one thing a person may control.

Especially when it is a character you write! says she.

You are whimsical! say I.

I think you feel better, says she.

Better? I berate myself morning and night! Look at the circles under my eyes!

They are no greater than usual, says she.

Perhaps, say I.

So is this what she learns, your girl in the red room?

The lesson that it is only her character which she may control?

You feel doubt, she says.

Always, say I.

I count the *characteristics* of character, first on one hand, then the other:

Character is the willingness to stand one's ground, though all would condemn you for it.

It is diligence, hard work, though one's prospects be few.

It is performance of one's duty, whether convenient or no.

It is *substance*, which is concern for what matters, like beauty and truth.

It is deep feeling for what is substantial.

It is kindness, though none may thank you for it.

It is endurance, a steady quiet through suffering, whether your own or that of another.

It is ability to know the character of others, to see through any *show* of character.

It is restraint, a corralling of turbulent nature.

I believe I have some measure of these *characteristics*; to them I add: effort to strengthen their force!

My *character,* this *girl in the red room,* shall have this *character.* It is by this character ye shall know her.

So sayeth the woman who must be told to wash her dress.

Day Once More

In the afternoon I featured all my selves. Queen Carlotta strode about, waving her scepter. Awake, she cried to her subjects. I would have you pay obeisance! Charley-Barley sat obediently, all diligence, watching Pater, awaiting instruction. Little Lotte trembled in the blackness, and ran to her papa's side to make sure he breathed. Charlemagne unsheathed her sword: Show yourself! she cried, ready to run *Editors* through, whether he be single or many. But it is as Carter Bell that I am happy, for that self unites all selves: as Carter Bell, I am imperious, admired, and fierce, soft and hard and strong, I am all things all together. I tremble, I shout, I roar, I cry. I remember, I forget, I make things new, I bring things back, I turn all things, and myself, upside-down. Above all, I am as my sister promised, as she made me: I am fearless, the guardian of castles, I take on all comers.

What shall I do, Carter Bell? What shall I do, big sister?

My Jane is small but she is not powerless! She keeps her power within. And she shall be rewarded! When she proves herself to my satisfaction, she shall be cared for. She shall not do without, though she be plain—plain in dress, plain in speech, plain in purpose, my plain Jane.

I pick up my pen, to see what happens next.

YOURS, CARTER BELL—

in which Charlotte, attempting to sell one novel, sells another

Dear Sirs and Mesdames:

Greetings, worthy publisher(s)! I write to tell you of a great literary occasion: the availability, at this moment, of *three* fictional novels by authors Carter, Emerson, and Artemis Bell, being relations and the authors of *Poems*, published by Universal Publishing. We do not continue with Universal Publishing, having little appreciation for their lack of energy on behalf of *Poems*, though they did promise much, and so seek alternate avenues to publication.

Artemis Bell, being the youngest, has written a fine tale of intrigue and satire, about a well-meaning Nanny, who witnesses much that is evil. Emerson Bell has written a highly original tale of great power and beauty of one family, in a singular, unforgettable style. Carter Bell, being yours truly, has written a tale of romance between a worthy Teacher and the Pupil who sees into his heart. We intend these novels to appear as a series of three, which shall surely heighten their appeal among the public.

Please find these novels enclosed!

We do require payment for these novels, both in advance and upon achieving their expected sales. You may reach us through me at the above address.

I remain,
Your faithful servant,
Carter Bell

Dear Sirs and Mesdames:

Greetings, worthy publisher(s)! I write to share with you my fictional novel, which I have but this month completed (!), entitled *A Teacher*, with the evocative subtitle: *A Romance*. You may be familiar with my name, as I am the co-author with Emerson and Artemis Bell, of *Poems*, published this year by Universal Publishing, to universal neglect (though the Poet Laureate of Vermont did call our product very "fine"). We do not continue with Universal Publishing, having little appreciation for their lack of energy on behalf of *Poems*, though they did promise much. Emerson and Artemis Bell have entered into arrangement with one other publisher, but I eschew that establishment, for it eschews payment in advance—or, I fear, payment of any kind!—and I am done with that! I am heartened to learn that other publishers (such as yourselves) are, by contrast, tireless in their love for literature, and do therefore remunerate authors; I therefore think that any of you would suit me quite well!

The novel in question (*A Teacher: A Romance*) concerns a worthy Professor and the Pupil who sees into his heart.

You may reach me at the above address.

Your faithful servant,
Carter Bell

Dear Editor:

I enclose herewith, *A Teacher: A Romance* for your consideration. Others, while declining to publish it themselves, have noted its energetic style and elevated subject matter. I look forward to hearing from you soonest possible.

Yours,
Carter Bell

Dear Mr. John P. Johns:

How astonished I was to receive from you not the customary three-line rejection but a three-page critique! I am humbled that while you have found fault with my *Teacher*, you, alone among all who have read it, have seen fit to offer a thoughtful response—and have requested to see other, longer work! I have such a work, which I have invested with even more interest. *Plain Jane* is very nearly complete; I shall send it to no other, and look forward to hearing from you at your earliest convenience!

Yours,
Carter Bell

Dear Mr. Johns:

Kind sir, you amaze me! You have had *Jane* but one day, and are certain she will do! This is excellent news! I could not have wished a better home for her, though I do wish you would reconsider *Teacher*. This book is a worthy predecessor to *Jane*, being not unconnected to her both in theme and language. Its appearance before the reading public would well prepare it for *Jane*, making my name better known among them and increasing her inevitable success. I'm sure you can see the merit of this approach!

On the matter of payment, I think you know that the sum you offer as *advance* is sparse compensation for a year's intellectual labor; I am confident, however, that *Jane* shall exceed your expectations for her, and my compensation shall then, eventually, approximate her worth—and so I accept your offer—gladly!—and look forward to hearing from you on matters of paper, illustration, typeset, and design.

Best to you,
Carter Bell

Dear John:

I appreciate your "notes" on the subject of the book's opening chapters. Sadly, I have many engagements at present and cannot act upon your suggestions. (I also fear that were I to apply my pen, cold now, to this work, I could not generate the necessary heat.) However, I would be glad to read examples of work that avoids the defects you have found in mine, so I too can avoid them in the next; merely send these titles to my attention and I shall be their diligent pupil!

I look forward to hearing from you on the matters of paper, illustration, typeset, and design.

Best to you,
Carter Bell

THE MISSES GREY—

in which a publisher spills some beans

WBEX Radio Archives: The Misses Grey

Produced by Felix Price of WBEX, the program is composed of an interview Deirdre Dent conducted with John P. Johns, senior editor at Grosvenor & Johns. Program length 18:20.

[Music: "Paperback Writer," The Beatles]

[Music fades]

DD: Carter, Emerson, and Artemis Bell have caused a sensation. Appearing more or less simultaneously, their novels, with their trenchant social criticism and compelling female characters, seem, each in its own way, to court controversy. Despite this controversy—and we'll talk more about that in a moment—their authors—or *author*, as some would have it—have famously refused to talk with the media. They will not appear in any public arena, or in fact let anything be known about their lives. We do not even know if they are male or female. Is their silence motivated by a simple desire for privacy, or is it, as some have suggested, a ruse to promote their books in a crowded marketplace, just as, surely, their simultaneous publication was designed to provoke maximum publicity?

The answers to these questions might have remained forever obscure were it not for Trudy Small, graduate student and performance artist from Carbondale, Illinois. Trudy Small, who uses the professional name Small Trudy, has produced a YouTube video in which she claims to be the author of all three books. The video has gone viral, garnering close to six million views. Now Small's signature red afro has started appearing on Plain Jane T-shirts and she is said to be negotiating the sale of her autobiography, though not, notably, to the publisher of *Plain Jane*, *Nanny*, or *The Heights*.

Carter Bell's editor, John P. Johns, is with us today in the studio, and he says enough is enough. Welcome, John!

JPJ: Hello, Deirdre!

DD: Let's start at the beginning, John. Why are you here?

JPJ: I'm here because Carter, Emerson, and Artemis Bell are three people, and not one of them is a graduate student from Carbondale!

[laughter]

DD: So who are Carter, Emerson, and Artemis Bell?

JPJ: If by that question you mean, what are their real names, I am not at liberty to say. I can, however, confirm that these are pseudonyms.

DD: Which we knew.

JPJ: Which most likely you knew.

DD: Why pseudonyms?

JPJ: They feel strongly that it's only by being invisible, as it were, that they can be true artists.

DD: Because of the satirical nature of their work?

JPJ: Because they are *retiring* sorts. They appreciate privacy. They cannot bear bright lights.

DD: So they are, in fact, women?

JPJ: I don't believe I said that.

DD: No one ever described a man as retiring! Unless gold watches were involved.

[laughter]

DD: But they are members of the same family?

JPJ: I think that's fair to say.

DD: Sisters, in fact.

JPJ: That I can neither confirm nor deny!

[laughter]

DD: You are the publisher of Carter, but not of Artemis and Emerson. How did you come to publish *Plain Jane*?

JPJ: It's a funny story. Carter actually wrote a first novel, called *Teacher*. He sent it to me in an envelope that had plainly made the rounds of other publishers, for when it was rejected and she got the package back, she simply crossed out one addressee and wrote in another!

DD: I won't keep bringing this up, but you just referred to Carter as both male and female!

JPJ: Did I? Anyway, that sort of thing does not endear a manuscript to a publisher, as you can imagine. *Do not try this at home!*

[laughter]

JPJ: But my secretary assigned it to a reader, who immediately saw that while the manuscript in question was not publishable—

DD: Because?

JPJ: It would have been a tough sell, let's leave it at that. Anyway, this reader saw that Carter Bell was the real thing. Instead of sending a form letter rejection, he encouraged h— . . . he encouraged Carter Bell to send another manuscript. It's hard avoiding pronouns!

[laughter]

DD: And?

JPJ: Carter Bell, it turns out, had a manuscript nearing completion, which he or she promised to send as soon as it was complete, which turned out to be that very week. The reader and I each read it in one sitting, and I immediately made an offer. Only twenty-four hours had passed since we received it.

DD: Just in case there's anyone in America who hasn't heard of *Plain Jane*, why don't you describe the book for us. What is *Plain Jane*?

JPJ: At the simplest level, it's about an "insignificant" girl who, despite her lack of good looks and social graces, manages through pluck and determination to achieve her heart's desire.

DD: Yes, that is it at its simplest level, but *Plain Jane* is also a fierce book, if I can call it that.

JPJ: It is fierce, I think you can call it that.

DD: Only a woman's work would ever be called "fierce," by the way.

JPJ: Perhaps. But you said you wouldn't do that anymore.

DD: Apologies! Explain why the book is fierce.

JPJ: It is a passionate book, an uncompromising book.

DD: Specifically, it is unsparing of curly-locked "Amelias," so-called, who are born with the ability to attract male attention and protection. It is unsparing of those men—most men, it would seem—who cannot see beyond those curly locks. At its heart, *Plain Jane* is an indictment of our culture's readiness to accept male fantasy as the basis of all story.

JPJ: Male fantasy?

DD: The pursuit and "capture" of "Amelias" as the only romance worth telling.

JPJ: Yes, much to the detriment of the plain Janes who constitute the majority of women. And this, I think, explains its appeal. That and it's a damned fine read!

DD: *Plain Jane* has definitely found its audience: already it's in its fifth printing. And I understand that it will soon be read in—how many countries?

JPJ: Sixteen! And counting! Women of all shapes and sizes now proudly wear Plain Jane T-shirts. All bootleg, I might add. Carter Bell has yet to see a penny from any of them.

DD: There are, however, many who feel betrayed by Jane's happy ending, as it (predictably?) involves romance with a man of wealth, power, and social position.

JPJ: To them I'd say, read the book again.

[laughter]

JPJ: Look, Jane is a character who is never given anything. Anything she's ever had is taken from her—her parents, her home, her dignity, her expectations of justice. She survives, and thrives, because she says, I rely on myself! I will be exactly who I am, accept myself exactly as I am—as a small, plain, *retiring* woman. I will not pretend to be anything other than what I am, in a vain attempt to meet some unachievable societal ideal. Much as she needs and longs for others, and a partner, she will only accept a man who is her equal, who can match her in character, wit, and passion. She is a hero, a modern American hero. She deserves her happy ending because she *earns* it.

DD: How much work did the book require on your end? How close was it to being in the state in which we read it today?

JPJ: We fixed the punctuation.

DD: That's it?

JPJ: We made some suggestions, which Carter Bell graciously declined.

DD: *Graciously!* Proof positive: Carter Bell is a woman!

JPJ: Whatever Carter Bell was, we didn't know it at the time. The book, which time will confirm is a masterpiece, was written in just over a year.

DD: That is remarkable. So you didn't meet Carter Bell when you published *Jane* but you did have cause to meet her eventually.

JPJ: I did. Word of the Carbondale charlatan reached us. We knew of course that the Small woman was not Carter Bell. But if Carter Bell was the author of *Nanny* and *The Heights*, we needed to know, if only because Carter Bell had promised us first refusal on a next book! So we wrote him, requesting clarification. Then one day my assistant buzzed to tell me that two ladies—yes, I think it's alright to say they're ladies.

DD: The gig is up!

[laughter]

JPJ: Two ladies wished to see me and wouldn't give their names. My assistant told them I wasn't available—I don't normally make myself available to ladies off the street—

DD: Do not try this at home!

[laughter]

JPJ: They would not be swayed: they had traveled a great distance, they said. I might have let them hang, but my assistant said, I think you want to see them. They are dressed very . . . *oddly*! I went to the lobby, where two very small ladies awaited me. Both wore prim, old-fashioned dresses and their hair was pulled up in tight buns. They made no attempt to be feminine. No makeup, no earrings. I don't know much about these things, but I'd say their dresses, which were rather gray, were home-made. Their shoes were sensible!

[laughter]

JPJ: Little did I imagine, then, that I was in the presence of genius. The older of the two handed me a letter. It was the letter I had written Carter Bell. She'd brought herself, and Artemis, to prove that they were three and not one—

DD: Like the Trinity!

JPJ: This was a joke Carter in fact made!

DD: Where was Emerson?

JPJ: Emerson did not come. I gather that Emerson is the most retiring of the three.

DD: A sister, then?

JPJ: I am sworn not to discuss Emerson. Already I have said too much.

DD: So you found Carter and Artemis charming.

JPJ: I did! I extracted a promise that we would meet that evening for a reading—

DD: Ooh, which one did you go to?

JPJ: I'm afraid I can't say without blowing their cover. I went to their hotel—which was more of a boarding house, really, one of those single-room occupancy places. Our meeting had upset Carter's stomach but still she wished to go—if I wouldn't be embarrassed by their clownish outfits, she said. You see, she knew! After the reading, I introduced them as the *Misses Grey*—yes, a pseudonym upon a pseudonym. They loved it. They loved being introduced to people who, let's face it, might look down on the Misses Grey but kiss the feet of Carter and Artemis Bell. They have a sense of humor, the Misses Bell.

DD: The Misses Grey!

JPJ: I should make clear that I am not Artemis's publisher nor am I Emerson's, though I would gladly publish their next books. I think they're wonderfully talented.

DD: What did you think of *Nanny*?

JPJ: Loved it. Wish I'd published it.

DD: Lots didn't love it.

JPJ: Of course! Look, everyone's got some Robeson in them. That girl cuts close to the bone!

DD: The environmental bumper stickers on the SUV. The family that recycles *constantly* but has three cars and two houses, which they only air-condition—

JPJ: When they *don't* have guests!

DD: So everyone can see how concerned they are about the environment!

JPJ: Meanwhile the nanny is upstairs ironing their organic Fair Trade cotton sheets.

DD: She's not invited to meet the guests.

JPJ: Exactly. So if people don't like this book, you understand why.

DD: Housewives who spend ten dollars baking for a bake sale that will earn eight dollars! Who spend weeks fundraising a thousand dollars, when they could work a proper job and donate much more than that.

JPJ: Exactly. And isn't that a metaphor for all the wasted energy of women in that book? The complacent Mrs. Robeson, the silly Misses Robeson, the nanny—what's her name?

DD: You know, I just think of her as Nanny.

JPJ: Trick question: she has no name. And of course, all that female energy is not just wasted, it's diverted, which causes great destruction. I wish I'd published that book. You can be sure if I'd published it, it wouldn't be filled with typos.

DD: And *The Heights*?

JPJ: Are you really going to make me shill another publisher's books?

[laughter]

JPJ: Okay, it's one of the great works of our generation. How's that?

DD: Plenty disagree.

JPJ: Ideologues, not readers. Look, *The Heights* is the negative to *Plain Jane*'s positive. If Jane is about how a woman might survive and thrive, her dignity intact, by acting exactly according to her nature, by which I mean, her *specific* nature, of course, not her *feminine* nature, whatever that is, then *The Heights* is about a woman who chooses *against* her nature and as a consequence destroys herself—

DD: Not just herself—

JPJ: Right. She destroys herself, and her marriage, and the children for whom she has given herself up, right down unto the generations.

DD: It's almost a biblical vision, isn't it?

JPJ: Damned tootin'. If *Nanny* shows us the social consequences of wasted female energy, *The Heights* shows us its spiritual and practical consequences.

DD: Is it a feminist book, do you think?

JPJ: Wow, who the hell knows. I don't know what a feminist book is. Do you know what a feminist book is? This is a book about a woman of great capability who *chooses* to narrow her choices to the point of absurdity. Her choice now is whether to puree organic carrots or organic peas for her baby's lunch, and believe me, she's convinced herself there's a right and a wrong answer. She *has* to believe there's a right and a wrong answer. Her sin, if you want to call it that, isn't that she makes her life trivial by becoming a super-attachment mommy—this isn't a mommy-bashing book, no matter what people say. Her sin is that she *chooses* the trivial because she's afraid of true choice, she's afraid of freedom, she isn't willing to *be* who she truly is. I think that's feminist. But I know some people, including quite serious feminists, disagree.

DD: They object to the violence, many of them.

JPJ: It is quite violent, but the violence arises from the main character's self-brutalization. Make no mistake: the author does not consider this mother a victim, no matter how brutish the husband. The decision not to choose is a choice for which we must take responsibility.

DD: Bookstores carrying the book in certain towns are being boycotted.

JPJ: Oy.

[laughter]

DD: When are we likely to see new work from Carter Bell?

JPJ: She assures me that she is hard at work on another volume—

DD: A sequel to *Plain Jane*?

JPJ: I hardly think so, but I do not know. She will not let me see it until it is quite done. I asked but she is adamant, and I shall not cross her!

[laughter]

DD: Well, that's about all the time we have, John.

JPJ: How it has flown!

[laughter]

DD: I hope you'll come back to talk with us again soon?

JPJ: With pleasure! Thank you, Deirdre.

DD: This is Deirdre Dent, with WBEX Radio, wishing you well till we meet again.

[Music: "Paperback Writer," The Beatles]

[Music fades]

Voiceover: This program was produced by WBEX Radio. All rights are reserved.

POINT FOR MR. FIVEPENNY!—
in which authoresses celebrate a New Year
(as recounted by Mr. F.)

Annie answered the door, shouting, *Master Fivepenny hath arrived!* and at once we flattened ourselves, for Emily chased Lotte with a spoon! Down the hall they charged, into the living room, Lotte dodging sister, spoon, and dog. Lotte feinted left, feinted right—Em was quite unable to reach her! Annie notched Lotte's victory on their whiteboard.

You are adept at escaping your sister, said I to Lotte, when she came to rest, her cheeks an enchanting pink. I looked pointedly at the board which showed her ahead in notches.

Today is a good day, she said. I have bested Annie in our who-can-last-the-longest-without-using-an-adverb competition, and I have offered Em a witty retort, to which she was unable to reply within the requisite four seconds.

She had a muffin in her mouth, laughed Anne.

I timed my challenge well, said Lotte.

So the game does not involve merely running and catching? I asked, good-naturedly.

You are a literal man, said Lotte. The game involves whatever we wish it to involve. Whoever has the marker . . .

The *magic* marker, said Anne.

The magic marker, decides.

That being I, said Anne.

That being Anne, said Lotte. Until I find a way to snatch it from her.

It shall never happen, said Anne, dropping the marker into her bodice.

So the rules are not plain, asked I.

The rules are never plain, said Lotte.

I am glad to find you in good cheer, said I.

Have you never seen us happy, Mr. Fivepenny?

I considered.

Not wholly, Miss Lotte, I cannot say I have.

She looked at me perhaps more carefully.

You are honest, for a man.

I do not know any other way to be, said I.

She might have replied, but Emily noticed me and said, Mr. Fivepenny, you are so punctual you have arrived two hours early!

Mistress Em, said I, I come when I am expected!

Expected by whom? Lotte asked.

Why, Master Bran, said I.

The girls looked at each other and laughed.

You have taken instruction from Master Bran, said Lotte. You *are* a literal man!

Em stirred a pot, from which wafted the aroma of a rabbity sauce; the spaniel rested at her feet. Anne was collecting linen bits and bobs. Lotte pulled up a stool.

You have returned from a vacation, said she.

You remembered! said I.

I did not, but your nose is burned. Perhaps you visited a lady? What think you, Em? Does Mr. Fivepenny hide a lady in his village?

Said Anne, You are docked a point, Lotte, for teasing a guest.

I protested: Lotte shall not be docked on my account!

You speak of me as if I were a boat, and you a tumultuous wind! cried Lotte.

I blushed.

What sort of lady will she be who wins your heart? asked Lotte.

A lady of dignity, said I, at which each girl laughed. I do not mean, I added, that she should be ever solemn, but her heart should be couched in goodness, and this goodness should affect her actions. She should know who she is, and be ever content with same.

While striving also to be better, said Lotte.

Naturally, said I.

But surely she has pretty dresses, said Lotte. And pretty curls. I am told gentlemen admire pretty dresses and curls.

I admire *character*, Miss Lotte, above all things. I believe you ladies taught me that.

Because we lack dresses and curls?

Because you are abundant in character, said I.

I am complimented! Lotte said. Give me a point!

We are all complimented, Em replied. You may admire his point, but *our* points are quite washed out.

Point for Em, said Anne, retrieving the marker from her bodice.

I did not follow their exchange—not fully—but I did enjoy it, fully!

I need a profusion of onion, said Em. Who wants a cry?

I could cut six profusion of onion and never shed a tear! proclaimed Lotte.

And I six dozen profusion! chimed Anne.

Then it shall be Mr. Fivepenny, said Em, for someone must cry!

Would you like these onions cut in narrow slices, or in small even squares? asked I.

I should like the onions *chopped*, said Em. No more, and certainly no less.

Point for Mr. Fivepenny! said Anne.

I endeavored to make myself both useful and pleasing to the Brontey sisters who, it should be plain now, are among my favorite people on earth—for whilst they be less conventional than many, they are cleverer than most and have always some surprising thing to say. And they treat me with kindness, which for a bachelor alone is no small thing.

When I had finished with the onion, I asked what Em cooked for supper, though I was peering over her shoulder and could plainly see.

This, she said, pointing to her rabbity stew, is All Good Things. And this, she said, pointing to bubbling greens, is Prosperity.

And for dessert, said Anne, she hath made Sweetness and Our Hearts' Desire.

But you shall not see these yet, Em said. Their nature is secret!

If Emily's food be as good as her naming, she shall gather many points, said I.

All Good Things and Prosperity shall be points enough for me, said Em, dropping a piece of the former for her dog.

The mood was less light-hearted when the good gentleman arrived, for he is a sober man, and we had to shut the dog in the kitchen, and guard ourselves, having drunk liberally of his port.

What, asked he, have you girls not changed for dinner?

We are wearing our best dresses, said Lotte.

I am glad to see you looking fine! Indeed, said he deliberately, it is *good to see*!

Point for Reverend Pastor! said I.

Every Brontey looked at me blank-facedly.

What is this? he asked then, examining the table, which I helped assemble beneath a painting of three girls. We are missing a place. Did you forget Mr. Fivepenny, my dears?

We did not, said Em, for there he is.

I am befuddled then, said he, for by my count there should be six.

Have you invited another person? asked Em.

Set a place for your brother, said he.

When the girls did not move immediately, he said, He will be here. 'Tis our New Year's Eve tradition and we have much to be thankful for.

The adjustment required much moving of items on the table, and an undeniable sense of closeness amongst the chairs. Lotte replaced one of the chairs with a footstool, on which she sat.

I moved to protest, and she said, You must not worry yourself, Mr. Fivepenny. I am a small thing; I have occupied lesser spots than this.

The others were not attending, so I pressed my case.

I am glad to see you so pleased with life! I wish I could add to your happiness!

You could not add to my happiness: when the present is perfect, it wants no addition.

What is this perfection? Can I be no part of it?

It is the feeling, Mr. Fivepenny, that at this moment all that is, is well. One does not regret the past, nor fret the future: everything necessary for happiness is right here, with us, right now. Have you not experienced the present perfect, Mr. Fivepenny?

I did not wish to educate Lotte on the finer points of grammar, which hold that the present perfect is concerned not with the *present*, perfect or otherwise, but with action completed that *relates* to the present. I did not wish to educate Lotte, for she is my heart's education, nor to enter into dialogue with her about *language*, as this is her proper domain: I wished to say that *she* was the only perfection I had ever known—but the Pastor called us to table:

Raise your glasses, said he, to the New Year. We have much to be grateful for, for all are healthy and I can see and return to my duties! Also, it is Annie's birthday soon. What shall it be, Anne—twenty-five? Twenty-six?

Twenty-eight, said she.

So soon! said he. Let this be a lesson: the years do fly!

'Twas a good evening. The Pastor entertained us with tales of his work; the girls provided rapt audience. Every so often I inserted a word and felt their gaze upon me, quite as if I were as great a man as he.

Have you anything to add, asked he, after we had consumed All Good Things, and much Prosperity, and made good work of our Sweetness, which was vanilla pudding, and Our Hearts' Desire, which was the same in raspberry.

Yes, said Anne, normally the quietest of the bunch.

She stood.

I am grateful that none of us is away, or demeaned by work, or forced by dependence to act with dishonor. To the New Year!

Emily then did stand.

I wish only that we should all be hale, one year from now, and reasonably content, to celebrate anew, said Em, and sat back again.

Overcome, I stood, though none expected it.

I am grateful, said I, to be here with you. You are as close to family as I presently know.

I attempted to hug the venerable Old Man, who instead extended his hand.

Charlotte stood, and looked at none of us directly.

I would have this moment stay, she said, for it is beautiful.

I thought *she* was beautiful! But there was silence as Emily and Anne looked for each other, then down at the table.

No, my master said. This shall not do.

Lotte looked at him, aghast.

Do you think words have no meaning? asked he. Do you think them quite without power?

No, Papa, of course not. Papa, what do you mean? I only mean that I would have this moment stay, for it is perfect, with you, with all of us together!

I'm sure—I said, but the Old Man would not have me speak.

With all of us together? Look around you. Do you not see that one of our group is absent? Do you suppose that all be *per-fect* with him, that we should wish an eternity of this moment?

Lotte's mouth opened but no word came out.

I would you had not said this, concluded he.

I would *he* had not said this, for her face had been shining, and the present had been as she'd said: perfect.

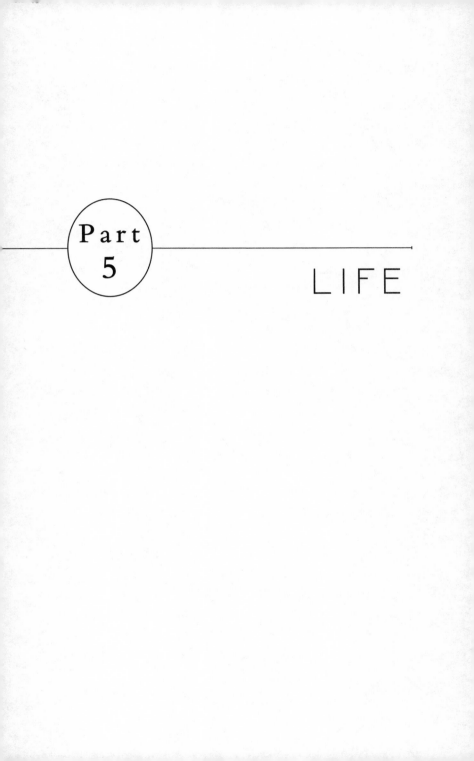

Part
5

LIFE

BLAZE OF GLORY—
in which Branwell nearly kills them all
(as recounted by Anne)

Last week, Brindle managed, through the agency of his *cigarillo*, despite *being asleep*, to set himself ablaze. I saw it as I passed our *living* room, which has become his *dying* room. For a moment, I thought, Let him die. So we might be free of him, and he also free, for Brindle cannot be saved. We may pull him from the fire, yet shall he burn and die, for the glory he could not have, our brilliant boy, our shining joy.

I did not let him die. I ran for Em, who, stronger than I, heaved him to the ground, then threw water upon him (there being a bucket, I'd forgotten, at the door).

He did not thank us for saving his life, nor did he regret nearly losing us ours. Rather, he said, Ye should have let me die, sister, I do so long to die.

Em said, Your way of dying is none so efficient: behold, a window!

Lotte, it goes without saying, heard nothing. She writes to Famous Authors we met as the Misses Grey. They seemed like ordinary folk to me, but Lotte cannot be satisfied with *ordinary* ordinary folk such as we, but only with extraordinary ordinary folk such as they. Is it no wonder that while Em fastens herself to new work and I prepare *another* book for publication, Lotte attaches herself to *correspondence*? It is only their tales now that interest.

Her mind was one with Brindle's once, their tales one tale, though he won the glory for them. Poor Lotte begged to share it, but Papa said, I have heard this tale, from Brindle; 'tis capital the way he sews it up! Sews it with a battle, a bomb, a round of gunfire from the ever-unexpected cavalry. Even then, it was Brindle destroy, Lotte make peace, Brindle kill, Lotte revive. He cared, then as now, for the grand gesture, the victory, the decisive blow. Unwilling to *earn* his place; he left the small matter of character, of structure, of *sense*, to her. He would never be a steady plotter, a boring *plodder*—he hadn't the patience for *middles*, he cared only for the explosive end. He would have the blaze of glory only, and only by *willing* it. Being unwilling to work for it, he has nothing. He gains no purchase; attached to nothing, he falls.

As a result of this fire, Brindle must sleep now in Papa's room. He keeps Papa awake with his ranting and sobbing, and coughs as if to break his chest (to better display his broken heart, perhaps) though this cough does not end his *smoking*. (Each of us has had her share now of this *catarrh*, turn after turn, in apparently endless rotation.)

Last night we heard a great roar, then Papa's calming voice: Son, there are no demons here! Let me help you, before it is too late! Whereupon Brindle, roaring again, called *him* demon, our father, and pushed him, or so it sounded, for furniture was displaced and Father did cry out.

There was a sobbing then. Whether 'twas Papa's or Brindle's we shall not know.

This has made Papa despondent, which adds heaviness to our house. To cheer him, Em suggests we offer good news, the best of which is this: that Lotte is a success, she has as Carter Bell written a book that is a success, by which we mean she has received reviews and remuneration. Really, Lotte says, I couldn't . . . I wouldn't . . . but quickly she is brought around.

What she doesn't say is: I will tell him of my book only if I can tell him of *yours*, for we are a success together, we have printed *good* books, all of us (and Annie soon shall have two!), even if the *public* does not see it, even if *reviews* do not mention it, even if *remuneration* does not reflect it.

What she says is, I shall do this thing, to gladden his heart, and puts on her best dress.

After it is done, she runs to us: I have done it! I have told him!

Her eyes are bright, brighter even than when we walked *incognito* amidst the writers of the city. He is greatly pleased! said she. I do believe he smiled and said, Good work, little Lotte.

Later, he brings us together and says, Your sister has done a good thing. She has written a book and it is better than I might have thought.

Of this faint praise, Lotte has written another book, of fulsome praise, and walks amongst us like an angel, supported by a heavenly cloud of praise, enough praise, in that faint praise, to last a lifetime, or maybe an afternoon, for no praise, for Lotte, is praise enough, not even faint praise. She shed tears, so happy was she, for her own sake.

I put my arm about her waist and said, Lotte, dear Lotte, your success is this, that you have written a good book, a *great* book, not that your father liked it a little.

She shook her head at me: I cannot think so, said she. I do not know how to think so.

Lotte! I said, Dear Lotte! You are marvelous as you are! I wonder you do not see it!

Do you wish to spoil my happiness? said she, pushing my arm away. Are you jealous of my small victory? What do you know of happiness?

What indeed?

DEAR LEGS—

in which Branwell dies (as recounted by John Brown)

Dear Legs.

Legs, I have awful news, and I am sorry to share it. Brandy, *our Brandy*, is dead! We thought him indestructible, didn't we? "You canna destruct me," he used to say—he'd produce a flask, or make up a word game concerning women's parts, or tell a story we'd half believe was true. He entertained with his opinion on everything: voting rights in Rapa Nui, how to mix cement, poetry none but he could understand. Mention any thing you had seen in the paper or on the news, and he would start. He did not have to look it up, he was never unsure. He was always one for accents and riddles and cheering a man on.

I wrote earlier about his decline after that woman's retainer told him they were through. He no longer laughed, or joked, or told tales, or promised to seduce our sisters and our aunts. He did not initiate discussion on politics or literature—or geography or minerals or the proper way to court a lady and make her "sing." He obtained mind-altering substances, and these made him volatile. He was not violent, but violence could be discerned within him. He might beg for coins, or slam his hand against the bar for the noise of it, or cry into his napkin—he might cry for death. He shrank—in size, but also in spirit.

I visited him his last day. He was too hot to lie within his bedcovers, yet shook as if in ice. His middle sister wiped his brow with a cool cloth and touched his brow and pronounced him hourly much improved, though he was not—she did this, methinks, to feel his face, so he might feel her hands, for it was not clear he could hear us. We said things as might encourage him, each taking a turn. I sat by him, early in the morning, and talked of that and this, the work I do now, my life in K—, whatever I could think of, for he did not reply, but looked at me askance and tossed and turned. Then he grabbed my arm with surprising force, and knew me. *"I am dying, John Brown,"* is what he said. Just that: *"I am dying, John Brown."* He was apprising me of this fact; perhaps he had just come upon it.

But he was not finished: *"In all my life,"* said he, *"I have done not one good thing."*

I might have argued, Legs, for he did only good for me, but who knows what scale of measurement a man must use in his final hours. It helps no one to tell a dying man that he is not, or to contradict his reckoning. Still his words did me in: I called his sisters, who replaced me. I withdrew to a far part of the room, where I stayed, with a view of his struggles, till it was done.

He sought the sister with the cloth. "Em," said he, "you were ever kind to me!" He sought the youngest. "Annabelle, you were a good girl, 'twas never your fault!" He sought the eldest. "Precious Lotte, I'll not abandon you again!" Each pronouncement caused a sister to cry out and hold her mouth with a hand. He did not mention that lady ever, the sole topic of his heart's discourse for three or more years; he had words only for his family.

The father, a good though wholly wrecked man, sat closest to him now. "You may yet be relieved," said he, "if you can name your crimes and repent them." Brandy was mute with dying, but that good man did not let go: he spoke with a tenacity that held me fast. "Speak to me," his father whispered, hands shaking. "Speak, son, say what you repudiate. The way shall be made easy for you then." This continued for some time, the son gasping and unable to speak, or even to fasten clearly on his father's gaze, the father holding Brandy's hands close to his heart. "Hear me, dear son, reclaim your innocence! I shall speak for you if you cannot speak for yourself, and you may nod, or offer an Amen—an Amen of the heart will do. I have been loose with my morals," he began—and maybe our friend's head did tremble in reply. "I have indulged. I have drunk in excess"—and maybe our friend's head did nod. "I have poisoned my body with opiates, I have abused my family"—possibly his lips moved. The old man, that pillar of strength, did not cry, even as his daughters cried, for there was no time for it: he continued with his terrible litany, holding Bran's hands fast that he might share his strength, through adultery and fornication and wrath and dishonor of the father and mother, any sin that you could think of, and when he had finished, it seemed Brandy's lips moved with an "Amen," whereupon the father broke down and wept, more tears than ever a man cried. Thus delivered, Brandy began his death. He shook and choked for breath and seemed to breathe his last until he found another. His shaking became convulsion till finally with courage I could not imagine he lifted himself away from his bedclothes, and somehow placed his feet upon the floor, one foot then the second, managing almost to stand, only to fall into his father's arms, there to die.

"My son my only son!" the father cried with new anguish. And where before he cried for Brandy's sin, now he mourned him and his great loss. "My son my beautiful boy! Do not leave me do not leave me! My son my beautiful boy!"

Brandy was but thirty-one: he was only thirty-one.

I left them then, knowing that the family should then be unto itself.

The father invited me to speak at the memorial. Not a dozen folk present but I broke down in unmanly tears. Had Brandy been there, he would have jumped up and said one million things. All I could say was, I miss him so, there will never be another.

I miss him, Legs, I really do.

John "Brownie" Brown

EVER AFTER—
in which Charlotte comforts a dying boy

There once was a boy

Take my hand

There once was a boy, who lived on a mountaintop far far away, with his father the King of Glass Town, and his three precious sisters

His five

His five precious sisters. They loved him so! His hair shone red like the sunrise

Lotte. Continue, please

Bran? I can't

Please

When he laughed, the birds stopped singing, just to hear him. When he smiled, the butterflies stopped flapping

Flying

The butterflies stopped flying, blinded by his radiance. The animals were his playmates

Bears

Really? The bears were his playmates: they brought him honey

Amelia

Already? The prince had his heart set on a beautiful maid named Amelia. She was lovely and

Tits

Branwell, you're going to make me cry

Tits

She had a comely pair of tits

Big

Stop it! Stop it, I can't go on

Sorry

She was lithe but womanly, how's that? She could play the harpsichord

Magic

She could do magic tricks?

Magic

Her effect was magical? You're shaking your head? She had magical abilities! She could fly! She made loaves out of fishes, she could disappear only to reappear wherever she liked. She was beloved by the whole kingdom. So they were betrothed! The whole kingdom gathered to celebrate their wedding feast, only—something bad has to happen

Kidnap

Of course! The lovely Amelia is kidnapped by evil Lord Strange, and Prince Branwell, a strapping lad and strong, set out

With

With his brave steed

With

His magic wand

With

You're pointing—at me? With his sister Lotte? With all of us? We go with you to rescue your lady? Okay, five sisters and the bonny prince set out to rescue Amelia, each riding a brave steed

Forgive

What? They forgive the evil lord? Never! The prince has to

blow his castle to smithereens, remember? There can be no forgiving the evil lord!

Me

Forgive you? Branny? You? Dearest brother, there is nothing to forgive. You're shaking your head. No, stop, Branwell, please, we love you, you are loved, please stop, here stop, let me, there's a handkerchief there

Pray

Pray? What? Pray for you? With you? Take my hands. Okay, let me hold yours. I don't know how to pray, but we can hold hands and hope, okay? We can hope for whatever you like

Papa

We'll hope for Papa, we can do that

Hard

Yes, it will be hard for him. You, too. This is hard for you. I know. No I will not let you go. Do not cry, dear boy, I will not let you go!

More

You want more? More hands? More people?

Rescue

More *story*! So Branny and his five sisters went to rescue the beautiful Amelia

After

After that? She's rescued. You want after that? The evil lord is vanquished and, triumphant

Happily

He lived happily ever after with his Amelia, who bore him many

Six

Six children. In due time, the proud king died and Branny became king of all he could foresee. His reign was wise and he was beloved throughout the land.

More

More? There is no more. There is only happily ever after

More

Before long his children had children, and they had children, and always there were children at the wise king's feet. In this way his legacy was assured

You

Me?

Happily

You

No, Branny

Happily

I can't tell that story

You

And his sister Lotte lived happily

Em

And his sisters Lotte, Em, Anne, Liza, and Maria lived happily ever after, having met Amelia's five handsome brothers, and soon they each had six children and their children had six children . . . You are happy now, I can see

Ever

Ever after. Squeeze my hand, brother, or just hold it, for we are on our steeds, we are almost there

OUR BOY IS GONE—

in which sisters mourn a brother (as recounted by Mr. F.)

Our boy is gone, writes Emily. He fell into Papa's arms and declared his readiness to die.

Thus did I learn of the passing of Mr. Brontey's only son. I did not know how I could be of service, only that I could, so I put on my black coat.

Mr. Fivepenny, Emily asked on opening the door.

She and with her Anne have performed the sad rites of cleaning and dressing. Branwell is a wasted thing, all bones and teeth and too-red hair. The suit they found is for a larger man.

I should like to report that he looks peaceful but he does not.

I did not know him as a carefree boy, only as an immoderate man. I was not loved but barely known by him, so my grief is theirs reflected or, rather, theirs inferred, for they go about their business. Charlotte, greatly nerved by these events, rests in her room and will not be seen.

Perhaps for a moment, say I.

Did she call for Mr. Fivepenny, sister?

She did not, I'm sorry.

When she calls for you.

I nod, uncertain that this day should come.

Anne appears smaller, Em larger. Death can make a person

shrink, or grow; I know this from our work. It also may make a person disappear—which is why I wish to see Charlotte.

Really, Mr. F., says Em. Can you not see that we have much to do?

Another time, says Anne, who coughs.

I devise a task, ministering to Mr. B.'s papers, which they cannot deny, and hope to learn through proximity how I may be of use. In the kitchen, Em and Anne discuss memorial, headstone, black dresses, where is Papa. I venture to Charlotte, knocking thrice.

Before I can be certain there is no reply, Em is upon me.

I have discovered a service you may perform, she says, and explains it.

But that is clear across town, I wish to say.

Immediately, I say, and it is done.

I am there the next morning. The body is away, Mr. B. is returned but shuts his door. Charlotte is abed and none may see her.

Can you advise the nature of her malady, I ask.

I think she would not wish me to say.

I merely wish, say I, to be assured that she is not afflicted by that which took her brother!

The sister is aghast.

No, Mr. Fivepenny, she is not thus afflicted. She *mourns*; that is enough.

It shall perhaps help if I take these dogs for a walk, say I, for they have befriended me.

Emily is surprised, and nods. I exhaust the dogs, forcing them to run for sticks.

When I return, I contrive additional work:

I believe you shall want those sheets laundered, I say, and take them away.

I noted that you were quite out of oranges; here be a dozen.

The sum owed by Branwell has been advanced to the bar.

I have obtained for Lotte some pastilles. (Still I am not admitted.)

The memorial is led by a certain Brown, for no Brontey can manage it. There are but few in attendance. I wish to take Lotte's arm, but she is upheld by her sisters, without whom she could not stand. I murmur a few words. She has the glazed look of all who mourn: my words are but sounds in air; she speaks with her eyes, which are liquid and urgent; it is to them I reply.

I buy her a volume of poetry, for the flowers on the cover, which speak to me of life.

You may return this, Mr. Fivepenny, Emily says, though she smiles. It shall bring you no favor. She promises to alert Lotte to my presence.

The dogs and I have become true friends. We play daily in the park, where I am led on a merry lead. This brings peace to Em, for it is she who must hold this house together, she who possesses this family's true fortitude. Their father disappears, saying only that he must *attend* to things. He would not be amidst his daughters' grief, is my conclusion, or perhaps he would not display his own, judging it too large for a house so small.

I am allowed to bring Lotte a tray. It is Emily's thinking that if I present it to her, she may be inclined to eat.

You have wanted quite urgently to see me, says my Queen. Do you perhaps have a message for me, to bring me from my funk?

She has drawn the bedclothes to her chin; her face is haggard: pale, malnourished.

You have not eaten, say I, and pull up a chair. This is my message, that you must eat.

Alas, says she, I thought you had some *real* message.

This is my message, this meal which Emily hath made you. This *mush*.

Chosen for its digestibility.

Thy message is mush?

Yes, and I shall feed it to thee spoon by spoon if I must.

You have helped my sisters.

I have done but small service, say I. I would do more.

You cannot do more, sir. This is what you do not understand. Our grief is *spiritual*, not *physical*. Our *true* brother left us years ago; we have already mourned *his* passing. What we mourn now is what he might have been.

Your grief may be spiritual, I say, but your *reaction* is physical. 'Tis not a *spiritual* response to take to your bed, 'tis not imagination that fails your frame but digestion! So I bring you what you need, which is nourishment and admonishment to *eat*. After which you may *stand*!

To stand on what? There is no floor beneath us, the ground has given way.

You shall find it sturdy enough if a sturdy friend be by your side, to prop you up and guide you.

At this my girl did laugh, which made her cough, which seized me with shame and fear.

Go, she says, her face white. You may return tomorrow. Leave the mush with me and go.

I return books to the library. I replace the fire extinguishers, which are grown old. I purchase tissues, and lozenges, for every Brontey has a cold, Emily most of all. I urge her to rest. Leave me to make dinner, say I. She laughs. Even I may cook a chicken! I protest.

Again I am allowed to see Lotte. Her eye is clear but her hand trembles.

You bring no food, says she, and I am glad to say she smiles.

Not so, say I, and produce pastilles.

Perhaps I owe you an apology.

For accusing me of arriving empty-handed?

No, says she.

For treating yourself so poorly, say I.

For treating you so, says she. I said before that you could not understand. I was not right to say that, without proof.

We have all experienced loss, say I. 'Tis a question of degree.

Is degree such a small thing, when speaking of a brother? I would suggest that it is a thing unlike any other. One may not understand if one has lost merely a cat, or an overcoat, though they had been with one much time.

Now you do treat me poorly! I do not say that losing a brother is like losing an overcoat!

Mr. Fivepenny, you exercise yourself! I speak hyperbole—I do that because I am small. To be heard, I use large language. Please, she says, be seated. Have a pastille—and now she raises herself somewhat. How can I explain? We are people of the imagination, my sisters and I, while you—correct me if I misspeak, do not feel you must again jump from your chair—organize your thinking in concrete terms.

I am a man of imagination, say I. Do you suppose your father and I could do our work if we could not imagine a different life, a better life?

In the end, I could not imagine our brother differently. Had

I been able to imagine him better, might he have become better, do you think?

Imagination requires faith. I must have faith if I am to imagine a better world.

I take your point, Mr. Fivepenny, and I tire.

Your sister needs you.

Which sister, why?

Emily. She needs you. She is not well.

Why do you say this?

She works too hard.

She is strong as an ox, she shall outlive us all.

When she coughs, it consumes her.

Emily coughs? Emily coughs?

Yes, I say, all in the household do cough.

All do cough? And she flings her bedclothes. I turn my head to avert my eyes from her nightdress. Emily coughs? Why did nobody say? Oh, help me, Mr. Fivepenny, can you not see that I fall?

I WILL HAVE A DOCTOR NOW—
in which Emily dies (as recounted by Anne)

Branwell's death has bleached my sister clean, scrubbing from her anything that is not *Emily*. Her cold does no better, but she persists. Ask if she's right, she shoos you away.

She brings Lotte a washcloth: If you are not able to clean yourself, I shall do it for you, but I haven't much time, so I will scrub you hard!

I tripped in the hallway—on nothing, there was nothing there, but still I found it difficult to rise. I contemplated remaining there, a fallen lump of Anne, for who has energy always to *rise*—but Mr. Fivepenny was there, extending five fingers and saying Oh Oh Oh five times.

It did me good to clasp his hand.

Lotte, up now, reads a review, written as if Emerson and Artemis were one vile person. Em is not amused: she waves the author, and possibly the reader, away.

Enough! she says. We've no time for foolishness.

I feel only loss of hope, which I tuck inside my pinafore: I had thought my words might instruct, or inspire change. Instead, they inspire vitriol. Or apathy. The opposite of under-standing. The opposite of justice.

Lotte suggests we shift to *her* publisher for our new books. It does not help that she has made her case before. You shall not have me, Em insists. I shall be only unto myself! she cries, and is subsumed by convulsion.

Em pauses to catch her breath after no large exertion. She is sicker than we thought and unwilling to have it known. I must speak on it with someone, I know not who. Papa is not here. Fivepenny would run for oranges. Lotte would interrogate, which Em will not allow.

She declines to join us for dinner: she has *snacked* already, which means she *snacked* yesterday, the smell and sight of food leaving her breathless.

She is diminished in frame, her fierceness enlarged.

We are to be visited by the Robinson girls. They ask if their limousine may make it through our narrow streets; Lotte says yes, so we may see them try. Emily shuts herself in the parlor so we must greet them in the kitchen. They are bedecked, bepearled, their hair held high. They do not see that I am pale and cough into my napkin; they see only that I admire and embrace them. I see them as they were then, wee things—not innocent, never innocent, but not far from it. Their frivolity doesn't offend me as it did then: it hides fragility. They *are* fragile, their hopes pinned to *things* which shall not satisfy.

Lotte says she came close to spitting in their tea. I weep, later, alone, because all of everything has fallen away. The girls are grown, the past is gone; we could not make any of it stay. We are not genii, we are not united, if ever we were; we can no longer imagine a future in which all of us are whole.

Emily feels pain in her side. I am afraid, but may not let her see. She has no patience for my fear. I touched her shoulder, by way of saying, I am here, and she flinched.

I think the air around us brings her pain. I wonder no one sees.

She has taken over Bran's room, once Aunt's room, once our living room, when we still lived—to not share her cold, says she, so she might be alone, think I.

At night, I creak into that room. She sleeps as her dog sleeps, with little jerks and fits. I cannot climb into her bed as I once did. We were one child, then, or so it seemed to me. I did not know the difference between us: the Emily part led; the Annie part said—Yes!

I watch her breath, which is my breath.

This awful moment, I see, is all there is, and all there will ever be: if the past is no more, and the future a short porch on which we may not rest, then there is only *this* and comfort must be found *here*, come what may.

My sister's eyes open, she grabs her mattress and gasps.

Ghoul, she says on seeing me. You must not *watch* me! Go!

Lotte approaches.

You have seen Em? she asks. She labors to walk to eat to breathe. I will broach the subject of her condition, she says—I want only the right time. Though discuss is a *misleading* word, is it not? If I wish Em examined by a doctor I must say, *Die, see what I care!* Which I cannot do, for she would not believe me.

Lotte does not await a better time: she accosts our sister upon waking. Enough! she says. 'Tis time! We must call a doctor! Do you think us unfeeling blocks of wood that we can be silent? How can we be silent? I do not remember when I last saw you eat, or smile. I cannot remember when you last *addressed* me, except to say, Washing's done.

She said much of this to the door, of course, for Em had shut it in her face.

Em is thin like a paper doll, though no doll could be so grim. Her cough is continuous, and terrifying. She is a phantom, who must stop to find her breath, or catch her side. She used to run stairs two, three, four at a time; now she moves slowly, foot by foot, to achieve the next room. She is a wraith, who would float away if she could—she weighs no more than a ghost's handkerchief. She holds nothing that might weigh her down, such as care or human attachment. She rises at seven, retires at ten. She sews, prepares our meals, cooks meat for the dogs, and brushes them, but slowly, slowly—she even attends to the investments she has made for us with Aunt's bequest.

To watch her peel potatoes is an agony.

I am silent. She can tolerate a silent person by her side. I do not attempt to do her work but when she does not look, I push the wash bucket closer to the sink; when she makes her way to the WC I peel three potatoes.

What troubles her? Papa asks. Em seems not quite herself.

Every day another piece of her is gone.

She is but thirty! says Lotte. Does she not want to live? It's not enough to say doctors *poison*: what experience has she of doctors! They saved our papa's sight; does she think they cannot save her? Is she so special she cannot be saved? Is she so strong she can withstand any assault? Would a day in bed pain her? What about five minutes? If I removed from this chair all aid to comfort, this cushion and this footstool, would she sit upon it? If not a chair, a bed of nails? *We want no martyrs here!* We've had enough of dying!

I feel a rush of love for Lotte, then. I lean in: she awakens as if from a dream. Enough, says she, pulling away so I may not kiss her.

She lives as she wishes to live, say I. How can we want her to be other than herself?

That is a monstrous thing to say, says she. Monstrous child!

How they suffer, each in her own way. Every moment of Emily's life is anguish; every moment a battle she must win: to lift herself out of bed, to put on a shoe—this is her purpose now, to step one foot after another—not to *live*, or find comfort, or come to any reckoning. She *shall* scramble the eggs, she *shall* write the shopping list—for twenty minutes if that is what it takes. Liver, apples, toilet paper. We feel a horrible awe watching her—out of the corner of our eye, for she will not *be watched*, nor may we *hover*—knowing what each move and every breath cost her. In this manner, she struggles to stay whole, to be herself, as she imagines herself to be. Lotte, meanwhile, fights to hold on to Em, as she imagines Em, or wishes Em to be. She will not let her be, she *cannot*: to let her be is to let her go, to know that she is gone.

I train myself to sit quietly in the dark, to need nothing—not as Emily needs nothing, not as rejection of what is, but as monks I am told need nothing, because there *is* nothing. I imagine myself an ice floe, floating, I imagine myself an island, with waves for company, each wave a breath, a rising, falling breath. I take whatever the moment offers: the texture of Emily's skin, the grim line hardening between her eyes, the sound of her small steps, the smell of lemon when she's washed a dish.

I shall read to you from my latest, Lotte says. Would you like that?

A reminder that neither Em nor I write, while Lotte, the most volatile of us all, produces volumes. She reads as she writes, in a dark room flailing, hoping someone will find her.

Her tale is of an heroic woman—I would say *sister* for

she is observed with a sister's cunning, a sister's love, but this hero has no need for *sisters*. She strides, she commands. She is brilliant (her brilliance unhidden; she will inevitably offend). She shall inherit her father's firm, and run it, but more important: she will learn lessons, which will humble her so she may marry well.

The narrator, who observes this hero, is a pale, feeble thing. Lotte reads but Emily does not hear.

Does she understand I write of her? Lotte asks.

I want to say, you cannot eulogize our sister with a dream, but she looks so hopeful.

I'm sure she does, I say.

I very much doubt it, says Lotte.

We need you, sister! Lotte says, standing outside Emily's door. Do we count for nothing? Can you not reestablish attachment to life, out of attachment for us? I would do anything for you. I would share every one of my breaths with you, I would give you half my life, for what good is twice that if you are not in it? I would comfort, and hold you, and hold your tears, you could spend all your tears on me, and I would spend all mine on you, if you would but take them—how is that not better than being alone?

When she hears nothing, she slaps Em's door with her hand, and cries.

Emily! Please! Emily, please! And lands on the floor, her face in her hands. I don't know what to do! she sobs, addressing me, or maybe herself. Tell me what I should do!

I try to imagine the time, when it comes. I shall not cling. I shall hold our sister loosely. You are well, I shall say, you are whole, your suffering complete! She will calm then, and smile; we shall both be at rest.

Em fell today retrieving the mail. She was carried, spitting, I'm sure, into the elevator by a doorman. The journey left her whiter than snow, and more insubstantial. Her eye fastens to nothing, her attention fully claimed by breathing. I do not know if she is here or already there. I fear her face, clenched, beyond white with its great black shadows. This night, she *could not* open the living room door! I sit now in the hall, by that room, my comfort the cold floor, *listening* wholly for any sound that is not grandfather clock, or dog. I would sleep at her feet but for the chance I might cough and wreck her rest, which could be her last.

She rises and I exhale. She dresses, but needs help with a button. Her throat rattles. She takes a piece of sewing but does not move the thread. There is only breath.

A doctor, Lotte cries. Emily, I beg of you, I am begging, please, a doctor!

I love you so much, Em, is what she wants to say: Can you not love me a little?

I stare at my book but do not turn a page.

At noon, Em has quite forgotten lunch, time is one stretched-out, laborious moment, breath after agonizing breath. Lotte and I pretend to sew, to read, but we only watch, and wait.

I may lie down a moment, Em says, who has never lain down in the day.

She lies on Auntie's couch, which was Branwell's couch. It is a dying couch: none may lie on it and live. Lotte runs over to remove her little boots, Em's feet are impossibly hot, and small. She tries to wave Lotte away.

Emmy, Lotte whispers, kneeling down before her, dear Emmy, tell me what to do.

But Lotte is not there for her. She does not see.

Lotte looks at me with a wild face and runs outside. I cannot imagine her purpose, unless it is to find a doctor on the street. I am here, Em, I whisper. I will be always here, but my whisper is soft and she cannot hear. I may not stroke her arm, I may not gather her to me. What may I do?

My sister is a shade, a shuddering shade, only a comma separating her from the universe, and on the other side: nothing! I cannot bear it! This is it, this is the moment—and beyond it: *nothing*! Emily, I cry! Emily! Look at me!

Lotte returns, with tulips, pink. Maybe this living thing will help my sister live, is what she thinks. She cannot offer the flowers, because her arm shakes and Emily cannot see.

I will have a doctor now, she says.

Again, Lotte, in wild tears, runs. I remain at my sister's side.

Emily's mouth opens quite hideously. I cannot let her go, *I cannot*!

Stay, Emily! Stay! Please don't go!

Who will see me when you have gone, who will hear me? is what I mean.

No, no, no, no, no! I cry!

She is not strong enough to cough; her body, a trembling leaf, shudders, then stills, and shudders again. I grab her arm so she may see me. I shout so she may hear: Who will be with me when *my* time comes? Who will say, You are whole, Anniebug, your pain complete? Can you say it for me now: Relax, Annie, I shall be with you always? Can you say it for me, please?

Stay, I say, *please*, when I should have said, Go.

Stay, I say, please, but she is gone.

LIVES OF THE POETS, pp. 85–86
—in which Emily has died

Scene: Close-up of Lotte's face: her eyes look "off-screen," her mouth is dropped open as if she might scream (but she does not), her face is white and contorted with grief.

Caption: Emily has breathed her last.

Scene: Sofa on which Emily lies is visible again. Lotte has been kneeling before the sofa, but now she has collapsed, her head hung low, her face not visible, her long gray dress billowing about her in a near perfect circle. Part of Annie's profile is visible in close-up on the left side of the panel: she has just returned to the room.

Annie: What's happened, Lotte?

Lotte: She's gone.

Annie: No!

Scene: Lotte remains collapsed before Emily's couch, but Annie has joined her. Her posture mirrors Lotte's: her face is dropped and hidden, her gray dress billows around her in a near perfect circle. Her arms, however, are outstretched, her hands touching Lotte's shoulders; Lotte has done the same. They look like grieving ballerinas.

Caption: The sisters comfort each other in their grief.

Scene: Papa's study is seen from down the hall, through its open door. Papa is seated at his executive desk, a paper in his hand. He looks at Lotte and Annie, who stand before him, Lotte somewhat in front, Annie allowing Lotte to represent them.

Lotte: Papa, Emily is no more!

Scene: A carpenter is nearly finished making a coffin in his workshop. Arrows across the length and width of the coffin indicate that the coffin is 5'7" long and just 17" across.

Caption: Emily's body was so wasted, she required a coffin just 17 inches across! The coffin maker reported that he had never built a coffin so narrow.

Scene: Two dogs, one medium-sized, one small, stand by a handful of black-clad mourners at a cemetery in front of a gravestone that says, Emily Brontey, 30 years old. The faces of the mourners—presumably Lotte, Annie, Papa, and Mr. Fivepenny—cannot be seen because of hats or the direction they face. The dogs bark at the headstones.

Dogs: Bark! Bark! Bark bark bark!

Caption: Emily's family were not the only mourners

Scene: Back at Haworthy House, the same two dogs stand in a hallway in front of a shut door, again barking. An arrow pointing to the door indicates that it is Emily's room.

Dogs: Bark! Bark! Bark bark bark!

Caption: The dogs would continue to bark for Emily for several weeks.

SAY NO MORE—
in which Annie ails

Lotte insists that Anne be relieved of New Year's Eve duty, in recognition of her, i.e., Anne's, upcoming birthday: soon she shall be twenty-nine! I may not be much of a cook, Lotte says, but I can at least manage stew! Mr. F. shall help me. Annie, luxuriate! Like a queen!

We are your subjects, Lotte says. Command!

Annie is no queen. She knows that. At best, she is an Under Princess, as when they were young. Annie never found a place for herself that didn't involve following, imitation, squeezing herself between, being the afterthought, the baby, the unconsulted one, the unconsoled. The one who said yes, why not. Lotte had been their ringleader, Bran their inspiration—those soldiers! What happened to them?—Em their spiritual leader. Emily the wise, Emily the infinite. Yes, Anne published one more book than they; did it change anything? Did it change anything at all?

Thinking on this does not help.

This is what ritual does: it forces us to recall! When the four of them, the six of them, sat at table, awaiting Papa's benediction. When Emily, carefree, experimented with stew and Anne found a turkey centerpiece at Goodwill. When Branwell broke a toe, and Lotte wore a wig. When Annie toiled at the Robinsons and no one sent a card. When she worked at Roe Head, and Lotte, merciless always, took the night shift on New Year's: time and a half, she said. A lifetime of new years, a lifetime and a half! But it does no good to think on this, no good at all.

Mr. F. arrives with a fuss and bother, dogs barking, Papa muttering, Who invited him? Lotte thanking him for the marigolds—so *autumnal*—so he might blush, also, tangleberry pie, which, due to its mingled berries, may serve as Sweetness *and* Our Hearts' Desire.

Once Annie had worried herself over him: could she, could she somehow, might he, somehow—but look at him! He stoops to kiss Lotte but cannot bring himself to touch her skin, he defers to Papa like a slave. He does not know what to *do* with himself! At the very least a man ought to know what to *do* with himself.

As if Annie knows anything about men! As if Annie will ever know anything about men.

Thinking this does not help.

Good to see you looking so well, he says, though he cannot bring himself to look at her.

Why they persist with this *celebration* is something Annie cannot understand. She wants only to be quiet by the sea. Lotte doesn't think her well enough; Annie thinks herself well enough to *decide*. Tiring of Lotte's excuses, she has bought their tickets herself.

Lotte will be surprised. To table, Lotte cries, all heartiness, as if she were a balloon blown tight: let go, she would sag. The metaphor sags, but Annie has lost interest in metaphor, she has lost interest in anything that is not as it seems. Nothing may be compared to anything: every thing is different, every *death* is different. The words *she died, he died* suggest an equivalence, but there is no equivalence. Every death is unassimilable, singular, none can be compared.

It definitely does not help to think of this!

Prosperity is ready, Lotte shouts, also All Good Things!

But it is too late: Annie *does* think of it, she thinks of everything: unassimilable death and being alone, centerpieces and hairpieces, death again and being alone. Mr. F. offers a hand, a big masculine hand, but she is lost to paroxysm. She collapses; he cannot bring her up. She rolls, clutching her side for the pain. She coughs, she weeps; she cannot rise.

WISH YOU WERE HERE—

in which Annie dies at the sea (as recounted by Charlotte)

Dear Papa,

I write you from the airport (hence the photo of the airplane on the back!) to assure you that all is well with Anne. A wheelchair shall be brought to take her on to the airplane, and one shall also meet us on our arrival. Moreover, I shall be permitted to board with her early, so we might avoid the crush of passengers. Also, the resort promises "easy hotel transfers," complete with drivers who shall meet us (with signs!) and transport us in luxury to our hotel! Anne sits quietly beside me, in good spirits, recalling with a smile the barking of incorrigible Rover III, and the consternation of airport officials!

We look forward to seeing you in two weeks' time.

Your loving daughter,
Charlotte

Dear Mr. Johns,

Thank you for your kind letter of condolence. I also regret that you did not meet Em. She was in many ways the organizing principle of our lives, though not our most sociable Brontey! She had not time to spare for most, including, sometimes, her sister. Her focus was ever inward. Her horror of public attention, her disdain of fame was absolute—had we not needed income, she would not have published The Heights. To the end, I believe she counted it—publication, I mean—her greatest, if not her only, error. It was this regret, I believe, which caused her to leave off her next novel, which may be for the best, as it contained material more disturbing than the first.

Thank you, by the way, for not mentioning her work in any future correspondence: I enjoy sharing your letters with Papa, & he knows nothing of either book, & would not approve it.

Yours,
Charlotte

Dear Papa,

You would smile to see dear Anne. She loves this beautiful place, and delights to sit either by the window in our bungalow (yes, we are situated in a bungalow just for us! On the sand!) or on a chaise longue by the sea. She forever watches the tide falling forward and going back; I believe she finds comfort in its reminders of life eternal. Men in livery wait upon her, offering her pink drinks with paper umbrellas, and inviting her to "beach barbecues." She rebuffs them with her usual mildness—they wish they could do more for her, as do I. Spring is warm here but I make sure her knees are covered with a light blanket. She wants very much to immerse her feet in the sea, but I do not allow it, the water being much too cold.

Yours, with affection,

Charlotte

Dear Mr. Johns,

It has been five months, but still I awaken in the night, remembering Emily's passing with fresh agony, still I awaken each morning crushed by her absence. I was able to save her once, at school, when we were young. I pulled her back to life—at some risk to my own—but could not manage it again, though I did try—she would not have it. Her spirit was strong, and would not be tied to anything, not to life, certainly not to me. Though I was tied to her. She was the nearest thing to my heart, my best, perhaps my only friend. Annie too. She has but little life left in her now that Emily is gone. She was always delicate, and now she ails. Think of us, dear Mr. Johns.

Yours, Charlotte

Dear Mr. Johns (John),

How kind of you to ask after Anne. Her prognosis is not favorable. She ailed during Emily's crisis, but said nothing of it. Grief for Emily further diminished her. Two weeks after Emily passed, Father sent for a physician, who examined Annie in our home. While he conferred with Father, Annie talked with unaccustomed brightness about small projects she might undertake for the betterment of the world. When Father emerged with the doctor, he called her to his side and on the sofa said, with all possible gentleness, My dear Anne. He could manage no more.

She has been more tractable in her illness than Emily, willing to try any remedy, no matter how vile, if only to please me, but none has helped, so now we are at the sea, hoping that the air here will achieve what useless medicine could not.

Charlotte

Dear Mr. Fivepenny,

We welcomed your card, with its fanciful drawing of a waving mouse & its message of Get Well Soon. Annie said she thought she'd seen that mouse here, running from a cook with a cleaver! I wish I could say she will Get Well Soon. She is emaciated, Mr. F., her arms thin like those of a child. She does not walk so much as creep, and pants with the exertion of it, or collapses in paroxysms of coughing; this morning she required the help of a steward just to manage three small steps. He carried her, Mr. F.—I could not watch. She claims to be at peace. She wants only to step once into the sea; I will not allow it, I cannot.

Thank you for acting as support to our dear papa. He is so hale that I forget he is past seventy. I dare say he knows our Anne may not return.

I feel a terrible rebelliousness of spirit.

Charlotte

Dear John,

Annie hath left us, on this beach she loved so well. Her last words were for me, she wished me courage. One does not need courage to continue on, I might have said, one need only be animal, for living is our strongest urge. It was she who needed courage, and she had it. Her face was calm—radiant, even. I felt all the world fail me when she let go my hand—I cried out and ran to the ocean & cradled water in my hands for her feet & washed them in seawater—and ran back & forth to the sea, crying out & cupping water, for whilst she lived I would not let her step foot into it for fear of the cold, thus she died not having felt the ocean. I collapsed then, on the sand, my arms upon her. How I came to our room, I cannot say. What I shall do now, I do not know.

Charlotte

Dear Mr. Fivepenny,

What we have feared, what we would least wish, has come to pass. Our Annie has left us. In pale & trembling quiet she left us, courageous to the end. Yesterday I was required to seek assistance to move her up some stairs—not long after, I called for a physician, who, marveling at Annie's composure, advised us that she had but hours to live. Set me down by the sea, she said, so I may watch the comings and goings of the waves, and maybe set myself with the setting sun, so we sat her there, I in a chair by her side, holding her hand, and hoping that some of my life, still strong, might flow into hers. She was quiet—peaceful, even, despite her difficulty drawing breath—& soon her hand was still. She was not yet thirty. Mr. F., I am resolved to bury her here. I shall tell my father nothing till the deed be done, for I cannot allow him to bury another child. Watch over him, please. I shall be in touch with you soon.

Charlotte

Dearest Papa,

Oh, how heavy is my heart that I must share this news with you: Annie, our little Anne, is dead.

She died peacefully, Papa, her face calm, her last words, sweet words for her family, whom she loved.

I have made contact with your colleague who does Good Works here. He advises me that it is quite impossible to transport our Annie home, so I have made arrangements to create a resting place for her here. She shall be cremated on the morrow & I will join her remains with the sea. In a few days I shall leave this place to rest a day or two at your friend's: his wife insists upon it.

My heart, however, is with you, & dearest Anne.

Charlotte

Dear John,

You are good to write. The few notes I receive here act as tether, connecting me to the world, which I find a strange & frightening place, where any person may be lost—for how can they be saved? I stay with a school friend of Father's—a good man with a good wife—but it is difficult to be among strangers, & every effort I make to "buck up" pains me like a knife in my heart. I do my best, which means my heart is sliced hourly. I tell my host that I write so he shall not disturb me with his good intentions—but writing also pains me, as I write of Em—and even there is in the narrator of Surely! something of Anne. Truly, there is no comfort anywhere, least of all at home, where I shall have to face my father, knowing that I can never make up for what he has lost. So I delay here. I think the quiet at home shall kill me.

Yours, Charlotte

Dear Mr. Fivepenny,

Papa writes to me of your good deeds. You read to him, you make sure he is not too much alone, you arrange outings for him, & see that he is not morose. You do the service of a son, while his daughter hides with strangers by the sea. I cannot thank you enough. Except to tell you that I have created an Assistant for my newest tale. He is not a major actor in my drama, for this would offend his sense of propriety, nor would drama adhere to him, but he is noteworthy for his kindness, his conscientiousness, his stolid uprightness. You shall like him, I guarantee it.

Yes, you have correctly the date of my return. I should like to say that you need not meet me—but I could not manage the airport alone.

Yours, Charlotte

Dear John,

Yes, my days are long and difficult, my nights are nightmarish: no sooner do I wake than I think of those who have passed, no sooner do I sleep than their faces come to me, and not as I knew them when they were young but as they suffered in death, first one, then another. I return home soon but know not how I shall manage. Still, I have been the recipient of much kindness. I had not known that people not tied to one by blood could extend themselves so fully. I have come to think kindness more important than any other human trait. I used to prize understanding above all—& surely understanding properly applied can be a form of kindness—but understanding does not require action which kindness does, & there is the difference.

I shall continue with my book—what else shall I do?

Best, Charlotte

Dear John,

Thank you for your welcome home card and flowers. I was both saddened & gladdened to receive them— everything is mixed now, nothing shall ever be just one thing again. I was held up by my sisters, my brother; when one by one they died, I died and die still. I was mortally wounded when young by the loss of a mother and sisters, but the remnant upheld me. Who upholds me now? Father? He tells me daily it is I who uphold him!

I have afflicted my narrator, John, I can make her neither move nor talk, nor leave her bed: she can only turn, fitful and feverish, or roll or moan, she cannot form speech, she cannot take action, none can help her! Who shall hold her up, if I cannot?

Yours,

Charlotte

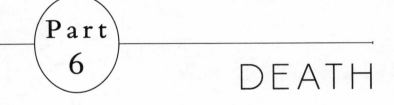

Part 6

DEATH

THE BETTER PLACE—
in which Charlotte, mourning, writes

Dear Diary.

I meet well-wishers at the threshold, wearing Emily's apron so they may know I'm *occupied*.

Always they speak of a better place.

Tell me of this better place, I wish to say, you who have always lived in *this* place.

You are right, I say, they live in my heart, certainly they are with me still, in that better place, but also here, with me, always, here, but also in that better place.

There is no better place, I wish to say. This was always the better place!

Things happen for a reason, they say, hands clasped.

Pray, what reason? Tell me this reason! I do not sleep for wanting to know the reason!

Time heals all wounds, they say.

Time has never healed a wound of mine.

Thank you for the casserole, I say, though there be none left to eat it.

Dear Diary.

The Assistant is come. Wearing a waistcoat and carrying tea.

Lotte, says he, 'tis time ye left yer bed.

Why? ask I. 'Tis warm here.

Yer father is afraid for ye, says he.

My father fears nothing now but death. He has already lost everything he holds dear.

Ye must hold him up, says he.

That's yer job, say I. Ye be well enough paid fer it.

I have not been paid this fortnight, says he.

Ye wish me to rise so I can assure yer wages? say I.

That is unfair, says he. 'Tis not like you, to be unfair.

I am not so good as you think, say I.

He hears you of a night.

I cannot sleep, say I. So I walk the floors; I cannot help their creaking!

He does not concern himself with floors, says he.

Ye know quite well that the bulbs he insists upon, to guard our house from fire, are weak and cannot support my reading, my eyes being weaker even than they.

He does not concern himself with bulbs.

If he be concerned with me, he might leave his comfort to comfort me, say I.

That's not his way, says he.

His way is to send an unpaid assistant, to tell me of his sleep.

I have taken the task upon myself, says he. For love of ye both.

I must stop disturbing his sleep with my wails and moans, say I. Message received.

This did not happen, of course. I wish it had so I might hate the man. Instead he said, I am here, should you need me, and I turned my head.

Dear Diary.

What kind of monster writes through grief? A monster who neglects her hair her punctuation her clothes. I keep a yellow pad under Bran's pillow so I might consider my narrator. She is abed, she tosses and moans. She mourns, but what does she regret? Only a wasted life!

I throw the notebook to the floor: Die, pathetic girl! She would *do something in the world*, but is held back—by lack of imagination, by her guardian, who guards her insignificance. She has no vigor, no fight: she yields, always she yields.

Why should she leave her sickbed? Do any note her absence? Certainly not the man she loves! She holds her passion for him always in her chest, though it leaks reliably from her eyes. *Yes*, I shall give her him in the end, *because that's what one does*: literature has nothing to do with life, there being happy endings in the former, endings only in the latter.

Emily, were she here, would smack me: Wake up, she'd say, get up, the both of you!

My protagonist shall be known henceforth as Shrimp: curled, boiled, her shell paper thin.

Dear Diary.

I dreamed a man was here. I leaned against him, he in a chair, I before him on the floor.

I told him—about my book, the choices I had to make. My narrator is prostrate since Annie died. I have let her lie too long and now she will not rise.

You can do this thing, he whispers. He smooths my hair. I am not your sister, I am not your brother, but tell me of her and together we may decide what to do. All shall be well, my dear, all manner of thing shall be well.

I cried out in waking! That I should never know this thing, not the love, nor the friend, nor ever the leaning back!

Dear Diary.

Mr. Fivepenny is glad to see me up. He toasts bagels, spoons herring onto a plate. I try to sit tall, but am weak and small and cannot manage it; my head lays on my arms again.

He spreads butter in addition to cheese, I suspect to fatten me: every day I become slighter through mourning.

You write, says he, *as if casually*. Forgive me, but I have noted the delivery of paper.

Should I tell him, about the narrator I wish to *murder*? I cut from this book literally now, with sewing shears. My handwriting is disguised, I scratch and crawl across the page, perhaps so I may not read the drivel there.

Mr. Fivepenny is so earnest: he holds his gaze: he expects an answer!

There is no writing, say I.

Dear Diary.

Annie flies. Demurely flapping, she floats above; her wings like fans refresh.

Bran is there, he's not there. Maria braids our Annie's hair.

A man in tails waits upon us, hopefully. Bats swoop. There is an aroma of roses.

They turn, waiting.

My heroine, say I. Em looks on me, all mystery. Branny wipes my brow with his cravat. She is prostrate, I say, she will not rise, I can find no purpose for her life!

Annie touches my hand.

What does she want, asks she.

I suppose she wants a man—'tis what she must want, no? *But I do not think this is it*. She has no courage to rise, say I, there is no one to tell her to rise, to give strength to her rising.

She wants a mother, says Em. Annie nods. A great whispering begins.

Dear Diary.

Did you have a mother? I ask Mr. F., when he visits. I have managed for the first time to put on a dress, and comb my hair, though nothing can hide the ravage of my face.

Her name was Sara. Why do you ask?

He sweeps the floor, inexpertly, though no expertise is required to gather a mountain of dust therefrom, for it is unswept in the months since Annie died.

Do you have pictures of her?

Photographs, do you mean?

I do mean photographs, I do not mean painted miniatures.

Oh, why is it so easy to be testy with this man? Is it because he is always there?

He laughs.

Photos, yes, I have some. Do you wish to see them?

Not particularly, I say.

If he is confused, he does not show it.

How to ask the question I want to ask?

What did she do for you? I say, though this is not it. It's not even close.

I suppose she did everything. Everything a mother does. She fed me, made sure I was warm, and went to school. If I was unwell, she tended me. That sort of thing.

Did she make you laugh? Did you have a secret language? Did you see yourself in her eyes? What did you see when you looked in her eyes?

I wait. I need to hear more. He retrieves a small dustpan from the closet, so he can sweep around the little table that holds the tulips he has brought.

And, I say.

She had birthday parties for me, she made me cake. She organized games.

Still at your birthday parties?

Yes, and at other times.

Did she tell you stories? About how life was supposed to be? About how you *were supposed to be?*

And when you hurt yourself?

And when you hurt?

She was a source of bandaids.

He laughed at this, as if it were funny. I put my head down. He was on all fours in an animal posture, reaching behind the armoire with a brush.

Yet you do not speak of her.

He untwists himself from the floor, a man again.

Is this for your book? he asks.

Yes, I lie, though this is also true.

You are the bravest person I know, says he.

I am not at all brave, say I. You don't know me.

I know what I know, says he. And you are brave.

Dear Diary,

I examine the grandfather clock, to determine if I might find a way to stop it. (It is enough that church bells play the hour—must I also hear each second pass?) Papa received this clock as token for his Good Works, so it would not do to be violent—but perhaps to subtly disharmonize its mechanics? Alas, I am unable even to open its casing. I could unplug it, but Papa, who notices nothing, would notice that, the source of sabotage no mystery. No good speaking to him of ghosts.

It is an affront, I explain to Maria, who sits on the couch, attired in a simple gown. I promise you, that clock did not exist when my sisters were alive.

I remember it.

You cannot.

She shrugs.

Do you see them as well? I ask. I want to see them, it is all I want, but seeing them is torment. It pains them to even open an eye. Why don't they rest?

They'll rest when you rest.

I am all they have, say I. How can I rest?

Dear Diary.

My father has retired after a long day serving *others*. I sit by the brightest of our dim lights, in the WC, a scratch pad on my lap. On the top writ large: *Mother.* A mother shall shake our shrimp out of her illness-unto-death, a mother shall give her something to live for, *since the shrimp may not have her gent till book's end*. I could give her talent or passion, which could, *theoretically*, offer solace, but that would require revision, and I shall not revise.

I am undeserving of my vocation, for I can think of nothing to put on my pad. I have no associations for *mother*, no sense of what a *mother* might do, nor of her healing action.

I leave the WC and clomp down the hallway: *clomp, clomp, clomp!* I slam every door, I clatter pots and pans. The dogs commence to sing.

Papa's head emerges, dozey in its nightcap.

Must you, Lotte? he asks.

'Twas not me, Papa; 'twas the ghosts. Did ye not hear 'em?

Dear Diary.

I lie in the high and mighty bunk, which I had as the eldest of four remaining, which Em took over for privacy till she was too ill to climb. Maria lies beyond the gap, where once lay Bran, dreaming of battles. She wears a tiara, reminiscent of our games.

When Mother was lost, I say, I didn't know what took her. You, too.

Those days were just as bad, says she.

Were they? I ask. Were they just as bad? (I think she is mistaken.)

You don't remember, says she.

I think I remember.

If you think they were not, you don't remember.

I don't remember nightmares. I don't remember crying always at anything. I don't remember thinking, *This is it how it shall be for the rest of my life.* I had hope then—that had to have made it easier.

You didn't have words, Maria said. That made it impossible.

Dear Diary,

A strange gift has arrived via Mr. Fivepenny. He delivered it this morning, after Papa left for work. A small packet, fragranced and tied with ribbon.

I am wearing Annie's socks, though he does not know it.

Your mother's letters, said he, to your father. He wishes you to read them.

I did not know such things existed, said I, hands shaking.

Truly, I had no other retort, I who am glad to tease Mr. F. for any small thing.

Why does he choose to share them with me now?

Mr. F. says he does not know, but I feel he is responsible.

I have sat on Auntie's divan three hours now, unable to let loose the ribbon. Mr. F. is long gone, wishing to leave me to myself, though he shall return for tea, having papers to gather then, or so he says. He shall bring a friendly ear, should I wish to speak, is what he means.

I believe I shall wash a floor. It has been too long since our worthy home was clean.

Dear Diary,

Our conversation, presented almost verbatim:

Me: Thank you for bringing bagels.

He: Do you wish to share one with me?

Me: I wish to have my own, thank you.

He (laughing): I did mean, do you wish to have yours in company.

Me: I'll set the table.

He (laughing and making a big show of slicing a bagel): How was your afternoon, Lotte?

Me: You wish to know about the letters.

He: Only if you wish to say.

Me: Perhaps. Do you wish tea?

He: Tea would be good for tea, thank you.

Me: Let me do that. They'll never fit in the toaster, sliced in that manner.

He: I'll see to the tea, then, shall I?

We (silence as I stand vigil before the toaster, he watches the kettle):

Me (back to him): I wish I had known her. Truly.

He (quietly): What did you sense from the letters? About her.

Me: She was a good woman, of lively intellect. A happy woman. Someone ready to entrust her future to a man she loved.

He: Is this what you remember of her?

Me: I remember nothing.

He: Nothing, really?

Me: I remember only what cannot be named: abundance, peace, surety.

Kettle (hissing, screaming):

He: Sorry, I didn't catch that.

Me (turning the conversation to other matters):

Dear Diary.

They do not help me know her, these letters. How cheerful she is! She knows nothing of tragedy, nothing of grief! "I look forward to our life together!" she writes. I wish to shake her: *Stop!* It is not too late! Don't think so well of your future! 'Tis short, 'tis dire! You will leave your husband, your "gay Paddy," alone. Only you see him as "gay Paddy" ("always ready with a joke"): when you are gone, so too will be "gay Paddy." Five of your children will die, the last the runt who should not survive! You will die too soon to tell me how to live, or how I might save them.

Dear Diary.

I have given my shrimp a long-lost mother, but still she lies abed! So I ask, is it only *comfort* we need in grief (a mother, in the language of literature)? Do we not also require *purpose* and *effort*: not just a *there-there*, but a *there-you-go*? Does my shrimp need a *father* now to push her into life? Are not two recovered parents more than any orphan, no matter how literary, may expect??

Dear Diary.

A recollection: our teacher, asking Em to write, as exercise: a Letter to Mother. Never did I see her response, for she did not show it, nor would she talk of it. To think there shall be no one in this world who remembers our teacher, who remembers *him*. Or Emily, as Baal made her, standing under the circular opening at the top of the Pantheon shouting, *Imagine!* Or sneaky Mrs. H., reducing rations so we might leave. Who will remember *me*!

This is the definition of aloneness, when no part of your past is shared with any other.

This puts to mind Emily's latest manuscript. It must be unfinished, as she labored on it only occasionally at the last. I have begun going through her papers. If I know my Emily, they are positioned not among poem drafts, nor even amid sketches, but in some perverse place.

I shall first check the pot where she stored the doggy bones.

Dear Diary,

I have found it, Emily's manuscript. It was behind her books, those stationed in our childhood cupboard. They appeared dusty, which is why I did not think of them: I forget how many months it's been. I brought it to the kitchen, then returned it to its hiding place.

I am not ready to look upon her words—her last words, for she said little enough in her final days. I ask Mr. F. what I should do. I imagine he will say, Read it, silly goose, how can it harm thee. Instead, he says: Burn it. It can do your sister no good.

Sight unseen, I ask.

T'would be best, says he. Do you not think? Your father would prefer it so.

He knows of this book? I ask.

He knows of no book. You have told him of no book, correct?

Of course not, say I.

And whyever not?

Because he would not approve, say I.

You have you answer, then, if you wish to do as he approves.

What *he* approves! say I, too briskly.

I shall never burn my sister's work. I may not read it, but I shall not burn it, and I wonder that Mr. F. thinks I might. If my father or some other *man* should come across it after I am gone and be shocked by what she's written, they shall get over it. I, on the other hand, should never get over the destruction.

I thought to give a father to my shrimp. What folly! Men *inhibit*! They restrict and constrict, and just as often hold one back. My protagonist shall act upon her own accord! Her newly found mother shall put her hand to her heart as she watches her child . . . do what?

I don't know! But she will *earn* her swain, I swear it! Up, child! Up you get! I shall move you—this is *my* job! Never shall you take to your bed again, not ever again.

MEMORANDUM—

in which Charlotte wants to take it back

TO: **Editorial Director**

FROM: **Features Editor**

RE: **"Plain Jane" interview**

Thank you for meeting with me about the C. Brontey interview. I do fully understand that this is a make-or-break piece for our spring issue; I welcome the "developmental feedback" and offer some thoughts here as follow-up:

1. **Lawsuit:** I cannot think CB will make good her promise to sue. She agreed to the interview; if she doesn't like what she said, she can join all other interviewees in the history of the world (not our problem). I have looked through every word of our correspondence and can find no agreement (or even request) that we confine our discussion to her sisters' books; if she said such a thing to a secretary over the telephone, that's hardly binding. Also, she hasn't one shiny penny with which to sue, her earnings (she told us!) having been given over to bonds for her dotage. I see no hindrance to our publishing the piece at first possible, but of course please do refer this

to Legal if, as you say, that makes you more comfortable. I only hope this doesn't greatly delay the piece—we are agreed its time is *now*.

2. **Notes:**

- CB's rationale for doing this "very rare" interview is clear: while we wished to discuss the publication of *Surely!* she wished only to "rehabilitate" her sisters. It's all she talked about: the reissue of their books (forthcoming), how each was a harmless homebody who didn't desire, much less invite, notoriety (her word was *scandal*). She made her sisters seem fairly *simple* (in the not-so-nice meaning of the word), as in, Emily & Ann wouldn't know a radical movement if it were served them for breakfast. For all that CB is radical herself, she is also entirely conventional. She wishes to be seen as *proper*. This conflict—shared by all sisters, perhaps—is more worthy of explication than her sisters' charitable works and "family values"! Our readers have sympathy with a woman's longing to "break free," esp. when breaking free does not mean treading too far from home.

- If we stick with the "woman of contradictions" motif (which has worked well for us in the past), there is also this: CB says she prefers a quiet life at home to the "busy" life of a literary superstar, but when the doorbell rings with a registered letter, she (I kid you not!) stopped our interview to read it! She does not, moreover, apologize for this piece of rudeness. Asked if she received good news, she says the letter is just a normal part of her correspondence with "literary luminaries," but her face lights

up in an unholy manner. Asked about these "literary luminaries," she becomes quite breathless, naming names and
describing events—though she then goes on to critique
the character of many of these "luminaries" (we will *not*
include these comments—they are too negative, and based
on what can only have been passing impressions) and
hastens to say she is always relieved after spending time in
such company to return to her little home. CB is clearly
stimulated *and* repelled by the literary world. Unless you
object, I shall make this contradiction clear. In service of
this, I hope to include some of the anecdotes we've heard
(e.g., the stunt she pulled at the Poet Laureate's house
last year after he'd outted "Miss Grey" as the author of
Jane and *Surely!*, and she told him off using semi-colorful
language, then spent the evening "supping" with caterers
in the kitchen). Our sources for these anecdotes are unim-
peachable. Again, I do not hope to "complexify" CB's life,
as you say, but rather to give our readers a CB they can
both identify with and reject, as it were (rather like the
approach we took with Romance Writer last spring). It's
true that this turns our piece into more of a feature than
an interview, but you've read the transcript: CB is terse
when not speaking of her sisters or Great Men; she offers
little in the way of new material.

• With the exception of this: As I mentioned in our
  meeting, she claims to have in her possession an unfinished novel by Emily. She immediately regretted this
  revelation, which is likely the real reason she wishes to
  scuttle the interview (this and a sincere reluctance to
  be "known" by the hoi polloi). She mentioned it in an
  apparently unthinking moment when I asked whether EB

was a one-hit wonder, assuring me that the power of this *fragment* is equal to or greater than that of *The Heights*. If true (or even, I suppose, if not) this is an electric claim, and one we should emphasize (pull-out box? comments by EB supporters/detractors?). The danger is that the piece will be memorable more for its reference to EB than its treatment of CB, but given the enormity of the claim, it's worth more than a mention. As long as CB threatens to sue, I suppose she will not be amenable, but she does live modestly: perhaps an appropriate sum would convince her to share an excerpt from this unpublished work, as a companion piece to our feature? That said, the sum would have to be substantial as she cried upon mentioning it, so great was her regret.

Photos: I've been through Jesse's photos again and prefer #186 (where CB points at EB's top bunk); #47 (where CB crochets—or whatever it is she pretends to do with yarn in that shabby-looking chair); #18 (where she pretends to write at the kitchen table—our readers will love that!). In close-ups, she's fairly scowling. She is not an *attractive* woman and she looks older than her 35 years, so I agree, we must reject those. If we want to hint (subtly!) at the missing sisters, we may also include #103, #104, or #107 (dogs in mourning, made-but-not-used bed, etc.). I also don't think another session, even assuming CB would agree, would yield improvement. Overall, our look is Solitary Writer Pensive and Melancholy—better than Solitary Writer Wants to Eat the Camera! A Sensitive Drawing that softens her features by way of portrait should do just fine; Frances could be just the one for it.

LOTTE: A LIFE! (CHAPTER 23)—

in which Lotte loses a friend (as recounted by a biographer)

We have seen how Lotte's friendship with her editor and publisher John P. Johns, originating in Lotte's eccentric first visit to the city with Anne, grew from Johns's early, somewhat disastrous efforts to introduce Lotte to literary society to more personal exchanges following the deaths of Branwell, Emily, and Anne. He appears the only one admitted to Lotte's private grief (we have said elsewhere that we distrust letters written to a late-to-the-party "Nell").

Reading Johns's correspondence from that time (that small portion which has been preserved), we understand why. He did not preach about the unknowable ways of the Divine or spout platitudes. Rather, he was direct and *kind*. He acknowledged Lotte's suffering and, as important, acknowledged he could not fathom it, having no experience with death, nor any kind of loss. He wished to be of service, however, and when she did not take him up on his first offer, he repeated it. His kindness manifested in ways that Lotte could best appreciate: he sent deli trays, well-chosen books of poetry; he did not let a week pass without inquiring after her health, her state of mind, her father's health and state of mind.

"Your kindness allows me to feel visible," she stated. "On those days I hear from you, everyone may see me, even the grocer!"

Thus trust grew and with it rare permission for Lotte to be herself. One might assume trust had grown as a result of Johns's role as editor—who could be more intimate with our "Minister of the Interior" than the editor of her words?—but, as we saw, Johns did not so much edit Lotte's novels as approve them. Rather, trust grew through the immediate and intimate medium of email. As spring approached, theirs was a lighthearted correspondence touching only rarely on her books (their professional business being conducted through formal letters sent by post):

> I wait in particular for my Publisher [she writes in her diary], for he has a peculiar talent for lightening my load. He makes me laugh, he affects interest in my life, such as it is (he knows he may not express interest in my work, it being much stalled)—just yesterday he challenged me to a duel! We shall each of us (when next we meet), on the count of ten, produce an anagram; he or she who produces the anagram least dreary shall be spared a shot in the eye. This is his game, only I may not prepare for it, for it shall be on a topic only he knows.

Lotte had, on occasion, attended dinners at Johns's mother's country estate in R——. Soon after Lotte's thirty-fifth birthday, they invited her for the weekend. "You shall be free to sit yourself on a hammock and watch the clouds," said he. "Nothing shall be demanded of you, except that you monitor the clouds! The clouds are better in R——, you shall see." Jeeves, he promised, would ply her with lemonade. She should even have an umbrella for her drink, should she wish it. "The clouds do make for very small rainfall then," was her reply.

Lotte visited the Johns on at least three such weekends. The chief occupation of these two friends then, aside from talking, and oh did they talk, was to hike. Lotte's shoes were sensible, but not suited to climbing hills. She was on her first visit provided with a pair of Mama's boots (though, she was at pains to note, she had to stuff them with paper, Mama having "outsized feet for a little lady"). Lotte told guests that first evening that Johns and she had on their walk conquered new land, planting at its height a flag containing an image of the QWERTY keyboard. "We have claimed this land for literature!" she exclaimed, and all at dinner clapped.

An historian present that evening stated in a letter that he could not see that Lotte was at all the awkward spinster he'd been led to expect; rather, she seemed flush with health, and triumphant, winning over Johns's friends with her lively wit and imagination.

"She was quite the littlest person I have ever met," he added.

It is worth noting, however, that this was, according to Mrs. Johns's records, an intimate gathering of six. Charlotte, as we know, wilted in gatherings larger than that. It is not surprising, then, that her second visit was not so successful: as Mrs. Johns noted in her social diary, "It was a tiresome business, trying to include that Brontie [sic] girl, as she would tend to look off when addressed. Also, she seems not to know what to do with silverware."

Despite the odd difficult moment, Lotte so enjoyed these visits that by the end of July she felt compelled to end them. "You have no idea," she wrote, "the desolation I feel on returning to my home. It is roughly equal to the joy I feel at your homestead. You and your mother see to my every need, including needs that were not needs before I met you (the need for conversation, understanding, companionship). Yet home is where I must be: I cannot deceive myself as to my fate, even for one weekend per month, and if one weekend of joy bring with it three weekends and four weeks of desolation, my constitution cannot tolerate the arithmatic *[sic]*."

So ended the visits—for the moment.

But the emails continued. Lotte's emails, those we still have, reveal her as playful: she gives Johns pet names according to his mood—Ogre Bear or Mr. Tipsy. She challenges him to greater heights of silliness, and apparently he obliges (we have few of his replies): she describes a dream in which she plays Sancho Panza to his Don Quixote: they attack a supermarket with truncheons of bread. He one-ups her with a dream in which they are Crusading soldiers who stop awhile to pursue calisthenics on the beach. Here one again sees a relaxed Lotte, an almost happy, all-but-unguarded Lotte—not the grim, silent Lotte of popular imagination.

Johns is probably the only person she knew outside her family who called to the child in her. As we read of their joking plans to write a children's book about "Mr. Clop-clop who tops himself with a mop," we remember six-year-old Lotte sharing imaginings, stories, and games with Branwell, and eventually her sisters, and how much she missed that creative sharing.

For all that Johns encouraged Lotte to be playful, did she view him as a friend and playfellow, or did she harbor stronger sentiments? We can only speculate, for Lotte will not give herself away. Nor will Johns. He has declined to speak publicly about her or to release their correspondence.

All we can say for certain is that for a time they enjoyed a friendly sort of banter. It may have been banter to buoy a depressive author, to ensure she did not collapse before finishing *V*. Or to ensure that a valued editor did not grow impatient. Their correspondence may have had as its engine nothing other than such practicalities. Or friendship, let's not forget friendship! Or boredom—each may have been bored in his or her little sphere. Certainly neither knew anyone quite like the other.

Three arguments support the notion that Lotte did in fact have feelings for Johns.

First, there was the intensity of her need. With the pleasure of their correspondence came that familiar, agonized waiting. We remember Lotte's anguished accounts of waiting for her *professore*'s "air-mailed letters, thin in all possible ways." If anything, the instantaneity of email heightened her anguish. No longer did she rush to the post office to ensure a letter was on its way before tea, then experience respite before she'd have to wait again. Now she had only to press *send*, and already she waited! For there he was, visibly "online"—why did he not reply?

"I am a rat," she wrote in her diary, "trained to push buttons with my nose. In exchange I receive a pellet. Only now the button delivers shocks that throw me to the floor, but still I press, press, for I must have pellets—how else may I survive?"

Make no mistake: a person who uses language such as this feels some measure of self-loathing. Lotte was disgusted that she could not control her cyclical feelings of anticipation, disappointment, elation, anticipation, and despair. She strove always to control her feelings, but here she could not manage it. So were these feelings for a friend? It is difficult to think so.

The second argument in favor of "feelings" is the "mysterious" three days in October, days in which their relationship—whatever it was—changed forever.

What happened during those three days? Again, we do not know. We know only that Lotte had been writing *V.* since spring, and by summer's end, she had sent Johns the novel's first half. Two weeks later, he sent her one of the formal letters that characterized their professional correspondence. In it, he approved that first half, but not without reservation:

"I am not sure your protagonist's young man is altogether worthy," he wrote, "but perhaps you intend to plump him with good qualities before the book is done?"

Lotte was elated. She wrote an official, almost giddy, letter by way of reply, assuring Johns that she had big plans for her "dear young man." Her editor would not find him wanting. He would be the best man ever to grace her pages, and so on.

When Johns did not reply, Lotte became despondent. The clinical depression that followed the deaths of Branwell, Emily, and Anne had lifted, but had been replaced by her more usual dysthymia. She was prone to nighttime terrors, extended black moods, protracted periods of sleeplessness, and difficult-to-pin-down aches and pains. After three weeks of waiting, she took to her bed, her constitution unable to "tolerate the arithmatic."

Why did he not reply? Was he bored with her, had his attention turned to another author, another woman, did he have a head cold, did his mother have a head cold? We have no idea. Like Lotte, we know only that he wasn't there.

Eventually Lotte sent an "official" letter, asking for a visit. It takes the usual formal tone of their professional correspondence. "There is a matter we must discuss; the future of *V.* depends upon it," she wrote. Again, Johns invited her to his mother's house.

We have no record of what happened during this visit. We know that Lotte purchased a dress for the occasion (its color: salamander), we see this in her meticulously kept accounts. We know she purchased for Johns a box of Cuban cigars, and a jumbo book of crossword puzzles, presumably for Mrs. Johns; we know she paid to have these wrapped "complete with paisley bow." This is all we know except that after this weekend, nothing would ever be the same.

Johns and Lotte would never meet again socially, they would never exchange emails, teasing or otherwise. Lotte now mailed her professional correspondence "in care of" a managing editor. And she "junked" her computer, not omitting to wipe clean its hard drive. (The report that she threw it out the window to land near her building's trash containers is apocryphal.)

These are the facts, they are what we know; beyond them, we know nothing. This turn of events suggests that someone's feelings during those three days were injured; given Lotte's extreme sensitivity, it is not unreasonable to assume that they were hers. It also seems unlikely, given their apparent falling out, that these were just "friendly" feelings.

Perhaps the most damning evidence (if damning it be) of the existence of feelings *on someone's part*, is *V.*, and with this, we have our third argument. The first half of *V.*, the portion Lotte sent Johns, concerns a woman (V.) whose qualities we associate with Lotte—intelligence, reserve, strong feelings kept under wraps, discernment, a rigid sense of social hierarchy, painful awareness of her place therein, wit, modest dress, a tendency toward depression.

V. becomes friendly with *Boyd*, a man whose qualities we associate with Johns—youth, beauty, social ease, gallantry, intelligence without intellectualism (plump enough with good qualities, one might have thought). Interactions with Boyd (and his mother!) prevent V. from breaking down, as do his letters, which are frequent at the start.

V.'s feelings for Boyd can only be inferred: she longs for letters but is this because she is lonely or because she has "feelings"? We do not know. What is clear is that Boyd does *not* have feelings for V.: he adores a certain *Amelia*. She is of a type familiar to us from Lotte's oeuvre: a fair-haired beauty, socially adept and of a certain class; she does not toil physically or mentally. It is probably this quality to which Johns objected when he thought Boyd might be "plumped," for Lotte cannot help but judge Boyd for his *boyish* superficiality, not to mention his naiveté.

So, in the first half of *V.*, a character like Lotte has feelings for a character like Johns. Given the conventions of a certain type of novel—the conventions of a *Plain Jane*, even, or a *Surely!*—the reader can easily imagine—assume, even—that Boyd would come around: by the end of the book, V. and he would be wed.

This is the half-manuscript Lotte sent Johns.

Was she trying to communicate something to him, through her novel? Read a certain way, it seems she offered herself to him; he could choose her or someone like Amelia. She is patient, willing to wait till he comes around, as surely he must.

We look at the language of his letter again: "I am not sure your protagonist's young man is altogether worthy." If this hypothesis is correct, if the first half of *V.* was, in a sense, a not-so-veiled love letter, why would she not read his response as encouragement: *I am not worthy of you.* Believing this, why would she not be elated? He would declare himself, and soon! Believing this, why would she not then be crushed and confused by his silence?

And Johns, what of him? Again, we can only speculate. The most frequent interpretation is that he was a callow youth—a boy, in fact—engaged in enjoyable correspondence with an author, who happens to be a lonely woman some years older than he (she was by then thirty-five). If he was flirting, he meant nothing by it. Or maybe he meant something by it, but was young and quickly changed his mind, perhaps with greater exposure to Lotte's sometimes-prickly, not-so-physically-attractive in-person persona. Innocent he may have been, in that case, but we cannot help concluding: he should have known better.

Less kind interpretations have him a manipulator, testing his powers of attraction with a woman who could little resist them. Only rarely do critics speculate that he genuinely cared for Lotte, perhaps even to the extent of falling in love. Certainly, she encouraged a side of him that was little exercised, an expansive side, a creative side, a side that was open to new things, new experiences. She had, in fact, "plumped him" with qualities no other may have seen. He may well have liked that image she had of him as being so much more than he so plainly was.

What happened, then, during those three days in October?

Again, *V.* offers clues—perhaps. After Lotte returns home from the Johns's country estate, she writes, over the next year and a half, an entirely unforeseen second half to that novel. Its narrative turnaround is one of the reasons *V.* will be read, studied, debated, and enjoyed for generations to come. If Lotte had simply followed the course established for her heroine—dim hero sees the light that is V., they live happily ever after—there would be little in this book to admire: *V.* would simply be *Plain Jane* redux, though featuring a plainer Jane, a Jane with less fire, less interest, a Jane with so little presence on the page she does not merit even a name.

Instead, as the second half begins, V. tires of Boyd: no sooner does he see through one Amelia than he is struck by another. V. takes fate into her own hands: she will not wait for novelistic convention to catch up with her, she will not wait at all! She instead finds a man who is everything Boyd is not: idiosyncratic, uninterested in contemporary taste, small, ugly, intuitive, intellectual, given to fits of temper, the very opposite of silly. A passionate and attentive man whose head could never be turned by an Amelia! What's more, he would never let two weeks pass without a letter! He is a man, in short, not a boy(d)—Lotte's idealized Teacher!

How do we understand this astonishing shift?

We must associate it with those three days in October. Something happened during those days, something connected, more likely than not, with the first half of *V.* If we accept this, we may also accept that the second half is Lotte's response.

On this score, we have Marlene Umlaut, who maintains in her seminal treatise on subversive "un-writing" that Lotte proposed to Johns at his family manse and when he turned her down, endeavored to "un-write" the event, making of *V.* a five-hundred-page I-take-it-back-I-never-said-that "erasure," belittling Johns and condemning him to a lifetime of Amelias.

Taking the opposing view is Polly Plume, whose excellent study, *Lotte Alone*, treats what she calls the "empty years" immediately following Annie's death. She suggests that it was Johns who proposed and Lotte, chagrined and humiliated—for she had never expected their lighthearted correspondence to come to this, and wasn't Johns very far from the man she imagined for herself?—turned him down, then wrote the second half of *V.* to convince him she wasn't the gal for him (nor he for her).

The only conclusion we can safely make is that in *V.* a character rather like Lotte is fascinated by someone rather like Johns, but chooses someone quite other, a man who is, in her view, superior. In settling the Johns-like character with an Amelia, we also understand that she judges him unkindly, regardless of how happy she insists their union shall be.

Johns was not amused. "I accept the manuscript as it stands. I would rather, however, that V. had chosen the lively over the dark-souled one, and do not think the former deserved an *insubstantial* lady. I think we shall find in the box office, as it were, our readers shall concur."

As we shall see, both of them were correct.

YOU ARE STILL HERE—
in which Charlotte finds a friend

Dear Nell,

Of course I remember you, Nell: pigtails, hemmed dresses, an aptitude for math? We engaged in brief, childish correspondence after I left school, proclaiming Devotion Eternal, though the space I held in your affection was soon taken by another—such is the way with children, and many adults, I have found! You are very kind to write.

The article you have read is, in its crudest sense, true. My sisters, the two who were left me when I knew you, are gone, my brother, too. They were taken so swiftly and in such short order that I am still, two years later, hollow with grief. Well-wishers besieged me then, offering platitudes from a bottomless wishing well. But you offer friendship! To you I say thank you from the bottom of my unwellness. You have opened my heart, normally a bitter, closed-up thing.

I was sister when you knew me; perhaps you can be sister to me now.

Dear Nell,

Thank you for your letter! You are right that some disapprove my distress. They insist on the softening effects of time, they marvel at how well I seem, always improving, everything, they say, always improving. Nell, I do not improve. How vexing! What to do with someone so felled by loss? A year has passed, two years: surely I've moved on! Nell, I shall never move on! Grief is an ocean tide (they say; also it is true): it ebbs, it flows, it ebbs, it flows. It gathers shells in its wake and returns them to the deep. What shall cause it to lose its force?

The first year I felt nothing; also I was in pain—I cannot say it better than that. The second year, I tried, as a ghost, to inhabit the world. That time was a shadow: it moved like a year, but lacked color and detail. As for the next, who can say? Do I fall to the floor when I hear that floor creak and think it is they? Not so often. Am I well? No, Nell, I am not! You thought I looked well on the cover of a woman's magazine? Nell, they altered me with pancake makeup a forty-minute hair styling a softening lens— they even changed the shape of my face, finding its squareness not to their liking! *She* looks well, I very much less so!

But, yes, as you've noted, I have released *Surely!*—my latest—to the wild, though the world cares little for her. I attract attention, *Surely!* very much less so. You are correct that this new book allows me my family name. It was Emily—the sister you did not meet at school—who insisted we cloak ourselves. I, aiming to please, agreed, though at the time (despite my modesty, which you know to be real and fundamental) I held dreams of literary success. I wanted—I hang my head to say it—fame and fortune—fortune, for obvious reasons, to secure my family's future, but fame? How foolish I was, and how wise Emily, for the spotlight was not for us. I have always been invisible (invisi-Bell, if you like); now I prefer it so. Become a Famous Author, and all you see are social faces—lies and fawning and courtesy of the falsest sort—and while these reveal a portion of human nature, it is a small and uninteresting portion compared with what you can observe unobserved.

After a certain blog shared our names with the public (it is legal, apparently, for so-called journalists to investigate one's waste, or the waste of one's publisher, and ethical for them to share what they have found), I begged another pseudonym for *Surely!* My publisher, an otherwise exemplary man, refused. He calls my name a "brand," as if I were coffee.

Dear Nell,

You ask how I occupy myself, now that I'm alone. Well, I saw into print a reissue of our *Poems* and my sisters' books, with corrections and new covers (no more housewives peeping through curtains at a mysterious *outside*). To counter lies spread by reviewers, who called my sisters crude and muckrakers, I wrote about their true natures in a Preface. But the world cares little for truth. It cares little for anything but *Jane*.

I travel occasionally in literary circles (often on the arm of my editor), but then I rush home a day or six early, swaddled in shame. Always I witness befuddlement: how to reconcile the impetuous Carter Bell with this quiet mouse? Then I upend conversation with a too-strong opinion, and all assembled fuss with their napkins and suggest retirement to the deck.

The writer's life is solitary, not played out at parties. We may choose a path that embraces what is current and passed around and seen before, or we can rely on her own selves, without distraction. It is only through the latter path, according to my experience, that we may find what is original, and beautiful, and true.

Though my interest in literary gathering is greatly diminished, I am not entirely alone. I enjoyed visits this summer at the estate of my editor, John P. Johns, till I was forced to suspend these, for enjoying them *too* much. He sends me missives, still, that delight with their light-heartedness and wit.

You ask if I write, though I disagree that the reading public eagerly awaits my next! I have begun new work (I call it *V.*), but it demands that I remember the past. It is hard, Nell, remembering the past! Writing is hard! Last night, I dreamt I was thrown from a great height; no one or thing could break my fall. I awoke panting and clutched my bedside. Writing is always this: the possibility that I may fall!

Little is needed to calm that fear: an embrace, a smoothing of the hair, a tender regard. You are still here, these gestures say, you live still. I once enjoyed such gestures from my sisters. Now I tell myself: you are but a drop of rain falling, you shall be absorbed into the sea!

I have not explained myself and for that I am sorry—it is only because you loved me once that I even try. I hope the next weeks bring you much happiness, and also a solution to that problem with your peonies.

Dear Nell,

You are kind, and delicate, in your query. My editor is not a "special someone." I do not have a "someone," special or otherwise, to offer comfort as I've described, nor do I expect one: I am thirty-five (we are thirty-five)! Fate hath decreed I be alone. There is something in me—do not protest, for likely you know what it is—that cannot be loved, not in that way.

I have accepted this fate, but it doesn't sit easy! Many is the day I would start a conversation, with anyone! The letter carrier is my chief target: I wait for him (I lie in wait), and mask my nervousness (will there be letters today?) as he sorts and distributes his gifts, asking whatever comes to mind: Is the weather, which I can see plainly from the vestibule, tolerable, what can he tell me of his route, which are his favorite books (he does not read), what are his favorite foods. He would think me a daft old thing were he not aware (from my mail) that I am a well-known thing. Fame gives me license to act with eccentricity.

If I receive a letter, then, for fifteen minutes I smile. I read the letter again, and again; I fairly wear out the ink for reading it. I put it down and pick it up again; I look to the back, as if some new paragraph might there appear. I tell myself I shall not reply immediately, lest the author, who is usually my editor, overestimate, which is to say, correctly estimate, my dependence on his missives, on him, and thence, from some perversity, offer less for me to depend on, but I cannot manage it: I reply immediately, then run to the postbox so my correspondent may hear from me tomorrow, and possibly reply. Then my vigil begins again, though it is often ten days before I hear anew, and on every one of those days, I subject my letter carrier to pointless chatter.

It is no better at night. At night I know my aloneness to be always, a fate so permanent it shall follow me after life, to whatever lies beyond. Is there a way to accept that it is emptiness that knows us best, emptiness which, in its own way, loves us? For it is only before emptiness that we are truly ourselves, and are truly seen, and are able, finally, to cast off childish desire.

Dear Nell,

I have not made myself clear: forgive me. I am so to myself I forget how to communicate. I do not wish a man's "guidance"; I feel well able to guide myself. I learned a painful lesson young when I asked a white-haired Laureate for advice, which he would not give. The lesson: do not wait for someone older, stronger, more established, certainly not more masculine, to offer a hand. Make your way across the field, up the mountain, through the valley—rest when you must, but continue! *Then*, if you are lucky, like Plain Jane, you shall find a companion for your journey, because your paths coincide; if not, at least you shall not regret the world you did not see, the person you did not become.

On the subject of men's guidance, you shall be amused to

learn that I have heard from another in my publisher's office—a certain JT—I forget his function. He is dour, and by dour I mean serious and upstanding and true to his word. He does not berate me with pity but instead suggests books I might read, any of which he would be happy to procure from his employer's stocks, for each is as good as the next and any would help me through.

He starred those on his list he thinks "worthy" of my fine mind.

I believe I shall stir myself to reply!

Dear Nell,

JT has in fact sent his cache of books, which arrived surrounded by newspaper and a mountain of packing tape. To prolong our correspondence (I admit it!), I asked which I should read first, being not so familiar with these Authors, who are none of them among those I met in the city. He replied again by flattering my intelligence. You should find most challenging the epic by . . . You shall be among those who fully appreciates the artistry of . . . His work reminds me of yours in his deft treatment of great themes such as . . .

After delivering his short list, which differed in no way from his earlier winnowing, he begged me to share my thoughts, for he values my mind, which, he says, is the most original he has known. He knows nothing of my mind that is not contained in my books, but I let this go.

At night when the light is dim and I should not, I read these books and formulate reactions. JT's replies are six times longer than mine, and always they hinge on some thought I have shared, which he calls *original* and *bold*. His praise has made me bold, so I share not just conventional opinion but also opinion that goes against the grain, for I have such aplenty, and he sees their value, even if he overvalues them, having few original ideas of his own.

I am grateful for his patronage, for it has given new structure to my days, or at least my nights, and new purpose to my pen, for I make no progress with *V*. He has asked if he may visit, to bring replacements for the books I have consumed. I have said yes, though I suspect his motive does not end with *words on a page*.

Dear Nell,

I may say it because you are my friend and will not (I hope!) admonish me: I became unhealthy in my anticipation of JT's visit. He promised books, but I thought he also promised . . . *himself*. I had no notion that I would want *himself*, but I wanted that he should offer it.

And more: perhaps (I thought, at night) union can thrive between those who share a mental life, who discuss books, who value ideas. I do not mean *imaginative* life: JT is a sober man, a serious man—he may respect my story-making, though story-making is not his way, so long, one suspects, as it takes place during fixed hours, and is put away thereafter. Nor do I mean his ideas, for as I have explained, he has few that are *original*. I mean *my* ideas, for I have enough for two and he finds they stimulate. Perhaps at thirty-five this is all I should expect: a companion, who respects me, or at least my sober thought?

This *fantasy* fueled not by sober thought but by imagining led, by morning, to overlong consideration of dress (though I have but three) and hairstyle (though I have but one), and the baking of biscuits, using a recipe of Anne's, which (tragically) lacked notation regarding temperature of oven, length of sojourn in oven, etcetera. Nell, you would not know me!

When JT arrived, punctually, with his *offering*—a dozen well-chosen books in a box, his sober suit, his downturned mouth—well, *I could not*. I could not be near him, I could not hear his discussion of *this* philosophical tract or *that* lyric poem, I could not offer my unpleasant biscuits, much less myself, I could not look him in the eye, so repelled was I by his precise beard, his tightly buttoned vest, his habit of saying, *In a manner of speaking*, and *I have heard tell*, his habit most of all of saying, *It should be this* and *It should never be that*, so repelled was I by his smallness, and his *smell*, which brought to mind a barber's perfume, an old virgin's mothballs, and his sense of unwavering rightness about everything. I directed him to sit on the farthest armchair, and when it seemed he might declare himself, I jumped up to say, *Will you look at the time*, the grandfather clock suddenly and for the first time ever my friend.

I avoided any possible embrace, or even handshake by, absurdly, waving as he departed. I think had he touched me, I might have collapsed, or at least voided my biscuits.

I shall not be handmaiden to a *brain*, Nell! I cannot! I must have union in everything—in wit, in body, in soul—I shall have a man who *stirs* me, who calls forth rather than quenches my passion, or I shall have nothing!

Thus hath sober reflection vanquished imagining, yet again.

Dear Nell.

It is some months since I have written—I am sorry! The fact is I quite broke down. I was troubled by difficulties with a quite different man—*my editor*! Then, as can happen, I fell into a black mood. I could not eat, I could not write *V*.—I could find no shape for it, or my life. I could not think for the ghosts that spat in my ear and devoured my dreams.

One night I took every belonging of my sisters and brother—Emily's bear-festooned apron and her tiny shoes; a pillow I found in the shape of an owl; Branny's odes and soldiers and moth-eaten vest; mixing spoons, notebooks, anything I could find—Aunt's moldy *sewing box*—and piled them in our hallway, as if to say what? Here is a battlement you cannot cross? On this side lay I, on that you may reside? I held and cried over and lay among these things, Nell, and felt my future lay among them, which is to say it was finished, it was over, it was done.

Good Mr. Fivepenny found me in the morning and returned me to my bed. There, for days and nights, my eyes they would not shut: every cell of my small frame felt the immanence of death. I could not breathe! Where would I find the air? My heart was a locomotive rushing to get out. It matters little that I knew my heart would not explode: equally I knew it would.

All this shall dispose you not to believe what I say next, for while that terror is done I again fear death, this time with cause! Nell, my chest is tight, my cough prodigious, I shiver through heat and sweat through cold, and I may have felt a pain at my side. Nell, these symptoms are familiar! I know what they presage! I have told nobody but you, as I cannot trouble Papa, given what he has lost. You are a praying sort, and a good woman who has accumulated credit with any who may have made us—pray for me, as I have not the means to pray for myself! And if I expire, as seems likely, please know that our friendship has offered much of the solace I have managed to squeeze from this world.

Dear Nell,

How are you, dear Nell? I still think with fondness of your visit a year ago, how you swooped in to make my home right, and charmed Papa (though he was in one of his moods), and administered to my illness, which you rightly diagnosed as flu, not sickness unto death, and brought with you charming board games we could play, such as I never played when I was young, and insisted, when I could stand, that I purchase a yellow dress. How good you are! I would wish you similar symptoms so I might similarly swoop, but I am not a ghoul, only someone who misses her dearest friend!

Your visit gave me courage, Nell: I returned to my book and it is done! The last third flew—I wrote it in a torrent, much as I began *Jane*. Unfortunately, my publisher and I disagree on its value; I am afraid the disagreement runs deep. I shall win this battle, though the cost be great, for nevermore shall he and I be friends.

You shall see that *V.* is different from *Jane*, and even *Surely!* At thirty-six, I have rejected the happy ending: in real life such are offered only to the lucky few and I choose now to write what is *real*: real fiction, wherein a real character—a woman, for I cannot write *really* about men, knowing nothing of them!—has a real life, in which she suffers really. There can be no coincidences, no dei ex machina to save her, her Prince Charming is deformed in all possible ways, as real men must be, if they are to resemble real women.

He pleases me, this prince, as does she, though they are not designed to please. She shall get him, *after a fashion*—I am not thoroughly disdainful of my audience!—but he shall not be the one we expect, nor shall he act as expected. Upon declaring himself, he shall disappear so my protagonist may fulfill her dreams without impediment. He shall smooth the hair from her face, assure her that she lives, but he shall do so from afar.

I have given you the ending, you must forgive! And read my book anyway, knowing that it is the journey that defines us, and never our reward.

HOW LOVELY IS THIS PROSPERITY—
in which a friend becomes sister

Lotte explains their various "traditions": meat standing in for
All Good Things, greens an augur of Prosperity, statements of
gratitude, a doubling of postprandial sweets. Nell is charmed.
Her own family (she is one of twelve) enjoys no such ritual,
being content merely to house, feed, and succor: it must always
be enough. But her friend has written, again begging her company. I cannot be satisfied, she says, with mere words on a page!
I must have my new "sister," especially on the New Year, when
no memory spares us. So Nell has graciously arrived.

Carrying exotic treats! Turkish delight. Candied apples. So
festive!

She is stunned again by Lotte's grip—how powerful is her
embrace! This is not *her* family's way—but Nell, thirty-five,
unmarried, a virgin still, decides it does her good.

Lotte insists she needs no assistance, but Nell poo-poos,
adopting an apron she finds, blue bears adorning, not noting
Lotte's distress. I shall be your sous-chef, Nell declares, then
explains the term. It shall have to do. So, chop, chop, I don't
mind the onion tears: I'm accustomed!

Nell's brothers and sisters are married; she is an aunt over
and over again—she takes charge, she *helps*. Let me get that, she
says. What can I do for you now?

She is pleased when good Mr. Brontey, whose work and

title impresses, shows her his awards (again), and the painting of "the girls," then pulls out her chair and toasts her: what an estimable addition she is to their New Year! Lotte agrees, Mr. Fivepenny agrees.

Mr. Fivepenny—well, he will not do. He is deferential, but keeps much to himself—too much. His gaze is for Lotte, though she does not see it.

Mr. Brontey sees it. Before Lotte has served Prosperity, he begins.

Has Lotte told you of the man she has met? JB, his name was. JD? JC?

For some reason he addresses Nell.

His name is JT, Papa, Lotte says, and I may have mentioned him, but he is of no account.

Nonsense! Papa thunders. One has only to spend thirty minutes in his company to know that he is a man of learning and accomplishment, a man of consequence, and *rectitude*.

He is a dull man, Papa, an ordinary man. This you would know had you spent thirty-one minutes in his company. Have you sufficient Prosperity, Mr. F.?

Plenty, murmurs Fivepenny.

Still, Papa says, I think him worthy. Shall we invite him to tea?

We shall not, Lotte says.

I wish you more acquaintance of his ilk, his quality, Papa says. He comes from good stock, he takes pride. You wither here, with no one to take your measure.

I am not alone, Lotte says, looking at her plate. I have my books, my correspondence. I have only to go the city and I am surrounded. People clamor.

How lovely is this Prosperity! Nell says, for her friend has not touched her food. Instead, Lotte clasps her hands on her lap, her knuckles white. Really, Nell says, you must give me the recipe—though Prosperity is nothing more than kale, boiled, with lemon.

Please do not interrupt. Or change the subject. This is important.

It is unclear if Papa speaks to Nell or to her friend, but she shall not oblige.

Mr. Fivepenny, Nell says, tell me something of your work.

Mr. F. obliges. Papa glares.

Part
7

LOVE

DOGWALKER—
in which Charlotte finds love

Dearest Nellie,

I shall not beat around, near, or in any bush, for the most extraordinary thing has happened: Mr. F. has declared himself!

I hope you can trust me when I say I did nothing to encourage his hopes which it appears he has maintained for months (if not years). I tease him, it is true, for he strikes me like a brother, being ever-present in our home, and teasable, with his pressed clothes, and tight opinions on any thing. Teasing does a man with pressed clothes and tight opinions good, and he welcomes it with good humor; whom else may I tease in this world if not him?

Nellie, you would not recognize him—he is utterly changed from the time of your last visit. For days he has appeared distressed, and I did not think to ask, for truly I do not give the man much thought! He declined tea and was woeful, and I think unwashed!—and I now understand why: he was coming to his resolve and this had made him ill! He could hardly stand! His hands shook and his eye twitched.

It happened thus: we had finished an evening entertaining certain helpers in my father's work, good people who volunteer their time for the poor. For such suppers, I make lasagna, because unlike my other efforts, this one often succeeds, and I can find many of the ingredients "ready-made" and do not have to trust too much to my own feeble skill, yet the outcome is such that it impresses. It happens also to be a favorite of Papa and also Mr. F., but on this evening Mr. F. would have none of it, and when a helper asked if he was well, Mr. F.'s voice cracked. Very well but not so well, was his inane reply. Which is to say, he added, my health is in order, thank you very much, but this he mumbled, and the conversation, led, as always, by my father, moved on. I thought perhaps Mr. F., had the influenza, and whispered this to him, but he insisted, with sorrowful expression, that he was not struck low by germs, nor food, nor the weather, nor any physical thing—rather, he suffered from sickness of spirit, though he declined in that company to explain, nor did I wish him to explain, obligated as I was to "chair" this meal, and unaccustomed to receiving confidences from that party. But I had an inkling then that he must be suffering in love, and how extraordinary to imagine him with a "lady friend," and then my thoughts turned to the subject at hand, which had everything to do with taxes.

Mr. F. helped me bring dinner things to the kitchen, a task he often undertakes. I was placing these dishes in the sink, when he said, Lotte, dear Lotte, I must speak with you.

Still I did not understand. Yes, Mr. Fivepenny, I said, turning on the water. I am all ears.

Lotte, said he, beloved Lotte, and on it went from there, I eventually turning off the water, and facing him in horror.

Does Papa know? I eventually asked when he had done and I had recovered my senses; he confessed that none did know except, now, me (and all who witnessed him tonight, I thought, for his behavior now seemed transparent!).

He does not believe that I can love him, Nell; he begged only to be heard, not considered, though the latter would make him the happiest man in the world.

I told him I would give an answer tomorrow, but only out of politeness, then I fairly pushed him out the door. Knowing Papa would be severely exercised, I decided to allow him his sleep, knowing that if I told him in the morning, he would have no choice but to go to work, granting space between his displeasure and myself.

Nell, I know from one small incident during your visit here that you think my father a tyrant, so I hesitate to describe his reaction the next morning, lest it reinforce that opinion. I have never seen him so distraught! Mr. F. is of dubious origins (says he), his future shall be undistinguished, he lacks brilliance and funds and any way of making himself Known. I do not disagree, but do not feel this is how we should judge a husband—or a man! Papa became yet more exercised, his face so red and puffed, I thought he might have an attack. He thrust his finger repeatedly in my face, and the words that came out of his mouth! Individually, they were words a civilized man might use, but in combination, they were hateful! Mr. F. was a snake, he was treacherous, he was evil, trying to <u>steal</u> me!

Mr. F. may be many things that would not suit—narrow-minded and ill-educated, with little in the way of imagination—his sole reading being political tracts, which always reinforce but never challenge his belief—but he is not—I know you believe me—<u>evil</u>! It pains me that my father should view him thus! It speaks to me of a want of human understanding, not to mention a too strong sense of injury. I have said nothing on this first day to defend Mr. F., not wanting to increase my pater's anger lest it reach dangerous proportion.

I wrote my refusal—my words were short and unequivocal—I would not wish to offer unnecessary hope—but my father has also written, using horrible language, forbidding Mr. F. to address me in our home. The long and short of it is that after seven years of irreproachable conduct, seven years of trusted, reliable, dare I say irreplaceable service, Mr. F. is become pariah, and I can effect no remedy! I cannot bring Father to reason, and the situation is untenable. Mr. F. is unwilling to make the promise demanded of him, so he cannot enter our home, and cannot therefore serve my father, as his office is here. In what my father describes as a childish tantrum, Mr. F. has therefore tendered his resignation, promising to work among the poor in a faraway land! I have no doubt he means it, but I do not wish it for him, for I do not think the weather or customs in any foreign place would suit, as he is an uncompromising man, set in his ways.

The volunteers had a "going away" party for Mr. F., though it remains unclear if he will go back to his people or in fact go far off. For the purpose of this party he was at last allowed into our house. It was a pitiful occasion. He scarcely heard what was said and when it was time for him to speak (for the volunteers believed he chose to follow a magnificent opportunity elsewhere) he could only gaze at me, his hand shaking so violently he spilled his champagne on the vest of one lady and could say only to those present, I—I—I.

I was cleaning the dishes—again! I must seem quite the drudge to you, Nellie, but alas, not to him!—when he left, and I thought him quite gone, and was sorry for it—but not too sorry—and went to the mailbox, having remembered our post, and found him in our lobby quite undone on one of those brocade couches intended for decoration (I am sure no one in twenty years has sat upon it). Nell, he was sobbing and not caring who might see. Sobbing not as a man sobs, with small discreet tears, but as a child sobs, his whole body aquake, if you can bring that image to mind. I went to him—of course I did: I am no monster. He will go for the time being to his people; he wishes me to write him. I told him that was impossible. I was glad of the opportunity to say that I was sorry for his distress and in no way shared my father's opinion of his proposal: I did not think him a "sneak" or "beneath me"; I merely thought him unsuited to my temperament, and I his. This did not ameliorate his feelings, though they did mine, for I have felt Mr. F. ill-treated, and wish it were not so.

Feel for me, Nell. I once wished admirers, but I have, as you know, resigned myself to solitude, and never did wish—much less expect—to be the cause of tumult or heartbreak.

I am likely never to see him again or hear from him. I shall think my life less for that. I had not known he had such passion in him, or such feeling.

Yours, dejectedly,
Lotte

Dearest Nell,

Thank you for your kind letter. It was exactly what I might have expected, and hoped: circumspect, yet generous. You applaud my decision, knowing what it cost me—yes, what it cost me, for with my rejection of Mr. Fivepenny I am bound again to confront my future <u>alone</u>. I have not your hardy family, Nell: I have only my father, who is, as you know, strong but old, and who, just this week, was laid up in hospital! He blames the situation which has lately passed between us, for while I have not countered his wrath, he knows I disapprove both his actions and his words. This brought him unhappiness, or so he says, though I have seen no unhappiness, only intemperate judgment brought about by an old man's wounded pride.

Yes, his pride! You defend him, but you are wrong: he does not consider what is good for me, except in so far as he assumes that I will be made happy by money, social advancement, and things I do not care about at all. You remember that he has pulled himself up from dirt, to use his colorful words, and would not have me return there (he has had no intercourse with his family since he was sixteen; perhaps he thinks their poverty contagious!). He cares not for human warmth, nor companionship, nor affection, having ever been one who did not need such things, who has fairly chosen <u>against</u> them, and not learned ever to display them. I say this and feel no little guilt, for as I say, he is in hospital, having suffered an attack. He looks no less imposing in his bed, though perhaps more measured for he is loath to "make a scene" which might be witnessed by Doctors, any of whom, he thinks, might make a match for me if only I would <u>try</u>. He has filled his hospital room with my books, hoping the Specialists might ask, which they do not, having on their mind (I'm sure!) the red-headed nurse who attends him.

In any case, I wish him a speedy recovery and ponder with realism what life will be like when he is gone—we are fragile, Nell! We may lose a person at any time, and when <u>he</u> is gone, I shall have no one left to lose. Can such as I live with no one? I have made do with this man, though he is not much company, because he is something, he is mine!

I might as well confess it, Nell: I have received letters from Mr. Fivepenny—six, in fact. I have not as yet replied. Such letters I never expected to receive from any man! He suffers, and I take no pride in it. He sees only good in me, he would protect me, and cherish me, and hold me against the cold. Did you know from your visit that he carried such depth of feeling? I did not!

When you met him, whenever I knew him, he was pleasant enough—attentive, certainly, and always kind—why until his last day he walked Emily's dogs, knowing this chore fatiguing for Father and painful for me. And we thought nothing of it, as if it were our <u>due</u>, when in fact the action was produced by a most delicate feeling, and never did he fuss about it or about anything he has done to lighten our load. So, yes, while we knew him to be <u>good</u>, we thought of him rather as we might a piece of furniture, something comfortable and always around. We did not consider—ever—that he held fathoms!

I pity him, Nell, I do! I understand what it is to hold feeling within, to keep it when it would burst through, I understand his restraint and I know its cost! I continue to feel sick for how my father treated him. And yet, in his latest letter he forgives him! He has forgiven my father's very real insult and wishes him well. He promises that if we were to wed, my father's comfort and security would be ever on his mind: he would do nothing to make the old man regret his consent. We could even live here, in this old apartment, together, if such were his preference.

I further confess: he will visit. And I have promised to write, though I shall not tell Father unless our correspondence progresses to something other, and I have a new decision made. This seems only fair to Mr. Fivepenny, who has been a good friend to me and my family, never asking anything for himself, until he asked for me. I hope my behavior does not shock you, Nell. I have not changed my mind about his suitability but I have agreed to at least . . . listen!

Yours, as ever,
Lotte

Dear Nellie,

You reprimand! This I did not expect! Because my father will not have him, I should not? I should not hear his words nor be in his presence? I will say it again, Nell, though you would not wish to hear it: you have the joy of your relations. You are reconciled, at thirty-seven, to spinsterhood, and you give reasons for how this may satisfy, but you are <u>not alone</u>! You have brothers and sisters, you have nieces and nephews! You have not seen the last of your blood in hospital, in his old age, infirm. I am our remnant, Nell—should I live to my father's age, half my life, and most of my life to come, would be in solitude!

I am less self-sufficient than you; those times when I have been left very much alone, I have suffered, and nearly died—do not pretend this cannot happen because I am "older now and wiser"! Do not censure me! It is unfair, and I need you, when my only family is against me, and all that happens spins my head and confuses. Please, Nell, please! I have made no rash decision—I have made no decision at all, just to hear a man speak. Do you know me to be rash, do you know me to decline duty, or to let it slip? Do you know me to ever do a thing for the pleasure of it or on a whim? How can listening to a good man speak be bad, how can it be wrong?

I remain, as ever, your affectionate friend,
Lotte

Dear Nell,

You decline to write—you are done with me, even as I need you most. Having you as friend has been my sole reminder that the universe, which often seemed only to strike at me, could be <u>good</u>. You break my heart, Nell, you really do.

On the next page shall be an update, but separated, should you wish to tear it to shreds without seeing even a word: I would not have it said that I forced you to know the details of what you think my sordid life.

You have perhaps continued to read, so I gather my courage and report.

Papa is home from the hospital and well. His doctors say we should have no concern, but Papa does not say this. He says, You must not disturb me, Lotte: any shock could be my end.

I do not believe this for one moment: he shall outlive us all! He has that strength and the conviction of his importance and place in this world.

I am sorry to hear it, said I, but I have something to say. Sit, if you fear for your health.

He sat, but spoke first: I shall hear no words on the subject of the Dogwalker (as he has taken to calling him); do not think to talk to me of this.

I will talk of this, I said, and you shall hear me. NO, said I, when he prepared to interrupt. I am of this household, and I would speak. I have seen him, we have exchanged letters. I shall continue to exchange letters, for I must know! I must know more, I must know if he will suit. You will allow this thing: indeed, you have no choice; it is already done!

I exclaimed this, and felt my heart close to explosion, for never had I spoken so strongly to any but my sisters, and oft-times Branwell.

I will not hear this, he said, roaring and stomping to his feet (health be damned).

You may well stand over me, I said, and look down upon me but never again shall your wishes stand over what I know to be mine, provided my wishes harm no one.

They harm me! he exclaimed. You harm me with your disrespect, not only of my person, and your disregard for my health, but our family name—to think you would ally yourself with that man who is but a secretary!

Papa! I cried. Look at me! What do you see? A beauty? I am no beauty! Look at this face! Look upon it as a man looks! You see, you look away! I do not please—in any way! I am too sensitive, too easily hurt, too ill adapted to the world. Do you see a rich woman? After settling Branwell's debts, I have little for myself, and no assurance that I shall make another penny with my art (for my work, dear Nell, has come to a halt)! When you are gone—yes, I say it!—I may well be impoverished! Who would have me then?

I fairly shouted these words, and he was not glad to hear them, nor was I to say them, for they nearly reduced me to sobbing, but I held myself in, and rallied the courage I had managed for thirty-seven years to hold in reserve, and shouted.

I have love in me! I cried. I cannot be satisfied a spinster, alone forever with my memories, having never a person to care for, never knowing love. You, Papa, have known love! You may have forgotten it—and here, Nell, I went further than I should—but you have had it. Would you hold that from me? Mr. Fivepenny loves me, Papa, he loves me with all his heart! He knows me, he knows my home character, he knows me when I am unguarded, when I am most myself, he has seen me in the worst and also in the best of times, he shall not be <u>surprised</u> by anything I am—he wants those things! He is not a boy, this is not a childhood <u>crush</u>, his are not ill-formed, <u>temporary</u> feelings; for years he has kept them to himself! His love will not go away—do you know what that means? Whatever else, he has convinced me of that, and has that no value, Papa, a love that will not fade?

Papa was fairly silenced by my outburst, having never seen anything like it.

I have not forgotten your mother, Lotte, said he. I am sorry you think I could—but he was not tamed.

A week has passed, Nell, a week of silence, during which I made none of my usual efforts to chatter or see to his comfort, and he has agreed, finally, to "allow" this correspondence, which in any case continues with or without his approval. Someday soon, Mr. Fivepenny shall be welcomed to our home, if only for a meal. I hope to have your blessing for this period of discovery—for again, I have made no decision—even if your blessing be as reluctant as Father's.

With all love,
Your Lotte

My dear Nell,

Still you do not write, and yet I write back. I pretend that you are true. I send a letter and imagine your reply. I read your loving words and smile—I know what Nellie <u>would</u> say, and yet I would hear you say it.

Nell, Mr. Fivepenny and I are engaged. I hope you read <u>these</u> words and smile!

It happened this way: he visited and we spent time together, in the open, as it were. We walked through our town, visited our small gallery to see the few pictures I like there, sipped coffee on the green. Mostly we talked, about everything, and with the honesty reserved for old friends. Then today he asked to walk with me in the park and found a bench for us there, which was perhaps known to him, which included at our back children playing so we might hear the sound of their games. Then, Nell, he knelt before me, good, kind Mr. F. (of course he is known to me now as "Art"), and said all manner of things, most of which I no longer recall, because as soon as he was on his knees I cried like an infant, knowing what was to come. He swore allegiance to me, Nell, he swore to remain by my side no matter what, he spoke of my beauty (and I did not interrupt to ask were his glasses working well) and my good qualities which, according to him, are both "legion" and "well known." In lieu of a ring he offered tulips, knowing these were Emily's flowers. At this

I collapsed into his arms, Nell, for what I understood is that he would take on all of our suffering, he would hold it, and me, and never let us go.

Never have I felt so peaceful and so glad.

He laid forth a plan for our life together, one that includes writing, should I be so inclined, and children, should we be so fortunate. We will stay in the apartment as long as Papa will have us. I have insisted—and he has agreed—that I create a will leaving my personal goods, such as they are, to my father, should I expire, so he shall not want in his final years. I feel that Mr. Fivepenny's plans are generous and honorable, especially given that, as I have recently learned, he has been offered better work elsewhere and is by no means assured of Father's position should Father leave us or retire. So he is most generous and loving with Papa, and given that, I can in good conscience say Yes!

I still have doubts, dear Nell: this is not the man I imagined when we were young. His tastes and mine are dissimilar, I cannot share the books on my shelf nor even the thoughts in my head—or rather I can, but would they resonate? Ours cannot be a marriage of ideas, but is that what we want, in the end? I can share my heart with him and, if you'll permit, my body, and he shall care for my spirit, and this may be enough. It must be, for I have decided: I will have him.

I told this to Papa the same night. He had been something less than civil during our supper, I am ashamed to say, though this may be because he is enduring a cold and only left his room to sup with us and was quite miserable during that time and not well able to breathe or speak. I chose not to overexplain my feelings and my thoughts, for I had no assurance he would understand, and indeed, he was dismayed and about to remonstrate when I explained the arrangements Mr. F. would make for his comfort and security.

You will not leave me? he asked.

Never, said I.

You will always be there? said he, very much like a child.

Always, said I.

You will care for me? Right here, in this house? Until I am gone? said he.

Till death do us part, said I.

And so, dear silent beloved Nell, we are to be wed. I hope that you can be happy for me.

Your affectionate,

Lotte

ILLUSION LACE—
in which Charlotte weds

Miss Charlotte Jane Brontey, thirty-eight, daughter of Mr. and Mrs. Patrick Brontey, became the bride of Mr. Arthur Fivepenny, thirty-six, son of Mr. and Mrs. Arthur Fivepenny, at a ceremony in the Park at eleven o'clock this morning. The bride wore a white illusion lace tea-length dress with a crochet lace overlay, scalloped hem and cuffs, cap sleeves, and birdcage-blusher veil. She carried a hand-tied bouquet of yellow, orange, and red tulips. She was attended by Miss Nell Mussey, who wore a rose-colored, embroidered dress with split flutter sleeves and ribbon-like appliqué in the skirt.

The bride was given away by Mr. Henry Jones, a colleague of Mr. Fivepenny, as Mr. Patrick Brontey was indisposed and unable to attend.

Mr. and Mrs. Fivepenny left on a two-week wedding trip to the south, motoring to visit Mr. Fivepenny's relations. For traveling, the bride wore a three-piece traveling suit with a toast-brown lightweight-wool short box coat and slim-fitted jacket chalk-striped in white and a dark brown skirt.

A TRULY NEW YEAR—
in which Charlotte shares wonderful news

Arthur is surprised to find his wife in fashionable dress, candles on the tabletop.

She stirs a stew in the kitchen, her hair curled.

She wears an apron he has not seen in a while, an apron with blue bears.

She sees him and flings herself upon him, in a manner that makes him glad.

What ho, says he. Is there occasion?

This, says Lotte, pointing at the stew, is All Good Things, and that stuff there, Prosperity!

And in the freezer, Sweetness and Our Hearts' Desire. Vanilla for you, chocolate for me.

But you depart from tradition! Art says. February has nearly passed!

Can you not guess? asks his wife, her face so soft, her eyes so full of tears.

Can you not guess what might make life new?

Arthur falls to his knees and clasps his wife's belly to his breast.

LITTLE NUT—

in which Charlotte, pondering motherhood, dies

Dear Peanut, for they say you are the size of a little nut, and little nut I imagine you to be, always my little nut, even when you are big and protest: I am a nut bush or a tree! I wish you to know something of us, your parents, little nut, in our imperfect glory, before you stand among us.

Your papa is a <u>good</u> man, even if he is stern, or has Ideas about how things should be.

What is goodness, you may ask. Why, goodness is many things:

It is sacrifice of one's self to ensure the happiness and well-being of others.

It is the placing of that happiness before one's own.

It is the envisioning of consequences, so your actions may contribute to that happiness.

It is a willingness to care for the small and unprotected.

A willingness to show affection, to lift up the dependent and the weak.

Your father is this kind of good. It is not just his work which is good, which places him indeed at the <u>forefront</u> of goodness, but his actions at home, where none but we shall see them.

And I, your poor mother. I can be perspicacious, but also dim; effusive, but prickly; I take pride in my restraint, then I burst out. I have passed many a gloomy day, but your papa lifts and steadies me. I hope that you shall meet only the good, kind, happy Mama; I see no reason why you should not.

As for our life, this is it: Your papa is up early to do his work; I am our family's housekeeper, which means I shop and occasionally dust and always make our meals. Your papa and grandfather do not complain, though they might, for I am a fearsome cook. The meals they like best are those in which I dress up a frozen dinner with frozen peas or, when we are flush, obtain fried chicken from the street. I help with their work, organizing their office and holding events, to demonstrate gratitude to Donors. I have also started a new book, which seemed urgent before my marriage, but does not call to me especially now.

Our life is peaceful, except when I make your father laugh, as his laughter booms, shaking pictures from the wall and threatening the crockery. Sometimes he makes me cry, though not from unkindness: I am unaccustomed to being the center of any soul's attention; his smallest gesture—the flowers he brings, the names he invents, his hand on mine—moves me, still.

When it was confirmed that you were among us, I experienced the most perfect moment—such peace, my peanut, such joy—not just in anticipation of you and all your peanut goodness, but because I saw that everything I had imagined about my life was wrong. I had been <u>resigned</u> to my "fate": I thought good fortune something we are <u>born to</u>. Instead, I learned, we can insist that fortune find us. I did this when I insisted on your father: I slapped fate and she revealed herself to be more adaptable than I'd thought. I will share this lesson with you, my love, I shall insist that you <u>persist</u>.

When I told your father about you, we shared that elevated moment, that present perfect, that repeats itself now whenever we gaze upon each other: we have made you, in love we have made you, something entirely good, therefore <u>we</u> are good, and happy. Whatever you may do in all your long life, we shall always have this, and for this I am grateful.

As for our qualifications to be your father and mother nut . . . I have examined your father and learned that he is excellent at:

Singing night songs, to encourage sleep.

Reading silly poems, that encourage laughter.

Pouring imaginary tea, for imaginary friends.

Playing chase, throwing a ball, flying kites, and hiding or seeking.

I do not know the first thing about such matters, but he assures me he knows not just the first, but the fifth, sixth, and seventh, so we shall be ready and well positioned to guide you! Where he gets experience at such things, to make such assertions, I do not know, but he is adamant about his skill—and we may believe him, for he is honest in all matters.

So you shall not want from him, ever. You will take pains not to interrupt him at his work, but he shall not bark at you if you do, provided it be important. If you misbehave, he will be hard with you so you might learn, but he will never lift a hand on you or say a vile thing—this he has promised, and it is a measure of his <u>goodness</u> that he is shocked at my asking—rather, he will use reason and clear language to <u>explain</u> badness to you, so you might reject it.

As for your mama, I shall love you devotedly. Such is my nature, to love what I love wholly, entirely, and without limitation or reason, so that while I hold opinions about a child's <u>conduct</u>, formed chiefly through observation of children whose conduct is <u>bad</u>, I may yet be a mother who excuses any behavior, out of love. My good qualities as a mother are these:

I can tell you stories, and you shall help! We shall tell stories together—to be certain they please you!

I can show you all the best pictures in our little town, and tell you how to view them.

I shall certainly remember your birthdays and make sure you have happy parties.

If we have the means, I shall buy you toys such as are likely to enchant you.

I shall see that you always have books.

I shall answer your questions, for children, I know, are curious, and it is well to encourage it.

I shall see that you have lessons in Latin, if such is your wish.

We shall strive to provide you with brothers and sisters, though you should not hold hope for this, for I am old like Sarah. I have been blessed by sisters and a brother, so too your father; we think being an only child a lonely business, so we will try.

I think, therefore, that you shall have a happy childhood. Please know that we, your parents, shall do our best to see that it is so.

Your loving Mama

Beloved kumquat! I have had to go to the grocer today to learn a kumquat's size and—yes!—its sweetness. It is a very satisfactory fruit! You should be proud to be an excellent kumquat; I hope you shall be equally proud next week when you are fig—I know we shall be.

I must advise, however, that despite your best kumquat intentions, you have made your mother sick. I am told this is usual, though I can scarce believe it: how can Mother Nature nourish a kumquat if its mother is forced every morning, and sometimes every noon and night, to lose her breakfast, lunch, and dinner? The nurse hath smiled her most condescending smile when I insisted it was wrong: This happens to all of us, said she (though I noted no ring on <u>her</u> finger). But I am glad to learn that I shall not vomit you up, nor starve you, nor even starve myself.

We have decided to put you in the living room, which does not please my papa, but he shall learn to love your little room once it becomes <u>your</u> room. To not overdisturb him, we shall wait till it becomes inevitable, then we shall sell Auntie's things to make way for crib changing table diaper pail toy chest—all the things I am told a Modern Boy must have. The lady at the store talked to me of <u>stencils</u> but I think I shall not be painting sailors on your walls, nor sailing ships, nor bailiwicks, nor candlesticks, nor bouncing balls, I hope you do not mind.

You shall like our little house, and we shall like you in it. It has been the site of much sorrow. Your aunties, an uncle, a grandmother, and great aunt all died here, and their dying still fills the air. It is hard to be in any room without sensing what has gone, but you shall fill every room with all things kumquat—your laughs and cries and runnings around and crawlings about, your playing and asking and insisting on things unreasonable like a little lord—till we learn to associate every corner only with you and the great holy wonder of you. We are full of hope now, dear fruit, for we see something in our future that is different from our past, and what that newness shall be we do not know but believe it shall be only simply fully and exactly good.

Your Mum

My darling peapod, I am in bed now more than I am out, for I am poorly: I can hold nothing in of what I eat. Your papa seeks to bring me things I love, notably bagels, and though the sight of them makes me ill, I smile and eat bites for him, then when his back is turned, feed the remainder to our dog. I very much do not like being abed, for while your papa is a most excellent and attentive nurse, he has Things to Do, as do I—like make your baby clothes, which I am determined to sew myself, as this will save us money and it is something I may do and know that your tiny overalls shall be well constructed. While abed, I shall not waste my time: I have found stories I wrote with your uncle and am reviewing them to see if any will suit, though the words of our manuscripts be exceedingly small and I exceedingly spent!

Your loving Mama Peapod

My sweet turnip, I shall be honest, my handsome and intelligent root vegetable: I am afeard, as the poets say. My mother died shortly after Aunt Anne was born. She was weakened by the birth, and did not long survive it. I am her age nearly, which is almost thirty-nine! I have ever been delicate; I fear I shall not manage.

There, I have said it, to you and no one else. Because I would see you toddle, and run, and climb, and soar! I would see you read your first book, then off to school, then make your way, and down the aisle. I would be there for all your triumphs— there shall be many! But where to find the strength? All assure me that this is normal, this level of <u>sickness</u>. But I can barely move my head, for all the walls spin, as do my insides; my head is heavy with emptiness and weighty air. It is only because it is <u>you</u> that I do not prefer death, but I am unwell.

Your loving Mama Turnip

My most dear-hearted child, I haven't the strength to open the book to learn what vegetable you must now be. I am guessing cantaloupe, due to the heaviness I feel, but it cannot be since you were turnip just last week: Can you grow when I give you nothing? Every day I take the broth my good husband offers: for your sake I sip till I am forced to bring it up. I try to keep myself alive, really I do, for you and your dear papa, who looks at me now with anxious and foreboding eyes, no longer the indulgent expression he wore when you were just a peapod and we thought me sick within the "great range of normal." I say "cantaloupe," because a cantaloupe might survive the loss of its mother, where a lentil, a fig, even a lemon may not.

It is with this in mind that I address you—I do not know that I can do so tomorrow, or even later today. My dear little one, you shall be strong, you shall be very, very strong, you shall fight with all the fight that leaves me, and all the power I once held with all my fighting against life and fate—which fighting hath brought me you, and here, so it is <u>good</u>! fighting is good!—you shall never give it up—and you shall live! It is alright for me to die if you may live. Be good to your papa, my beautiful cantaloupe, my good, strong cantaloupe, for he shall be sad when I am gone. He holds me up, your papa, even when he does not know it he holds me up, and—this is lesser known—<u>I him</u>; he shall do the same for you, and you, when you are older, or even now, for him. This is what our life is for, my one and only cantaloupe: so we can hold each other up, and know that we in turn are held up. I think there is little else, certainly little as important as that.

Your sadness shall be different from your father's, and he is not likely to know it: he will miss what he has had—what he waited too long to have—and he will assume your feelings the same. But <u>you</u> will miss something you've never had, something you do not know and cannot name, you shall feel a hunger you cannot sate. This, then, is my wish for you, that you do better than I. Demand affection from your father, and attention; he shall give you both, and gladly, and more, if he knows it is needed, and then you shall grow up fine, and bold, with the good qualities he will share with you. He shall make of you a fine cantaloupe, indeed!

The boundaries begin to burst between here and there: beings crowd this little room, the <u>qualities</u> of our lost ones swirl, hoping for a place to land: your uncle's brilliance, Auntie Anne's steadfastness and clarity, Em's genius and self-sufficiency—how you would have loved these souls, how they would have loved you! Maria's care and sacrifice, Eliza's willingness to serve, my mother's, well, my mother's love, they are <u>here</u>, with us, every day, they hope to fill you, to be part of you. You shall participate in what they were, or are; I sense this, with gladness—so they shall not die! I think I could gladly die if I knew that this were true.

Forgive the mystic vision, little fruit—mayhap I shall explain myself better tomorrow in words you—and I!—can understand and may all our dreams come true.

THE BELLS—

in which a widower grieves

The bells across the way have been removed, deregulating the Old Man's hours.

From his bed, he calls for his daughters, his son: *someone* should serve him. I wish him to sleep: awake, he will curse me, wanting Em, baby Anne, Bran, or the small one, *what is her name*. He calls even for Maria, Eliza, gone so long I did not know them.

Fivepenny! he shouts, remembering me. *Fivepenny! Fivepenny!* He throws *something* to the ground. Pliny, perhaps, or another tome he keeps by his side but does not read.

If I do not attend, he shall soil the bed—out of spite, I believe, but who can say.

At breakfast he reminds me that Charlotte left her estate— this is what he calls it—to him. He seems to think this gives him *rights* of some kind, over me, I mean. I am not his idea of a son-in-law, he says, as if I could forget. He *objected* to our match, he says, deciding now that he knew his beloved daughter—his *beloved* daughter—could not survive it.

You know something about subjecting a woman to *child-bearing*, I think but do not say.

As often, he is harmless. He dresses in his waistcoat and shows me Branwell's painting of the girls, from which Branwell effaced himself, using rare good judgment. Could stand on any wall, the Old Man exclaims, meaning any museum wall, any great person's wall. In fact, it is only Anne's face that reminds me of girls long gone. Though coarsely executed, her portrait captures something of her diffidence: she would escape the back of the canvas, if she could. Lotte's face is softened—it is *prettified*—while Em looks surprised (Em was never surprised).

Our employers know nothing of the Old Man's diminishment. As his "assistant," I do his work and my own, and suffer his abuse. I know he has complained to them that I lack "diligence," by which he means I am *different*, my ways are *different*; also, I live while his son has died. When he has gone I shall "apply" to do his job and be told I lack stature and qualification. My labor to date shall mean nothing. I promised Charlotte I would care for him and I will, but I have written my people: when the time comes, they shall give over the east wing. I do not wish the Old Man harm, but may it be soon.

Perhaps I shall do no more good works when I am home, perhaps I shall just stand at the dunes and stare at the ocean, as Charlotte did, when, newly wed, we visited that place. We could stay here, I thought then, amid plenty, away from the noxious air of this town; she could make friends of my sisters, and live in ease, among people who care for her, she might be happy, she who in the end yearned only for simplicity. But I would not say it, for she would not hear it. Instead, I watched her stand at the dunes and stare at the ocean—as if thinking, the world it comes and it goes, the people in it, events too, out they go and in, in and out, in and out, and we abide, through no fault of our own we abide. And kicking bits of sand over the edge, as if to say, the ground we stand on, it is no ground at all.

I did not disturb her standing, her kicking and her staring. She drew one strength from standing alone, another from standing with me. She misplaced the former in the end, over her excitement at attaining the latter, for she was too long without love, too long asked to stand alone. Had we time, I would have pushed her, gently, to recover some part of her solitude, if she could stand it, for from it she derived her *true self*, which I loved, and from it also everything she made and I hold dear.

I have been going through those things she made. I can destroy nothing that holds her words. Emily's pages are deranged, they do her no credit, so I have burned them, along with her brother's ramblings. I have learned that the Old Man cuts up Charlotte's letters, to give pieces to any who ask. I do not think he does so for *money*, but rather to be the one who does the giving, for they clamor, her "fans," deluging us with emails and calls. I have retrieved what letters I can from his room. They shall remain safe in my possession, even when they speak ill of me.

As they do: my assessment during those years was not wrong: Lotte would tolerate without especially *liking* me, despite my good offices. Heaven only knows why she relented.

I know why she relented. She'd reached a "point of no return": she'd talked herself into a dark corner. The "lifeline" I offered— when I had no other option, when I would either have to reach out my "assistant's" hand or leave forever, so long had my heart hurt for want of her—reached her. She was no fool: she would either grab for me, or float away to die. Lotte was never a fool.

I am a fool. I fool myself to this day that she loved me, though I know that she loved being loved by me. It is easy to love a woman who has never been loved, for she makes your love, however understated, seem the strongest *death-defying* love ever known.

If only.

It is wrong, I suppose, to walk through a house that once lived thinking, This shall go, and this shall go. All of it shall go, except Charlotte's writings, a few of her things, for as long as they smell of her, Emily's recipe box. The rest—the Old Man's vaunted library, with its first editions and crabbed marginalia, this rotten furniture, the old Aunt's sewing paraphernalia, which *still* dress a sideboard in the "living" room, that noxious (too loud) *clock*, Branwell's soldiers—it all shall go, very much as those awful *bunks* went when we wed. The family shall vanish, except as remembered by me, and their readers, who of course know nothing.

You should have seen that she was ill, the tyrant says, a vein pulsing in his neck. *I* would have seen, he insists, had I been allowed to see, had you reported truth to me and not lies. Instead, you kept her from me! My own little Lotte!

I did no such thing, but it is true: Charlotte gained no comfort from him. I spared her the need to *answer to him*, and when there was no hope, I kept her for myself. Had she been able to speak and admit what she felt, she would have said this, that she wanted me alone. She was tired of loving that man, who only took from her—her youth, her good nature, her money even—giving nothing in return but the sense that she had ever done wrong, had never been enough, was a poor replacement for what *he* had lost, which was everything, while she was nothing.

To me, she was everything.

When there was no hope, I locked her door, and slid into her bed, where I could hold her face, and mop her tired tears.

But, she would say, and I would say, *Shh*. And she would say, *But*, and I would say, *Shh shh* there is no need, and she would relax. I think all her life she wanted only this: to let her words go and simply be, in another's arms. She had no words in the end, just a shuddering into my chest, my heart. *Shh*, I said, there is no need, and she relaxed into death.

I'll miss her more than I can say.

CUT—

in which Papa mourns

The sound of a home movie rolling. It displays on a screen in a living room. An old man attends the projector, watching.

Annie, age 6, on camera. She holds a sock doll. Her blondish hair in wispy braids, she wears a blue-and-white-checked pinafore.

Annie: This here (*pointing at the doll*) is Miss Folly. Miss Doramar Folly. She is my favorite, at the moment.

Silence, as Annie looks at the camera.

Boy's voice, *off-screen*: Lord Weevil is honorable!

Girl's voice, *off-screen*: He is a cad! Look at what he's done to Lady Lazymere. She's quite undone!

Boy's voice: She ought to have given more thought to her conduct!

Girl's voice: That is . . . ridiculous! He is as much to blame for her . . . condition as she!

Boy's voice: But he is a man, a gentleman!

Girl's voice: No difference!

Boy's voice: You are intolerable, and a know-it-all! No one can work with you!

Sound of door slamming.

Annie: That would be Bran and Lotte, working out some business to do with Glass Land.

Silence, as Annie looks at the camera.

Annie: I mean Glass Town. I think they disagree about something.

Annie continues to look at the camera.

Man's voice: Tell me more about Dolly.

Annie: Folly. Miss Folly.

Man's voice: Miss Folly.

Annie: She is a schoolmistress. It's her job to make the little children learn. Sometimes she beats them, when they're bad.

Man's voice: Surely not!

Annie: Children can be very bad.

Man's voice: I did not know that. I know no children who are ever very bad.

Annie smiles for the first time, showing a gap in her teeth.

Annie: I am, sometimes.

Man's voice: Is that true? I can't believe it.

Annie, *still smiling*: Sometimes I steal things. Like candy. From Em. Not from Lotte. Lotte always knows how much she has. Then when I'm asked about it, I lie.

Off camera

Branny (*shouting*): What's more, you're an idiot!

Sound of door slamming.

Man's voice: What to do about those two?

Annie: They don't mean it. They're just playing.

Man's voice: So show me where Miss Folly has her schoolroom.

Annie tilts her head at the camera in puzzlement.

Annie: It's not real, Papa. It's only make-pretend.

Off camera

Lotte: *AAAAHHH! I hate you! I hate you I hate you I hate you!*

Man's voice: CHILDREN!

Silence

CUT

Four children stand before the camera, Bran, age 9, in front; he wears knickers, his wild red hair is uncombed. Annie wears a pale yellow pinafore; her hair is in wispy braids. Two older girls, brown-haired, wear braids and pale-colored "pinnies." They fidget and look at the camera.

Branny: So these are the very best of the books we have made.

He extends his hand, and three or four tiny booklets, approximately the size of postage stamps.

Lotte: Not the very best. There are better but he won't show them because his name isn't first.

Papa (*off camera*): Shh, Lotte, let your brother speak.

Branny: They contain many adventures, as pertain to the gentlemen and ladies . . .

Lotte: And servants and paramours . . .

Papa: Lotte!

Branny: Of a magical land, where none do die . . .

Lotte: Except those who deserve it, and a few very remarkable ladies who die of love.

Branny: Make her stop interrupting me!

Lotte: It is our story and you're not telling it right! Look, Papa, at my scar, where Branny knocked me down.

She displays her elbow, on which rests a dirty-looking bandaid.

Lotte: He is forever knocking me down.

Branny: I did not! I didn't touch you!

Lotte: You did too, he did too!

Branny: I only poked you, like this.

Lotte: Stop IT! Papa, make him STOP!

Branny: But I didn't *do* anything!

Middle girl: He is a lout sometimes.

Papa: Em, you will not talk ill of your brother; Bran, you must never hurt your sisters; Lotte, you will not tell tales.

Lotte: But we are telling tales! About Glass Town!

Papa: That is not what I mean.

Branny, *turning, fists high*: OUCH! Someone pinched me!

CUT

Em stands alone in front of the camera. She is wearing a white dress she may have outgrown; her hair is pulled back in a single ponytail, though long wisps escape and frame her face.

Em: You wish to see the landmarks of Glass Town?

She turns and walks out of the room. The camera follows. She arrives in a children's room: two parallel bunk beds and a chaos of blankets, books, and clothes strewn about.

Em: It is not usually like this. This is for the game. Usually we are very tidy.

Silence as Em looks at the camera.

Em: So this (*pointing at a closet*) is the land of Trod, a very unhospitable land where knights must prove themselves by jousting and also by privation.

She walks out of the room, almost as if marching, impressed by the solemnity of her role.

Em (*pointing at the kitchen*): Over here is the great harem where noble ladies are kidnapped and forced to marry swains. Sometimes it is also a schoolroom, or a great room for dancing.

She walks out of the room, past the children's room, to the bathroom.

Em: This is the dungeon, for obvious reasons.

CUT

Four children lie on their stomachs on the floor, a star, their heads almost touching. They appear not to know they are on camera. Bran fiddles with a toy soldier, but the girls are intent on each other.

Em: I tire of Lord Fancypants.

Bran: Lord Fanderant. Call him right!

Em: I tire of Lord Fancyrant. I find him a self-satisfied boor. I was happier when he was dead.

Lotte: But I revivified him.

Annie: He wasn't really dead.

Lotte: He only pretended to be dead, so he could fool the lout Seymour.

Em: He didn't *pretend* to be dead: Branny killed him, with a rocket!

Lotte: But I changed that. Listen, if he's alive, he can foil the lout Seymour, who . . .

Em: I know, who would otherwise ravish Queen Elinor of the Mountaintop.

Annie: Because Fancypants wouldn't be there to protect her! I think he should be alive!

Bran continues to play with his toy soldier: the soldier is walking about, shooting things.

Branny: Brrlsh! Brrlsh!

Lotte: Besides, Fanderant isn't a boor; he's just very knowledge-able about politics and botany.

Em: He needs to stop talking and *do* something, otherwise there's no *story*!

Lotte: That's why he needs to go to Mountaintop *right now*!

Annie: Are there fairies in this one, I can't remember?

Em: Okay, let him go, but if he begins talking about medicinal herbs, Branny throws a rocket.

Lotte: The herbs were so he could pretend to be dead!

Em: I don't care. Medicinal herbs, rocket.

Branny: It will be real this time! *Keflew!!!*

CUT

The four children, maybe a bit older, wearing slightly more formal clothes, by the kitchen table.

Papa: Can you make for me a map of Glass Town?

The four children nod, each reaches for the pencil he proffers.

Papa: Bran can do it.

Branny smiles and pushes his sisters with his elbows so he can have more room with the paper. He begins to draw. The camera cannot see the table.

Lotte: No, pencilhead, you've got it wrong: the duchy of Din is on the other side of the mountains!

Branny: Not today it isn't!

Lotte: But that doesn't make sense! Duchies don't *move*! If it's not on the other side of the mountains how can the tribe of horsemen rain down on them and steal their crops and jewels? Give me that pencil! *Give it to me!*

Branny elbows his older sister viciously; she doubles over. Her agony may be genuine.

Lotte: Papa!

Branny lifts his map and pushes it toward the camera.

CUT

The four children, again wearing different clothes, perhaps a little older, sit in a row on the sofa, the three girls, then Bran. The hair of the girls is down, Bran's is uncombed, wild.

Papa: What do you imagine your lives to be like when you are old?

Em: How old?

Papa: Very old. Like me.

Em nods.

Papa: You can go first, Em.

Em: I shall never marry. I shall live in the woods with my dog. I shall have a stable of dogs, and live maybe on a mountaintop, where none shall find me. I will sing songs there and be alone.

Lotte (*interrupting*): I too shall never marry! I shall only write books all day long. I shall travel all over the world, and live with Em and Anne, and also Bran if he behaves himself.

Papa: What sort of books will you write?

Lotte: Very good books, with adventures and people falling in and out of love. Chiefly noble ladies but also servants of obscure parentage.

Papa: Really?

Lotte: Oh, yes! And they shall be long books, and they shall sell for a very lot of money!

Papa: So you shall make us all rich, then?

Lotte: I hope so! I really hope so!

Branny: I am going to make a very lot of money! I am going to be famous and rich!

Papa: Bran, you must wait your turn. And you, little Anne?

Annie: I don't know.

Papa: You don't know?

Annie: I know that I should like to live to be very, very old, because I think very old ladies tend to be happy. They always have sweets in their house and it is nice to visit them. And I shall want to live always with Lotte and Em. I will live with them until I die.

Papa: Do you also imagine you will never wed?

Annie: I would like to have six babies.

Papa: Then you shall need a husband.

Annie shrugs.

Branny (*shouting*): It's my turn! I should be first!

Papa: Branny, you must be patient.

Branny: But it's my turn to say what I will do. Even if you just go by age I should never be last! I am going to be rich and famous, more famous than them!

Papa: You must wait your turn. I am now talking to your sisters.

Branny, impatient, jumps off the sofa.

Branny: No! It's me now! It's my turn now! I'm going to be more rich and famous than them!

Papa: Branny, sit!

Branny (*pointing at his sisters*): Pow pow pow pow I got you now all of you are dead!

ACKNOWLEDGMENTS

My interpretation of the lives of the Brontë family is indebted to the Brontë novels—*The Professor*, *Jane Eyre*, *Shirley*, and *Villette* by Charlotte Brontë; *Wuthering Heights* by Emily Brontë; and *Agnes Grey* and *The Tenant of Wildfell Hall* by Anne Brontë—as well as the following books: *Charlotte Brontë: A Passionate Life*, Lyndall Gordon; *The Brontës*, Juliet Barker; *The Brontës: A Life in Letters*, Juliet Barker, ed.; *The Early Writings of Charlotte Brontë*, Christine Alexander; *Emily Brontë*, Winifred Gérin; *Emily Brontë: Heretic*, Stevie Davies; and *The Brontë Myth*, Lucasta Miller.

Thanks beyond thanks to the exceptional Robin Black and Juliet Grames, whose readings of *Half-Life* (when it was *much* longer!) made all the difference; Alice McDermott (and her group at Sewanee!) also offered kind feedback on a particularly important section of the book. Warm thanks to A.L. Kennedy, David Lynn, Tobias Carroll, David Daley, Sari Wilson, and Josh Neufeld, who chose pieces from this book to appear (in slightly different form) in their lovely journals and anthologies. Seeing those stories in print lifted me during the decade it took to write this book.

I intended to write about the Brontës long before I started *Half-Life*. The book's eccentric form, however, could only have come about as a result of three extraordinary months at the MacDowell and Yaddo colonies. Additional residencies, all of them wonderful, sustained me while I drafted and redrafted (and redrafted) the book: Djerassi Resident Artists Program, Virginia Center for the Creative Arts, Millay Arts, Art Omi: Writers, Passa Porta, and Dora Maar House. Thank you, thank you also to those who helped me get to these beautiful places: Jim Crace, DW Gibson, Elizabeth Kadetsky, Jodee Stanley and, again, Robin and Juliet.

I could not have asked for a better, kinder, more sensitive editor than Mark Doten: every word was as important to him as it was to me. Gratitude galore to Janine Agro, Bronwen Hruska, Rachel Kowal, Erica Loberg, Rudy Martinez, and Steven Tran for making every stage of the publication process a pleasure, and for doing their jobs so darned well. Thank you also to Jaya Miceli for the gorgeous cover, NaNá Stoelzle for her thorough copyedit, and Mia Manns for her exacting proofread. Working with Soho Press has been a dream! And every day I thank my lucky stars that Gail Hochman and her team at Brandt & Hochman are on my side!

Finally, more gratitude than I can convey to my friends and family. Ten years is a long time to write a book; it took a village to keep Rachel merry. With love to my parents, who always made me feel I could accomplish anything I set my mind to, I dedicate *Half-Life* to my brothers and sisters who, probably without knowing it, hold me up, and always have.

NOTE

Pieces from the book have appeared, in slightly different form, in the following journals and anthologies:

"Half-Life of a Stolen Sister," *Bridport Prize Anthology* (UK, 2011)

"Dead Dresses," *Kenyon Review* (Vol. 37, No. 1, Jan.-Feb. 2015)

"Dear Sirs," *Vol. 1 Brooklyn* (http://www.vol1brooklyn.com/2013/04/21/sunday-stories-dear-sirs/)

"Present Perfect," *Five Chapters* (2014)

"Lives of the Poet, pg. 85," *Flashed: Sudden Stories in Prose and Comics* (Pressgang, 2016)